"If Stephen King and Jim Butcher ever had a love child then it would be Alan Baxter."

—Smash Dragons

"I was completely blown away when I read this. A classic hero's journey with a cast of real three-dimensional and really interesting characters. The world he's built rivals anything by Jim Butcher…his prose is fluid and engrossing, and he balances action with pace and provides wonderful vignettes of really descriptive prose. I'm reminded of Benedict Jacka and Kevin Hearne…"

—Kylie Chan, author of the Dark Heavens, Journey to Wudang, and Celestial Battle trilogies

"Kick ASS!"

—Sean Williams, *New York Times* #1 bestselling author

"I had a lot of fun reading Alan Baxter's *Bound*…It's a teeth-gnashing, shadow-chasing, magesign-riddled sexy beast of a thing!"

—Margo Lanagan, award-winning author of *Sea Hearts* and *Tender Morsels*

continued…

"A genuine page-turner from a major new writer."

—*The West Australian* newspaper

"…an escalating adventure that mixes epic dark urban fantasy with thriller pacing… The pressure doesn't let up the entire novel. Baxter's trimmed down the prose to fighting readiness and come out swinging… I'd compare this series to Jim Butcher's work in terms of Urban Fantasy, though whereas Butcher riffs off hard boiled tropes, Baxter most definitely riffs off the thriller genre."

—Sean Wright, Adventures of a Bookonaut (review)

"I highly recommend *Bound* to anyone who likes a good supernatural action thriller."

—Traci Harding, bestselling author of *The Ancient Future* and *The Timekeepers*

"…a relentless whirlwind of magic, sex, and violence. *Bound* is a rollercoaster of gritty magic, evocative settings, and brutal action: a solid intro to a new urban fantasy series."

—Billy Burmester, *Aurealis Magazine*

"Alan Baxter delivers a heady mix of magic, monsters and bloody fights to the death. Nobody does kick-ass brutality like Baxter."

—Greig Beck, bestselling author of *Beneath the Dark Ice* and *Dark Rising* (Alex Hunter series)

ABDUCTION

ALEX CAINE.BOOK 3

ALAN BAXTER

RAGNAROK
PUBLICATIONS

ABDUCTION: ALEX CAINE #3
Ragnarok Publications | www.ragnarokpub.com
Publisher: Alan Bahr | Creative Director: Jeremy Mohler
Abduction is copyright © 2017 by Alan Baxter.
All rights reserved.

Published by Ragnarok Publications
5601 NW 25th Street
Topeka, KS 66618

ISBN-13: 9781945528422
Worldwide Rights
Created in the United States of America

Editor: Gwendolyn Nix
Cover/Interior Design: Shawn T. King

For everyone fighting a battle;
May you find the strength to never quit.

Alex Caine woke to a soft creak in the floorboards of his old weatherboard house. From a fitful sleep, he was instantly alert, tense, heart hammering. *Breathe*, he told himself as he forced the nerves to subside. Just Silhouette returning from a trip to the city to feed. She jokingly complained about the commute, but taking people from the small country town where they lived was far too obvious, so a two-hour each way journey once a month or so was a necessary hassle. The price of eating people was something Alex still struggled to come to terms with. But he loved her.

He glanced over at the clock and anxiety riddled his chest again. Three am. Far too early for Sil to be coming home. He squeezed his eyes shut for a moment to gather himself, and images of broken chunks of an obsidian city flashed through his mind, hundreds, even thousands of people cast tumbling into the Void to blink out of existence, as if they had never been. Hundreds more crushed or maimed as Obsidian slammed back into the mortal realm. All of it focused through his consciousness and power, through the energy of the Darak stone embedded in his chest, a living part of him.

You saved thousands of people, Silhouette repeatedly reminded him.

But I killed thousands more. I've felt the Void. I know what I did to them! he would counter, the pain a black hole in his soul.

The intensity of the events never ebbed, even for a moment.

Alex centered himself. He was a warrior, a fighter against all odds. He remembered the words of his Sifu: *When the battle rages, put aside fear. Of course it is there, but you can make time for it later. When you fight, there is only the moment, nothing else.*

He opened his eyes, nerves barely steadied, and sat up in bed. The darkness was absolute, no streetlights for miles around his two acres in the valley, and no moon this night. But Alex had a preternatural vision that out-performed anyone he had yet met, arcane or mundane. He let that vision open, watched through normal space for shades and planes of magic, for the auras of any intruders and the magesign of their activity.

An aroma rose, sickly sweet and cloying. He had been to a seaside resort in England once, years ago, and visited a shop that made candy, sticks of rock with the resort name running right through them. The smell there had been the same, intense, hot and sugary. Only this had a layer of something else over it, something oily.

The sensation of magesign in the house swelled. He slipped from the bed, quietly pulled on a pair of loose cotton pants and a plain T-shirt, a frail shield against the vulnerability of nakedness. Someone was in his house, doing magic. The 'sign swelled again and he saw the shades of some kind of searching spell, tendrils questing through the rooms, seeking. He gathered his own power, closed his shields, hid himself from everything, even light. Invisible in the darkness, he flexed his fists and waited.

A movement beyond the door caught his eye. Then another. At least two people stalked his home. The sickly stench grew thicker, the sensations of spell-casting stronger. He recognized the flavor of arcane energy, similar to that which had pulled him and Silhouette and the others through to

Obsidian just a couple of short months before. Silhouette had said it was Fey magic. A tremble moved over Alex's skin. Were there actual Fey here? Sil had promised this couldn't happen without plenty of warning. How had they slipped past the wards? After all the work Armor had done to protect him, as desperate as they were for him to join them, why weren't arcane alarms going berserk?

And besides all that, the day before had been Lughnasadh, or Lammas, the thin day, when the Fey had power to pass between Faerie and the mortal realm. They shouldn't be able to threaten him now, and not again until the next thin day. Was all of Armor's recent work for nothing?

Silhouette's dread of the Fey disturbed him. She was hard as nails, old and powerful, for all her apparent youth and beauty, and she feared very little. But the Fey put her on edge. As a Kin, mixed blood Fey and human, she knew intimately the nature of the creatures. As a first-generation Kin, rare even among her own kind, she knew perhaps more intimately than most, and if one thing absolutely terrified the love of Alex's life, it was the Fey. Utterly evil, she had called them. Was it possible some trod the boards of his home?

He searched his memory, tried to remember what he had lately read. He had thought it wise to learn all he could of the Fey, and Kin, and the otherworld of Faerie, but Silhouette scowled and shook her head, dismissing the majority of literature on the subject as simply the musings, mythology and misconceptions shared by humans. *Faerie is no fairy tale, Alex,* she had said. *It is evil and other and inconceivable and best left out of mind.*

But as Armor were so keen on him and Silhouette joining them since the Obsidian Incident, he had access to a vast of array of knowledge from their centuries-old archives.

He moved again, silent as an assassin. He tried to get a better view from the room, but the architecture worked against him. He needed to see more, plan a course of action, but doing so might give him away.

The Obsidian Incident. Such a toothless misnomer for the horror of what had occurred, the lives lost. They had given him a lot of time to deal with the traumas of the Incident, and he had tried to use that time to learn. Although, he had often been too tired, unmotivated. He slept a lot, fell easily into black moods. PTSD, the Armor psychologist had told him. Post-Traumatic Stress Disorder.

He had learned about the thin days. He and Silhouette had sat nervously through the previous twenty-four hours, wondering if they would have to fight or flee, use some of the new protective measures, but nothing happened. *The Fey may not come at all*, Silhouette had said, though they knew better. There would be some attempt at retribution for the blow he had struck against them. But it had to be a thin day and they had planned for that with scrupulous attention to detail. How were the Fey here now?

Alex jumped as shades of movement shifted in the darkness near the bedroom door. Even now his mind was wandering, his focus weak. *Pull it together, for fuck's sake!*

He crouched and moved, watched an intruder's aura, their shades plain to him as they passed into the large bedroom. He could see shifts and colors of others in the hallway beyond, definitely more than two, maybe four or five. His heart hammered. The shades were like nothing he had ever seen, warping colors like oil on water, but all overlaid with deep, dark shadows, black light masking the true nature of their psychic signatures. It hurt his mind to read them, made him nauseous as he tried to decipher intent.

The thick darkness of the night masked their physical presence. He had no idea what they looked like, and their slippery auras made it impossible to guess their shape. An enemy he had no idea how to engage. The one in the room hopped up onto the bed he had so recently vacated and crouched. He got the impression of a dog sniffing a scent. The claggy, sugary aroma filled the room as others hurried in, drawn by some silent signal.

Alex, holding his breath, moved painfully slow towards the bedroom door. However well they saw in the dark did not matter as his magic rendered him completely invisible. His own shades were locked down tight, concealed in a shell of mundanity. If he could leave the room, perhaps he could get to his car and escape. Or head to one of the more heavily warded areas in the garden, his newly erected stone circle, ancient methods for modern protection. He would grab his phone on the way through the house, call Silhouette for advice, draw on the services of Armor. Anything was preferable to engaging with whatever prowled his bedroom. Even without Silhouette's warnings it was clear to him that these things were incredibly powerful, dangerous in ways he could not fathom, and he desperately wanted to avoid any confrontation.

He took a deep, silent breath as he neared the door, drawing it into his belly, using his extensive training in *chi gung* to steady heart and mind. In preparation to slip out the door and into the hallway, he softly let the breath out again.

Sharp movement on the bed and the intense scrutiny of several beings hit him like a series of blows. Before he had time to even register surprise they were on him.

Alex cried out, all pretense of stealth become irrelevant, and thrashed around. He felt blows connect in the darkness, heard high-pitched squeals of pain and frustration as his Darak-enhanced strength and masterful technique delivered devastating attacks. But it wasn't enough. Even as some creatures fell away, others slammed into him. Sweet, sickly, oily blows rained down, struck his head, neck, body. Pain blossomed all over him and something else, something arcane and malevolent, filled the room. No, it filled his mind. As he fought, magic like he had never felt before infiltrated his very being and tightened about him like steel cables. It was similar to the enchantment the Autarch of Obsidian had used to bind him and his power, except instead of wrapping him up like a straitjacket, it wove tendrils of shackling through every fiber of his core. His chest pulsed and burned. The Darak felt incandescent against his flesh.

With a roar, he used his elemental specialty and drew heat from every corner of the house, agitating together a huge ball of radiant flame to burst out from him and incinerate his attackers. If he burnt down his house, he was past caring.

In the sudden glaring orange glow, he saw twisted faces and raised thin hands. His heart double-thumped in terror at the cold, broken shape of the things before him, even as they squealed and fell away, wreathed in tentacles of twisting flame. But it was not enough, there were too many, and as the magic continued to tighten about him, the blows returned. His bedclothes and curtains crackled with licks of fire, casting an orange dancing light through the room. The long, sharp, gangly creatures were quick in uncanny, sticklike, jerky movements as some batted out flames and others wrapped a glistening, oily rope around him. His shouting and thrashing grew more contained. Their elongated, hollow faces, the skin a deep green-black like the thickest algae scum of a darkened swamp, shifted slowly from concentration to some twisted semblance of joy.

As some beat out the last of the flames, one leaned forward, its eyes a flickering amber in the dark-again room, and hissed something. Its breath was the heaviest, sweetest, most nauseating thing Alex had ever breathed and darkness covered his mind like a hood.

CHAPTER
TWO

Claude Darvill studied the lie of the bones on the scrap of black canvas and scowled. He knew he was missing something but could not place what, and his frustration grew. The reading was confusing. Tendrils of volcanic smoke drifted snake-like around the dark gray rock he used as a table for his tools of magic. His breath steamed in the frozen air. With a noise of annoyance, he gathered the small, yellowed bones in his fist again, and once more whispered the incantation. He let his questing mind be free, sent his desires out into the aether and cast the skeletal pieces across the rough black material. They fell exactly as they had before, far too accurately for any hint of chance to enter the reading.

"Fuck." Squatting, Claude rubbed his hands together for warmth and stared.

"Perhaps something interrupts the result?" a small voice behind him suggested.

Claude didn't take his eyes from the divination. "You think, Sigmund?" His voice was heavy with sarcasm.

"I just meant…"

"I know what you meant." Claude stood suddenly, making Sigmund take an involuntary step backwards. Claude smirked. He enjoyed how much he scared the small Icelandic 'tour guide.' The man came highly recommended through a mutual friend, but this fellow was an obsequious and annoying little toady. Darvill had no time for such people. He turned his gaze to pierce Sigmund's blue eyes, which widened under a mop of curly blond hair. "I find things, Siggy, you understand that? It's what I do and I'm fucking good at it. No one, in fact, is better at it than me."

Sigmund nodded, playing nervously with the hem of his jacket. "Of course. But I was just going to suggest that perhaps it might be worth figuring out what is interrupting the magic rather than simply trying to force your sight in spite of it."

Claude frowned. "Hmm. Perhaps you're onto something there." His admission was grudging, but genuine. If the source of the interruption could be found, and circumvented, the divination would be clearer.

"Is there a ward of some kind, perhaps, preventing your sight?" Sigmund asked.

"No. Something more…physical than that. And the read I am getting is contradictory somehow. There's a misalignment about the result I can't see through. That fucker Alex Caine—how I wish I had the means to kill him—told me my father died in Iceland. That *he* killed my father here. He promised to take me to the site, but Armor kept us apart, sent me away. Caine would never have kept that promise anyway, the bastard. But I feel my father somewhere nearby. I've spent months tracking his psychic signature. I know I'm close. So close I can almost smell Robert Hood's foul fucking aftershave. If Caine killed him here, there should be some trace of that death, some echo of his mind ending. Maybe even some fragment of physical evidence, however tiny, however inconsequential." He balled his fists. "There should be fucking *something*!"

He crouched again, stared at the scattered bones of ancient crows, imbued with the magic of shamans centuries dead. These were his most powerful tools, his most accurate, and they told him he was right on top of what he sought. But nothing anywhere near confirmed that.

"A physical barrier," he muttered to himself. He stood again, looked around. Nothing but gray-black stone and shale, desolate as the moon, covered with a layer of snow and ice. The snow lay thicker on the higher ground in the distance. It crunched under his booted feet even on the thermally heated ground on which he stood. Tussocks of hardy grass and scrub dotted the landscape, shifting in the cold breeze. Charcoal-colored volcanic ash covered a lot of the land despite the snow, far from the neat and civilized inhabited areas of the island. There was simply nothing here.

Assuming Sigmund would follow, not really caring if he did or not, Claude strode off across the rocky ground. Taller formations and hills off to one side caught his eye and he moved towards them. As he wandered between them, he muttered incantations of finding and echoes of old magic bounced back to him. He caught a hint of something familiar and paused, closed his eyes to concentrate. He sensed a tiny flicker of psychic signatures he recognized, wisps of old magesign. Alex fucking Caine and his Kin bitch, Silhouette. They had definitely been here, many months ago. Other powerful signatures echoed too, dark, malevolent. He was close. Alex certainly had not lied about killing Claude's father in Iceland.

A cave mouth yawned darkly from between two tall, leaning rocks and Darvill entered, flicking a flashlight on as he went. Someone had lived here, a monastic existence of utter simplicity. The few possessions were still in fairly good order, though dust and hints of ash covered everything. No one resided here now, but they had not too long ago. Could it be something as simple as caves getting in the way? Were his divinations being blocked by complicated cavern systems, confusing his seeking mind? Could plain rock be that obstructive?

Darvill's eyes widened and he turned from the cave. As he ran back the way he had come, he barreled into Sigmund and knocked the slight man onto his arse. "Out of the way!" Claude yelled.

He slipped and stumbled on the loose shale and ice as he scrambled to his makeshift table and stared at the crow bones. He gathered them in a shaking fist and rattled them between his palms, muttering slightly different words of magic. He cast them across the canvas and stared, mouth opening in shock and anger.

"Not caves," he whispered to himself. "Actual solid rock is between us. And he's not dead!"

ilhouette drove through the dim glow of false dawn, satisfied. Kin didn't need to feed often and, unlike so many of her kind, she certainly wasn't of the mindset that humans were nothing more than cattle. But she did enjoy a good feed and had long since come to terms with the requirements of her life. While the killing would never sit well with her, the feeling of a sated Kin hunger was unlike anything else. Her guilt was little different to the carnivore's empathy for the cow, but she tried to pick her victims carefully.

The highway heading south stretched gray and straight beyond the reach of her headlights, leading her back to the rolling green hills where she lived with Alex. She would never have considered herself a country girl, but he had shown her how idyllic it could be. And the city was only a couple of hours away. Sydney provided plenty of opportunities for feeding. It hadn't taken her long to sniff out the dens of iniquity populated by criminal and violent lowlifes who exploited decent people everywhere. Hell, every time she fed it was a public service.

She grinned wolfishly in the dim light from the dashboard. Tonight had been particularly fun, breaking into a closed-door poker game and playing with her food before eating. They honestly thought they had the upper hand. For quite a long time, considering. It wasn't until she actually shifted into her favoured panther-like form and took out the throat of the muscular bouncer by the door that anyone thought her anything but an unfortunate idiot who had stumbled into her own worst nightmare. How that situation had swiftly reversed.

She grinned again, remembering something Alex had said not so long ago. *You're like some strange cross between Batman and Catwoman. Except neither of them eats the bad guys they bring down.* She glanced at the bag on the passenger seat, bulging with cash from the game and quite a few other items of value from the night's victims—watches, rings, necklaces and more. She preferred the Catwoman comparison.

There was something about thin days that made her hungrier than any other time and made the sating of that hunger more satisfying too. Something to do with her half-dose of Fey blood, she presumed. The days made Fey power stronger and that must affect the needs of the Kin, first-generation, especially. Everyone knew the urge to feed was at its strongest on those days. Most Kin dens tried to manage it, insisting some members resist feeding to prevent too many deaths at once, which might risk discovery. It had been hard for Silhouette to avoid feeding until the dangerous twenty-four hours had passed, but she had certainly made up for it.

The last thin day had been the December solstice when they had been sucked through a vortex of Fey power into Obsidian. She sighed. That had ended well, all things considered, but Alex was still having trouble dealing with it. It had taken a terrible toll on him.

Then Imbolc had come around, a time of renewal in the northern hemisphere of her birth. She lived on the other side of the planet now, so it was actually Lughnasadh that just passed. She had trouble getting her head around it. But still a time of change. They waited out the day and night, terrified of Fey retribution, but nothing eventuated. A few days a year of extreme vigilance was a small price to pay in the long run, and since Alex had truly committed the Fey anchor stone to the Void, it would only ever be those few days forever more. But the threat did nothing to help Alex's ongoing trauma with the events surrounding Obsidian.

Her thin day hunger, deferred but finally sated, made her feel strong. It was weeks until the next one. Perhaps she would wake Alex when she got home and they could celebrate the event. First, she would fuck him silly, then introduce him to some old Pagan rituals, a bit of Kin magic to help him refind his focus. Perhaps help him shake off his melancholy, if only for a little while. She knew his road to recovery was likely to be long and undulating, but she was determined to do all she could to ease the journey.

She pulled off the highway and onto twisting roads leading between the green hills of dairy country. A soft smile played at her lips as she thought of the different ways she could wake Alex to immediately dispel any annoyance on his part at such an early rousing. Dawn smudged the sky pink and purple, the hearty sun about to breach the horizon behind her, and as she pulled along the dirt driveway of their house, her heart froze.

The front door stood open in the dim half-shadow of early light. The ice around her heart cracked as it began hammering double time. The hairs on her neck rose. She killed the engine and braked to a halt twenty meters from the house. "No, no, no…" she muttered under her breath. Maybe he was up early…she knew it wasn't true. If anything, getting Alex out of bed before noon at the moment was hard, his mood lethargic and sullen. Something was wrong.

She slipped from the car and smoothly flowed into her feline form as her feet touched the ground. Her clothes melted into soft gray fur, her features rounded out. She dropped to four paws and padded low and stealthy through the shadows of hedges towards the house. A low growl rose in her chest as an aroma sent shivers of panic through her. The sickly, sweet stench was unmistakable. Fey. It wasn't possible. *Shouldn't* be possible.

Anger and grief battled for primacy in her mind as she slunk through the obviously empty house. The sick-candy scent grew stronger as she moved towards the bedroom. There had been many Fey here. The soft early light showed damage and burn marks across the bed, carpet and curtains and Silhouette tipped her head back and roared. Alex had clearly fought, but he was nowhere to be seen. Barely an echo of his presence remained, buried in the horrible, overpowering remnants of Fey manifestation.

Silhouette stood up onto her hind legs, and morphed back to her human shape as she ran for the kitchen. She snatched up the phone and dialed with shaking fingers.

After two rings, the phone was answered. "Sal's Pizzeria, can I take your order?"

"It's Silhouette. Put me through to the Commander right away." Her voice trembled with rage and fear.

"May I take your order please?"

"Oh, fuck me." Silhouette squeezed her eyes shut. There was protocol for a reason. "Large thick crust, half supreme, half meat lovers, anchovies all over and a bucket of Coke."

The voice at the other end became casual. "Thanks, Sil. Sorry, you know how it is."

"Sure, sure. The Commander, please!"

"Just a sec."

There was a click and the most frustratingly lame smooth jazz hold music piped through. Silhouette tapped her foot, ground her teeth.

"Silhouette?" The Commander's voice was gruff and thick with sleep.

"They got Alex!" Silhouette cursed the high panic in her tone. She sucked in a quick breath. "The Fey, they've been here, there's been a fight, and Alex is gone."

"Sil, are you…"

"Yes, I'm fucking sure! How did this happen? Yesterday was the day, not today!"

"Silhouette, take a breath, please. This is serious, but let's try to stay calm." The Commander's voice betrayed no further hint of his sudden awakening. "Now I don't doubt your assessment, but are you sure they've taken him?"

"He's not fucking here!"

"You're sure? There's no…body?"

"What?"

There was a pause, then, "Are you sure they haven't just killed him, in cold revenge?"

"How did they get him today?" Silhouette demanded. "This can't happen!"

"I'm sorry, Sil, really I am. But search—make sure he's been taken."

Silhouette paused, teeth clenched in frustration. The Commander had a point. She started moving from room to room. "I'm looking now, but I can't feel him."

"If they came for Alex, took him away, there must be something else at work, no? Fey are complex and evil, they operate on the bigger picture. If it's not simple revenge, what are they doing? I know this shouldn't have happened, but as it has, let's reduce the angles and decide on a course of action."

Silhouette shook her head, terrified that Alex might have been killed. "They know about the Obsidian situation; their ridesprite escaped Nicholas Haydon. They know Alex truly cast the anchor stone into the Void. It is genuinely lost." She shivered as she moved from the house towards the garden, searching. "You're right, Commander. If they came, why didn't they just kill him?" A more horrible thought occurred to her. "Unless they've taken him somewhere to make him suffer…"

The Commander sighed. "Perhaps, Silhouette. Keep looking. It's morbid, I know, but make sure, if you can." There was noise and movement on the other end. "Sil, hold on a minute." The Commander's voice became muffled. "What is it?"

A conversation ensued and Silhouette took the opportunity to move quickly around the overgrown gardens. There was no trace of anything out of order. The Fey had obviously surprised Alex while he slept, there had been a fight, and Alex had come off worst. She was relieved to confirm that his corpse didn't mark the end of the confrontation, but it terrified her to think what that might mean. What did they want with him? Were they going to torture him for revenge? Had they abducted him to Faerie? But it wasn't a thin day, so they couldn't have gone back. Only on thin days could the Fey travel between realms.

Her heart tremored as the thought of facing Fey rose in her mind. But she loved Alex and she would go after him, even if it meant going where she least wanted to ever be. She would follow him to Faerie if she had to. But they *couldn't* have gone back today.

"Silhouette, are you still there?"

"Yes. Commander, what are we going to do?"

"Well…" The Commander's voice was strained. "Something's come up here, I have to go, but…"

"More fucking important than this?" Silhouette was astounded.

"Silhouette, calm down. I have to go, but a team is on its way and they will conduct a full survey of your house and grounds. We will find out all we can about what's happened to Alex and we will act."

Silhouette bit down on her anger rising like a wave of lava. "Commander, I'll go after him if I have to, whatever that entails."

"I understand. And we'll help. A team is coming. Other things are happening, Sil, you know how it is. They always are. Hang in there."

Silhouette breathed heavily into the phone, impotent and furious.

"Wait for the chopper, Sil. We'll sort this. It's what we do, right?" The Commander tried to inject confidence and authority into his voice, but Silhouette could hear his concern. And if he was afraid, she was beyond terrified.

"Okay."

"I'll call you back a bit later." He hung up without waiting for a reply.

The wait for the chopper was excruciating, but it gave Silhouette time to confirm there was indeed no trace of Alex anywhere near the house. She stood in the center of the recently erected stone circle, supposedly a safe space for them to retreat to should the Fey set off alarms by arriving. The circle was an expensive and powerful construction, the rock imported from Scotland, the wards created by the best teams in Armor. As were the other wards throughout the house. None of it had worked.

After Obsidian, Armor had really stepped up to ensure Alex's recovery and protect his and Silhouette's future. It was partly because Alex was valuable to them, but it had quickly become apparent that Armor genuinely wanted to help Alex as he had helped them. And they wanted him to join up full time, of course. Silhouette was glad for their new allegiance. But as she stood among stones that buzzed with magesign and ancient power, a deep sadness welled in her. All the effort had proven useless.

A thrumming rose through the hills and a sleek, black helicopter appeared over the ridge. She watched it descend on approach and eventually settle on the grass not far from the house. She remembered the last time a chopper had come from Armor. That had been the start of the whole Obsidian debacle. She wished Alex had never taken that job, but it was easy to wish in hindsight. She had encouraged it, at the time.

Black-clad operatives hopped out as she ran, half crouched, to meet them.

"We have to know what happened," she shouted over the rotor noise to the first of them. "Please, any tiny clue."

The dark-skinned woman nodded, gave Silhouette's shoulder a squeeze. "We've got this. If there's anything to be found, we'll find it. We'll get him back. I'm Gwen. I know we're only supposed to use Jane and John Doe in the field, but we're all operatives together, right?"

"Silhouette."

"I know." Gwen gave a sad smile. "I should warn you, opinion is a little divided on the situation here."

"What?"

Gwen turned to the two men who had followed her from the chopper. "You guys head out to the property perimeter and work your way in towards the house. I'll start inside."

The two men nodded. They both had sour expressions. One looked at Silhouette with undisguised disdain.

"What's the problem here?" Silhouette asked as the men ran off.

"The long-haired fellow is Dan. He lost two good friends during the Obsidian Incident, killed by escaping Kin. The skinny guy is Jack. He thinks Alex should have stayed in Obsidian and sacrificed himself along with everything there, left it all in the Void."

Silhouette was horrified. Alex had met with several fairly bluntly stated opinions since the Incident, she understood the anger of people who had lost friends and loved ones, but to suggest Alex should have cast himself into the Void was unconscionable. "He removed the most powerful item in Fey history," she said, aghast. "Alex saved the mortal realm from the Fey ever getting a permanent hold here again."

Gwen nodded, mouth set in a grim line. "I know. I'm on your side. You can imagine, the flight here was…tense. But everyone's experience of something like this is different."

"I need help here, not enemies in the people who are supposed to be my allies!"

"They'll do their job, I promise you. They've sworn as much themselves, don't worry about that. Just don't expect too much in the way of friendship. At least, not from them. Not now. They'll come around."

Silhouette watched the two men trotting out towards the fence line where Alex's property backed on to broad, rolling dairy paddocks. "I'm glad *you're* here," she whispered.

"I am. Trust me, they'll do all that's required of them and I'll do more."

Silhouette nodded and led the woman away from the slowing rotors towards the house. "I'll show you where he was taken."

As Gwen set up complicated equipment in the bedroom, the unique Armor melding of technology and sorcery, Silhouette cursed herself again for leaving Alex. If she had stayed, perhaps they could have fought together. She racked her brain, trying to figure out what had happened. How it had happened.

Her phone interrupted her thoughts. "Hello?"

"Silhouette, it's the Commander."

"Oh, you've got time for me again?"

"Sil, there are always a million things that need my attention, you know that. It's just the nature of our organization. But I am one hundred per cent committed to helping you guys. They there?"

"Yes, setting up now. You couldn't send a team who wasn't glad to see the back of Alex?" She heard the venom in her voice and regretted it. The Commander had been nothing but supportive, almost fatherly to them both since their return, but she boiled with rage, guilt, and fear.

"I'm sorry, Sil," he said. "Our numbers are thinned right now. Gwen is in charge and she's on your side. The others will do their job."

"So she said. You really couldn't find any others who don't hate Alex?"

"He made many enemies with his actions. Give it time. People will come to understand."

Silhouette nodded, determined to not give in to her roiling emotions. She had never been as close to anyone in her many centuries of existence as she was to Alex and it scared her how much of an effect it had. But she was not some snivelling girl and she would fight to get him back. She intended to affirm that resolve to the Commander. "Any further ideas on how it happened?" she asked.

"Some ideas. What about you?"

"It's possible the Fey came through yesterday, when they could travel on the thin day. Their power is massively reduced if they're trapped in the mortal realm on any other day and they can't return again until the next thin, but it's possible they planned exactly that to take Alex off-guard. Wait somewhere, come the day after we expected them. Even weak, if there were enough of them…"

"I thought the same thing. Our wards and alarms?"

"Nothing as far as I can tell. It's clear Alex was surprised in the bedroom. They came while he slept and he got no warning."

"Bastards. But why do it like that? If they could avoid the wards, why wait and trap themselves here until the next thin? Why operate on a day when they're so weak?"

Silhouette stared through Gwen and the equipment at the foot of her bed. The bed she shared with Alex. "I don't know. I get that coming a day late would catch him unawares, but not the risk of having to stay here." She took a shuddering breath. "But if that is what happened, they must be somewhere in this realm still and that means we can find them, right?"

"I hope so, Sil. With any luck, Gwen and her team will uncover some clues to work with."

CHAPTER FOUR

Claude Darvill stared at the man before him with undisguised hatred. "Can't be done?" he asked.

The big civil engineer shrugged broad shoulders, and gestured around. "Look at the terrain. And these conditions. Even if we could get a vehicle in here, you're asking that we dig through solid rock. It can be done, but not by my team or equipment."

Claude pulled the battered leather broad-brimmed fedora from his head, ran one hand over his sandy hair. "So I need a better team with better equipment."

"Yes, I suppose you do."

"Any chance you can recommend someone?"

The big man scowled. He clearly didn't like Claude, but that was the least of Darvill's problems. "You might try a more commercial outfit," he suggested. "Someone used to corporate development. But getting the required people and rigs out here? Big ask."

Claude nodded, replaced his hat. "Right. Well, thanks a fucking lot."

The engineer turned and walked away without another word. He climbed into the cab of his pick-up truck and drove away with a spin of tires, snow and gravel spraying in an arc as he went.

Claude turned and whistled. Sigmund hopped from the driver's seat of his battered four-wheel drive and jogged over. "Gone to get his stuff?"

Claude laughed without any humor. "No, he's fucking useless. Perhaps I underestimated the scale of the groundwork required. We need a bigger and more organized outfit. Drive me back to town, Siggy."

"Right." The small man trotted to his car, blond curls bouncing.

Darvill stared after him, grinding his teeth. More like Shirley fucking Temple than a genuine assistant. He needed quality people around him, professionals. Time to use some more of dear old daddy's real money and influence. He pulled his phone out, tapped a quick-dial number.

It only rang once. "Jean Chang."

"Hello, Jean. Claude Darvill."

"Yes, I recognized the number. I'm glad you rang. You okay?"

Claude smiled. She genuinely cared, this one. "Yes, I'm fine. I need your expertise again."

"No problem. What can I do for you?

"I'm giving you a promotion. A big one. Pay will reflect that."

"Yes." Chang dragged the word out, voice betraying her suspicion of what her sudden raise might entail.

Darvill laughed softly. "I like you, Chang. You're smart, bloody good at your job and you care about the details. I need you in the field with me."

There was a moment's silence at the other end, then, "Okay. That will require that I make some significant changes if you want me away from London and the Black Diamond office for any length of time."

"Consider it a permanent reassignment. Whatever your salary is now, double it. Fix up any loose ends in London and get the board to arrange your replacement there. I want you out here with me in twenty-four hours."

"And where are you, sir?"

"Iceland."

"Okay."

She didn't even flinch. Not a moment's pause. Claude liked that. "I'll email you details and I'll email the board to back up what I'm telling you now. And before you leave, I need a serious earthmoving company who can cover very rough terrain out here and excavate through solid rock."

There was rapid tapping at the other end as Chang's fingers flew across a keyboard. "Right. Anything else?"

Claude smiled. No questions, no hesitation. "Not for now. Hop to it."

"Yes, sir. I'll text details as they become available and I'll see you before this time tomorrow."

"Attagirl."

Claude hung up and strolled over to the four-wheel drive.

Sigmund leaned out of the driver's side window. "Everything okay?"

"It will be. Get me back to town." He couldn't wait to be rid of this ridiculous and useless assistant and looked forward to the arrival of the willowy and darkly attractive Chang.

Gwen stood, lips pursed. She ran a hand over her loose afro, smoothed it back to replace her black cap. "Weird," she muttered.

Silhouette swallowed her nerves. "What's weird?"

"Come and look at this." Gwen shifted a small monitor so Silhouette could see more easily. The screen was hooked up to strange equipment with glass tubes and copper wiring. An antenna like a small satellite dish oscillated gently on the edge of the bed. Gwen pointed at the screen. "Watch here. It's hard to interpret, so don't expect to see much, but I'll try to explain. Anything with a strong presence, beings with heavy magesign, leave a kind of echo behind, right?"

Silhouette nodded. "That's why we mask all the time."

"Right. But Fey don't mask. They don't care, too arrogant. So if they've been around, they leave pretty obvious traces. Imagine this sensor is a bit like an ultrasound. It doesn't see an image, just bounces back against information. Except what it bounces from are traces of magesign."

"Right."

"Now watch."

Gwen triggered the machine, adjusted a couple of dials. Images shifted across the screen, like static shadows on a television poorly tuned. Sudden bursts of clearer interference flared. "Here they come," Gwen said. She pointed to a patch of snowy reception. "That's one Fey. There's another. Then, there are suddenly lots." A burst of brightness flared off to one side. "But what the hell is *that*?" Gwen asked. "There was nothing there, it didn't enter the room, just appeared out of nowhere. No realmshift, just there."

"Alex," Silhouette whispered.

"What?"

"You wouldn't believe how good Alex is at masking. That's him giving up his cover."

Gwen's eyes widened. "Wow. Okay, that makes sense."

The confusing images were converging on each other, and massive bursts flared and died. "That's the fight," Silhouette said, a hollow hunger clawing at her gut.

Gwen frowned. "Yeah. It's a *big* fight." The confusion of magesign and activity died and faded, smears of interference moved off the screen. "And that's Alex being defeated and them moving away. They have Alex with them. If he died then, it would show in his 'sign. So, they took him alive."

Silhouette was partly relieved, but her concern no less intense. "How?"

"I don't know. We'll have to see if we can track where they went."

"You can do that?"

"Maybe. Depends on the strength of the signal. Given Fey are so blatant and care little for secrecy, we might be lucky. We have the signature now." She detached the oscillating dish and clipped it to a hand-held paddle, like a metal detector used by airport security at check-in gates. A cable ran from the end of the device which she plugged into a wrist-mounted screen she wore. She pointed the tool with one hand, watched the screen on the other. "This way."

Silhouette shook her head. "You have some cool toys."

Gwen grinned. "Armor money and an unrivalled R&D team. Magic and tech can be powerfully combined. Come on."

They moved slowly through the house, down the hallway towards the front door. Gwen paused, back-tracked, moved on again. She walked into the kitchen and stopped, turned in a slow circle. Her face slowly creased into a frown. "That's…"

Nerves rippled through Silhouette's gut. "What is it?"

"Not possible."

"What is it?"

Gwen shook her head, tapped buttons on her wrist monitor. "Wait a minute." She went back to the bedroom, returned with another device. She plugged it into the first. "Signal booster," she explained as she studied the readouts on her arm. "What the hell…?"

Silhouette was losing patience. "Please, Gwen, what the fuck is going on?"

Gwen shook herself, switched off the gear and turned to face Silhouette. "Sorry, I'm distracted. These results are unusual, but I can't interpret them any other way. The attackers dragged Alex through this far—I don't know why, I'll have to study more. Once they got here, the trail ends."

"Ends?"

"They went somewhere else. There's a massive burst of realmshift here—you know when beings travel between realms?"

Silhouette's heart began pounding. "Where did they go?"

Gwen made an apologetic face. "That's the thing. I can't tell for sure yet, but all the frequencies seem to match the Other Lands."

"Faerie? They can't travel between here and there except on thin days."

"Supposedly."

"They're a day late for that."

"I know."

"So what the fuck, Gwen?" Silhouette heard the anger in her voice and put a hand to Gwen's shoulder. "I'm sorry, it's not your fault. But seriously, what the fuck?"

Gwen covered Silhouette's hand with her own, squeezed. "I'm not sure. Let's try to find out more."

She put her equipment down and pulled a small radio from her belt. "Dan, Jack, check in."

The radio crackled, then, "Jack here. Dan's with me. We've run a full perimeter. No activity and no signs of struggle or magical activity. We're about to spiral in, see if we can pick up anything."

"Don't bother. Far as I can tell, it all happened here in the house. Bring your gear and we'll see if we can fine tune what I've found."

"Roger that."

The radio went still and Gwen hooked it back onto her wide canvas belt. She thrust her hands deep into the pockets of her Armor-issued black combat pants. "We'll find out what happened."

Silhouette nodded, sadness welling up from somewhere deep inside. "They took him back with them, didn't they?"

Gwen shrugged.

"I don't know how, but they did," Silhouette said, her voice betraying the depth of her fear.

"Looks that way."

"Will you be able to figure out how?"

"Possibly. It'll take a lot of time. We have the gear to search out the kind of magic used, we can track certain aspects of it. But it's like unravelling a huge ball of knotted twine. It's time-consuming, fiddly work. But we will find out all we can. Why don't you go make a pot of coffee or something, try to rest and gather yourself."

Silhouette smiled crookedly. "Do you want coffee? 'Cause, you know," she gestured at herself, "Kin."

"Oh, yeah. Of course."

"And I just fed."

Gwen nodded, her black skin paling slightly. Silhouette took a dark pleasure in the woman's discomfort and felt immediately guilty about it.

But when emotions built up in Silhouette, she had long since got used to letting her monstrous nature to the fore, a shield against her human frailties.

"I'll go and leave you to your work," Silhouette said. "Tell me if you need anything."

"I will."

"How long do you think it'll take?"

"Give us a couple of hours."

Dan and Jack came into the house and Silhouette nodded to them, ignoring their scowls of disapproval. Fuck 'em. They didn't have to like her or Alex as long as they did their job. She wandered outside, drawing deeply of the fresh, grassy air. Impotence swelled in her, made her flex her fists until the bones creaked. She wanted to fight, to rend with tooth and claw. She needed an enemy to engage and pour her hate into, but there was nothing on which to focus her rage.

Flashes of the grainy, monochrome screen came back to her. The flare of Alex giving up his cover, the huge bursts of magic as the battle was met. The sudden deflation of all activity. They had overwhelmed Alex quickly and thoroughly and that bothered her more than anything else. Alex was a fighter to his marrow, an absolute warrior. The fact he had been beaten so easily had two possible causes. One was there were simply so many Fey with so much power that he couldn't stand against them. Frightening though the concept was, it was infinitely preferable to the other possibility nagging at her mind. Had he just given up?

His demeanor since Obsidian, his struggle to come to terms with all that had happened, kept him bedridden some days when at its worst. Had he faced down a mortal enemy earlier today and simply given in to his despair?

Silhouette hissed in frustration. She refused to believe that until it was proven. Alex, her Alex, was a warrior and he fought. She had seen that happen on Gwen's screen. He had pumped masses of energy into the battle even though it was so short. He had been surprised and overwhelmed by numbers, nothing more. And she would find him, even the odds, and get him back. Or they would both die, side by side, fighting.

CHAPTER FIVE

Jean Chang took a deep breath as she disembarked from the Black Diamond jet in Reykjavik and headed through customs. Quite suddenly, her life was on a new trajectory and she had mixed feelings about it. Claude Darvill had appeared in her life, in the day-to-day running of Black Diamond, in a very unexpected way. First Hood and Sparks disappeared, then, as they desperately looked for the leaders of the global corporate entity, Darvill arrived. Hood's son, with magical and charismatic power none of them had experienced before. John Turner still hadn't forgiven Darvill for his sand trick in the boardroom that first day. None of them knew Hood even had a son until then.

And just as quickly, Darvill disappeared too, leaving the board to run Black Diamond again. There was little out of the ordinary on the surface. Hood regularly disappeared for extended periods, and the board was used to operating without him. But recent events were clearly out of the norm and Chang had sensed a fundamental shift in operations. She wondered if Hood or Sparks would ever return. She wondered how things would be under Darvill. His disappearance had greatly perturbed her. Then, he briefly returned only to go quiet again. Now he was back and asking for her personally.

She remembered the first boardroom meeting, Claude identifying himself by that gorgeous dragon tattoo across his chest and stomach, the act of magic. He was a rugged man and handsome in a rough way. He was smart as hell, too. Jean had always known she outsmarted the vast majority of the board, but Hood had never given her credit for it. Darvill recognized it immediately, used her as his only liaison. Now, she saw the opportunity to move from an office into something more interesting, more tangible. Her rise through Black Diamond had been fueled by a desire to know more about the arcane goods Hood bought and sold. They all knew the everyday activities of Black Diamond— investments, corporate takeover, mineral wealth—were a by-product of Hood's primary business, and a cover. Many of the board chose to ignore it, but not Jean Chang. She wanted to know. She wanted a part of Hood's esoteric world. And he had barely given her a second glance, the sexist fuckwit.

Then Darvill came along and homed straight in on her and made her feel truly worthwhile for the first time in her career. But the trip to Iceland after organizing all he had asked of her gave her pause. Hood and Sparks were gone, no one knew where. Or if they would ever be back. Had she let herself in for more than she could handle? Would she be the next to disappear? With Darvill or without?

A four-wheel drive carried her away from the city, the driver babbling on about something she could not be bothered to follow. As she stared at the snow-covered landscape, the cold light of realization began to dawn on her. What was she walking into? She gripped trembling hands together in her lap. She would not baulk. Frightening it might be, but she was strong enough to face it.

The journey was long and fairly boring, though the view kept Jean's attention and helped her ignore the nagging worries. The driver, whose name was apparently Sigmund, eventually gave up on his attempts at small talk. The view became slowly more bleak and Sigmund finally pulled off the road onto an unsealed track. Before long, he turned away from that and bounced and slipped across country for several miles.

"Nearly there," he said, pointing ahead.

A grouping of rocks and low hills, dark against the frozen land, stood among the shale and pale tussocks of hardy grasses. The edge of a bright blue tarpaulin poked out from among the edges of the stones, another four-wheel drive vehicle parked nearby. Jean smiled as she saw Claude emerge from the shadows, using one hand to shield his eyes as he watched their approach. He disappeared for a moment then reappeared, cramming his wide-brimmed leather hat onto his head. He wore his signature khaki pants and heavy linen shirt, a scuffed brown leather jacket pulled tight over the top. Indiana Jones cosplay was never so accurate—he even had the leather satchel. All that was missing was the whip. But the Indy comparison must not be made in his presence. How could he not be freezing in that getup?

As the car pulled up, Jean hopped out, straightened her jeans and zipped her padded Gore-Tex jacket against the chill breeze. She was glad for the hiking boots she wore, tipped off by Darvill's request for heavy earth-moving contractors on site. She shouldered her backpack, crammed only with essentials, and held out her hand. "Hello, sir."

Darvill's smile was warm. "Ms. Chang." He shook her hand, his own rough but warm. "I'm so glad you're here." He leaned past her. "All right, Siggy, you can fuck off now."

The small man was surprised. "Sir?"

"Fuck off. Send your timesheet in to head office once you're back. Make sure you claim for today's driving hours."

"Oh. Okay. That's it?"

Darvill rolled his eyes. "Fuck me." He looked back to Jean. "You see why I so desperately needed some real help?" Without another look at the dismissed man, he led Jean away, heading for the tarp stretched between rocks.

Jean avoided the burning temptation to look back. She could imagine Sigmund's puppy-dog eyes as he watched them leave. She felt sorry for him, but he had failed where she would succeed. Darvill was the sort of person who never wanted to have to ask for anything twice. She'd realized that early on and made it work for her. She had no time to offer failures any sympathy. As they ducked under the tarp, the car started up again and the engine faded as Sigmund drove away.

The tarp shielded an open area between rocks where Darvill had stashed all kinds of gear, warmed by free-standing, gas-powered space heaters. Big plastic tubs were stocked with food, multi-packs of bottled of water sat piled on top. Ground surveying equipment and other tools were stacked opposite. The end of the tarp, shivering in the icy breeze, covered the entrance to a cave. The sunlight was filtered blue by the material, made the place feel like an undersea grotto. Darvill led her into the cave and a sudden close warmth. An oil burner sat in one corner, camping gas burners for cooking beside it. A small dishevelled cot was opposite.

Darvill pointed. "I've got a camp bed and sleeping bag for you. We'll set it up here in the warm later. Sorry about the poor accommodation and lack of privacy."

Jean shrugged. "I'm sure I'll cope."

"That your only bag?"

"Yes, sir. Never been a girly girl. I don't need much. I only packed for a few days and figured I could always buy whatever else I needed."

Darvill grinned, clapped her on the shoulder. "Good girl. Smart. Hopefully we won't be here too long, but you never know. You saw how far it is to the nearest town."

"Yes, sir, I noted that on the way in."

"Good. If you need anything, take the car out there. I'll have errands for you, anyway. You set yourself up an expense account?"

"Well, I still have my board accounts."

"Excellent. Use them. Put your stuff down there and follow me."

He strode from the cave. Jean threw her bag down and hurried after him. What the hell was he doing out here? She had heard Hood often refer to his main man in the field and had a strong suspicion it was this man—the son none of them knew Hood had. He must be the one who sniffed out the rare artifacts, negotiated with strange mages, hunted down the people Hood needed for deals. She smiled at the thought. Darvill was more like Indiana Jones than she had ever realized, if her assumptions were correct. So what had he found out here that needed to be retrieved with rock-cutting equipment?

Darvill stood in the middle of an unremarkable patch of shale. He turned as she caught up. "You ready for anything, Chang?"

"Yes, sir."

"Sure?"

"Well, I hope so. I guess until I know what it is…"

"Brace yourself. I need your help and I don't want you flaking out on me."

"Whatever it is, you can rely on me." She stood up taller, hoping her resolve truly matched her words and posture.

"Good girl. When's the rock cutter arriving?"

"First thing tomorrow. Following your email, I gave them the location and they said they'd be here before nine. Took a huge bonus in their pay to get them to come right away, but you said cost was no object."

Darvill nodded, lips pursed. "Black Diamond coffers can cope. Let's hope this crew is up to the job. They're going to have to cut deep." He stared at the ground by his feet.

Jean followed his gaze. "What's down there, sir?"

Darvill sniffed, met her eye with an intense gaze. "My father, Chang. And he's in a lot of pain."

Jean stared into Darvill's eyes and could think of nothing to say.

Silhouette sat among the stones of the circle of protection that had proven to be anything but. For nearly two hours, she had stewed, worrying. When Gwen called out, she was up and running to the house instantly.

"Well?" she demanded.

Gwen's face was grim. "Definitely Faerie."

Silhouette nodded. She had known in her heart that would be the answer. "No question?"

Gwen shrugged, moving aside as Jack and Dan packed up their gear. "There's always doubt. This is magic, not science, however much we bring technology to bear. But it's a very slim doubt. Everything points to the Fey dragging Alex here, unconscious we think, and from here they performed a ritual and travelled back to the Other Lands."

Silhouette gripped her blonde hair back with both hands. "Fucking how? The thin day was past."

"I don't know."

Silhouette slumped onto a kitchen stool. "Without their anchor stone, how did they do it? Something must have changed."

"Or something we didn't know about is happening."

"Wouldn't we have had evidence of it before? Well, wouldn't you? Isn't that Armor's fucking job, to know this stuff?"

"Yes, it is. And maybe someone higher than me in the organisation does know something."

Silhouette stood decisively. "Let's go. I want to talk to the Commander."

Gwen nodded, turned to the other operatives. "Load up the chopper, lads. We're going back."

Silhouette looked around herself, bereft. She felt terrible leaving the house, but staying was pointless. Alex was long gone, taken to the worst place she could imagine. Even as someone who had been to Obsidian, the thought of Faerie filled her with a darker terror. Regardless of her concerns, it looked like she was going to the place she feared most and

Armor had better have ways of helping her.

The chopper journey was frustrating. She wanted to be doing something. Gwen radioed in once they were airborne and gave the Commander a full rundown of what she had learned. She told him Silhouette was coming in.

The ride over the beautiful rolling hills of the New South Wales south coast and on over sprawling Sydney suburbs didn't take long, but Silhouette worried and fidgeted the whole way. She cursed herself again and again for leaving Alex. If she had stayed, perhaps they could have fought together. Or perhaps they would have both been overwhelmed. At least she was in a position now to help him.

The chopper settled briefly in the Sydney Botanic Gardens to drop her off and left the moment Silhouette was out. Gwen and the others were returning to the hangar with their gear. Silhouette ran through the grounds, past open-mouthed tourists and office workers, staring as the helicopter swept up and away over the picturesque and famous harbor. She jogged out of the gardens and on through old streets to the magnificent edifice of St. Mary's Cathedral. She slowed as she made her way around to the Armor HQ secret entrance at the side of the building and stood beneath the cold eye of the camera above the door. After a moment, the door clicked and she pushed it open. Dark steps went down to the small anteroom which led to the operations room. Silhouette swept through, nodding to the people there. They all returned her greeting stoically. She wondered if they had heard about Alex. If they cared. Maybe some were glad, like Dan and Jack.

The Commander stood as she knocked and strode into his office. He stepped around the desk and took her into a firm embrace. He was a giant of a man, with gray-white hair cascading over his shoulders and a huge handlebar mustache. He pressed her against his chest for a moment, planted a fatherly kiss on top of her head, and returned to his seat. She sat opposite him.

"I'm so sorry, Sil," he said, his eyes dark. "This is messed up."

Silhouette nodded, determined to not give in to the grief churning inside her.

The Commander poured them both tea, pushed a cup across the desk. "How did they so easily get by our barriers?"

Silhouette sipped. It tasted like metal. "I don't know. How much do you really know about them? How effective were your wards, really?"

"Clearly not at all. We thought we knew better, but they appear to have power beyond our ken."

"And how did they travel back? We thought they were waiting for the next thin day to take him away. We would have had weeks to hunt them down. But Gwen is convinced they went directly back."

The Commander nodded, staring into his cup.

"Fucking how?" Silhouette yelled.

The Commander raised his eyes to meet hers and his gaze was filled with sadness. "The great power the Fey had was in their anchor stone. When it was in this realm, it made every day like a thin day. They came and went between here and the Other Lands at will. That's why the Eld cast that anchor stone out into the Void."

Silhouette nodded, impatient. "Yeah, except there were members of the Eld who were greedy and built Obsidian around that stone and used it to live large in their own pocket world. Alex fucked that for them. He truly cast that stone into the Void, destroyed Obsidian. It's all gone. That's why they hate him."

The Commander sat with his tea cupped between massive palms and stared patiently across the desk, waiting.

Silhouette narrowed her eyes, anger rising. What the fuck was he waiting for? A terrible realization rose in her like a rush of adrenaline. Alex's power was primarily through his bond with the Darak, a stone of power. It was a part of him, embedded in the flesh of his chest, beating with his heart. But the Darak was a piece of the Fey anchor stone, removed from its host by massive Eld magic, used to cast out Uthentia.

The Darak was what started all their problems, and then the Fey used it and Alex to get to Obsidian. They wanted their anchor stone back, used everyone to that end. But Alex had beaten them. They had all been concerned the Fey would come for revenge, but that wasn't it. "They want the Darak," Silhouette whispered.

The Commander nodded. "We should have thought of that, eh? They must have used Alex himself to travel back, his bond with the Darak making him a living version of their stone, at least a part of its power. Alex did indeed finish the work of the Eld, casting the anchor into oblivion forever. Except he didn't cast out all of it."

Silhouette paled, anguish washed through her. "But Alex and the Darak are one. They can't be separated. It would kill Alex if they took the stone, but it would kill the stone too. He gave it life—isn't that what your scholars said when they examined him after the Incident?"

The Commander nodded again, set his cup down. "So, I'm guessing they maybe know something about it we don't. Or they plan to use Alex as their tool."

Silhouette trembled with fear and rage. "We can't let them have him."

The Commander's face was grim. "But what can we do? I'll have to talk to some experts about this."

"The same experts who came to our house and posted those wards? Who built a stone fucking circle in our garden?"

"Silhouette, I know this is upsetting…"

"You have no fucking idea how this is, Commander! All Armor has so far done for Alex is send him on a mission that nearly killed him and, as a result, has led to his abduction to about the worst place imaginable. You'll forgive me if I don't trust you or your experts anymore." She knew her anger was really at the Fey, but she honestly rued the day Armor had entered their lives. Certainly, Alex had been lost and seeking direction after the business with the Darak and Uthentia, and she had thought maybe that direction was to be found with this shadowy organization. Now, she just wanted to have Alex back and all these people could go to hell.

The Commander reached across the desk, took her hand. "Silhouette, I understand your rage, really, I do. But the Fey would have found a way to Alex with or without us. Once he had recombined the Darak, created that power to get their influence into Obsidian, they would have found a way to make that happen. And, if I might be so bold, only through our help did you all get out of there again as cleanly as you did."

Silhouette barked a laugh, shook him off. "Clean! Alex is traumatized beyond belief. He's felt the Void, Commander. He has the deaths of *thousands* on his conscience and he knows how terrible those deaths were!"

"And he saved thousands more and we have to help him come to terms with all of that. My point is, we can still help. Don't hate us for what happened. Let us help."

"How? What are you going to do?"

"We have sages, bookworms and brains who specialize in the Fey. Firstly, let's consult them. Get an idea of how we might proceed."

Silhouette stood. "They've taken Alex to Faerie and we can only assume they want the Darak. If they have a way of getting it, that will almost certainly be bad for Alex. And even if taking it didn't kill him, they would kill him afterwards anyway because they're evil and they hate him. Or they're just going to use him like a living key. Fuck that. I'm going to find a way there and get him back."

"I can't allow that, Silhouette. Not yet."

Silhouette's mouth fell open, incredulous. "Allow it? Who the hell do you…?"

"You're part of Armor now, whether you officially work for us or not, and I have a responsibility to protect you and the organization. We need to move carefully, strategize." The Commander pressed a button on his desk. The office door opened. Two black-clad operatives blocked the way.

"You can't hold me here!" Silhouette yelled.

"I'm sorry."

Silhouette turned to the door and the two operatives moved as if they planned to tackle her. Behind them the looming form of Jarrod appeared, his enormous Maori frame, a head bigger than either of them and twice as wide, imposing. His brow creased in concern. "Silhouette?"

She had never been so pleased to see her half-brother. "If you have any love for me, Jarrod, get me out of here."

The Commander's chair scraped as he stood. "Stand down, Jarrod."

The big man looked past Silhouette to his commander, then back to his sister. Silhouette pleaded with her eyes, silently begged him to intervene. With a subtle nod, he grabbed the operatives around their necks and hauled them back. Without pausing for a second, Silhouette bolted forward. "Thank you!" she said as she passed him.

A klaxon blared and the Commander yelled, "Hold her, for her own sake! Jarrod, you fool!"

Silhouette pushed through a suddenly confused and milling operations center and dove for the door even as security grilles dropped. She felt something clip her heel as she ran, ignored the stab of pain. She took the stairs in a headlong rush and burst out into the busy plaza of St. Mary's Cathedral. Without waiting to see if she was being chased, she ducked left and right through the crowd and kept running until her lungs burned. Whatever Armor may or may not suggest, her course was clear. The last twenty-four hours had proven Armor knew next to nothing about the Fey and the Other Lands, not really. But she was Kin. First-generation at that, a full half-Fey. And she knew people. Alex needed her and she planned to find a way to get to him.

J ean Chang waved the huge excavator over to one side of the site. What had been nothing more than open scree and a clutch of rocks, snow and ice the day before was quickly becoming a major work effort. It had taken some serious paperwork and no small number of bribes to circumvent the various bureaucracies involved in an operation of this scale, but Black Diamond pockets were deep.

The excavator was followed by an enormous vehicle bearing a huge circular saw on an extending arm. Its hooked serrations were frightening to behold as it cruised past and hissed to a halt. The driver hopped down and looked quizzically in her direction. She pointed to Darvill in conversation with a small group of contractors.

As the man nodded and moved away, Jean checked her tablet for details of arrivals. Everyone booked was here with the exception of the government overseer. And screw that guy. She had tried to assure the pen pushers that he wasn't needed and now he wasn't here anyway. If he showed up late, she'd deal with him, but she certainly didn't plan to wait for him before letting the work commence. Claude would not stand for that, and more money would motivate the contractors to ignore protocols.

She strolled towards the group who were deep in discussion. Claude had insisted she use his first name, told her to treat him like a partner, not a boss, even though she was tasked to do everything he asked without question. She was okay with that, happy to serve and rise in the organization. She wanted to learn more, extend herself and her experience. But this was a sudden and disconcerting change of direction. Mr. Hood was in the rock, Claude had said. In agonising pain, inside the very ground. How was that possible? How could he live down there? How had he gotten there? Claude had no answers for her and simply wanted to get his father out, and she could understand that, but there was something else bothering her. She had tried to bring it to Claude's attention, but he had not been interested to listen. It still bothered her. If Hood was down there, and somehow still alive, what would getting him out again mean? No man could survive being buried in solid rock. So what, exactly, would they be letting out? She knew Claude recognized her concerns as valid, but he deliberately chose not to think about it. Filial love or insatiable curiosity? Maybe both.

"I don't care if you have to get a new fucking star in here," Claude was saying as she joined the group. "Find a way to get light in, use generators and whatever else you need. Screw the expense. Daylight is too short here right now. This site runs twenty-four seven and that area gets excavated as soon as fucking possible."

One of the men turned to his companion, rattled off something in Icelandic. The other man hurried off. "He will organize arc lights," the contractor said in English. "What about the excavated material?"

Claude's brow creased. "What?"

"The rock and earth we clear from the area marked. Where do you want it?"

"I don't give a shit. Just pile it up somewhere. You can always shovel it all back in afterwards."

Uncomfortable murmuring ran through the group. "What are we excavating?" one man asked.

Claude shook his head. "It's too complicated for me to explain right now. Suffice to say you need to dig in the area marked." He pointed to a section of loose shale and pale grasses, a square some ten meters across marked with tape and spray paint. "Keep digging until I tell you to stop. I understand it's confusing, but you're getting well paid to do what you do. Just dig a fucking hole."

"How deep?"

"Until I tell you to stop!"

"The loose material on top is only about a meter thick. Below that it's solid rock. It's going to take quite an effort to clear the area marked to any depth, but even then it's not a big footprint and this is very volatile country…"

Claude held up one impatient hand. "I don't care!" He pointed to the giant rock saw. "That's here for a reason. The area is big enough. Start digging, right now."

The contractor turned to his fellows, spoke again in Icelandic. They muttered resigned consent and moved away to their vehicles.

Claude turned to Jean. "Finally! Well done organizing this lot."

She nodded, smiled. "No problem. What now?"

"We wait."

"What are we waiting for exactly?"

Darvill narrowed his eyes. "What do you mean?"

"Are we really waiting for your father to be dug from solid rock? It's really Mr. Hood?"

Claude laid an arm across her shoulders and turned her towards their cave camp. "I know it's hard to understand, Chang. Trust me. Let's have a cuppa."

CHAPTER SEVEN

Silhouette walked along King Street, bustling as it always was at any time of day or night. Traffic crawled bumper to bumper and every tribe of Sydney trod the pavements, passing secondhand clothing and bookshops, every other doorway leading into an eatery. Back before the Obsidian Incident, when Silhouette had asked Wilhelm the fight organizer where she could get Fey ingredients for her healing concoction, he had directed her to a fetish shop in Newtown. That dealer had Fey connections and it was the only lead she had anywhere in Australia. She checked Wilhelm's card again, her memory hazy after her time away, and turned into a side street.

The narrow road was littered and dirty. Graffiti and primary colored posters advertising gigs and protest rallies overlapped each other on the walls between shops. Residential terraces started half a block down, but right before her stood a black-painted storefront with a square plate-glass window. The same cursive script as the card adorned the space above the window, *Leather & Lace*, while mannequins inside modeled exactly that. The fashion du jour seemed to be a kind of Victorian/sub-dom hybrid. One mannequin wore the same outfit as last time she had visited with Alex. Emotion welled in her as she remembered the day.

Alex had pointed to the fitted leather bodice, red laces pulled tight across the front. "You'd look great in that."

Silhouette looked from the bodice to Alex and back again. "You're right. I would look freaking hot in that. Buy it for me?"

Alex popped one eyebrow. "Really?"

"Fucking no, you dumbass!"

They had both laughed, though Alex was clearly disappointed. She stared at the bodice again. If she managed to get him out of this, she would come back here and buy that thing, wear it for him.

She pushed the door open and entered the shop. A Fields of the Nephilim track played, from the *Dawnrazor* album. She had fond memories of the late eighties in London. A very buxom girl in a huge lace and crushed cotton dress, with an ivory whalebone corset pulled tight, nodded a greeting from behind the counter. "Help you?" she asked. Her eyes narrowed. "I remember you. Need more stuff already?"

"Something like that," Silhouette said, forcing a friendly smile onto her face. "Crabapple here?"

"Sure." The girl pursed her lips. She raised her chin and a burst of magic briefly lit Silhouette's senses. After a moment, an answering pulse came back.

"He'll see you," the girl said. "Remember the rules: no touching, no magic, no haggling."

"I remember," Silhouette said.

"You know the way." She pointed to a door behind the counter marked *Private*.

Silhouette gave the girl a tight smile. She pushed open the door and headed into a room beyond. There was a table and a small kitchenette, sink, kettle, microwave, fridge. Another door led from the room. She went through into a dim corridor and a strong, sweet smell like burnt sugar. Her senses roiled, stomach tightening. It was a Fey odor. Were there actually Fey here? Crabapple was Kin, a dealer in Fey goods, so he obviously had contacts, but she had always dealt with dealers because only idiots dealt direct with the Other Folk. Let the dealers take the chances. But her mission was too important. She pushed on.

Along with the odor drifted a sensation of something she had never felt before. Oily and sweet like the smell, overlaid with a creeping malevolence. Like the sensation of someone secretly watching, only amplified a thousandfold. For all her long life as a Kin, Silhouette had never faced a Fey in person. She had hoped she never would and any sane individual would feel the same. Now, she was trying to find a way to their realm. The human half of her reeled, desperate to turn on her heel and bolt. The Fey half yearned for something beyond conscious thought that made her very uncomfortable.

She pulled herself up tall. "Hell no. I'm not balking at this." Her voice sounded tremulous and she ground her teeth as she continued along the corridor, dimly lit with weak bulbs concealed in the ceiling. After a few meters, three steps led down to another door. Written on it in letters made from twigs twisted together was *Crabapple*. She knocked.

"Come in."

When she opened the door, the greasy sweet smell intensified, washed over her. Crabapple sat behind a huge desk. He was an old man, wrinkled like a walnut, his skin a deep tan. Almond eyes almost lost in folds of skin glistened, dark brown in the low light. "Hello again," he said. "So lovely to see you back." His country Chinese accent was strong, but his English impeccable all the same, almost as if he enhanced the accent deliberately—an affectation Silhouette found strangely irritating.

She stepped into the office and hissed, her form shifting briefly between her human appearance and the wild, panther-like cat she favored. In the corner, out of sight from the door, sat a creature that turned her stomach to water. Tall and thin, it seemed to be made of night and shadows. Its face was long and angular, its eyes glowed a soft amber like coals burning low in a campfire. Coldness wafted from it, as though it were a fridge door left open.

The creature rocked back, laughed heartily. "No need to be rude, dear!" One long, stick-like arm raised and flapped at her, the movement uncanny, almost flickering, like an over-cranked film or one of those jerky old black and white movies.

Silhouette gathered herself, enforced her human form. On closer inspection, the creature's skin seemed like thin, leathery bark and, though shadow and cold seemed to manifest around it, the skin was a deep, oily green-black. In such close proximity, the burnt-sugar sweetness was almost enough to make her gag. "You're Fey!" she growled.

Tension crackled in the air. The creature sat forward and stared hard at her. "And you have blood like mine enhancing your human weaknesses, you Kin bitch, so you might want to show some respect."

Crabapple chuckled, slipped half-moon glasses onto the bridge of his nose. "You knew I got my stuff from somewhere. You're really that surprised?"

Silhouette breathed deeply, determined to control herself. She didn't take her eyes from the Fey. "I'm first-generation Kin. One of you fuckers raped my mother. Don't expect any respect from me."

The creature's face split in a grin, revealing a double row of sharp, black teeth. "Ah! Your father was pure! No wonder your essence is strong."

"My *father*," Silhouette sneered, emphasising her disdain with the word, "is nothing to me."

"You may like to think so, but he's everything that you are."

Silhouette shook her head. "My mother, my *human* mother, was the only parent I ever knew and her influence was strong. Since her, only Kin."

The creature chuckled. "Deny it all you like. You're first-generation, there's not many like you."

Silhouette reminded herself that outside thin days, Fey were weak in the mortal realm. How weak, she had no idea, but chose to concentrate simply on the fact they were reduced. She would not be intimidated by this bastard. "You live here?" she asked.

"I made a powerful enemy in Faerie and was cast out, imprisoned in this realm and stripped of my power. If I ever return, I'll die. Supposedly. So I've carved out a bit of a business here. I'm very good at sneaking back and forth."

"How do you bear it? Don't Fey hate the mortal realm? Isn't that why you fuck with it so much?"

The creature hissed laughter. "Don't presume you know anything about us, whelp. But I'm different to most. I like the order here. It's partly how I became an exile. But I don't owe you a life story. Get on with your business and be gone." It flicked one long-fingered hand jerkily towards Crabapple and sat back in its chair.

Silhouette's mind raced. This was a potentially useful development. Presumably this creature had just returned on the thin day, bringing its illicit merchandise with it, and was busily transacting its business. She had hoped Crabapple might be able to point her in the direction of someone, or something, that could help her get to Faerie. Well, terrifying though it may be, sitting right before her was exactly what she needed. "I've actually got something in mind that you might be able to help me with more than him."

Surprise registered on the Fey's long, sharp face and Crabapple spluttered. "Excuse me, young lady. You don't come in to my office and start making deals without me!"

Silhouette turned to the old Kin. "I'm sorry, I don't mean any disrespect. How about I pay you a finder's fee?" She did nothing to hide the sarcasm in her tone.

The Fey spoke, its voice deep. "What do you need, Kin?"

Crabapple jumped up, came around to stand between them. "Kreek, do you mind! What's happening here?"

The Fey, Kreek, stood swiftly, rising to over seven feet tall. Silhouette couldn't help noticing his large, branch-like penis swing free. He stuck one long arm out and pointed a sharp finger at Crabapple. "Silence! You and I do business and you do very well. This, I think, is…something else. She has bought from you before and no doubt will again. Be content with that."

Crabapple sighed and slunk back to his chair. Kreek folded himself back into his own seat, rested pointed elbows on knees like gnarled tree limbs. He tilted his head like an inquisitive dog, regarding Silhouette with curiosity.

Silhouette endured the scrutiny. She would need to tread carefully, maybe show this thing some respect after all, whether she felt it or not. She needed his help.

"What do you need of me?" Kreek asked. "If it was simple Other Land ingredients, you would trade with him."

Silhouette nodded. "I need something he can't give me."

"Which is?"

"Access to Faerie."

Kreek's eyes widened, his knife-scar of a mouth curving into a smile. He began to laugh, a low rumble in his narrow chest that bubbled out into a raucous hoot. "You *want* to go to Faerie?"

Silhouette considered all she had heard so far, took a gamble. "You've been cast out, right? I'm guessing you have little love left for your kind."

Kreek's laughter faded. "Perhaps."

"What if I told you I have a plan to really piss off some of your Folk? If I can get there, that is."

"I'd say you were one deluded Kin bitch and you would be dead in minutes." He held up a stick-like finger. "No, correct that. You would be enslaved in minutes and spend a long, miserable life suffering in service to whoever over there was lucky enough to catch you first. You'd be quite a prize."

"I'm prepared to take that chance." Silhouette's chest fluttered with nerves as she realized the truth of her words. She had always been a pariah, always a loner. In Alex, she had finally found someone she could love, someone to commit to. He wasn't Kin, and she was done with her own kind, but he was strong enough, with magic enough, to live a long lifetime like she would. She wanted them to live that life together, and she would be happy to die or become enslaved in an effort to rescue it. Of course, she would much rather survive the attempt and get Alex back. "Get me to Faerie. Give me some tips on how to survive there. Please."

Kreek tilted his head again. "You mean it, don't you? What a strange one you are." He sat back in his chair, chin resting on the backs of his hands, and stared at her. The perusal dragged on, became uncomfortable. Silhouette refused to budge, refused to show anything but a steel resolve, though she had trouble looking at the dark creature. Her eyes kept trying to slip aside. "What's in it for me?" Kreek asked eventually.

Silhouette shrugged. "What do you want? What would I have to give you? I promise to strike a blow against the Fey if I can. Is that not good enough? To know you helped get me there, to fuck with the Folk who exiled you?"

Kreek chuckled, shook his head gently. "Possibly. You fascinate me. I'm certain I'll only be sending you to a terrible fate, but perhaps I can help you. Just for the fun of it, eh? I'm sure I'll think of something you can do for me, some time."

Silhouette nodded, knowing she had made a deal with evil. Like taking a favour from the Mob, one day she would have to pay for this and it would not be pretty. But she had little choice and opportunities like this would not be easy to find elsewhere. "So you'll help?"

"Let me finish my business here and make some arrangements. Do you know an oceanside place to the east of here called Gordon's Bay?"

"No, this isn't my town. But I'll find it." Not wanting to spend another moment in the cloying confines of the small office, she turned and left.

The polluted noise and bustle of King Street was a blessing after the sickly closeness of Crabapple's. The Fey were evil, simple as that, and Silhouette didn't trust for a minute that Kreek was completely exiled or completely powerless. They never told the truth. Never! But she needed his help and would have to hope he kept his end of the bargain. She had a few hours to wait before meeting him at Gordon's Bay. She had no idea why there, but would have to play along. If the fucker was simply setting her up to kill her or worse, she would deal with it. Somehow. Or die trying.

An old pub stood imposing on the corner a block down the road, its brick and tile frontage inviting. She decided to have a steadying drink or two before finding a bus to the eastern suburbs.

Claude Darvill strode angrily through the worksite, shouting orders. People reluctantly nodded, grudgingly agreed. If it wasn't for the seemingly bottomless coffers of Black Diamond Incorporated, Jean Chang wondered if these workers would be putting up with a fraction of Darvill's abuse. But he was throwing money at them almost with abandon and they grit their teeth, took his cash and did as he asked. As ever, currency greased the most recalcitrant wheels and silenced moral misgivings.

The enormous saw whined a deafening scream as it sliced into solid rock. Water sprayed in a thick jet over the work, cooling and suppressing dust, steaming up into the cold air. The topsoil and shale sat in a huge mound off to one side which Darvill had taken to standing atop to better see the progress of the excavation.

A front-end loader moved into position, lifted out chunks of carved rock and moved them beside the mound. They cracked as they were dumped, the sound echoing across the desolate land. Darvill nodded, his face stark in the paling glow of an overcast sky as twilight began to wreath the land around them.

Chang still harbored doubts, reservations about not only the process itself and what exactly had happened to Hood, but about Claude too. His zealotry increased by the hour, his need to finish this job. She was concerned for his sanity and, by extension, her safety.

An enormous hissing and searing jets of steam drew her attention. A yell went up from the workers and the giant saw truck backed up. The hose was directed down into the slowly deepening hole and more steam clouded out, billowed angrily up towards the darkening sky.

Chang hurried up the mound to stand beside Darvill, her feet slipping and sliding in the loose material. "What's happened?"

Claude stared at the hole with a disconcerting intensity. "They've struck a pocket of something."

More shouting and men running back and forth. A worker was helped to the tents where the men rested, cradling his arm and moaning in pain.

The foreman jogged up to them, pointed back at the injured man. "He's been seriously burned. Steam."

"So replace him." Darvill didn't take his eyes from the hole.

The foreman scowled. "We've hit a volcanic seam. There's enormous heat down there, magma probably."

"So?" Darvill tore his eyes from the scene at last to stare daggers at the foreman.

"So we can't work in such conditions. It's too dangerous."

"You are just getting to exactly where you need to be. Keep cutting away that rock above."

The foreman's eyes widened. "What? We could release any amount of contained geothermic energy. Did you see that steam geyser?"

"Yes, I saw it. Be more careful, but carry on. You want danger money? Am I not paying you e-fucking-nough?"

The two men stared at each other for several seconds. Eventually, the foreman lowered his eyes. "Our equipment could be destroyed in the process."

"Then I will pay to have it replaced. Have someone put in an order now to make sure any equipment needed is ready immediately."

The foreman shook his head and trudged back down the mound to talk to his workers. There was hand waving and angry looks but they moved away and restarted the machines.

Darvill put an arm across Jean's shoulders, squeezed her into his chest. "We're nearly there!"

"Molten rock," Chang said quietly. "What can survive in molten rock?"

"I find things, Jean, and I've found my father. I know he's alive down there. I can't tell you how, I have no explanation for it, but don't you think it's amazing? Finding out will be incredible."

Chang endured the rough hug, thinking that incredible it may be, but it wouldn't have been her first adjective of choice. Terrifying, maybe. Or unnatural.

The whine started again as the huge circular saw lowered into rock on the opposite side to the area still jetting steam. The water hoses were increased, a second water tanker moved in, and the whole worksite began to feel like a giant outdoor sauna, humid and hot, as steam billowed like winter mist all around, pushing the icy air away. More cuts were made and several times the machinery was hastily retreated as the volatile geology tried to fight back. The workers slowly sectioned off a larger portion of the rock shelf they were cutting through and a sudden, deafening crack caused cries of alarm.

A chunk of rock the size of a large car split away from the edge and sank into roiling, bright red magma. The saw vehicle tipped at an alarming angle and its engine screamed as the driver over-revved it to drag it backwards. Huge tires spun, shot gravel and chunks of rock through the air, and the heavy vehicle bounced and skidded in reverse.

Smoke and steam flooded up from the hole in the ground, like the crater of a volcano in miniature. Men staggered back from the sudden and intense heat, other vehicles hastily retreated.

From atop the mound, Darvill and Chang had an excellent view into the hole, glowing bright red like illuminated blood. Jean shook her head, a sense of relief washing through her. Nothing could survive in there, even the rock itself was melted.

And something lapped up at the side.

A moment of surreal calm and silence fell across the site. All eyes turned to the unnaturally shifting lava that crept up over the edge of sheer-cut rock and dragged itself away from the hole. The mass popped and steamed, bright redness rippled black as it cooled rapidly in the night air. It arched upwards, a curve of lava the size of a man standing up against gravity. With a roar of agony, arms emerged, rising from the globular mess. The arms thrashed up and down, chunks of searing hot rock and gobbets of lava flew off in all directions. Workers were hit and fell screaming, or ran for cover holding burnt flesh or scorched clothing.

The lava man staggered forward, shaking off more thick, red heat, howling in torment. It turned and flicked one arm deliberately at a truck driver cowering some few meters away. A huge globule of lava flew from the creature's arm and slammed into the unfortunate man's chest. He screamed as the molten rock ate swiftly through clothing and flesh and he fell lifeless to the ground.

The burning man stopped some three or four meters from the hole and stretched its arms skyward, yelling incoherently to the firmament. With slow, deliberate movements, it began striking at itself, knocking away chunks of rock and sizzling lava. Its flesh, impossibly, glowed pale and unburnt through the gaps. It dragged hands over its face and roared as it tore away the hell-coating of its prison.

Jean Chang was vaguely aware of Darvill's frantic breathing and disjointed murmurs beside her. Her entire body shook with shock, horror, disbelief. How could she possibly be seeing what eyes told her was there?

Within moments, Robert Hood, CEO of Black Diamond Incorporated, stood naked and hairless as ever, thin and wan in the arc lights, unblemished flesh steaming in the cold. He tipped his head back and a high, manic laugh rippled up from his chest, to burst out towards the heavens.

ilhouette walked along the footpath above Gordon's Bay, trepidatious both for her awaited contact and the possibility that Armor might have tracked her down. A part of her wondered if Armor were perhaps leaving her to her own devices. She didn't doubt for a minute that if they really wanted to, they had the means to find her, be those methods arcane or technological. Or both. Maybe the Commander had decided she was less trouble out of the way and at least now he didn't have to commit any assistance to her cause.

She wished Jarrod was here to help. Other than Alex, Silhouette had no friends or family she could rely on. At least, she hadn't until she met Jarrod and realized they had a connection in their Fey blood. She would have appreciated the big man's hulking presence and reassuring calm. His mother was Maori, from New Zealand, and Jarrod was fiercely proud of his heritage and cultural tradition. She wanted more time to learn about him, his history. And about the possibilities of their kinship. She toyed with the idea of calling him, asking him to come with her, help recover Alex, but she tossed the idea aside. He would almost certainly say yes and she was under no illusions about this endeavor. It was quite possibly a suicide mission. Besides, for all she knew Jarrod was locked up in an Armor cell for helping her. She hoped not.

Alex might already be dead, she might never find him. She would probably be caught and killed, or worse. But she had to try. After centuries of never fitting in, always treated with suspicion by the Kin-born for her first-generation blood, always so removed from her humanity by the needs of being Kin, in Alex she had found love and purpose and direction. She didn't want to be alone any more.

She stopped walking, heart hammering with the realization. She stared out to sea, looking over the rocky shore of Gordon's Bay, a small inlet between two larger beaches. She was being thoroughly honest with herself. After so many years of living a loner life, she had had enough. Alex—and only Alex—offered salvation. She laughed quietly, shook her head. "Damn you, Caine," she whispered to the gathering gloom of twilight. "I'm fucking coming for you."

A man strolled casually towards her and she froze. He stared with an intensity that fixed her to the spot and she knew without a doubt that it was Kreek. He appeared as a fit-looking man in his forties, shoulder-length hair loose about his head. He was tall, but not as tall as in his Fey form, and moved with an agile grace, nothing like the stutter movements of the Fey in their natural state. Silhouette wondered briefly if that was a condition of being in this realm. The shapechanging certainly seemed to remove it somehow. Another Fey mystery. Kin shapechanging was a benefit of their Fey blood. She wondered what else they inherited from their evil progenitors and realized, not for the first time, how little she knew of her true heritage. How little any Kin knew.

"Silhouette," Kreek said with a nod as he approached. "Looks like it will be a lovely evening."

She returned the nod, lips pressed into a tight line.

Kreek laughed. "Relax, please. I'm not going to eat you."

"Why did you want to meet here?"

"Isn't it nice, by the ocean?" Kreek pointed out over the gently undulating seas. "Can you imagine, if you go that way and, assuming you miss the northern tip of New Zealand, keep going, you won't find land again until you reach Chile? Such a massive expanse of water. Inconceivably vast."

Silhouette frowned, wondered where he was going with this. "There's a fuckton of islands scattered throughout the Pacific Ocean. You'd probably hit one of those first."

Kreek smiled, slowly lowered his hand. "Indeed. You're right, of course. But those islands are so scattered, it's quite possible you'd miss them all. Quite possible too that you would be blown off course, end up circling away from Chile. Spend an eternity adrift on an expanse of ocean hard to actually imagine. Oh, you can look on a map and work out distances and consider the nature of the planet. But imagine, for a moment, yourself, tiny and insignificant, adrift out there. Thousands of miles away from this or any other shore." He turned sharply, pinned Silhouette with his gaze. "*Can* you even imagine that, tiny Kin?"

Silhouette swallowed. "Your point?"

Kreek smiled again, his face softening. He turned back to stare across the water. "Do you have any perception of the size of Faerie?"

"Not really."

"Hmm. Nor does anyone else."

"What?"

Kreek strolled to a bench beside the path, sat to continue his perusal of the sea. The sky on the horizon was darkening through indigo towards night. The sky above still shone a pale blue as the sun slowly set far behind to the west. He patted the seat beside him and Silhouette reluctantly sat, leaving a large gap between them.

"The Other Lands are soaked in magic," Kreek said. "It shapes and reshapes them constantly. A kind of chaos rules there. They are a place of contradiction and change. Constant change. Nothing like you would be able to understand here. In this realm, there is order, and that is what the Fey so enjoy dismantling."

Silhouette was growing impatient. "Again, your point?"

Kreek looked at her, his mouth twisted in a crooked smile. He was quite beautiful in this form and that bothered Silhouette more than his true form she had seen at Crabapple's.

"You truly hate me, don't you?" he said.

"I hate all Fey."

"You are a full half-Fey yourself."

"I hate that, too."

Kreek nodded, looked back out into the darkening sky. "You're very much in love, clearly. That or absolutely batshit insane."

"Quite possibly both," Silhouette said with a reluctant smile.

"Hmm. My point, as you so annoyingly keep requesting, is that navigating the Other Lands is next to impossible for non-Fey. You, as a first gen, might have an easier time, but you will have to indulge the Fey half of yourself. Let it out."

"I don't even know what you mean by that."

"You will when you get there. If you go."

"I am definitely going."

"Fair enough." Kreek took a packet of cigarettes from his jacket pocket. "You know, it's most likely the Lady herself who has your lover. Want one?"

Silhouette's heart jumped. She waved away the offered smoke. "What? How do you know? I didn't tell you…"

Kreek held up one hand. "Please, don't insult me." He lit the cigarette, drew deeply. "Echoes and portents, they ring through this realm like bells. I'm Fey. I know what goes on with my kind in this place."

"You're not really an exile, are you?"

"I am one very unpopular fellow in my home. But word has a way of traveling to interested parties and I have a network which keeps me very well informed. Not much happens on thin days around here that I don't know about. And I know some of the Lady's people came for a human the day *after* the thin and took him back straight away. That interests me enormously and you know why."

Silhouette was disturbed by his knowledge, but it made a kind of sense. "I don't know what I can tell you, give you, but I really need your help."

"I know you do. And I will give it to you. But you will return the favour by telling me everything you know. Now and later. I want all the information you have, always."

Nerves rilled through Silhouette's chest. "I'm not tying myself to you forever."

"You will if you want what I can give you."

"Why?"

"Information is power. You know that."

They sat in silence. Kreek smoked his cigarette, blue-gray smoke curling gently around his head in the soft, warm summer breeze. Silhouette's mind raced. What would it mean to give this Fey her allegiance forever more? And after this, assuming she survived, let alone succeeded, she planned to have nothing to do with Faerie ever again. So what would she have to tell him? What information could he want? She wondered if he would be interested in Armor secrets and how he might trade those. If she could really betray them.

A darker thought occurred to her. If she could save Alex, she would have his assistance again. If this fucker pushed her too hard, Alex would help her end him. Between them they certainly had the skills to take out one exiled Fey. Didn't they? And if they did, Faerie wouldn't care, as he was hated there anyway. They might even earn some favor that way. As if. Any success would only put them more in the sights of Faerie anger and Kreek was Fey and therefore almost certainly lying. He could be working for this Lady right now for all she knew.

Paranoia sank over her like a fog. She had found him so easily. Surely this was a trap, set up by the same people who had abducted Alex. This was just more of their plan. A trembling passed through her hands as she panicked at the thought. Was she being played?

"Difficult, isn't it?" Kreek said quietly, smoke drifting from his mouth.

"What is?"

"Deciding what's real and what's not. Who to trust. Which way to jump. Imagine an entire realm like this, and you are part way to imagining Faerie."

"How do I know you'll help me?" Silhouette asked.

Kreek laughed. "You don't."

"Then why should I trust you?"

"You shouldn't. By all the arms of chaos, girl, you should never trust a Fey."

Silhouette shook her head, sank her face into her hands. She had to jump one way or another and without this infuriating creature she had nothing. Consequences would have to be dealt with later. All she wanted was a way to save Alex. And she almost certainly wouldn't survive anyway, and that made everything academic. "How do I get to Faerie?"

Kreek smiled, ground his cigarette out under a boot heel. "After you tell me everything you know."

Silhouette took a deep breath, wondering how much she could get away with leaving out. She would do her best to tell this bastard as little as possible and claim ignorance on all the details. "Alex is bonded with a power stone," she began.

Jean Chang and Claude Darvill stood atop the mound of moved earth, staring down at the naked form of Hood. Engines revved and voices yelled as the site workers ran for vehicles and fled the area. Men screamed and cried for help, some answered, some abandoned. Darvill was plainly happy to let them go, their purpose achieved.

Chang tried to still the violent shaking of her hands, tried to breathe down the furious beating of her heart. Hood swept his gaze back and forth, took in the enormous machinery and tall arc lights. He looked back towards Darvill and nodded once.

Darvill nodded back. "Hey, Dad."

The site sank into eerie quiet as the last of the vehicles sped away. The hiss and sizzle of the open ground and the occasional moans of dying men were the only sounds. Darvill tapped Chang on the backside, spurring her into motion. They descended the mound to stand before Hood.

"Are you…okay?" Claude asked.

Hood rumbled with laughter. "Fuck no, son, not even close. How long have I been down there?"

"Several months. I'm not sure exactly."

Jean tried to survey the Black Diamond CEO without being seen to stare. Surely this wasn't the same man.

Hood turned, pinned her with his gaze. "Who's this? I recognize you…"

Chang jumped, sucked in a quick gasp. "Jean Chang, sir. I was on your board. Mr. Darvill seconded me to his personal assistant recently."

"She's been enormously helpful," Darvill said. "Let's find you some clothes and I'll tell you all about it."

Hood began to nod, but the movement flexed into a writhe of agony, his face twisted in a grimace. His fingers rose up, hooked like claws, and he barked an inhuman sound. He shook himself, his face dropping calm once more. "Yes, some clothes," he said, as if nothing had happened.

"Are you okay?" Darvill put a hand on his father's shoulder, whipped it away with a hiss. "You're so hot!"

Hood laughed. "No shit, Sherlock." He gestured back at the bubbling hole in the ground.

Darvill nodded, his face concerned. "You're okay, then?"

"Will you stop asking me that? For now, I'm as well as can be expected." Hood's face twisted again, his lips suddenly animated as he muttered something fast and guttural, the words completely unfamiliar to Chang's ear.

"Sir, can I get you anything?" she asked, desperately hoping she might be sent away on an errand. Far away, with any luck.

Hood looked at her, laughed, shook his head. "Just some clothes."

Darvill pointed towards their rocky camp. "This way."

It took several minutes more for Hood to cool down enough to put on clothes. One scorched shirt was enough to convince them to wait. Chang busied herself making tea and pouring Hood glass after glass of cold water while the two men talked.

"I know it was Alex Caine," Darvill said.

Hood grimaced, nodded while he guzzled water and held the cup out for more. "That fucker. I mean to see him dead. Tell me you haven't killed him already. I want that pleasure."

"No. I was strangely trapped with him…It's a long story. Anyway, he told me he'd killed you and I came here, tracked down the site, just to be sure. Imagine my surprise when I felt you alive down there."

Hood tipped his head, offered a crooked smile. "Imagine." He clenched, his body folding almost in half as he gasped and hissed guttural words again. Within seconds he sat up, his face calm. "Tell me everything about how you met that bastard."

Darvill gestured vaguely. "That…thing that keeps happening to you. You need something? Maybe we can…" He petered off, lost for words.

"What, exactly?" Hood demanded sarcastically. "Get me a doctor? Take me to emergency. 'Hello, there, sorry to bother you, my father has just been fished from burning magma where he's been trapped for months and he's not feeling too chipper.' Think they have a pill for that or something?"

Darvill began to offer an apologetic reply, but stopped as Hood was racked with spasms again. He muttered and spat, looked heavenward and barked out staccato words. Seeming to pull himself together, he stared into the mid-distance and said, "What would you have me do, exactly? We want the same thing, no? Leave me be." He snapped his eyes back to Darvill. "Caine. Tell me how you know him."

"Who were you talking to?"

"That, son, is a longer story than I'm prepared to go into right now. Suffice to say that Alex Caine is the reason for *all* this." He gestured at himself, face twisting briefly into a grimace of pain. "Tell me *your* story."

Darvill nodded and explained about Obsidian, from his initial efforts to track down his missing father, to his entrapment in the city with Alex Caine, to their subsequent escape. By the time he had finished, Hood had finally stopped drinking water and had managed to dress in some of Darvill's clothes, khaki pants, white shirt, heavy leather boots. Father and son looked identical in clothing, but so different in every other respect.

Jean Chang eyed them both, wondering who Darvill's mother had been. She must have had strong genes. Both men were thin, but where Hood was scrawny and wan, Darvill was wiry and tanned. Hood was completely bald, had been even before his sojourn underground, while Darvill had shaggy sandy hair. But in the features, they were most different. Hood's small, dark eyes and upturned nose gave him a reptilian cast, mean and repellent. Darvill had stronger, more rugged features, a heavy brow, Roman nose.

Throughout Claude's story, Hood had repeatedly fought off attacks like small seizures, time and again muttering and arguing with himself in a language hard to hear, impossible to understand. The words were difficult to even conceive, let alone decipher. Darvill would pause each time, back up to repeat the story, until eventually it was all out.

Hood nodded, his expression thoughtful. "You have some sympathy for Caine, now?" he asked. "Given that he saved you from this Obsidian place?"

Claude laughed. "You know, I did a little bit. He was a stand-up guy in there, did the best he could by everyone. And, let's be honest, your methods of acquisition are often, shall we say, unsubtle."

Hood nodded, flinched, smiled. "Granted."

"Yeah. So I thought maybe he had only been defending himself and *had* to kill you. I wasn't happy about it, but if you were dead I would have to deal with that and do the best I could by the company. But now, after seeing what he *actually* did to you? Fuck him and the bitch he rode in on. I have no sympathy for that."

"Good. Because he did worse than kill me. He cursed me, in the most painful way possible. These months, which could have been years or minutes—in that kind of agony, time has no meaning—have been more than anyone should have to bear. I wished he had killed me. Every second down there, I wished he had killed me." Hood blanched and cramped up again. Muttered, swore. "But fuck him, you got me out."

"And do you think you'll be okay?"

"No, son, I will never be okay. But I will be a lot better when Caine is dead."

Darvill nodded. "Then we can make that happen. I've kept vague tabs on him since the incident. With Jean's help, we can track him down no problem, I'm sure."

"Good. We really need this one?" Hood gestured to Jean and her stomach tightened.

Darvill looked from his father to Chang and back again. "We do. I rather like her."

Hood made a face of disgust. "Hmm. Well, for now we'll keep her. But I have a powerful killing urge and it won't wait until we find Caine. I need to rend and destroy, Claude, so you two had better make that happen for me one way or another. Or at least, you'd best keep cleaning up behind me as we go."

"Dad, get a grip. I just pulled you from magma. You're hardly in a position to be making demands of me now! Show some gratitude."

"Oh, really?" Hood stood up, flinched, and backhanded Darvill across the cheek before his son could react. "You always were a difficult child."

Darvill's eyes flashed fury. "What the fuck would you know? It's hardly like you were ever around."

"We really going to bicker about this now?" Hood roared. "Or shall I just kill her?"

Claude cast Jean an apologetic look. "Let's all try to stay calm. We'll do what we can for you, but leave her alone."

"For now, I will. Let's go."

"Where are we going?"

"Haven't you listened to a word I've said? We're going to find Alex fucking Caine. *You* tell *me* where that is." Hood doubled over again, stood abruptly and shouted broken words. He turned away and slammed punches repeatedly into the wall of the cave. Every strike chipped out chunks and flakes of rock, but Hood's hands were unblemished. Tipping his head back with a roar, he dragged hooked fingers like claws through the rock wall, leaving channels an inch deep in the stone.

Darvill turned to Chang. "You'd better see what you can do about tracking Alex Caine. Start with the file on my laptop called 'Caine.' Quickly."

Jean nodded and hurried away, stomach churning. What the hell was happening here? She wondered how she might extricate herself from this situation. She thought of her maternal aunt in the countryside north of Guangzhou and decided that might be just far enough away to serve as a place to hide.

S ilhouette reached the end of her story and night had settled deep and black around them. A streetlamp glowed a sick orange on the bend of the coast path some fifty meters away, seeming a world unto itself. She felt dirty, a betrayer. Kreek's attention had been rapt as she explained the Darak stone Alex bore and their suspicions of how the Fey used it. He made her backtrack and explain what happened in Obsidian. If anything, one thing she felt slightly better about was her previous concern that she was being played. Kreek's joy at hearing the tale seemed truly open, uncontrived. She wondered again just what his story was, but he seemed genuinely thrilled at the strife Alex had caused Faerie. He seemed to at least partly share her disdain for the Other Folk, his own kind. *The enemy of my enemy is my friend*, she thought wryly, and questioned the dangerous illogic of that old chestnut.

"And that's all I can tell you," she finished. "I'm convinced they've abducted Alex and they're going to try to separate him from the stone.

I need to get to him before they do, because if the process doesn't kill him, they will as soon as they have what they want."

Kreek chuckled. "I doubt it. I'm sure they'll do all they can to split Alex from the Darak and keep him alive for many years of suffering and torture. No one does things against the Fey like your Alex has and gets away with it. Especially against the Lady."

Silhouette flinched at the thought. "I have to get to him. Save him."

Kreek nodded, rested his chin on the points of his fingers as he looked out over the dark ocean. Silhouette's sharp Kin night vision plainly revealed the lascivious smile he wore in the darkness. A gentle sugary aroma seemed to hang around them, reminiscent of the cloying thickness of the air in Crabapple's office. Where it had been overwhelming while Kreek wore his natural form, now it was subtle, almost pleasant. Almost. She wondered if all Fey smelled this way, even in their human disguises, the scent reduced, but not gone. But it would only take a bit of cologne to mask it.

"I will help you," the Fey said, eventually. "I actually hope you succeed, as I've never seen anyone do anything before that would upset the Lady like the things you've described."

"You keep mentioning this Lady," Silhouette said. "Who is she?"

"Faerie is a chaotic land, mostly untamed madness. But, in as much as any kind of order exists, a large part of it is ruled by the Lord and Lady of the Fey. The Lord sleeps, has done for countless centuries for the benefit of all Folk, but the Lady still commands there. At least, she commands those among the Fey who have decided to be her faithful. Nothing is absolute in Faerie and there are regions where the Lady is not known, I'm sure. It's a lawless place for the most part, but many Fey defer to the Lady and her unnatural magical ability. No one has ever commanded the kind of arcane strength she wields. Except the Lord, who is more powerful still by all accounts." Kreek chuckled softly. "I don't miss her rule, that much I can tell you. She is a capricious and twisted monarch. Regardless, suffice to say the Lady will be the one who has been orchestrating the events you've described, and she will be the one most aggrieved by Alex's actions."

"And she has Alex now?" Silhouette asked.

"Almost certainly. And she's the one from under whose nose you will have to try to steal him. Can you imagine how hard that will be?"

Silhouette felt despair rising and refused to give in to it. "Are there others like you in Faerie? Who might help me?"

"Possibly. Who knows? I can get you there, and I can give you a couple of tips on how to survive and navigate. But as for what you'll find along the way? That's your journey."

A woman strolled along the coast path, her demeanor confident. She was good-looking in a dark way, face angular, framed by long black hair. She wore tight jeans and jacket, also black. Silhouette eyed her sideways, suspicious of everyone. Was this Armor come to drag her back?

"Hello, Magdalena," Kreek said. "Just in time."

Magdalena tipped her head in greeting. "How are you?"

"Perfectly well, thank you."

"And this is the foolish girl in question?" Magdalena eyed Silhouette up and down. Her gaze was like that of an adult surveying an unruly child.

Silhouette tried to feel the woman's nature. She certainly emanated age and power, but it was hard to place. "Who the fuck are you calling a foolish girl?"

Magdalena smiled. "You want to go to the Other Lands, therefore you are foolish. You are female and young, therefore you are a girl."

Silhouette snorted. "I might look young, but I've been around a while." Who the fuck was this woman?

Magdalena sneered, shook her head. "Don't patronize me, you fool. I know exactly what you are. Do you have any clue of what I am?" She leaned forward and hissed, long canines extending from her upper jaw as her face hardened, eyes elongating into slits. She stood back, her face normal again.

Silhouette was confused. "You're not Kin, but only Kin act like that."

The woman tipped her head back and laughed. "You think Kin playing at being vampires are the only ones? Those try-hards should get a life." She grinned at her own joke.

"There are no actual vampires," Silhouette said. "It's just a Kin affectation."

Kreek laughed softly. "Well, yes, a lot of Kin live as affected vampires. It's a fashion choice. But the *educated* Kin knows there is such a thing as the real undead too—true vampires who stalk the night. Magdalena here is walking proof of that."

"Seems you don't know half as much as you think you do," Magdalena said.

Silhouette scowled. The dig about educated Kin had not escaped her notice. She was well aware of the shortcomings in her knowledge of her own kind, but every Kin she had ever known in her long life had thought vampirism only a Kin lifestyle. She wondered what Kreek considered an educated Kin. She wondered too just how much had been kept from her, or how much knowledge she had arrogantly assumed without much evidence to back it up. She hated the way this bastard and Magdalena made her feel like a child. She had hundreds of years under her belt, for fuck's sake. It was a reminder that no matter how long someone lived, there was always something more to learn. "I've been a pariah most of my life, so yes, I'm sure there's a lot I don't know, much I haven't been told." Refusing to be shown up in her embarrassment, she went on the attack. "What the fuck is this blood drinker doing here anyway?"

Magdalena hissed again and Kreek held up a hand. "Please, ladies, enough. You need to get to the Other Lands and that can only be achieved in certain places. Magdalena is here to take you to one of those places, as they repel Fey on anything but thin days. Don't ask me to explain why, it's one of the many mysteries surrounding the strange relationship between this realm and Faerie. Maybe you can ask the Lady when you see her. It will ward off the Fey aspect of you too, so you'll have to fight to get in."

Silhouette let out an expansive breath. She nodded towards Magdalena. "Fine, thank you."

The vampire smiled thinly, her eyes narrow. "We don't have to be friends. I'll show you where to go, but I don't plan to stick around."

"Fine." Silhouette turned back to Kreek. "So, what do I need to know?"

Kreek took a small box from his pocket and opened the lid. Inside, nestled in dark silks, was a small ring, silver with tiny runes exquisitely carved all around it. "This is an amulet that will help you pass through Fey portals. It will also help to enhance your Fey nature. The spell is bound into the ring. Once you wear it, the enchantment will become part of you. Don't lose this. It will help you find portals back again, should you survive long enough to seek one."

Silhouette took the ring, slipped it onto her index finger. It was a snug fit; she certainly wouldn't lose it. A buzz of magic, sweet and oily and unmistakably Fey, gusted through her hand and up her arm. She fought a powerful urge to rip the thing from her hand. "I don't like how this feels," she said.

Kreek smiled at her viciously. "Good. That means it's working. I encourage you to accept that, if you hope to survive over there. The only other advice I have for you is this: seek the ice mountain and the palace atop it. That's where the Lady lives and is almost certainly where Alex is being held. I doubt I'll ever see you again, but if you do make it back, remember our agreement. You can find me through Crabapple. I'll know too, so don't try to hide from me should you return." Without waiting for an answer, Kreek stood and walked away to the south.

Silhouette sat on the bench, somewhat stunned. Something dark and malevolent swelled in her, like the feeding urge, only deeper. She swallowed, steeled herself. *I am a powerful motherfucking Kin and I do not take shit from anyone*, she reminded herself. "All right, then." She turned to Magdalena. "Shall we? Is it far?"

Magdalena smiled, gestured northwards along the coast path. "This way."

They walked in silence. Silhouette wanted to engage the vampire in conversation, prove she wasn't in fear of the nightwalker, but the truth was that she did harbor serious concerns. Magdalena was an unknown quantity, an untested power. It was hard enough getting her head around the idea that there were actual vampires in the world. She decided a stony silence was equally effective. Let this creature show her what she needed, then forget her.

"You're quite brave, you know," Magdalena said.

So much for a stony silence. "That right?"

"Yes. You're an idiot, but you're brave. I respect that."

Well, bully for this bitch. "I'm glad you do." Silhouette really had no idea how to respond.

"You must really love him," Magdalena said.

They rounded the headland, headed down towards Bronte township, the small beach deep in shadow below the pathway. "Yes," Silhouette said. "I really do."

Magdalena sighed wistfully. "I'd like a love like that someday."

Silhouette barely managed to contain a derisive laugh and realized the vampire was being absolutely serious. The weight of her love for Alex hit her like an out of control truck. "Is it far?" she asked, to cover her sudden rush of emotion.

Magdalena pointed across the park behind the beach. "Up there, through the bush reserve. Only a few hundred meters. Probably why Kreek chose to meet you here."

"And to give me his little ocean lecture."

"What was that?"

Silhouette did laugh this time. "Nothing that bears repeating."

Magdalena chuckled and Silhouette glanced across at her. Were they suddenly friends now, united by an understanding of deep love? Fuck that. They walked on in silence and strolled into the dark of the trees behind Bronte park. A small gully with a creek through the middle ran back, narrowing as it rose towards the densely populated urban center, where the truly wealthy could afford coastal Sydney property and daring renters hung on to tatty Art Deco apartments in crumbling blocks.

Before they reached the steps leading up out of the valley, Magdalena turned up the south slope and led the way to a natural clearing, raised a few meters above the gully floor. A huge Port Jackson fig tree filled one end of the clearing, its massive buttress roots like wooden waves.

Silhouette felt a nauseating shift in her gut and chest. The ring on her finger grew warm and pulsed something greasy through her. Her vision sharpened and she felt both emboldened and scared, but another sensation rose—a malevolence, a desire to fuck things up, to kill and confound. She realized this was the enhancement of her Fey nature Kreek had warned her about. What bothered her most was how much she liked the feeling. Her eye was drawn to the deep buttress roots of the fig tree. She moved towards it.

"Wait!" Magdalena's voice was urgent, tinged with fear. "Don't open that thing while I'm here."

Silhouette paused, looked back over her shoulder. "I don't know how."

"Yes, you do. You'll feel it as you approach. But push on. The Fey part of you is what gives you knowledge of it, but it will also be repelled because this is not a thin day. The human part of you would not be able to find this place, but it won't be pushed away. Do you understand?"

"Not really."

Magdalena laughed. "You'll figure it out. Think of it like a recipe, where you have to get the proportions of ingredients just right. Good luck."

Without waiting for an answer, Magdalena turned and seemed to fold in on herself in shadow. She moved preternaturally fast and Silhouette sensed more than saw her run out of the gully to the east.

Silhouette turned back to the tree. So, she needed to juggle the human and Fey aspects of herself. She walked forward, let her Fey nature rise, simultaneously repulsed and excited by it. A pressure built against her as she moved, pushed her away. She forced down the rising Fey nature, concentrated on her humanity, on her love for Alex, her need to get through. The pressure eased and she moved forward again. It took several attempts, back and forth, but she slowly made her way between the roots. As she began to wonder what would happen next, the tree split from the ground up with a deafening rip. A deep blackness welled from within. The ring seemed to grip her finger, burning hot. She pushed against the repulsion of her darker nature, tried to hold down the fear rising through her and pushed forward.

"Fuck you all!" she yelled, stepped into the darkness and fell.

Jean Chang barely held back tears as Darvill made phone calls to organize disposal of the body. Hood sat on the edge of the hotel bed, glistening red, grinning maniacally.

"Did you not enjoy that?" he asked.

Chang gripped her teeth together to avoid screaming.

The young man who had wheeled in the room service trolley lay outlined by a quickly spreading pool of his own blood, almost black against the dark carpet. Hood had simply reached up and torn the man's throat out with his bare hand. He had tipped his head back in laughter as arterial spray painted the bed, the floor, and Hood himself.

Hood's bloodstained visage was demonic in the low light. "I asked you a question, bitch!"

"No, sir," Jean said quickly. "I did not enjoy that."

Hood laughed again before twitching and curling in on himself. He fell back onto the bed in a fetal ball and muttered under his breath.

Darvill hung up the phone and turned to Chang. "Someone is coming. Thankfully we have contacts everywhere."

"I can't do this," Jean said, swallowing against a rising urge to vomit. Her heart hammered in her chest. "I did not sign up for this."

Darvill nodded, looked down at the dead man. "I have to be honest, it's not what I expected either. My father is certainly...changed." He snapped his head back up, his gaze intense. "But you've seen everything."

Jean shook her head, eyes wide.

Darvill reached out, pressed his index finger against her lips. "It's not an option to go anywhere, Ms. Chang. You're in or you're out. And by out…"

Hood was suddenly beside her. She hadn't seen him move. The man's blood-spattered face was perfectly calm. "By out, he means dead. By my hand. You would not believe how strong the urge is to kill. Even now, right this very second, I'm desperately resisting the strong desire to snap your pretty neck!"

Chang knew a no-win situation when she saw one. She had survived many a corporate meeting by remaining cool when things appeared to be falling down around her. This was no different. She willed herself to believe this was no different. "Okay, fine, no problem. Then I'm in."

Hood hissed and spun away, moved jerkily around the room like a marionette with a speed-freak operating his strings.

Claude smiled. "Good girl. I'm glad, because I need you. You really on board?" His eyes were hard.

Jean nodded, for the moment not trusting her voice.

"Good. Now, we obviously have something to deal with here."

Chang glanced at the man on the floor, his ruined throat, his dull, staring eyes.

Darvill flapped a hand. "Not that fucker, that's dealt with. Which, incidentally, should have been your job. I don't intend to do your work again."

She nodded, far too much, far too fast. "No, fine, okay. Sorry, it was all a bit sudden. I won't let you down again."

"I mean him." Darvill gestured to his father, who was crouched down, breaking the edges off a wooden desk with his fingers and biting the strips of wood into smaller pieces. "He's going to need some serious management. Stay with me, use that clever bloody brain of yours and help me manage. Right?"

"Right."

Darvill turned to Hood. "Dad, if we help you find Alex Caine, do you think that will help you find some…equilibrium?"

Hood rose to his feet, spun around, punched a hole in the wall. "Equilibrium? Ha! Good choice of words, son. I feel about as far from fucking equilibrated as I possibly could. Is that a word? Well, it is now. I'm unequilibrated. Haha! Fuck you!" He stared at the ceiling and his face twisted in effort. Chang could hear his teeth squeak together from her spot across the room. Hood grunted and let out a shout. "I will decide!" he yelled. With a clear effort of will he pulled himself together and turned back to Darvill. "I have to be honest with you, son. Finding Caine is by no means a cure for my current condition. However, I will deal with controlling this state and you help me find and kill Caine anyway, because it certainly won't fucking hurt. It's something that needs to happen."

Hood sat on the edge of the bed again, for the moment seemingly back in control of himself.

Darvill stared at his father long and hard, brow furrowed. Chang wondered if he was weighing up the possibility of running from this situation. "You have the details of Caine's home and so forth?" he asked her.

She jumped slightly at his sudden attention, cursed herself inside. She needed to be stronger than this. "I have. You've been there before."

"Yes, very briefly. Looks like we need to go there again. You've organized the jet?"

"Yes, sir. It will be ready to leave in an hour."

Darvill pulled the room service trolley over, maneuvering it past the dead hotel employee. "Then we eat now and get our plane in an hour." He turned to his father. "It's a long flight to Sydney. You going to be okay?"

Hood nodded, teeth clenched so tight the muscles in his cheeks writhed like worms. "I've mastered many things in my life, son. This is just one more."

Darvill uncovered the food, gestured Jean towards an armchair. "Sit. Eat."

Chang sat before her legs gave out beneath her, but refused the sandwich Darvill held out. She did her best not to see the dead man, the blood, the rent flesh, the hanging trachea. "Thank you, I'm not hungry."

CHAPTER
TEN

Alex sat in an icy cell, ravenous, exhausted, furious. Strange light streamed in through a high window, from one of the numerous suns that seemed to come and go at random in this mind-fuck of a land. His nose was thick with the candy sweet smell he had first encountered when they came for him. Here, it was like he swam in it. His cell, seemingly made of ice, was sometimes frozen to the touch, other times pulsing with living warmth. Sounds drifted to his ears from far below the tower where he was held—screeches and hoots, sometimes shouts of anger or bursts of laughter. The land of Faerie existed out there in all its incomprehensible mystery and it was driving him slowly insane.

He put his hand over the three shards of the Darak embedded in the flesh of his chest, felt the beat of his heart through them. And something else. They were hot, swollen somehow. Since the moment he had been caught, since that sickening, soul-tearing journey slid to a close and he had been dragged roughly across rolling paddocks of thick, undulating grass, the Darak had seemed to expand with a greasy heat and pressure. Where it had always pulsed in perfect time with his heart, it seemed now to stutter, at once in time with his heart and also slightly off-beat, as if responding to something other. Something outside of his body.

The Fey had carried him roughly, at first trying to hide his vision with their hands and bodies, then tearing off his T-shirt to wrap it about his head to blind him. Sounds had changed as he was dragged through open places, then a chattering area with a harder floor that felt like cobbles beneath his feet. He had been prodded and driven along a steep winding path and eventually into somewhere cold and echoing, then up numerous steps, only to have the T-shirt taken from him after he had been thrown into the cell. They hadn't returned it and he wore nothing but the light cotton training pants he had pulled on as the Fey invaded his home. He should be colder in this frozen cell, but whenever he thought he might start to freeze, the temperature changed and all sensation shifted. But hunger tore at his gut constantly.

For the thousandth time, he probed with his mind at the magic binding him. It was similar in effect to the spell he had been put under in Obsidian, where the Autarch had shackled his power, only this version was so much stronger, tighter, more complicated. He had been able to wrestle his way out of the Autarch's enchantment, but this one was locked through him, tight as steel wire. A million steel wires, networked and webbed all around him and within him, binding his magic down. Where the Autarch's entrapment had been like a straitjacket, binding Alex's magic inside, this was altogether more invasive, winding through him, shutting every part of his talent down at source. He could not feel his magic inside, and that terrified him. Had his ability been replaced with this intrusive enchantment?

At least his vision remained—that preternatural ability to see shades and magesign that had always been with him, since long before this new world of the arcane had opened up. But currently, there was no detail to see. The shades he could make out were alien and confusing, colors and combinations that confounded his ability to interpret, that wove and slid through everything. Magic permeated this place like air. He felt impotent and weak. He felt human again, all the powers he had built up removed. It infuriated him that it was the feeling of humanity which made him feel the most incapable. What had he become?

Ever since Welby darkened his changing room door, his life had tumbled more and more into ruin. Every time it seemed like he might be getting on top of things, something worse came along. The chill of the Void echoed in his soul and the lives of all those he had lost in Obsidian howled at his conscience. And now he was abducted to fucking Faerie and it seemed they were planning to take their time killing him. He had no idea how long he had languished here. Certainly hours, maybe days. He had had enough. He was ready for death and it couldn't come soon enough. It was the only true peace he could imagine.

He stared up at the window as he used his mind to probe and worry again at the sorcerous binding. The pale purple sun seemed to be high, another shifting behind it. The second shone a pale, incandescent blue, almost white. The light here confused his eyes, the spectrums mixed and contradictory. In the icy whiteness of his cell, everything was too bright.

The door, made of the same ice-not-ice, slammed open.

"Time to see the Lady, hominid!" The Fey in the doorway was like all the others he had seen, tall and spindly thin, its skin a green-black, bark-like leather. Female, recognizable only through its lack of a penis. He had been unable to see any other distinguishing features between the sexes of the Fey he'd encountered thus far. She moved with a sinuous grace, but subtly jerking through the smooth movements, like a dancer in a strobe light. She emanated a sense of immense, contained power as she strode across the room and pulled him roughly up by his shoulder.

"Who the fuck is the Lady?"

The Fey laughed, a cracked and guttural sound. She leaned forward, her long, narrow face and burning amber eyes inches from Alex's own.

"The Lady is the authority behind all of Faerie. Show some respect." She hissed laughter, her breath a sickening, cloying, sweet gust.

He was dragged stumbling along a frosty corridor and managed to find his feet after a few meters. He shrugged off the painful grip of the Fey. "I can fucking walk, thanks."

The Fey laughed again and strode alongside. She morphed and shifted into the shape of a human woman his height, beautiful with long, straight indigo hair and startling blue eyes. Her nakedness was breathtaking for a moment, before diaphanous gowns in a variety of azure shades wafted around her. The stutter-strobe of her movements ceased with the new form. "You'd better be prepared to grovel for your life," she said. "The Lady is most displeased with you."

Alex barked a laugh. "You assume I value my life."

"You don't?" The Fey's brow creased as she tipped a glance at him.

Alex ignored the question, stared ahead. He recognized a small part of himself that rebelled against his current mindset, that screamed for him to start rending flesh. It was the fighter in him, the core of his being. He had always been first and foremost a fighter and now he hated that part of himself. He looked across at the fine-looking woman walking beside him and knew a despicable creature was concealed by that pleasant veneer. The warrior in him wanted to lash out at her, purely to fight, but another part knew it was pointless. There was a time when he would have fought, regardless. Was he really just giving in, or was he biding his time? He knew he stood no chance against a Fey without his magic and right now he was weak, powerless. Human. The Darak burned and throbbed impotently against his flesh.

The Fey woman led him through a high, arched doorway and down a spiraling staircase. He had vague memories of being dragged up it before, but blindfolded by his T-shirt it could have been another. A day ago? A week?

At the bottom, they turned along another corridor which led into a large room with benches down either side. At one end, tall wrought-silver gates stood open. Beyond them, a courtyard bathed in the twisted, multi-hued light of the outside. The other end was dominated by huge double doors, peaking in a steep arch some six or seven meters above the ground. The doors were of a heavy, dark wood, inset with shining silver making an intricate tree, branches twisting and reaching towards the top. The silver glowed with its own light, pulsing slightly, the branches undulating and weaving mesmerizing patterns. The Fey woman pushed one side open into a huge room, high vaulted ceilings and intricately carved columns. Strange flora stood in massive vases all around, complex tapestries and paintings hung from the walls depicting portraits and battles, landscapes and monsters. Balls of light bobbed and drifted high above. The floor was carved to resemble tiles, but everything—floor, walls and ceiling—was the strange not-ice like his cell. At the back of the massive room stood a raised dais, and atop it two beautifully carved thrones. They were a dark wood, almost black, with intricate designs of vines and leaves twisting up the legs and over the arms. The back of each was engraved with three suns in a pattern of arcs that reminded Alex of crop circles.

As they entered, Alex's breath began to puff, the air dropping to a shivering sub-zero. The woman smiled at him, shifted back into her wiry Fey form. "Over there." She pointed to a mirror-bright door behind the thrones.

"Not coming?" Alex asked.

The Fey smiled, mouth a thin scar in her wood-like face, and shook her head.

Alex walked into the enormous throne room and the heavy door with the argent tree closed behind him with a solid *thunk*. He found himself alone and the urge to bolt almost overwhelmed him. But he knew he was being played. The Fey were evil, conniving creatures. Silhouette had warned him over and over again. They lied, they played, they fucked up everything. They lived for chaos and disruption. He was under no illusion that he only seemed to be alone. He strode across the room towards the small silver door, determined to face whatever was before him with his head held high. He reveled in the thought of walking to his death with pride.

By the time he reached the door, he was shivering uncontrollably, the cold biting deep into his bones. His bare feet were numb against the floor. He looked at his reflection in the polished metal, shocked by his gaunt appearance. Maybe it was the strange mirroring that made him look taller and thinner than his athletic, firmly muscled six-foot frame. He certainly hadn't lost condition in the short time since his abduction. He pulled himself up straight, squared his shoulders. He lifted his right arm, stared for a moment at the reflection of the tattoo on his upper ribs, a private reminder, usually concealed by his biceps. Four circular lines making eight directions in a globe, like the sketch of an atom. For Alex, it signified the eight angles of attack and defense. While the *bagua* itself had many interpretations, fighting was always at the heart of Alex's philosophy and everything else related to that. If you kept all your angles covered and all angles prepared for attack, you would prevail in a fight. Whether that fight was a physical battle or life itself, the same principles applied. A shiver of something other than the cold rippled through Alex's chest and he realized it was shame.

The fight is not over until you're out cold on the floor.

His Sifu had probably drilled that detail into him more than any other. Never give up. For a moment Alex felt strength return. He was essentially powerless in this unnatural land, but he enjoyed the brief sensation of focus. He had no idea how long it might last before the melancholy set in again, but he held on to it and pushed open the silver door.

The space inside was gloomy and wood paneled. It was warm and smelled strongly of a cloying incense that combined with, rather than covered, the sickly, sweet stench of the Fey and Faerie. It was not a large room, bore no furniture other than a glass sarcophagus on a plinth in its center. Lying in the clear coffin was a Fey, easily over seven feet tall. He was plainly male, and thicker, more heavily muscled than any others Alex had seen, though he had not seen many. He lay with his arms crossed over his broad chest. His face was calm, eyes closed, but Alex felt sure he wasn't dead. He had no explanation for why, but there was a heavy sense of waiting around him, not death.

"Beautiful, isn't he."

Alex jumped, spun around. There was no one with him, just four dark walls, one interrupted by the shining door, under a similarly dark, low ceiling.

"It's all your fault, you know, *human*." The voice was feminine and harsh, so full of hate and bile that Alex felt it fall across him like a shadow.

"What is?" he said loudly, pleased his voice rang with strength.

"Everything!" The word hissed in his ear with a rush of candy-sweet breath and Alex jumped back. A willowy Fey stood there, more than a foot taller than him. She wore a blood-red leather dress, tight about her with the hem splitting into straps that writhed across the floor like snakes as she walked around the sarcophagus and looked at the Fey within. She was the first clothed Fey Alex had seen in base form.

He tried to see her shades, get some measure of her with his powerful vision, but Fey auras were entirely alien to him. He saw power there, unbelievable age and power, but the information was useless. Anything beyond that was simply confusing, incomprehensible. These creatures were unlike anything he had ever known.

"You have no idea of the love we have," she said quietly. She morphed into human form, still retaining her incredible height, but her swampwood skin became milky pale, wavy tresses of thick black hair fell over her shoulders. Her face was high-cheekboned and harsh, but possessed of a strange beauty, enhanced rather than marred by the retention of the glowing amber eyes of a Fey. Her red dress still writhed. "Do you?" she demanded.

Alex shrugged. "Nope. I have no idea what the fuck any of this is."

The woman gestured tiredly and Alex was racked with a searing pain. Lightning bolts of fire raced throughout his body, following the network of internal binding that bestilled his magic. He collapsed to the floor, crying out against the agony. The pain eased and he remained down, gasping.

"You will refer to me at all times as my Lady, do you understand?"

"Yes," Alex managed between pants.

Pained lanced through him again. "Yes, my Lady!" he screamed and the pain eased once more.

The Lady walked around the sarcophagus, never taking her eyes from the body within. "This is the Lord," she said in wistful tones. "The other half of me. We ruled this land for so long, like no one before us had ever managed."

Alex breathed deeply, desperate to settle his racing heart and regain some focus. He pushed himself across the floor, hunched into a corner, back pressed into the wooden walls.

"We don't know order here," the Lady said. "Not like you do. Magic pervades our world and makes order a fallacy. It's the price of eternity. We never die, did you know that?"

"No, my Lady," Alex said to her back.

"We *can* die, of course. We can be killed. But without intervention, we are eternal. For that, we live in a kind of chaos. For the most part, we're happy with that. But it's also why we are so fascinated by you pathetic creatures. Humans particularly, but everything in the mortal realm interests us. Do you realize why?"

"Because we die?" Alex asked. He quickly added, "My Lady," as pain tickled into his chest. He breathed out slowly as the promise of agony abated.

The Lady laughed softly, a sound like wind through dry autumn leaves. "Yes, I suppose so. But not so much *because* you die, but *why* you die. You have order in the mortal realm."

Alex frowned. "My Lady, I don't see much order in the world I know."

"Of course not. That's because you don't know true chaos. But the reason you die is because you have order. Order comes with a cost."

She fell into silence, slowly circling the Lord's body, staring down at him. She ran one finger along the glass edge, pressing harder as she went, the pale flesh of her fingertip spreading until the glass sliced in and she drew a deep red line along that trickled down the clear sides, inside and out. After a few moments, she moved her hand away and turned to face Alex. She held up her gashed finger and eyed him dispassionately as he watched her finger heal. She rubbed her palms together and the blood that had covered her hand was gone. Alex looked to the glass coffin and that too was free of the scarlet stain.

"Do you know what that cost is, you feeble flesh?"

Alex shook his head. "I'm not sure I follow, my Lady. Death?" He was infuriated at how easily he used her honorific name already, trained like Pavlov's dog, but he did not want to feel that searing agony again. He yearned for his power back.

"Death is a result of order, because the cost of order is entropy. We have eternity, but we live in the chaos that this much magic causes. You have order, because you have largely driven magic from your realm. Those of you in possession of it live unnaturally long lives, no? But all things there wither and die, some much sooner than others. Most humans and animals have a lifespan that barely registers, pathetic moments between the ticks of the eternal clock. Others among you have discovered some power with what you call the arcane and you live longer. Others are afflicted with various life-extending conditions, or they carry our blood and their lives are longer still."

That last was a reference to Kin, Alex realized, and his heart ached for Silhouette. *I'll tell you something of love, you evil bitch.*

The Lady sniffed, turned back to her Lord. "But regardless of length, there is entropy and eventually all things die. Why am I telling you this, human?"

"I don't know, my Lady." He suspected it was an elaborate way to set him up for death, but he refused to play her games.

"It's hard for pathetic creatures like you, however long-lived you might be, to comprehend the time we experience. We entertain ourselves in many ways, but few compare to playing in the land of order. The *mortal* realm." She said the word mortal like it was a despicable disease. "My Lord conceived of a plan to give us access to that place all the time. You see, the realms work in mysterious ways and the connections between this realm and yours are fragile and tenuous things. Only for brief moments can we cross over, so *very* brief, and if we miss our return, we are stuck there for periods too, our powers greatly reduced. It is most frustrating."

Alex knew she was talking of the thin days, the solstices and equinoxes and others scattered through the year he couldn't recall. He kept quiet, let her talk.

"My Lord's plan was genius and used extensive magic. You see, we needed something over there that was a connection to the true power here. Something living, but not subject to entropy. My Lord devised a way to leave his heart in the mortal realm and that gave us free rein between the worlds."

Alex frowned, confused. "His *actual* heart, my Lady?" How could something live without its heart?

She smiled sadly as she turned to look at him with pity. "Yes. Time, you mayfly. You brief instant. You have no conception of it. He devised a way to lay in repose here while his heart resided in the mortal realm. 'Take a while,' he said to me. 'Enjoy yourselves over there.' He knew I could return his heart when I missed him too much and chose to revive him. A century, by your standards, or an eon. No matter. And I could still do that, of course, if I only had his heart." The Lady's amber eyes glowed like fire in the small, dim room as she fixed Alex with her gaze.

Realization dawned as he sorted through the bizarre tale she was telling. "His heart was the anchor stone," he whispered, trembling at the implication.

The Lady raised her arms above her head, morphed back to her Fey form. Her blood-red dress swirled around her body like thick smoke. "You cast my Lord's heart to the Void, you pathetic creature!" she screamed and Alex buckled and writhed as pain pulsed through him in neverending, agonizing blasts.

CHAPTER ELEVEN

Silhouette tumbled into Faerie and vomited. The gateway gave out into a mirror replica of the location she had stepped through, only twisted in every way. Weirdly hued light washed the land, strangely bright. Three suns traveled overhead in varying arcs, purple, blue and orange. The grass she landed on was bluish-green, both dark and pale at once, depending on the angle of her eye. It shifted beneath her in a nauseating wave and seemed to be many writhing tentacles of semi-translucent flesh more than blades of vegetation. She vomited again, tried to crawl away from the living turf on shaking hands and knees, but it was everywhere. She squeezed her eyes shut, determined to ignore it while she clawed for some kind of equilibrium. The sickly candy aroma of the Fey permeated the place, thickening in the back of her throat. The magesign present was overwhelming. Magic drenched her senses to a degree she had never imagined possible, threatened to drown her mind. It was all too much and her gut rebeled.

After what seemed an age of retching uncontrollably, she managed to drag in a breath and scoot back into the cover of heavy, strange-shaped leaves. She wiped her mouth on her sleeve, stared out into the bizarre land as her human nature battled the repulsion of her Fey blood. Distances seemed to flex and warp; faraway hills seemed suddenly near, then far again as she tried to focus. She was among tall and ancient trees, their bark gnarled and deep-wrinkled. The ground beneath the gently squirming grass was dark, almost black like rich potting mix. Her mind began to adjust to the mesmerizing depths of 'sign that permeated everything.

She gathered her own magic and shifted into her panther form, better for camouflage. Her clothing morphed into thick smoke-gray fur and her vision shifted. But something interrupted her transformation, pain stabbed at her right paw. A wave of panic made her heart race as she wondered if this fucked-up place was going to have a detrimental effect on her abilities. The Fey bastard could have warned her about that.

She shifted back to human form and her finger burned where Kreek's ring gripped it. She slipped it off and hung it from a heavy silver chain she wore about her neck. The chain had been a gift from Joseph, her Clan Lord. The Kin who had saved her and her human mother when they had been lost and confused. Had taken her in, raised her in Kin ways, kept her as close as a daughter after her mother died all those centuries ago. And she had turned against him for Alex. She wondered if he would ever forgive her for that. She hoped he would. She pressed the thick rope of silver to her lips at the thought of Joseph, then pushed the sentiment away.

As she hung the chain back around her neck, the ring's influence settled through her again, its oily malevolence heavy in her mind. At least it worked this way as well as on her finger. She shifted form again and the transition came easily. The chain, restricted from shifting by the ring, sat nestled out of sight in the deep fur of her neck.

The nature of the realm around her became a little clearer, a little less confounding through her panther eyes. She slunk through undergrowth, moving quickly from the Fey gate in case any other creatures might come by. A sensation in her heart did nothing to dispel the remaining nausea.

She felt the darkest parts of herself rising, ebbing through her blood. It was her Fey nature, she knew, the tainted blood that made her what she was. That she always tried to resist. It was the dichotomy of all Kin, to embrace the powers of their kind without truly acknowledging the source. In this place, ignoring her heritage was impossible.

The fur at her hackles bristled. Someone was watching her. She paused, scanned slowly around. Eventually her gaze rose up into the trees and a large, multi-colored cat caught her eye. It perched on a branch, hunched tight, its eyes piercing red. Its mouth was split in a horribly wide smile of sharp, interlocking teeth. They stared at each other for several moments. The creature's rictus grin exuded pure malice and evil. Slowly, it faded from view, all except its beaming teeth, that eventually hung disembodied in the air. With a flash, they winked out. Silhouette stared hard at the spot. Was it still there, invisible, or had it gone? Was it a threat? Was it really some monstrous incarnation of the Cheshire fucking Cat? She could feel no presence up there anymore and slunk nervously away.

With no idea where she was or where she needed to go, she stayed in the shadows of the woods and kept moving. Kreek's words about being adrift on a massive ocean haunted her and she wondered if her actions were folly. As she moved away from the gate, the sensation of nausea eased, but was replaced by something else. Isolation, loss, loneliness. Without the sickness in her soul, the full impact of the place settled over her. Its strangely undulating ground, its eye-confounding light, the completely alien sounds all around, the utter drenching of magesign, everything conspired to make her feel smaller and more insignificant than she ever had before.

Her senses spiked at the sudden realization of silence. The various sounds of birds and other unseen creatures had been disconcerting in their otherness, but not nearly as frightening as the instant lack of sound that suddenly surrounded her. She sank low to the ground, sniffed, scanned, her attention piano wire taut.

"What is it?" a voice said, part wonder, part amusement.

"Not of this place," another said.

Silhouette lifted her gaze to the branches interlocking above her head to meet half a dozen pairs of eyes looking back at her. The creatures were crouched on the branches like fat owls a meter or more tall, but their feathered bodies, in varying shades of red, brown, umber, were incongruous with their ape-like heads. She growled deep in her chest, a bass rumble of warning.

Laughter rippled around the group as others emerged from the foliage. "From the mortal realm?" one said.

Another clapped its wings against its sides, and then reached out from beneath those wings with long, sinuous arms. "I think so!" It dropped from the tree, reaching for her.

Its brethren dropped with it and Silhouette leapt to one side and bolted through the trees before they could land on her. Hoots and shouts burst out behind as they flapped and ran and crashed through the wood.

She ducked left and right through the trees. *Brilliant. Only been here five minutes and I'm going to get eaten by a pack of giant fucking monkey birds!*

She skidded to a halt as two dropped in front of her. Realizing the others were coming in from behind and having no idea where or how many they might be, Silhouette roared and leapt forward. Time to take the fight to them. She struck out with one mighty paw. Long, hard, sharp claws extended and caught it by surprise. It tumbled to the ground, screaming as it pawed at the rent flesh of its face. Not waiting for a reprieve, Silhouette kicked back with her hind legs, catching the second creature in the midsection, driving it back. She dropped forward onto the fallen one and tore out its throat in one swift and savage bite. Branches snapped as others dropped through the trees all around her.

The next few moments were a blur of rage and fright, feathers and blood. Screams from the creatures were disturbingly piercing, almost like the femme fatales of old movies, contrived and impossibly high-pitched. They fought back for a moment, but Silhouette's ferocity knew no limits.

Her frustrations and fears from losing Alex boiled over and she let her fury out, set it to work on rending these creatures to pieces.

With five dead around her and a sixth spasming limply against a tree, the others crashed and howled away. Shouts for mercy and promises of revenge retreated with them. Silhouette stood, head low, panting for breath as the adrenaline of the fight ebbed. The black Fey part of her rejoiced inside, begged to be released.

Silhouette realized she could fit in more with this place if she did let it rise, even slightly. She remembered Kreek's words about accepting the influence of the ring and her own nature. She raised her head, looked around. She had run to the edge of the woods and faced down into a valley. At the head of the valley a township of some sort nestled, buildings scattered as if they had been shaken like dice and tossed across the valley floor time and again, piled atop one another. Dark wood walls and black slate roofs, cobbled streets and all manner of beasts and creatures. Parodies of cattle and horses stood around or pulled wagons. Sounds drifted up to her, hisses, wheezes and clanks. Smoke rose from chimneys and some wagons rolled without creatures pulling them, strange engines pulsing magesign at their rear. She could feel the massive magic of the place even from so far away, powering everything like buzzing arcane batteries among the machines and livestock. And among them all stalked the tall, spindly creatures she recognized as the Fey. Like Kreek, their woody sinuousness moved jerkily everywhere she looked. Tiny in the distance, they were nonetheless clearly all as tall, if not taller, than Kreek had been.

Silhouette looked down at her gray paws. With a sound of resignation, she slunk back into the trees, away from the corpses of the apebirds, away from the pathetic mewling of the one taking altogether too fucking long to die, and into deep shadow. She sat back and shifted into her human form.

Shapeshifting was a rite of passage for all Kin. Finding your shape was a moment to be savored. Almost all found some form of predatory mammal—big cats, wolves, bears. Kin believed their true nature existed within their totem form, within their animal nature. Many chose to live without shifting often, or only partly shifting to enhance their monstrousness, half human, half beast. Others chose to affect lifestyles like the horror stories of humans, vampires or werewolves. Although recent experience told Silhouette that she still had a lot to learn on those scores.

Regardless, older Kin practiced other forms. Shifting to the totem shape came relatively easily and became second nature with practice. Forcing another form took far more energy, practice, dedication. She remembered the Council of Obsidian, the medusa-like serpent of one, the rickety shape of another that she now recognized as having a heavy Fey influence. She wondered how long it had taken them to perfect those horrific arrangements. For most Kin, their totem appearance was enough.

But she realized now what Kreek had meant about accepting her Fey nature. The horrible creatures that had attacked her had recognized her as different. If she wanted to have any chance of moving freely through Faerie, she needed to move unnoticed.

She fingered the ring at her throat, twisted it back and forth on the silver chain. She let its Fey influence soak in more deeply, gave in to its cajoling. At the same time, she relaxed her grip on the oily, dark presence deep inside herself, her Fey heritage.

She recalled the conversation with Kreek. *Navigating the Other Lands is next to impossible for non-Fey*, he had said. *You, as a first gen, might have an easier time, but you will have to indulge the Fey half of yourself. Let it out.*

I don't even know what you mean by that, she had told him.

You will when you get there.

In this place, with the power of this amulet, as a first gen, she knew it would be easy.

This is what he had meant. Kin-born folk would not have a strong enough Fey influence in their being to shift the way she needed to, but she was half-human and half-Fey. Equal parts. In the mortal realm, her human half took precedence in form, her Fey nature made her Kin and her totem was the gray panther. In this twisted realm, it was reversed.

Her Fey half was strongest and she had to let it out.

She brought to bear everything she knew about shifting. Slowly, so very carefully, she let a Fey form leak out of her being. Hanging on tightly to her mind, to her human thoughts, her Kin identity, she let her limbs elongate, her skin darken to the swampy green-black she had seen on Kreek. Like trying to hold a weight from rolling downhill, once she began to loosen her grip, momentum took over and the transformation was swift and complete. She cried out, in despair as much as pain, as her body shifted into a shape it had never known before. With it came that slick malevolence, the evil need to corrupt and disturb that was the driving force of the Fey.

She bit it down and rose unsteadily. She felt stretched and fragile, but as she began to walk, strength and confidence came into her movements. She looked down and realized there were no features to the body, no breasts. Her genitals were an almost invisible simple split at her crotch. Thinking back to Crabapple's office and her first encounter with Kreek, she remembered his unmistakable masculinity, the brief flash of his hanging penis to prove it. Was that all there was? Did the lack of breasts signify they were nothing like mammals? But they raped humans and interbred, created Kin. Did they need to emulate human form to do that? There was more magic than biology at work there, she knew. *Like evil fucking tree people or something.* A smile tugged at her thin, lipless mouth. This form felt powerful and good, but she refused to give in to that lascivious self-pride. She needed to remember who she truly was.

And a part of her, a part she tried desperately to ignore, suggested that maybe, just maybe, this *was* her true self.

Darvill ground his teeth as he drove the hire car along the southern freeway out of Sydney. That bitch, she had such potential.

"Let it go," Hood said, staring out the window at the Royal National Park whipping by. The Pacific Ocean was a broad, seemingly endless expanse beyond it.

"Let it go? Dad, the bitch ducked and ran. Literally ran away from us. I trusted her."

Hood grunted. "Proof you can't trust anyone but family."

Darvill nodded, accepting the truth of that. He cast a sidelong glance at his father. At the thing his father had become. Was he still family? The trip to the airport had resulted in two more killings by his father's bare hands, but fortunately, the clean-up guy from the hotel was still with them and had gone straight to work. That had proven to be good forward planning on Claude's part. Then, the long flight to Sydney aboard the private jet had been eventful. Darvill had managed to talk his father down from killing the pilot, though that had been touch and go for a while. Then, Chang had fallen firmly in Hood's sights, and it had taken considerable effort to protect her. Then, the cow just fucked off the moment they got to Sydney. Ran away into the crowd, taking her small bag and who knows how much Black Diamond money and tech with her.

"We'll track her down after we take care of business here," Hood said, still staring out the side window. "You should have let me fuck her up on the plane like I wanted to."

"Yes, I should have. Now I want to finish her myself. You might have to let me take that one, okay?"

Hood barked a laugh. "I approve of the sentiment, but no promises."

They drove in silence for a while. The one advantage of the long flight, after Hood had been convinced not to kill Chang or the pilot, was that he had subsequently sat in some kind of forced meditation for hours. Darvill had persuaded him of the need to try to control whatever urges were owning him and Hood had seen the sense of that. It seemed he had been, to some extent, successful. The man was almost recognisable as Darvill's father once more. Almost.

Claude smiled to himself. Riding with the old man again, just like the old days. His father had not been around much while Darvill was a kid, but his influence had been manifest often. He had encouraged Darvill's occult studies. And when Claude had turned sixteen, his dad had become a regular feature in his life, sharing the field experience and grooming Claude to be his main outside contact. He enjoyed that time together and, if Hood could maintain this new level of control, Darvill thought he might enjoy finding out just what his father had become, and where that might take them. Regardless of how much he had come to empathize with Caine during the Obsidian Incident, it was all shattered now. He wanted to finish Caine and his bitch Kin lover. And that would only be the start of his adventures with his newly powerful father.

"The urge to murder, son. It hasn't gone away."

Claude glanced at Hood again, wondering if the old bastard was reading his thoughts. "You can keep a better hold on it though, right?"

"For now. But I don't know for how long. You've killed. You know the thrill."

Claude shrugged. "Sure, depending on the circumstance. Ending someone intent on ending you carries a great satisfaction."

"It's the ultimate, the power over someone's life. It's clearer to me now than it ever was."

Claude laughed. "You were always so happy to manage the business and make the money. You left the magic and the mayhem to me once you knew I was up to it. Changed your mind now, eh?"

"No, just decided to embrace a more hands-on aspect of the life. I never left it all to you. There were many things I did for myself. But change, son, it's inevitable and we have to roll with it. The only certainty in life is change. And I have a powerful need to kill."

"We're only an hour from Caine's place. Hopefully we'll find him in and all your killing urges can be sated."

Hood twitched and shuddered in his seat, muttering under his breath, but he said no more.

The drive was uneventful, the freeway giving way to narrower single lane roads and eventually to the rolling country so recently familiar to Darvill. Hard to believe it had only been a few short months since he had last been here, looking for Caine to find out what had happened to

Hood. Now, he returned with the man himself, all that shared experience in Obsidian fresh, and the urge to kill strong in him also. He grinned. He almost felt sorry for Alex and Silhouette. But this time, he was in control. He had no need to endure an alliance of which he wanted no part and it was time to make Alex pay.

He pulled into the driveway to Alex's house and a large, black Land Rover with opaque tinted windows blocked the way. A man in all black combat fatigues waved a hand and approached.

"The fuck is this?" Claude said. He wound down the window.

"Can I help you?" the guard asked.

"Here to see Alex Caine," Claude said, with a dashing smile. "We're friends from out of town."

"He's not here at the moment, I'm afraid. Maybe you could come back. I can take a message."

Claude put a hand on his father's leg as Hood began to growl in annoyance. "We've come a long way, we can't just turn around."

The guard's face hardened, all civility evaporating. "You'll have to leave now."

The passenger door flew open before Darvill could react and Hood leapt from the car. The guard jumped backwards, bringing a small automatic weapon up from his hip as Hood slid across the car's bonnet. The weapon barked and flashed, deafening in the country quiet, and Hood's shirt danced and shredded under the hail of automatic fire. It didn't stop him for a moment and he grabbed the guard around his throat with one hand, lifted him high and slammed him headfirst into the ground. The man's head burst like ripe fruit. Hood straightened up and roared with laughter.

Darvill slipped quickly from the driver's seat as the sound of pounding feet approached, responding to the gunfire. His father would be unstoppable in the short term and they needed someone alive. More weapon fire and shouts of alarm rang out, then screams of pain and Hood's maniacal laughter. Darvill rounded the Land Rover and saw three more people rushing towards Hood and one man standing by the house, his face ashen, talking urgently into a phone.

Darvill ran for the lone fellow, glancing back as he went. Hood ducked a burst of point-blank fire and came up to punch the man to the ground. With an animal roar, he grabbed one of the man's legs, stood on the poor bastard's hip and wrenched hard. The leg tore free and the man screamed briefly before falling unconscious. Hood swung the dismembered leg wide like a baseball bat, slammed the gory stump into the side of another guard's head even as that man riddled Hood with more ineffectual bullets. Blood and body parts began to rain in all directions.

The mayhem was a good distraction for the man on the phone and Darvill snuck in behind and slipped his arm about the man's throat. Locking his other elbow into the man's back, he squeezed a choke hold on and the guard thrashed briefly and quickly sank asleep. Darvill lowered him as his father strode along the driveway. He was covered in dripping scarlet, his clothes ragged, his face split in a lunatic grin that chilled Darvill's bones.

"Ah, you took one yourself!" Hood said, disappointment in his tone.

Claude held up both hands. "He's not dead, but don't kill him! Not yet! We need to ask him some questions, yes?"

The guard moaned and shifted as he came around. He froze at the sight of Hood, instantly awake again.

Hood frowned. His hands clenched and loosened quickly, his face twisted as he clearly fought some internal battle. After a moment he drew a deep breath and his rage seemed to dissipate. "Yes, I suppose you're right. I wonder what's going on here."

"These people are Armor," Claude said. "I recognize the look. Caine worked for this group and that's what started the whole Obsidian thing. If he's gone and all these fuckers are here, something serious must be going down."

Hood stood tall, stretched his arms high. He dragged his hands back down over his face, his clothes, revelling in the feel of the blood and gore that coated him. He spread it around like a salve and it seemed to calm him further. "Ahhh, okay then. Let's interrogate this bastard."

"Don't kill him," Claude said. "I have to make sure there are no more."

Hood nodded and, for the moment at least, Darvill believed him. He ran a quick jog around the house, in through the back door, and swiftly checked the rooms. It seemed everyone had responded to the mayhem out front and all paid dearly. He returned to find the sole surviving guard propped against the wall of the house, his eyes wide as he stared in open terror at Hood. Hood stood stock still, a statue in red.

Claude crouched beside the man. "Name?"

"John Doe."

Claude laughed. "Of course."

The man said nothing.

"You're Armor. I'm not asking, I'm telling you. I know about you and about Alex Caine. Now before that fella at the gate met an untimely demise, he told us Caine isn't here. He wasn't lying, it turns out. So where is he?"

Doe sniffed, swallowed, never taking his eyes off Hood. "I'm not telling you anything."

"You were on the phone, so I can only assume reinforcements are on their way." Darvill leaned forward and yelled, "Which means we do not have time to fuck around!"

Doe flinched, but said nothing, still staring at Hood.

Claude sat back. "Tell me where Caine is. What's going on here? Why all the Armor personnel?"

Doe clamped his jaw shut. Hood moved forward, Doe's eyes widening again as he came. Hood crouched and picked up one of Doe's hands. The man tried to pull away, but Hood's grip was like a vice around his wrist. He pulled Doe's index finger out straight and took the fingertip between his thumb and the first knuckle of his own index finger. Staring into Doe's eyes, he squeezed suddenly and Doe's fingertip burst with a crack of bone and a spray of blood as the nail detached. The man screamed and thrashed, but Hood refused to let him go.

Darvill grinned. He could get to enjoy field work again with his old dad. "Answer my questions," he said to the panting operative.

The man shook his head, gasping for breath.

Hood dragged Doe's middle finger free and promptly crushed the tip of it with his iron grip.

Doe screamed and paled further, his white face flushing a sickly green. His eyes fluttered on the verge of passing out and he sobbed. "Stop, please!"

"Answer my questions," Darvill said calmly.

"I can't!" Doe screamed between sobs and the tip of his ring finger erupted in a spray of crimson. For a moment, the operative sank unconscious from the pain, but Darvill slapped him awake again. He sobbed and gasped for breath, snot smearing across his mouth and chin.

Hood held up the man's arm where he gripped it about the wrist and squeezed. Bones ground together, popped and cracked. Doe wailed and beat the ground beside him with his free hand. "I don't know I don't know I don't know! They didn't tell us! They said only that Caine had been abducted and we had to stand guard at his house in case anyone or anything came for him. Some of the guys think they can feel Fey influence here."

Darvill tipped his head to one side. "Fey? They think the Fey abducted Caine?"

"I don't know," Doe sobbed. "Only maybe Fey have been here."

Darvill sat back on his heels. "I don't know a lot about what happened in Obsidian," he said thoughtfully to Hood. "Even debriefing me afterwards, these fuckers were careful to give very little away. But I'm pretty sure Caine pissed off the Fey with his actions there. I'll explain later." He turned back to Doe. "So I'm guessing your bosses know a lot more?"

Doe nodded dejectedly, his breathing ragged with pain and fear, his body racked with tremors. "Please, let me go," he said, almost too quietly to hear.

"Tell you what," Claude said. "You tell us where the local Armor

HQ is and we'll let you go."

Doe looked up, eyes wild. "I can't do that!"

"You won't, you mean. Because you most certainly can. In Sydney, I presume?"

Doe shook his head. Hood flexed his fingers around the man's wrist, like he was crumbling something to sprinkle on the ground. Bones ground and popped and Doe screamed.

"Tell me where it is," Claude said.

The man had some strength, Darvill was prepared to give him that. It took several more bones and three times passing out before he finally gave up the location of the Sydney Armor HQ under St. Mary's Cathedral. He'd even, to his credit, tried giving a false location the first time, but Darvill was not easily fooled. Claude strolled back to the car as Hood finished the job. The man's screams echoed through the country air.

Hood joined him in the car moments later, his face calm and satisfied.

"That'll see you right for a while, will it?" Darvill asked.

Hood nodded, eyes low like a man on a drug high. "Oh yes, that'll do me for now."

Claude started the car. "Good. Let's get out of here, before that bastard's back-up arrives. We have to drive two hours back to Sydney. I tell you what, I'm getting some powerful déjà vu right now. But this time, it is definitely going to end differently." As he drove, he marveled at his father's display of physical power. He was not only invincible, impervious, but had returned from the magma with seemingly superhuman strength. Just what had Robert Hood become?

In a café in the central business district of Sydney, surrounded by people and bustle and noise, Jean Chang sat and trembled. She stared at the screen of the small tablet on the table next to her undrunk coffee. The tiny tag she had attached to the inside of Darvill's satchel on the flight was performing perfectly, marking his location as somewhere two hours or so south of the city. She could only assume Hood and Darvill would stay together, and she knew Claude would never leave that satchel behind. He wore it constantly. She logged the information and picked up her cup with shaking hands. The coffee was cold, but she sipped it anyway, hoping it might help to settle her agitated gut. She wondered if she would ever stop quaking.

A dialog box popped up on the screen, alerting her that the tag was moving faster again. They must be back in a vehicle. She frowned as the blip moved northwards. Were they returning to the city? Already? Was Caine dead? If so, she wondered what that meant, what their next course might be. They were bound to come after her. She thought again of Guangzhou, but wondered if anywhere on Earth would be safe from those two. Or, if they hadn't found Caine, had they discovered some lead to his whereabouts?

She made sure the tech was recording all the relevant data, made notes of her own and sipped more cold coffee. And for the hundredth time wondered just what the hell she was going to do with all this information. She should keep running, find somewhere to hide where Darvill and Hood would never track her down, if such a place existed. But some part of her, the decent, human part, felt the need to do something. She had known all along that Hood and Black Diamond were far from law-abiding. She knew their business was nefarious. She had chosen to accept that as she built a career. But cold-blooded murder? Wholesale slaughter? Such horror was beyond the pale for anyone. She had been a fool to think it was any different, really. The kind of wealth and power Black Diamond wielded did not come from playing fair or nice, but she had never considered anything like this.

Alex Caine had clearly done what he did to Robert Hood for a reason. That Hood was now free again was terrifying. It should never have happened and she was directly responsible for it, at least in part.

She had no idea what she might do with the information she gathered, but she would gather it nonetheless. Someone, somewhere, could surely use it. Darvill had been anxious for her to track down an organization called Armor when he had originally been looking for Caine, before his disappearance. Perhaps she needed to continue that work. Not for Darvill now, but for herself. For everyone else. She needed allies and if Darvill was an enemy of Armor, perhaps they were best suited to be her friends.

The agony pulsing through Alex seemed eternal. The Lady had no concept of time in mortal terms and she brought all that patience to bear on torturing him. The agony had become all-consuming, nothing existed but wave after wave of torment, and Alex begged for death.

Mercifully, at least momentarily, the pain eased. Alex unashamedly sobbed, curled into a fetal ball on the floor of the chamber. He pressed his face into the strangely warm wood and howled.

After a time, as his cries eased to short gasps of breath, the Lady spoke again.

"You have no idea how much I want to kill you, tiny mortal. But I can't, not yet. So I will have to make do with this."

"Just fucking kill me, bitch," Alex said through clenched teeth. He screamed as pain lanced through him again.

"I knew those cursed Eld had removed my Lord's heart," the Lady said, as though they were simply conversing over afternoon tea. "But

I also knew those greedy Kin had built something around it, too stupid to see through what they had so audaciously managed to achieve. So I could get it back if I was patient. So, I waited. We tried many times to influence events. The Darak is a part of his heart. A part of him. You feel it beating even now, don't you?"

Alex pressed a hand over his chest, noting again the double stammer of his pulse, his own and something else. Could it truly be this Fey Lord's lifeforce he felt?

"You have a piece of my Lord in your hideous meat body!" the Lady screamed, and agony flashed through Alex again.

As it abated, the Lady said, "I knew we would eventually find our way to it. And sure enough, along you came. I thought Uthentia might finish you and we would get access to Obsidian then, for he was ever our beast. But you defeated our trained godling. I still find that remarkable and you should rejoice that for a while you earned a modicum of my respect. But while he is powerful, Uthentia is a dumb brute. A blunt instrument. Chaos is one thing, but chaos without mind is formless, directionless. No matter, I thought, I can still use you. And that's what I did. But you destroyed Obsidian and actually did what the Eld had failed to do all that time ago, you arrogant, despicable, *meddling ape!*"

Alex braced, knowing the torment was coming again, and it did. It racked his body in electric heat, pushed into his bones as though they were splitting and bursting apart. Merciful blackness took him.

As consciousness returned, there was a moment of peace before the echoes of his torture shuddered through him. Alex squirmed and pulled himself up into a sitting position, hugged his knees to his chest. Finally opening his eyes, he jumped to see the Lady reclined on a chair opposite him. He was back in the white cell, featureless but for the Lady and her seat and the window high above. An orange sun was just visible, seemingly setting. The blues and purples were less evident, the remaining star cast everything with a fiery glow.

The Lady had resumed her human form, the red leather dress tight about lengthy curves. She sat forward. "So, what to do with you?"

"Fucking kill me."

"Not yet. The last chance for my Lord lies in those shards buried in your fetid flesh."

"So take them!" Alex yelled, and buckled as her pain thrashed him again.

"You must learn some respect, worm. I am not going to kill you, you will not force me to do so, therefore I suggest you show some respect to avoid all this discomfort."

As the hurt lapsed, Alex sagged to the floor again. He dragged himself back upright, determined to remain strong in the presence of this bitch. If she wasn't going to kill him, he certainly wasn't going to let her break him.

"I cannot simply take the Darak from you," she said, "or I would already have done so. Your bizarre actions have created a situation unprecedented. By your strange magic, bonding as you have with that piece of my husband's heart, you have afflicted it with mortal entropy. And therein lies the problem. If you die, the stone dies. If I remove the stone, it is still afflicted with mortality and will die. You may have a long life by the standards of your kind now you've released your arcane nature, but it is still an insignificant tick in the greater scheme of things."

"So what do you plan to do, Lady?" Alex asked, genuinely curious.

"I have the most intelligent Fey—at least, all those I can really trust—trying to work out a way to remove the stone and the stain of entropy you've given it. I'm studying you too, in detail." Alex's skin crawled. "I care not if it kills you in the process," she went on, "but I do care for the last remaining chance of reviving my Lord. We will find a way. There is magic for everything if you look hard enough and wield power enough."

Alex rubbed a hand absently across his chest. "Will this be enough to revive him?"

The Lady shook her head, her face a picture of misery. "I do not know, but it's all the chance I have and I will not squander it."

"And you plan to keep me here until you figure out how to safely separate me and the Darak?"

"Safely for the Darak, yes."

Alex nodded, his mind churning with possibilities. "Return my power to me and I'll help." He meant what he said. "I will gladly return this to you if I can. Perhaps, if you reconnect me with my power, reconnect me with this," he tapped the shards, "I might be able to figure out a way to separate it from myself. Just like I figured out how to bond with it in the first place."

The Lady laughed softly. "Foolish animal. For one, I doubt you have even an inkling of what might be required. Secondly, I would not risk returning your powers to you, for fear you might somehow escape. You are sputum in the pit of irrelevance other than your possession of that stone, but I will not make the mistake of underestimating you. Others have done so to their detriment."

Alex nodded, looked at the floor. "So we just wait for you or your boffins to come up with something? What if they never do?"

"I have a lot of patience, don't forget," the Lady said, lazily raising a hand. "And I can entertain myself with your suffering in the meantime."

Arcs of pain burned into Alex and he writhed across the floor. But among the almost all-encompassing agony, one thought persisted, like a tiny light on the darkest night. She wasn't prepared to kill him right away, and that was an opportunity. He would be damned if he would give her the satisfaction of winning. He knew he had no chance of defeating her without his powers and no chance of getting them back trapped here. But if he could kill himself, her plans would be thwarted and the last laugh would be his. He had truly had enough. The cold of the Void lived in his soul, the lives of so many weighed on his conscience and now he was the only thing standing between the mortal realm and the return of true Fey power. His death would be a great personal relief and maybe some small repayment for all the hurt he had caused. She would leave him alone eventually, and he would find a way to die when she did.

Silhouette's movement felt smooth, but she saw the stutter-jerk of her limbs as she tentatively walked forward from the trees. It was a more disconcerting sight in her own form than it had ever been in another's, even if her own shape was currently so alien. The body she wore, that sheathed her soul and mind, felt ancient and cold about her. The Fey in her blood bubbled up, coated her sense of self in that sweet, oily, candy sensation that was now more than a simple odor or aura. It had become her very being and she did her best to avoid thinking about what a comfort it was. *It's this place, this fucked-up place. I only feel right in this form because I'm in Faerie.* She shook her head. Yeah, right. She felt right because she was half Fey.

She pushed the thoughts from her mind and concentrated on ensuring her disguise was complete. The physical appearance was one thing, but even from so far away she could see that nothing masked its aura like arcane folk did in the mortal realm. Magic was normal here and every creature wore its power with pride. The massed, convoluted, overlapping shades of magic and magesign in the town below her were hard to parse. She had to blend in on that level too and that meant letting her greasy Fey aspect stand forth. Hanging on to her self, her Kin self, deep inside, she relaxed and let the disguise take her.

It felt good.

Without pausing to consider the implications, she strode towards the settlement. Get this done as quickly as possible and use the ring from Kreek to find a way out. The sooner she was back in her own world, the better.

Buildings began on the outskirts of the town, scattered along the valley walls like farmsteads. Some did indeed seem to be farms, growing strange crops with stranger beasts roaming enclosed paddocks. As she got closer to the habitations, Silhouette's woody Fey feet slapped cobblestones and the magesign in the air was a constant static. She had never before experienced so much magic, so freely used. Even with her own eldritch skills really quite well developed, the whole place made her feel like an infant, fumbling and basic in her knowledge and ability.

Many Fey in the town wore their natural form, but others paraded in all kinds of shapes. Some wore human-like skins, though usually with some affectation of height or color or face. Others took bodies like animals, in full or in part. One group she passed appeared to be constructed of nothing but artistically entwined twigs and branches, their voices a rustling susurration as they talked animatedly.

The buildings were random and confusing, using no real order and adhering to no known rules of physics. Some had narrow ground floors with wildly spreading upper stories, others were tall and crooked, level upon uneven level. She paused outside a circular structure that rotated gently on a bed of pure energy, the sorcerous cushion sparkling in the strange orange light of what seemed to be early evening.

"Come in, come in!" said a spindly Fey by the door. "Food and entertainment, I'm sure you'll have something to trade."

Silhouette nodded, wondering how business was done. A system of barter by the sound of the invitation, but it must be quite complex and advanced to keep a society like this functioning. At least it seemed some things were familiar in this place. If there were establishments for entertainment, if there were employees spruiking at the door, then some semblance of society and economy existed, and maybe she could sniff around for information like she would in her own realm.

She nodded again to the Fey on the door in what she hoped was a casual fashion and stepped inside. He seemed to look her up and down as she passed, almost sniff her like a dog, and she flashed him a look of annoyance. At least, she wanted that to be portrayed on her unfamiliar Fey features. He returned her a crooked smile which did nothing to ease her mind. Without waiting for any more discomfort, she hurried inside and was pleased to see a bustling crowd.

Her heart hammered, surrounded as she was by the things she feared most. The magesign and sickly presence of the Fey was thick in the air, dizzying. She moved to one shadowed corner to get her bearings. The place was packed, a raised central stage, currently unoccupied, dominated the space. At intervals around the circular walls were bars serving all manner of food and drink, some with huge roasts of disturbingly shaped carcasses, others with bottles of vibrantly colored drinks. Fey milled everywhere, many in natural form, many in pretty much every other shape she could imagine. One drifted past as a floating globule of clear liquid, like a sentient mass of water. It had no features, no extremities, and yet she recognized it for what it was and even got a sense of its individuality. Its aura was smug and self-obsessed. Fey equivalent of a dandy, she wondered, full of itself. She thought of all the science fiction she had seen over the years. The Mos Eisley Cantina in *Star Wars*, the *Babylon 5* space station, with their eclectic mix of aliens. None of them were a patch on this place; they seemed almost normal in comparison.

The din of conversation was a dull roar, a white noise of massed life, the sounds of glass and ceramic chiming through. The atmosphere was stiflingly hot and close. Silhouette wondered how long she would be able to endure the densely-packed Feyness of it all. And yet, as she breathed and tried to calm herself, allowing everything to wash over her, it became less offensive. She even began to feel slightly at home.

Raucous music pounded out, thumping and harsh. Everybody in the place turned to face the raised circular dais.

"Let's go! Feeding time!" a voice roared from somewhere, everywhere at once.

The center of the stage dropped away out of sight, every Fey present surged forward. The center rose again and upon it were dozens of creatures, some like the strange farm beasts she had seen on her way in, so many varying beings she had no hope of identifying. With a gasp, she saw several humans running and pushing through the throng of life on the raised area, eyes wide in terror.

But nothing up there stood a chance. The crowd rushed over the stage, some keeping their Fey form even as their jaws flexed impossibly wide, bristled with razor teeth. Others shifted into animals, parodies of mammal predators or monsters of all kinds, scaled, feathered, clawed and wild. Screams and howls ripped forth as blood sprayed and the crowd bayed for more.

Silhouette stood her ground, at once dismayed by the sight and excited by it. She had to resist the urge to fly forward and join the frenzy as her stomach ached for the feed. She was used to the feral nature of her own hunger, she reveled in the animal kill when she caught her human prey, but this was something else. Like sharks turning on their own as soon as blood flared in the water, the entire congregation had gone mad. She saw Fey battling each other over portions of food, ripping and tearing and eating each other's flesh as they did so. Nothing on that raised dais was out of bounds.

Within minutes, the frenzy died down and Fey staggered from the stage. They laughed and clapped each other on the back, compared wounds and brandished stripped bones like trophies, all animosity from the feeding seemingly forgotten in an instant.

"One hour till the next round," the ubiquitous voice boomed out and the crowd returned to socializing, drinking, purchasing the pre-prepared and altogether boring by comparison fare. A number of Fey wearing red tunics moved through the crowd, talking to those who had partaken, collecting tithes and promises, it seemed, in payment for the entertainment enjoyed. Silhouette narrowed her eyes, tried to figure out how the system worked, but it was opaque in its details.

"Prefer to watch, do you?"

The voice right by her ear startled her. She looked over her shoulder to see a Fey beside her, gnawing on a long bone. He was slimier than any she had yet encountered if his aura was any indication. He wore it like a flasher in a park reveled in opening his coat to unsuspecting girls. "Just getting the lay of the land here," she said, as casually as she could manage.

The Fey laughed. "Lay of the land? All roundhouses are the same, no?"

Silhouette pushed down a sudden panic. "Sure, but each has its own vibe."

"Yes, I suppose it does."

They stood in silence, Silhouette thankful her gamble had paid off. It stood to reason that even if this roundhouse thing was common across Faerie they would vary like pubs and clubs did at home.

Silhouette took a deep breath before taking a chance. "The Lady caught that human, I hear."

The Fey laughed raucously. "You hear? We all heard. I don't expect she'll have any luck. Our days of playing in the mortal realm have long been curtailed. It'll stay that way."

"What makes you say that?"

"You really think she has any chance of separating that human and his prize without killing both? I have no doubt she will persevere for a long time, but she won't succeed. And eventually she'll kill him trying and we'll all suffer her wrath again. Then, that too will pass, as all things do." He turned a crooked eye to Silhouette and she didn't like the look he gave her.

"Surely, she'll figure out a way eventually. You don't want free rein over there again?" Silhouette was certain he would be able to see her chest moving as her heart pounded against it.

The Fey shrugged, looked away. "Of course. Who wouldn't? I'm a realist, is all. It's been this way since the Eld. Nothing is likely to change there. The world of mortals will soon burn out anyway. Maybe one day we'll find a new playground."

They lapsed into silence again and Silhouette turned over what he had said. The Lady was indeed trying to get hold of the Darak. She needed to do it without killing both. The stone on its own could die? Regardless, hope fluttered in Silhouette's stomach. Alex was likely still alive and would possibly stay that way for a while yet. His presence seemed to be common knowledge in Faerie, so perhaps she could learn more.

She turned to ask another question and caught the Fey looking at her, eyes narrowed. Too late she noticed his mind probing and stroking across her. In the maelstrom of magic in the place, it was almost impossible to feel.

"What are you?" the Fey asked, a half-smile tugging at one side of his mouth.

Silhouette swallowed a flood of panic and made a dismissive noise as she swept away and hurried through the crowd. Nerves jangling, refusing to look back to see if he followed, she strode out of the roundhouse.

"Not good enough for you?" the Fey on the door asked.

Silhouette threw him a smile. "I'll be back later." She turned and walked as fast as possible without running away from the rotating building. A carriage with chrome and brass pipes, clanking and hissing with steam and magesign, rounded the next building and blared a horn as Silhouette danced out of its path. She yelped as it clipped her hip and hurried away. As she turned down a side street, she glanced back to see the Fey from inside talking to the one at the door, both looking at her with amused interest.

Idiot! She cursed and muttered as she strode along, turned left and right randomly to put as many streets and inhabitants between her and those two as she could. Her disguise was one thing, but these creatures were wily and wise. Disgusting they may be, but they were highly intelligent, suspicious and cunning. She needed to get away from this town before they decided to organize any kind of search. Hopefully they would consider her a curiosity not worth their time, though deep down she knew that was unlikely.

Darvill and Hood stood outside St. Mary's Cathedral, the huge sandstone edifice towering over them. The wide open space out front crawled with tourists and lackluster teenagers riding skateboards. The side area and door they had found was relatively quiet. The door itself was small, wooden, with iron studs and a heavy black ring in the center. Beside it was an electronic pad, and a camera stared unblinking from above.

"They know we're here then," Darvill said, nodding towards the lens.

Hood pursed his lips, brushed down his clean new suit, fresh off the rack at a store on the way into town. "This is probably about to get ruined. Cheap rubbish anyway. Stay behind me, they're probably armed."

He raised his arms and strode forward, bringing both fists crashing into the door. It shattered into a thousand splinters under the blow. Darvill marveled again at the man's strength.

Steps led down to another door, similar to the one above. Hood smashed it just as he had the first and a small room lay beyond, a simple office. A man stood from hiding behind the desk, a small sub-machine gun swinging up from his hip. The report of automatic fire was deafening in the enclosed space. Rapid pops of the bullets slamming harmlessly into Hood's body were just audible over the gunfire. Hood smashed one fist through the wooden desk, grabbed the stunned man and tore his head from his shoulders. Blood arced from the ragged stump of neck, painted walls and ceiling scarlet.

Across the way, a steel door with another scanner beside it stood between them and further progress. Hood walked up to the door and began pounding on it. The steel was thick. It dented slightly under Hood's barrage, but refused to give way. As his father stared in annoyance at the barrier, Darvill picked up the gun from the floor where the headless guard had dropped it. He moved into the corner beside the steel door and crouched.

Hood grunted and moved to one side. He raised his arms again and hammered at the wall beside the steel. Chunks of sandstone flew and dust billowed out. In moments, Hood tore out a great section of wall and the steel door shifted in its destroyed mountings. Through the clouds of stone dust, Hood walked into a hail of automatic weapon fire and searing blasts of magic.

Darvill hunched tighter into the corner as the mayhem played out. Over the cacophony of gunfire, screams ripped through. Yells of anger and barked orders turned to howls of agony, often cut short just as they began. Crashing and splintering cracked and snapped among the other noise.

Darvill shifted to the edge of the hole in the wall and peeked around, staying low. The Armor command center was a mess of destroyed equipment, broken furniture, and rent bodies. Limbs and heads lay scattered among the debris, blood pooled and splattered all around. Sparks jetted from smashed consoles. He moved into the room, gun held before him. Hood pounded through a tall glass wall and faced a double rank of men and women in black, one row crouched in front of another. The first row fired assault rifles while the second seemed to be working together, casting some powerful magic.

Hood slowed, as if he was trying to walk into a gale force wind. His limbs became sluggish and he roared as he strained forward, some few meters from the ranked Armor agents. He reached towards them, fingers hooked into claws, grimacing as his movements slowly froze into inaction and hundreds of bullets bounced ineffectually off him.

Darvill shifted position behind a mostly destroyed desk and raised his weapon. Aiming carefully through the narrow gap it allowed, he riddled the standing row of agents with Uzi fire. They bucked and danced like puppets and their magic shattered. Hood surged, suddenly free. He fell upon the Armor members and tore them limb from limb. A woman came running from a side room with a gleaming sword, bright with magesign. She raised it high as she ran and brought it down across Hood's neck and shoulder in a double-handed strike. It made him hiss and spin to face her even as she jerked backwards from Darvill's shots and collapsed dead in the corridor.

A small gash in Hood's shoulder, shallow, barely through the skin, closed over in seconds. There was no blood, nothing to mark where it had been. Any normal person would have been cleaved in two by such a blow. Darvill narrowed his eyes as he looked at the woman's weapon lying among the devastation.

Hood continued through the complex, like an avenging angel delivering nothing but destruction everywhere he passed. The only real challenge had been the moment the operatives had managed to combine their efforts and hit him with magic far greater than any individual seemed able to bring to bear. Darvill smiled, glad he had played a vital part in the raid by shooting that group. It was easy to feel somewhat in the shadow of his father as events progressed.

He followed, kept low behind walls and broken furniture. As he passed the woman he had shot, he slipped the sword's scabbard from across her back. Thankfully his hail of bullets hadn't damaged it. He turned to the weapon on the ground. It was a little over a meter long, the hilt maybe one-fifth of that length. The blade was slightly curved, some four centimeters deep, ending in an upward-sloping point. It was essentially a Japanese *katana*, only a little larger, the blade a little deeper. Claude had a deep affinity for swords, had studied the arts of swordplay many times in his life. This weapon filled him with wonder. The hilt, rather than the traditional sharkskin-wrapped wood with leather bindings, was carved ivory, a design of interwoven serpents, shiny and smooth with age. He ran one finger along the carving and it felt warm, slightly giving, entirely unnatural. It would certainly not slip from the grasp, even wet with sweat or blood. The *tsuba*, the hilt guard, was cast bronze, a slightly disquieting design of circles and lines, exquisite in execution. Its symbolism would require research. The temper line ran a smooth, undulating wave along the length of the razor-sharp blade. The weapon exuded powerful magesign. With a smile, Claude slipped the sword into its scabbard and slung it across his back. He moved on in the wake of his father.

Shouts rose from the depths of the complex, more gunfire, more screams. A voice rang above the others, "Protect the Commander!"

Darvill ran forward. That one they needed to keep alive. He jumped a pile of bodies, or at least the mauled parts of bodies, and dropped into a crouch outside a door. A window to his right shattered as a broken corpse flew through it, hitting the opposite wall with a wet thud. His gun raised, Darvill leaned into the room to look. A huge man with a massive walrus mustache was backed into one corner, his hands knotted in a strange configuration. His magic was old and intense. Several more bodies lay around the room, one man squirming weakly in obvious pain.

Hood stood before the big man, growling a feral noise deep in his chest, clearly restricted somehow by the man's spell. Darvill stepped into the room, his gun leveled at arm's length. "Dad, don't kill him. We need to talk to him."

Hood glanced around, face furious.

"Dad!" Darvill yelled.

Hood shook himself, saliva sprayed from his lips. He cried out, stretched and twitched, suddenly became still. His face calmed. He pulled a chair upright and sat, one ankle resting on the opposite knee, a contented smile on his face. He gestured. "All yours."

Darvill nodded once and popped a bullet into the Commander's knee. The old man screamed and dropped, clutched at his leg. To his credit, he began his incantation again almost immediately. Claude sensed the magic wards going up, but was across the room in a flash, the weapon pressed to the old man's temple. "Stop. Or I will kill you."

The Commander quietened mid-spell and scowled at Hood. "What the hell is this?" He looked up at Darvill. "I know you, from Obsidian. I thought you were on our side."

"I had to ally with Caine to get out," Claude said. "But I was never on your fucking side."

The Commander pointed at Hood. "I recognize him, but I'm not sure..." His eyes widened, realization dawning.

Claude smiled. "Remember now?"

"Robert Hood. CEO of Black Diamond Incorporated. Alex Caine put you away, I thought."

Hood lifted his palms, shrugged. "I guess I got out."

"*What* in all the realms are you?"

Hood chuckled. "That's actually a very tricky thing to answer."

Darvill jabbed the Commander with the gun barrel. "We'll be asking the questions. It's Caine we're after. Where is he?"

The Commander rumbled a deep laugh. "Oh, your timing is terrible." His eyes narrowed. "If you're here, you must have forced some information from one of our people. I dread to think what you did, they're trained not to speak."

"You should use the old cyanide tooth capsule or something," Claude said. "Everyone cracks eventually. But he was good. Tried to give us false locations and everything."

The Commander nodded, a deep hatred burning in his eyes. "So you've been to Caine's place, and you know he's been abducted."

"What about his bitch girlfriend?"

The Commander raised an eyebrow. "Silhouette? She went after him. I'm hoping she failed to find a way. We're still looking for her. Well, we were…"

"Where?" Darvill yelled.

The Commander flinched, scowled again. "Faerie. The Fey are mad at Caine and found a way to get him."

Darvill gestured at the devastation around them. "Seems you can't actually protect much at all, old man." A suspicion settled over him. "Why are you being so free with this information?"

The Commander started laughing, shook his head. Dizziness tickled at the edges of Darvill's vision. He realized his grip on the gun was loosening. The Commander's face hung slack, already pale from the pain of the kneecapping. His eyes drooped. "You're already dead," he managed in a slur before his chin fell to his chest. Drool ran from his lips.

Darvill fell to one knee, put a hand out to prevent falling flat on his face. The ground felt spongy under his palm. Or was his hand the spongy thing? As blackness closed in from the edges of his vision, his last thought was, *Fucking gas. Last chance countermeasures.*

Jean Chang sat among crowds of tourists and office workers in front of St. Mary's. She pulled the broad brim of her new sun hat low, sinking her face further into shadow from the harsh Australian summer sun as she watched the side of the cathedral. The tracker still worked and Darvill was somewhere under there, not moving much. She had thought to move a little closer, but didn't dare. She had no idea why she was even taking this risk—how safe was she really among these people? But she wore a heavy weight of responsibility for the presence of Robert Hood in the world. She might not be much of a field agent after all, but she was good with information. So, she would gather what she could.

The blip on her tablet started moving. She hunched down, watched the screen, glancing up occasionally. After a minute or so, Hood emerged, carrying the limp form of Claude Darvill.

Chang gasped. Hood moved away from the building into the shadow of a low wall and lay Darvill down. He leaned over his son, shouted and pumped the man's chest, tipped his head back and blew air into his lungs.

Jean couldn't see any obvious injuries, but she couldn't see much detail at all from such a distance. She jumped when Darvill suddenly bucked and twisted on the ground. He cried out. Several people had paused to watch the two men when Darvill rolled to one side and vomited noisily. People quickly moved on.

Chang watched wide-eyed as Darvill continued throwing up violently for several minutes. Eventually his father dragged him to his feet and half carried him, staggering away from the building. Claude had a sword strapped across his back. That was new. Jean huddled under her hat again as they moved through the crowd only twenty meters or so from where she sat, panic fluttering in her stomach. Stupid to have come so close, there was no need for it. But what were they doing? What had happened to Claude?

When she was sure they were well out of sight, the blip on her screen showing them moving across Hyde Park, she snuck up to the door from which they had emerged. It was smashed in and smoke drifted gently up the stairs. No way was she going down into that mess. Uncertain what to do, she returned to her spot in front of the cathedral and kept an eye on their progress on her screen. She felt safer in the crowd, and safe in the knowledge they were moving away from her. *Just watch*, she told herself. *No need to get too close.*

CHAPTER THIRTEEN

Alex did his best to ignore the icy bands biting into his wrists and ankles. Spread-eagled on an inclined, intricately-carved wooden tabletop, he closed his eyes and tried to think of anything except the Fey moving around him, probing, prodding, testing. Though when he closed his eyes, he saw the bodies of so many desperate lowen, tumbling into the Void and winking out of existence. Even here under these conditions, those horrors were branded into his mind's eye.

The Fey magic was horrible as it slipped over and through him, like a thousand spiders running under his skin. He recognized parts of it, sensed and guessed at others. They focused most of their attention on the shards of the Darak, tested the edges where the pieces bonded seamlessly with his chest.

Occasionally they muttered to each other. A sharp pain made him buck off the table and his eyes popped open in shock.

"Lie still, fucking human!" the Fey leaning over him said, a sharp scalpel in his hand. "If you cause me to damage you too soon, there will be hell to pay."

Alex shook his head, clenched his jaw as the Fey leaned over him again. He was tempted to time his next movement, shift his body up to meet the blade as it descended. But there was no guarantee of a fatal stab. As if reading his thoughts, another Fey leaned in and pressed hard hands into his hips. With him pinned to the table, the first creature lowered the blade once more. Alex hissed in pain at the heat of the slice. His skin parted alongside one of the shards and blood welled up. The Fey mopped at him, leaned in close for a look.

"Capillaries and nerves, would you believe it?" he muttered.

"Into the stone?" the other asked.

"Yes, it's actually growing into him. Or he into it, whichever you prefer. It is an organic part of him."

"Well, that much we assumed. But can we excise it?"

The first Fey stood straight, staring at the freely bleeding slice in Alex's chest. He shook his head. "It would have no blood supply, and it relies on one now. We need to return the stone to its original state before removing the pieces. Or at least isolate it artificially. I don't think it would survive excision and then turning. Even if we had a clue how to turn it, in or out of this fucker."

Alex smiled to himself. They were at a loss and they knew it. All this testing and poking and cutting was just flailing in the darkness of ignorance. That gave him time. For what, he was not entirely sure, but all the while these fools were flummoxed, he had an opportunity to plan something. Or perhaps…the thought was too much to consider. He had to assume Silhouette, and subsequently Armor, were at least vaguely aware of his situation by now. Would they launch a rescue? Would they be able to?

Perhaps he didn't have so much time after all. If they were able to save him, that would mean this risk still existed—the risk of his possession of the Darak and the value it held for the Fey. It all needed to end. He needed to end, and all the suffering he had caused would end with him. And the nightmares would cease.

The Lady strode into the room, eyes dark with fury. "Well?"

The two Fey jumped, standing almost to attention in surprise. "We're still exploring the possibilities, my Lady," said the one with the scalpel.

"And?"

"Nothing conclusive yet, my Lady. But we have several more avenues to investigate."

Alex laughed aloud. "You have no fucking idea," he said. "Tell her the truth!" He bucked and howled as the Lady's pain lanced through him.

"Don't you dare prove him right," she said, and swept from the room.

The first Fey turned back to Alex, rage in his amber eyes. "You think you can beat us?" he hissed. "Meat sack!"

Alex chuckled. "You're already beaten."

Silhouette walked quickly from the town, striding along the valley in the burning orange glow of Faerie twilight. Night seemed to be falling, though she wondered if another sun would rise before the orange one had fully set. Was it ever truly night here?

Magesign swirled all around, different to that in the settlement, but no less potent. Distances also confounded her eye. As she went, the land seemed to slip and shift beneath her. She would be looking at a forest hundreds of meters away, blink, and it would be suddenly right in front of her. She turned up the valley side, looking for higher ground, and after a good ten minutes realized she was heading downwards again, the valley twisting strangely away from her.

After an hour of walking, regularly checking behind for signs of pursuit, she made a startling realization. Intent had a direct effect on travel in this fucked-up place. She looked up the gently sloping ground to her left, to a copse of trees standing like sentinels on the ridge. She decided to go there, started moving. She closed her eyes, kept the image of the copse in mind, opened them again. She was standing among the trees.

If she let her mind wander while moving, the land seemed to take its own course and she meandered randomly. Or she inadvertently considered somewhere else and was drawn there. But if she concentrated, she could traverse wherever she pleased. She moved to the edge of the trees, looked out across the land from her high vantage point. Undulating green rolled seemingly endless in every direction. She saw a few settlements in the distance, some nothing more than soft light smeared in the expanse of the darkening landscape.

A loud buzzing interrupted her thoughts and a shadow passed over. A giant dragonfly, at least five meters long, flew by. It took a second for Silhouette to realize it was mechanical, hinges and cogs worked smoothly as diaphanous, glass-like wings beat the air making the loud burring sound. Yet the mechanics were powered with magic, magesign curling around it like smoke. A Fey sat atop the thing, riding it. Silhouette moved into the shelter of the trees, watched it cruise by. She looked across the skies and realized there was other air traffic, tiny dots moved through strangely fibrous looking clouds. All manner of machines and balloons, mostly so high she hadn't spotted them before. They exuded a similar amount of magic to everything else, the air swamped with the thick static of arcane power.

A weight of despair descended on her. This ridiculous place, so alien, felt like a wide open maze. The skin she wore, the shape she was forced to maintain, disgusted her and thrilled her simultaneously. She wanted to be free of it. She wanted to be free of this hell. She toyed with the ring on its chain about her neck. She had the ability to find a way home. Kreek had been right in his analogy of being lost at sea, but she had a way out. She turned a slow circle, the land flexing and moving as her vision passed over it. What chance did she ever have of finding Alex?

Maybe she should simply ask where the ice mountain was and risk discovery. If she could find a lone Fey travelling, perhaps she would have a chance to fight or run if things turned sour.

"He's not in yet," a voice said.

Silhouette supressed her surprise, turned slowly. A Fey stood behind her, leaning against a tree. "Isn't he?"

"No. Should be back soon. How many did you want?"

Silhouette's mind raced. "I hadn't decided yet."

"What do you have to trade?"

"Maybe I should discuss that with him."

The Fey laughed, shrugged. "Fair enough. Most don't have the guts to deal direct, but if you do, more power to you. Wanna wait inside?"

Silhouette really didn't want to go inside anywhere, but she did need information. Time to take a chance perhaps. "Sure."

The Fey wandered off through the trees. Silhouette followed him into a thicker stand of heavy, dark wood and did her best to hide her surprise again when they came to a huge house built from the forest itself. Trees grew together, formed walls as their branches formed windows and doors. Leaves gathered along the top of openings like eyebrows and the roof high above them was a dense canopy of rippling green. Magic was thick about the place, as it was everywhere, but not least in the wards sealing it like a bubble from the rest of Faerie.

She followed the Fey in through a high front door, the wards tickling but not impeding her. They were for something else. They entered a large hall lit by flickering brands of not quite natural fire. The walls and floor and ceiling were all smoothly connected, a naturally grown hollow in the middle of a giant tree that just happened to be the shape of a great hall. Several humans, mostly children, moved morosely about preparing a huge feast on a massive central table. The shields, Silhouette realized, were to keep these unfortunate souls in.

The Fey turned to her. "Name's Fack."

Silhouette suppressed a juvenile grin. She nodded. "Sil."

"Strange name."

"I like it."

"Fair enough." Fack looked her up and down, shrugged and turned away. He gestured vaguely around the room. "None of these are for sale. All of them with the yellow mark."

Silhouette looked, wondering what the trade was and realized all the humans present wore yellow armbands. These bastards traded in people.

For service as well as food, it seemed. The Fey were a complicated race. At least as Kin she knew how everything worked. She fed on people, but lived among them, to some degree lived as they did. Here the rules seemed to shift and undulate as much as the confusing landscape.

"They seem busy," Silhouette observed, as much to make conversation as anything. She needed to find a way to ask about the ice mountain and get out before she was too deeply trapped.

Fack grinned at them, amused by their increasingly fervent activity. "He's due back any…" He was interrupted by a rush of sound and a ringing of bells. "Well, right now."

Fack hurried away and the servants disappeared like roaches from a light turned on. Silhouette found herself alone in the great hall, the huge table almost bowed under the weight of fruit and meat, bread and vegetables, desserts and cakes, her only companion. It was like something from a fairy tale and Silhouette smiled immediately at the irony of the thought. The food was soaked in magic. As she tried to see more clearly what it was, some kind of controlling enchantment, Fack reappeared from a side door, dressed in a strange finery of leaves and branches. The front doors burst open and a crowd of about a dozen children stumbled in, eyes wide in fear and confusion.

Behind them strode a huge man. He was seemingly human at first glance, heavily muscled and dressed only in green leather breeches and boots. His skin had a verdigris sheen. But he was not human. His hair was tumbling moss and his eyebrows thick leaves. Two huge antlers sprouted from his head. His face was hard, though handsome, the brow heavy, the cheekbones high and sharp. He slammed the doors and gestured at the table. "Eat, children! It's all for you!" His voice was a deep baritone, carrying through the room like a bass note.

"Erlking!" Fack cried. "Welcome home." He morphed into human shape, wearing a red uniform like a toy soldier. The children gasped and gaped. "This way, kids," he said, all friendly and open. "Eat, drink, enjoy!"

Some of the children openly sobbed, terrified. Others stared nervously at the riches before them. Fack slowly herded them all to it and helped them to eat and drink. Even the most scared he convinced to nibble on a strip of crispy bacon or a sugary doughnut.

Silhouette swallowed her disgust as the kids became trapped forever by the insipid magic in the feast.

"What do you need?" the Erlking rumbled.

Silhouette realized he was addressing her. "I'm here to see what you have to offer, actually, not to deal right now."

The Erlking made a noise of disgust, flicked one massive hand at her. "It always changes. Come back when you're ready to negotiate."

"The Lady is interested in your stock," Silhouette said, heart racing with her audacity.

The Erlking laughed. "I'm no follower of that bitch. There are Erlkings far nearer to her ridiculous monument. Why come to me?"

"Let's just say she's collecting." Silhouette desperately tried to parse the information she was getting. There wasn't one Erlking, but several. Some were nearer the palace, which meant she was currently still some distance away. But what did distance mean in this realm? She racked her brain, trying to remember all she could of Erlking mythology. She knew of old ballads, Germanic and Scandinavian legends of siren-like kings and their daughters luring humans away. It was all so much nonsense, completely useless in the very real environment in which she found herself.

The Erlking tipped his head, the muscles in his thick neck bulging at the weight of his antlers. "Collecting. What's that sour bitch up to now?"

Silhouette tried to stay in character. "Beware how you speak of the Lady!"

The Erlking roared with laughter. "Fuck you, little Fey, in *my house*! Your Lady is a capricious and pointless despot. If she wants any of my stock, tell her to come herself and beg me for it." He strode from the room, wide eyes of children following his exit. They seemed to relax when he was gone and returned to eating with vigor. They were lost to the enchantment. Doomed. She realized the children's attention had shifted to her, tall and frightening in her Fey shape.

Fack strolled up to her, still in his human form. "You're taking a bloody risk, talking to him like that. None of the Erlkings care about Fey politics, you know that."

Silhouette shrugged. "I still expected him to show some respect."

Fack barked laughter. "What are you, new here?"

Silhouette's heart fluttered, but she kept her cool, laughed with him.

"Why is the Lady collecting human children?" Fack asked.

"No idea. I just do as she asks."

"You're a long way from the Lady's influence. There are at least three Erlkings more suited. How much variety does she need?"

Silhouette shook her head, leaned casually against a wall. "I don't presume to question my Lady's desires."

"Maybe something to do with that human she's already got, the one who fucked up our fun."

Silhouette blanched, hoped Fack didn't notice. "Probably."

"I can talk him down a bit if you want to make an offer for something here," Fack said. "I know how to deal with him."

"No, not right now. Perhaps I did come too far afield. I'll go to the other Erlkings and start there. Who's nearest again?"

Fack turned his attention from the feeding children to look her up and down. "Who's nearest?"

"Where's nearest?" Silhouette said. She felt like she was drowning. They were all Erlkings, did they not have individual names? Had she made some fundamental error in the distance and geography of this horrible realm?

Fack's magic swept over her, probing, rude and insistent. "The fuck are you?" he asked quietly.

Silhouette refused to give in to rising panic. *Move fast!* She shot out one hand, clamped it around Fack's neck and squeezed. He gagged and thrashed, shifted back into his Fey form as his magic built up quickly. Silhouette cracked him hard in the temple with her free elbow, stunned him. His power drained, his eyes swam.

"Where the fuck is the ice mountain?" she demanded.

"Wha...? You're not Fey..."

Silhouette hit him again. "Where is it?" She squeezed harder.

Fack choked, scrabbled at her fingers crushing the breath from him. "Follow the blue fucking sun!" he managed to get out.

He was regaining strength, the surprise of her attack past. Silhouette could take no more chances. She moved her shape, elongated her maw to a predatory jaw full of long teeth, shifted her grip and tore out his throat. He howled silently, air rasping through the ragged hole, and thrashed. Silhouette slammed him into the wooden floor, hardened her hands with long claws and smashed through his body, tearing at organs and flesh. His blood was a viscous green, his internal parts fibrous and tough. Still he kicked and squirmed, his hands clawing up at her. *How do you kill these fuckers?* She dimly registered the screams of the children as she ripped through Fack's chest cavity. She saw his pulsing heart, swollen and almost black. She tore it free and his movement ceased.

Before anyone else could show up, praying the Erlking didn't come thundering back in, Silhouette bolted from the wooden hall. Outside, night had fallen. The clouds shimmered with an unnatural light. Three moons drifted across the sky, casting everything in a wan blue glow. She was momentarily reminded of the light in Obsidian and cast the terrible memory quickly from her mind. She turned away from the Erlking's domain and ran, long Fey legs eating up the ground as she blinked across great distances, looking for new shelter. She felt like never stopping.

In a hotel room in Sydney's Chinatown, Claude Darvill puked again, wondering when his intestines would curl out of his raw throat and he would finally sink into the blessed oblivion of death. He rubbed his eyes, his vision slowly returning to normal.

"Come on, son, you're made of sterner stuff than this. Remember that voudoun you told me about in Port-au-Prince? Ha! If you survived that, you can get over this."

Darvill looked across the room at his father as he slumped back onto the bed again. "Fuck you, Dad," was all he could manage, his voice weak.

Hood smiled, hands twitching and busy in his lap. "You sleep it off, I'm going out."

Through his haze of pain and nausea, nerves rattled in Darvill's chest. "Where are you going?"

"To rape and murder. I want violent, non-consensual sex, followed by blood and splintering bones."

"It's too risky." Darvill hid his disgust at the casual depravity, tried to appeal to the logic of not getting caught.

Hood laughed. "What's the risk? I get caught, I kill them too. I am fucking invincible, son."

Darvill's thoughts flitted briefly to the new sword across his back. "Them not being able to hurt you is one thing. But we don't need the heat. They'll send more and more against you and we won't be free to move where we want."

Hood scowled, lips shivering as he muttered. He tipped his head back and yelled, "Fuck you, I will decide!" And Darvill knew his father wasn't addressing him. "How long till you can move on?" Hood asked.

Darvill simply wanted to die, to curl up in a ball and expire, but he needed to keep his father focused. The old man certainly seemed to be developing a greater level of control over whatever haunted him, but it was hard to guess how long it might last. The mass killing under St. Mary's should have satisfied him for longer than this, surely. "I can go now," Claude said. "But what's the plan?"

"I want Alex fucking Caine. Same as always."

"But he's been abducted to Faerie. Shit, is that even possible?"

"You told me about Obsidian, son. You know the other realms exist."

Darvill nodded. He couldn't deny that. "So what do we do?"

Hood stood, his eyes darkly furious. "We go to Faerie and get that little cunt so I can kill him. Why is this so hard for you to grasp?"

"Let me rephrase the question," Darvill said with a sneer. "How do we get to Faerie?" He pulled himself into a sitting position, head swimming. Whatever gas he'd ingested, it was messing with him in a hundred different ways. He was in no doubt that if it had been any more he would never have woken up again. It seemed his father's immunity extended to many forms of attack. Hood had been completely unaffected.

Hood raised his palms. "We just walk right in."

Darvill's head pounded, his gut roiled, his vision blurred. He had little time for his father's overzealous attitude to everything. He shook his head, raised a questioning eyebrow.

"This thing in me," Hood said. "This fucking thing Caine gave me knows the Fey and Faerie intimately. I can't explain it to you, but I have knowledge and experience you wouldn't believe. I know the Void, I know so many realms. I can see through dimensions into the shapes of things unfathomable."

Darvill held up a hand. "You're not making any sense. My brain hurts too much for this shit. Basically, you're saying you can get us to Faerie?"

"Yes. I know it. I've been there before. At least, part of me has. We just need a gateway. Find us a Fey gate and I can open it."

"Right. So *I* need to find a gateway. You can't do that bit?"

Hood shrugged. "I have to do everything? Come on, son, I'm trying to include you here. Did I save you from that place for nothing?"

"I don't even know what a Fey fucking gate is!"

Hood slumped down into a chair again, put his feet up on a small coffee table in front of it. "You're the seeker, Claude. You have all those great finding skills. I could probably track down a Fey gate, but you could do it quicker. Here."

Hood stood swiftly and slapped a hand to Claude's forehead. Jolts of energy crackled through like electricity, made Claude cry out in surprise and pain. Sensations of another place rocked through him, vistas confusing to the eye and mind. He realized it was Faerie he saw. "Feel it!" Hood yelled. "Know it!"

Darvill pulled away, fell backwards off the bed. "All right, enough! Too fucking much, in fact." If he thought his head had throbbed before, he was mistaken. His skull flexed fit to burst. He pulled himself into a kneeling position, lowered his head to the floor like a Muslim at prayer and groaned. The pounding pain began to ease. "Okay," he said in a weak voice. "Just give me a minute."

"What's that across your back?" Hood asked. "You get a new sword?"

Darvill sat back, kept his face as neutral as possible. He was enjoying this newfound mayhem, but recognized that it might quickly spiral out of control. He had no idea if the sword was a *Get Out of Jail Free* card against his father, but he didn't want to jeopardize the possibility. And besides, it was something special, almost alive. He had barely explored its potential yet, but recognized its unrivalled potency. "I picked it up in that Armor base. You don't remember?"

"I don't remember much, to be honest. Bloodlust, son. It's a wonderful thing."

"Yeah, I can imagine. I thought it looked cool and kinda valuable. They're not going to need it any more."

"Very true." Hood walked to the door. "So, come on then. Let's go."

Darvill raised his hands. "Wait a minute. I have to do my thing first. It's easier here where there's peace and quiet." He rummaged in his satchel for a thick charcoal pencil and began marking sigils of finding on the tough carpet. "Now shut up a minute while I find us a gate."

Jean Chang watched with interest as two more people wearing all black approached the broken door in the side of St. Mary's Cathedral. They conversed with tense faces and angry gestures. The one who had arrived first grabbed the sleeve of another to prevent her rushing downstairs. He made a phone call. After ten minutes or so another man joined them, a big, dark-skinned fellow with long black hair and a heavy brow over a handsome face. Maori, perhaps, Jean guessed. Or from somewhere in the region. He carried a large sports bag and took a gas mask from it.

He put the mask on and, gesturing to the others for patience, went in through the broken door.

Chang watched patiently. The three remaining people by the door shuffled around. After several minutes, the large man re-emerged, pulled the mask from his face. His handsome visage was distorted in anger and grief. Chang watched the four of them talk and argue for a minute before she made a decision. Taking a deep breath to steady herself, she walked towards them.

Conversation ceased as she approached. They watched with suspicion.

"Hello," Chang said.

The big man nodded, stepped forward to take charge. "Can I help you? We're a little busy here."

She held out her hand. "My name's Jean."

He looked at her hand, back to her face. "Jarrod." He shook, his massive hand engulfing hers completely.

"Hi, Jarrod. Listen, I'm not sure what happened down there exactly, but I know who did it."

The posture of all four changed instantly. From wary patience they became alert, avid. Jarrod held up a palm to stem their questions before they had a chance to start. "How do you know?"

Jean looked around the group. They all wore matching black cargo pants and T-shirts. They had utility belts like policemen and shouldered satchels. There was an air of professionalism about them, an almost military discipline. But who were they? Could they be part of the Armor group Darvill had been so keen to track down? "I need to know I can trust you."

Jarrod smiled, nodded. "Understandable. You can. I can't tell you too much about who we are, but we're the good guys." He gestured down the stairs where tendrils of smoke still drifted like lazy ghosts. "Someone attacked our headquarters down there. They've killed a lot of our colleagues and virtually destroyed the place. I need to know anything you know. Please."

"Are you a religious organization?" Jean nodded towards the towering sandstone wall beside them.

"No. Once maybe, in a way, but not now. We're secular and only interested in the safety of the population. Does that matter?"

Jean hugged her bag to her chest. Inside was the means of finding the perpetrators these people so desperately wanted. And they looked like the kind of organization that might have a chance of succeeding in stopping the hell she had helped unleash. Perhaps she could ease her conscience. But she needed to see it through. She needed to know, to be part of the solution. And she wanted to feel safe. "I'll only tell you what I know if you keep me with you."

Jarrod started to protest and Chang held up a hand to stop him. "This is non-negotiable," she said. "For my own protection as well as for my own reasons. I'm capable and have tech that will definitely help you." She hefted her bag for emphasis, wrapped her arms tightly around it again, pressed it against her chest like a shield.

Jarrod sighed. "Okay."

Chang allowed herself to feel some relief. "Do the names Robert Hood and Claude Darvill mean anything to you?"

Jarrod's eyes widened in shock. "Yes. Yes, they do."

Jean nodded. This was the right decision. She told him everything.

lex paced the icy cell. He ground his teeth, frustrated, angry, riddled with pain. The brief reprieve from the ministrations of the Fey afforded him little comfort. His chest burned where they had cut around the shards of the Darak. The very fibers of his being ached from their intrusive magic. Apparently, they were procuring humans from some strange dealer in order to test a new raft of theories, to see if those humans survived before they tried on him. More deaths on his conscience.

He stopped, looked around again. An empty square space offered zero opportunities for self-harm, and they knew it. He had no bed, let alone bedclothes. And even if he had a sheet to twist into a rope, there was nothing to hang himself from. At best, he could knock himself senseless against the wall, but that was pointless. He yelled, an incoherent noise of frustration, and resumed his pacing.

The window high above was a square of darkness. Two moons had drifted past, though no stars were visible. He wondered how long the night would persist. He stopped pacing, turned to look up at the darkness again. The window was too high to jump for. But he was a fighter, in peak condition. Maybe he could make it. He moved under it, crouched, leaped. As he reached up, his fingers were more than a meter from the aperture's lower edge. With a grunt of annoyance, he tried again. Maybe a centimeter or two higher. He might be in great shape, but no mundane human could make that jump. If his magic was unbound, he could make it easily, and far beyond.

He turned his back to the wall, slid into a sitting position. Again, he turned his attention inwards, probed and prodded at the enchantment binding him. So complete, he saw not even the tiniest opportunity to manipulate it. The Lady made the Autarch's magic seem like a child's toy. With a roar, he stood and leaped, and leaped again, reaching for the window.

The cell door banged open and the Lady strode in, wearing her human shape. Alex fell to the floor as her whips of agony thrashed through him.

"You think to throw yourself from the tower like a love-struck princess?" she demanded. She raised her hands theatrically and her magic flooded out, her 'sign blinding. The room shifted and warped, the walls stretched, the ceiling shot upwards. The window was dragged up with it. With the only opening ten meters above the ground, the Lady turned to Alex and stared down at him. "Perhaps that will stop you trying, imbecile. Understand, you are utterly powerless here."

Alex snarled and jumped to his feet. "Fucking kill me!" He slammed into the Lady, hammered her with blows and managed to actually drive her back a few paces before her torture tore through him again. Though he tried to fight it, she proved herself right. He was powerless.

He writhed in pain as she moved back across the cell. "Pathetic!" she said with a laugh and slammed the door closed behind her.

Alex lay curled on the floor, bereft.

Silhouette sat in the shadow of trees, in the darkness of night. Follow the blue fucking sun. The only information she had was useless until the day came around again. Was that just a matter of hours? She thought she had put a lot of distance between herself and the Erlking and didn't know if she had run towards the ice mountain or away. And how did you follow a sun anyway? It wasn't like a distant star, static in the night sky. The sun travelled across the land. In the mortal realm, she could follow the sun from east to west and what good would that do?

Perhaps following the blue sun meant heading in the direction where it rose in the morning. It was her best guess so far, but she still felt as though she was swimming in molasses and slowly sinking.

A sound in the trees distracted her melancholy. She looked up to see a group of the huge ape-headed birds she had encountered on arriving. They seemed to be roosting, heads slumped onto their chests. The noise came again as one shuffled, shifting the branches and leaves around itself. Four of them up there. Silhouette nodded to herself. *Time to get proactive.*

She climbed as quietly as possible into the lower limbs of the tree directly beneath one of the creatures. Its ape feet were curled around the branch, gripping tightly. She reached slowly forward and clamped one hand tight around its ankle. It woke with a violent burst of movement and noise, crying out. The others woke with it and screamed like furious chimpanzees as Silhouette dragged the one she had caught to the ground. She slammed one fist into its face, stunning it. "You want some of this too?" she yelled up at the others.

"Help me!" the one on the ground cried weakly.

Silhouette shifted through her panther form and back to her Fey shape, made herself as monstrous and dangerous as she could. The three remaining creatures fled.

"Your friends are shit," Silhouette said to the one she held.

"What do you want? I'll get it for you. Anything!"

"Actually, I just want information."

The creature stilled beneath her. "What is it?"

"Where's the ice mountain? And the Lady's palace?"

"Same place. Her mountain is the palace."

Silhouette gripped the thing's throat with a long, Fey hand. "And where is that?"

"Just go there. Just go."

"How do I get there?" Silhouette yelled.

One spindly arm emerged from under a twisted wing, pointed uncertainly. "That way? That way, if you like, and on till morning. Or right now. Just go." Its ape face was confused, like it was speaking to a child.

"How far? How long will it take?"

The creature shook its head, frowning in consternation. "As long as you want. Just go. Fold that way. Here, there, all the same."

Silhouette remembered her travels thus far, the distances seemingly arbitrary, adjusted with intent. Fucking Kreek could have explained this concept to her and made her life a lot easier. But of course, he was Fey and they liked nothing more than corruption and lies and games. Why would he make it any easier for her? She looked along the creature's still outstretched arm. "How will I know if I go off-course?"

"Off-course?"

Silhouette growled with annoyance and wrenched the thing's throat and head in opposite directions. The bones in its neck crunched and disintegrated. It squealed, high and shrill and brief, and lay still.

Follow the blue sun. She realized it was probably simply a figure of speech in this messed up land, a nonsense phrase. She stood and walked in the direction the ape-bird had pointed. It was as good a choice as any. *Ice mountain,* she repeated over and over in her mind. She let the landscape twist and warp beneath her. The normal rules of physics held no sway here. She swallowed the nausea traveling seemed to give her and closed her eyes. After a few paces, keeping her mantra rolling over in her mind, she opened them again, saw ridged hills in the distance. She let her desire to go there to the fore and found herself striding up rocky green flanks. She blinked again and saw a huge white edifice towering above her. The top of the mountain was a palace. It wasn't built atop the rise, but carved from it. The mountain itself became a huge, icy palace at its peak. A pathway wound up from the green hills, zigzagging up the pale flanks. Silhouette concentrated on the foot of the pathway and she was there.

The mountain palace gleamed in the light of three moons. After all her panic and concern and blundering around, it was done. Fucking Kreek and his lost at sea monologue. She pictured herself and Alex ripping that bastard to pieces and it momentarily gave her strength.

But what now?

She couldn't simply wander in and get Alex. This Lady was a powerful monarch, even if not everyone here conceded to her rule, and Alex her most prized prisoner. A village lay nestled in the crook of two ridges not far from where she stood. A few Fey and other creatures strolled languidly through its streets, though the place seemed quiet and calm under the mantle of night. A couple of strange vehicles moved. A long, cigar-shaped balloon descended as she watched and a Fey appeared on a rooftop to tether it in place. From the small gondola beneath it, three more emerged and disappeared inside through a doorway on the roof.

Silhouette watched it all from a distance, like observing a puppet play. She needed to get the lay of the land, decide how to move. Perhaps the Fey in that village were among the Lady's most faithful and would have reason to come and go from the mountain. Surely, there must be something to learn down there.

She made her way towards it, following the ridge as it sloped gently down. She didn't try to fold the space between even though she was getting the hang of it. She needed time to think. Repeatedly she looked up to the palace, high above her. It had all the hallmarks of the impregnable fortress, the only obvious entrance from the path leading up. She could make out a courtyard at the end of it and huge double gates that shone silver in the night.

She looked back towards the village and the cigar balloon recently moored there. Could she commandeer something like that and approach from the air? Even if she had to steal an aircraft, given that she had nothing to trade, she had little idea how to pilot one. And even then, surely the palace would defend itself, and in this land of ubiquitous magic, that defense could be swift and deadly. Frustration burned in her gut.

Shouts and commotion erupted from the village. Bolts of energy and sounds of breaking wood and screams of pain. Silhouette dropped into the lee of a rock pile. The village streets were suddenly filled with Fey and someone came striding through the throng. The Fey buckled under the assault, snapping and flying, tossed around like dolls. The person doing the damage was tall and thin and pale and human. And bald. Silhouette's heart hammered in her chest. Impossible! Hot on the heels of the pale man, another came, looking for all the world like Indiana Jones brandishing a long, gleaming sword swirling with magesign. His swordplay was expert and Fey limbs were sliced free, heads rolled.

The two men cut a swathe through the village, shielded from the offensive magic of the Fey by a glistening ward of energy that seemed to emanate from the man with sword. *Admit it*, Silhouette thought. *That's Claude Darvill and Robert fucking Hood!* How was that possible? Darvill was one thing, but Alex had buried Hood forever. And they were here in Faerie? The protection they walked under reminded Silhouette of the magic Darvill had used in Obsidian to protect Haydon. But in this case, the physical was let through and the shield rebuffed arcane energies.

What kind of weapon did Darvill wield that could rend Fey with such ease? And Hood literally tore them apart with his bare hands. Such strength. They marched through the village and mounted the path leading towards the mountain top. They were coming for Alex.

CHAPTER FIFTEEN

S ilhouette tore her gaze away from the mayhem below. She had to get to the palace before Hood and Darvill, no matter the cost. They were a fair distance behind and seemed to be enjoying the carnage. Perhaps it would delay them.

She ran back towards the path up the ice mountain. Her long, thin Fey legs ate up the distance and she blinked, dragged herself through the land with each breath, folded the space between her and the courtyard high above. Several Fey emerged from the frozen citadel as she approached, looked down to the village. With any luck, these would slow Hood and Darvill, too.

She burst onto the courtyard, staggered by the size of the huge silver gates towering over her, intricate and beautiful, like finely wrought lace, gleaming in the blue-white light of Fey moons. The courtyard was carved from ice, but it wasn't cold. At least, not as cold as she had imagined it would be. As the thought occurred to her, the chill drastically increased. She could not wait to be out of this twisted place.

Trees dotted the courtyard edges, mighty, ancient oaks and yews and other types she had never seen before. Among the crowding Fey, she slowed her pace. She needed to remember caution. Some of them cast curious glances at her, but perhaps they thought her flight was related to the chaos below.

A huge tearing sound rent the air and all turned to see one of the massive trees split from roots to crown. From the yawning blackness within, the Erlking emerged, his face a mask of fury. Silhouette cursed. What next? She ducked behind a small group of stunned Fey, hoping he hadn't seen her. But he didn't even pause to look around the group. Head down, antlers forward as if for battle, he strode into the stronghold. From the gaping tree, more creatures appeared, hot on the Erlking's heels. They looked like heavily muscled dogs, walking tall on their hind legs. Their backs arched in a wave of vicious spines, their snouts short and snarling, hands long and tipped with glistening black claws. More and more stepped from the darkness and marched into the palace. Several of the Fey present ran back inside, their apprehension palpable, while others continued down the path towards the village.

With a confused shake of her head, Silhouette slipped inside with the dozens of marching dog-beasts. They entered a large room with benches down either side. Before them stood huge, arched double doors, dark wood, inset with a shining silver tree. The tree glowed and twisted, like it was whipped by a strong wind. One side was open, leading to a huge throne room with high ceilings and carved columns. The ice-carved chamber was scattered with plants in large vases, tapestries, paintings. Several Fey milled about inside, an air of tense concern heavy among them. As the Erlking and his soldiers marched through, they crouched into readiness. The air became charged with the tension of imminent battle.

At the end of the room, two large thrones sat on a raised dais. On one throne a regal Fey woman reclined. She leapt to her feet in outrage at the Erlking's approach.

"What is the meaning of this intrusion?"

The Erlking shoved aside any who dared to stand between him and the woman. "Lady of the Fey," he said, voice dripping with disdain. "What do you mean by sending your emissaries to kill my servants?"

Silhouette felt something colder than the ice stir in her belly. This was her fault. The Erlking presumed she had told the truth about looking on behalf of the Lady, and she had killed his best servant. And this was the Lady. And Hood and Darvill were rending their way up the mountain. Could things have turned more to shit? Suddenly, every enemy she could imagine was in one place.

The Lady walked down to stand nose to nose with the Erlking. "You have some nerve showing your horns in this place!" She gestured to two guards standing nervously beside her. "Go and ensure our *guest* doesn't get any ideas while this idiocy prevails." She put her hands on the Erlking's chest and shoved him away from her. Pandemonium erupted as dog-beasts and Fey clashed with roars and bursts of magic. The Lady braced as the Erlking dipped his antlers and bullrushed her.

The clash of their impact shook the hall. The two guards instructed to protect the guest ran from the room. Silhouette saw her chance and took it, hightailed it after them, a grin spreading across her face. Perhaps the havoc in Faerie this night would work to her advantage, after all.

The Fey ran through a door in the corner of the throne room and up a spiral staircase, taking the steps two or three at a time. The sounds of battle below intensified, the roar of the Erlking, the scream of the Lady. And more distant sounds of fighting, presumably Robert Hood battling his way up to the courtyard. How the fuck was that Robert Hood? Darvill must have done this, the fool!

Silhouette's blood chilled and she ran on, up and up, level after level. The sounds of fighting faded below. The Fey ahead of her turned along a corridor and called out something she didn't catch to companions unseen. She slowed her pace, snuck along the passage. At the end, it opened into a room with several doors along one side. Four Fey moved towards one of the doors and looked in. They nodded and muttered to each other.

Silhouette ducked out of sight as they turned back towards her.

The palace shook, massive pulses of magesign washed up through the structure. A strange, almost animal klaxon sound rang through the air. The four Fey became agitated, arguing. One gestured to the door they had looked in before, another towards the corridor leading away. They were clearly torn in their duty. Silhouette took a chance.

She ran forward. "The Lady is battling an Erlking! We need to help her."

They looked at her in confusion. "We know!" one said. "Can she stand against one? And his beasts?"

"There are dozens of them down there!" Silhouette said, the desperation in her voice not feigned in the slightest. "They're tearing the place apart!" As if to confirm her words, the palace shook again as if bombs were going off below.

For a moment, she thought they would call her bluff, regardless. Then, as one, they bolted for the corridor and the stairs leading down. Silhouette turned to run with them, took a few paces, then dropped back. Hoping they wouldn't notice her absence, she ran back to the door they'd looked in. It was solid, a slab of ice. What had they been looking at?

She paused, took a deep breath. *Remember where you are.* Everything about this place was magic. Fey magic, which was an intrinsic part of her. No matter how much she denied it, it was in her nonetheless. She willed the door to reveal what it held, looked between the shades and planes of enchantment that wove through everything. A panel cleared in the ice and Silhouette gasped. Alex lay inside, bleeding and battered. He stared blankly at the ceiling above him. Only the tiny movements of his chest gave her the relief he wasn't dead.

She drove her mind through the door's magic, looking for some way to release it. Muffled explosions rattled up through the floor. Voices of anger and pain carried with them.

Silhouette's heart hammered, her hands shook. *Come on, come on, come on!* And there it was, the lacework of Fey magic locking the door into place. She stripped it out, working at it like she might deconstruct a Kin ward. It was slow and fiddly work and not entirely familiar. The palace boomed and shook. She heard several sets of footsteps pounding towards her. "The Lady is moving!" a voice shouted. "Protect the Caine!"

Silhouette tried to concentrate only on the door as the footsteps pounded closer. *I just want to get in there!* she screamed silently and nausea twisted her gut. This place, it was ridiculous. Could she just…? She looked into the cell and willed herself inside, blinked. She stood beside Alex's prone form.

He started, scrambled back on hands and heels, face racked with pain. "Fucking kill me already!" he yelled.

Silhouette's heart cracked. "It's me," she said, and shifted back to her human shape.

Alex's eyes widened before his face twisted in grief. "No, surely not."

"Alex, we have to…"

"Kill me!"

"What?"

Alex moved onto his knees, reached out to her like the supplicant Christ. "It's all me, Silhouette. Everything is because of me. They've taken my powers, so *you* have to kill me. You *have* to!"

Silhouette grabbed one wrist, hauled him to his feet. "Fuck that, Iron Balls, we are getting out of here."

Alex resisted, shook his head. "Even if we do, they'll only come again. It can only end with my death, don't you see?"

"Alex, Hood is free. And he's here."

"What?"

Frantic voices argued outside the cell door.

"Alex, please, we have to go." Silhouette was distraught at the total despair in Alex, but she refused to let him give in to it. "We need a Fey gate, Alex, and we can get home. Then we can deal with everything else."

"Hood is here?"

The cell door slammed open and three Fey strode in. They paused for a second, stunned at the presence of Silhouette with their prisoner.

"Grab them both!" one yelled.

Silhouette, her grip still tight about Alex's wrist, ran for a gap between them and kept her eyes on the open room beyond. She blinked and forced the space to twist around her. The Fey roared, grabbed at them as she pulled Alex through, their surprise buying her precious moments. She hauled Alex along as the three gave chase.

"Fucking run, Alex!" she screamed and he finally found his feet.

"We have to deal with Hood!" he said as they ran.

"Yes, but not here! At home."

A wave of burning energy slammed into them from behind, knocked them flying. They slid facedown across the icy floor and fetched up with a jarring impact against a wall. The Fey were on them in an instant. Through stunned eyes, Silhouette saw another door opposite the one she had emerged from earlier, more steps leading down. She dragged against Alex's arm, used her considerable strength to fling him towards the stairs.

"Run!"

She met the assault of the Fey. Her vision swam as one mighty blow cracked across her jaw even as she delivered a similar blow to another. Alex refused to run, turned to face the fray. He drove a kick hard into the back of one assailant, sent the tall, dark Fey stumbling away. Even without his powers, he was a formidable fighter and a new fire burned in his eyes. A massive concussion shook the citadel, the ground cracked beneath their feet, sent them all staggering.

"They're tearing the place apart!" one of the Fey yelled.

Alex grabbed Silhouette, dragged her away.

"We can't hope to beat them!"

Silhouette's magic was nothing compared to the Fey, or even Alex for that matter, and his skills were clearly shackled. Prisons in this realm could only work against the shackled or the mundane. Desperately, she gathered enough energy to put up a ward between them and the Fey and they ran for the stairs. Her shield lasted less than a second, but it bought them a few paces head start. As they rounded the wall and hurtled down the steps, the ice behind them exploded in shards of glittering white. Blue Fey fire crackled through it.

The palace shook again, stairs crumbled out beneath them. They slipped and fell, barely controlling their descent as the stairway became a slide of broken ice. Fey magic scorched down from above, barely missed them as more walls cracked and fell. The wall to their left shattered with another rattling boom from below and the multi-blue of Faerie night painted the white space.

Vertigo twisted in Silhouette as she looked out and down, the palatial fortress merging with the mountain in a sheer drop, hundreds of meters to the shadowed green valley below. Dozens of Fey rushed along the winding path from the town, stutter-stepping through folded space, like timelapse photography, to help their Lady. Halfway along the path, they met the carnage of Hood and Darvill still fighting their way up. More Fey, entangled with dog-beasts, battled in the courtyard and somewhere inside the Lady and the Erlking had to be still engaged, the entire structure suffering with the might of their combat.

Silhouette looked down. Some twenty meters directly beneath them, a huge dirigible drifted, heading for the courtyard. Without thinking, as the stairs under their feet cracked again and more blue fire arced down from above, she grabbed Alex and hauled him out through the gap, leaping with all her strength away from the walls.

All other sound was torn away by an incessant rush of wind. Silhouette registered Alex's stunned, wide-eyed face beside her even as tears whipped across her cheeks. Their clothing slapped at their limbs. But his jaw was firm, his focus entirely on the dirigible below. Time seemed to slow and speed up at the same time and the rushing air suddenly ceased with a *whump* as they hit the stiff, leathery balloon.

For a terrifying second Silhouette thought they might bounce off, but it sagged under them and they sank into its depths. The dirigible shuddered and shifted in the air, its flight interrupted by their unexpected impact. Alex and Silhouette clawed their way across the leather, towards the icy wall sliding by not three meters from them.

"Drop and slide!" Alex yelled and slipped out of sight.

Silhouette was an instant behind him. For a second she was falling again, then the icy side of the mountain hit her with a breath-stealing impact and she was sliding, a random, hectic course down a steep crevasse. The ice was rough and hard, burning and grazing with friction as she slid. Alex hurtled ahead of her, wearing nothing but light training pants. She couldn't see his face and was thankful she couldn't see his pain.

The crevasse narrowed and steepened and for a moment they were in free-fall, before striking hard ice again. They bounced and shifted, bones jarring, teeth rattling. Alex gestured frantically to his left, dug his heels and elbows into the ice to shift his course. Silhouette matched him, trusting whatever he had seen. They surfed over a frozen ridge and skittered out onto a natural ledge on the mountainside. Alex flipped over, dragged with his hands to slow his momentum. There was no way he would stop in time. Wide open space yawned beyond his feet.

Silhouette let herself fly free a moment longer, drew alongside Alex and grabbed his arm in one hand. She shifted the other to a panther paw, large, black claws extended. She gouged into the ice, crying out as she felt her claws start to tear free, her shoulder stretch open in its socket. But they slowed and, legs hanging over a sheer drop, finally stopped moving.

Both flat on their bellies, gasping for breath, racked with pain, they hauled themselves onto the ledge and took a moment in silence.

"That was fucking invigorating," Alex said eventually.

Silhouette couldn't suppress a laugh as she looked over at him. The despair, at least for now, had left his face. They kissed, hard and urgent.

Silhouette pulled away. "We have to keep moving."

A deafening crack ripped through the air as one massive wall exploded out into space. Huge chunks of ice flew free and came tumbling through the sky. They scrambled close to the mountainside as the deadly rain fell by.

"Who's doing that?" Alex asked.

"The Lady and an Erlking are having a bit of a disagreement. And

Hood is yet to get there. With any luck they'll all kill each other."

Alex raised one eyebrow.

Silhouette shook her head, tipped him a wry smile. "I'll try to explain later. Here." She pulled her pouch of healing powder from her belt, dipped one finger in. She rubbed it into her gums, offered some to Alex. He copied her action, eyes fluttering as the healing effect through his body was almost instant. "Not perfect, raw like that, but it'll help for now," Silhouette said. "Come on."

They turned back to the descent and began traversing the treacherous mountainside, heading for the green valley floor below. Silhouette knew she could move easily, fold her way down, but Alex didn't have the Fey blood she did. He had to go the long way. And he had said they'd taken his powers. What did that mean? Taking care, using the edges of crevasses and the natural features of the rock beneath, they slowly worked their way down. The incline leveled out considerably as they moved, the way becoming less daunting by the step.

Silhouette took the ring from its chain around her neck and slipped it back onto her finger. It swelled its oily presence through her as she concentrated, let her desire for a Fey gate sit at the forefront of her mind. Her gaze was drawn to a forest of shifting trees not far from the mountain's base on the opposite side to the village. The movement of trunks and canopy confounded her eye, as if the trees all occupied two or three different, but close by, places all at the same time. "We have to go there."

Alex looked, grimaced. "Great. I have no power, Sil. They bound me up better than the Autarch ever did."

Silhouette pointed to the Darak, smeared with Alex's blood. "All we need is that and I can do the rest. We'll deal with everything else at home."

"It's Fey magic, Sil."

She nodded. "I know a Fey now."

Alex clearly chose not to question that and they concentrated on climbing down. Eventually they hurried across the level grassland, heading for the shifting trees.

The battle above quietened, but they were too far away to see any detail. There was frantic movement up there, but who moved and who might be dead was a mystery.

"We have to assume Hood survived," Silhouette said. "It's a question of who else lived."

"I doubt the Lady would fall," Alex said. "Could this Erlking have beaten her?"

Silhouette shrugged. "I have no idea. We have to assume not, I suppose."

"She would run rather than lose a fight." Alex tapped his chest. "There's too much at stake."

Silhouette ducked into the trees. "Come on."

The wood was sickening to the eyes, like a television not properly tuned in, the picture dancing and flickering in and out of phase. Except it was three-dimensional and all around them. The trees reached out, wavering branches snatched at their hair and clothes. Alex grunted as he snapped and wrenched at the clamoring limbs. Silhouette concentrated on the pull of the ring. It led them to a pile of almost spherical rocks, piled into a high cairn. At the base was a dark opening.

Silhouette pointed. "This is it, but I have no idea where we'll find ourselves on the other side. Somewhere in the mortal realm, but it could be anywhere."

Alex pressed his hand to his chest. "Anywhere is better than this. That thing hurts me, whatever it is. Let's just go through."

Silhouette wondered if releasing her Fey nature would prevent her access to the gate, but she knew the Darak would open it for them. It was independent of Alex's own powers in that respect. And she had Kreek's strange ring. Hoping it would let her through, she gripped Alex's hand tightly and they stepped forward. A vortex of color whirled into the darkness in front of them. Silhouette felt her Fey self repelled by it. Nausea dragged at her.

"Help me through," she said. "Alex, drag me through!"

Without asking why, he dug his feet into the ground and pulled her along. The swirling vortex sucked them away. As they went, a blood-curdling scream rang through the air and was whipped away like a leaf in a storm wind.

Robert Hood held the decapitated head of the Erlking by one blood-soaked antler, the creature's neck a ragged, bloody stump where it had been torn free of the body. "Where is he?" he yelled.

Fey and dog-beast bodies in various stages of dismemberment littered the courtyard. The palace stood behind them, broken and tumbling. Chunks of it lay scattered everywhere, more littering the pathway and the valley below. What little remained of the structure spiked into the sky like a shattered tooth.

Claude Darvill held his sword across the neck of one Fey, who shook her head side to side widely, fear and denial. "What are you?" she wailed.

"Answer the fucking question!" Hood screamed.

"He escaped, didn't you hear? You felt the gate open and heard the Lady's distress, no? She ran for him after you started fighting the Erlking, but must have been too late. Why did you attack the Erlking anyway?"

Hood looked momentarily confused, stared at the blood-soaked, antlered head. "Just fucking felt like it, I guess. Though it was a strange compulsion." His eyes narrowed and he snapped his attention back to the Fey. "Caine escaped?"

"He must have. A gate triggered. And I can't think what else would have made our Lady scream like that."

Hood tipped his face to the triple-mooned sky and roared in raw fury. Darvill whipped his sword aside, the Fey's head spinning away as its body crumpled to the ground.

Hood lowered his face, stared levelly at his son. "That was quite a scrap!" He grinned broadly.

Darvill nodded, his own grin matching his father's. "It really was, huh!" He looked at his new weapon. "This thing is fantastic." He slipped it back into the sheath across his back.

"You and I, son, we can rule the world. But first, Alex Caine must die. How can he possibly have escaped that?" He gestured angrily at the collapsed edifice.

Darvill shook his head, chewed his lip. "No idea. But it seems he did. And this Fey Lady had him prisoner for a reason."

"So fucking what?"

"So she's likely to be after him again. We need to move or she may get him first."

Hood tapped one index finger against his temple. "I've got lots of Fey knowledge in here thanks to my new passenger. And you know what it tells me? It says that bitch is stuck here until the next thin day. We can go back when we like because we're not Fey, and I know how to trigger the gates. But she can't."

Darvill smiled, pleased with the news even while he remained very concerned about what exactly his father's passenger was. "Well, let's you and I get back home. This place freaks me the fuck out."

Jean Chang quietly sipped tea as Jarrod talked urgently on his phone and his friends worked. They tapped at laptops and tablets, distilling what they knew. The safehouse in the Sydney suburb of Rockdale, to the south of the city, lived up to its name. She felt secure. For how long, she didn't know, but at least for the moment she could rest.

Jarrod's voice was tense, his knuckles paling as he gripped his mobile tight. "No, Sydney is devastated. Everyone is dead and most of the equipment ruined. I've sealed it and set the pump-out into operation. You'll have to send a team in to recover what they can and deal with the dead." Pause. "No, it's a fucking mess. No one died clean down there."

Chang looked away, shamed as she observed his obvious distress. She had caused this. Not alone and certainly not through her own desire, but she bore responsibility.

"Alex and Silhouette, yes." Jarrod listened again. "No, I was trying to find her because she went after him. We lost her. We have to find them and figure out what's happening." Another pause, longer this time. Jarrod's jaw tightened as he listened. "No, sir. I'm sorry, but my priority is my sister. There are three more operatives here who can meet with your contingent when they arrive." Pause. "Yes, sir. I'll tell them."

He disconnected the call, slipped the phone into his pocket. He turned to his companions. "London is on the case. They've mobilized a team from Melbourne and experts from Auckland to fix up the Sydney situation. And someone from London is on the way here too. You guys wait for a call, then team up with them. See if you can start any kind of rebuild in Sydney."

"Alex fucking Caine caused this," one of them said, eyes dark. Her mouth was set in an angry line.

Jarrod nodded. "Yes, he did. But none of it is his fault. He's trapped in this, has been from the start."

The woman stood, jabbed an angry finger towards Jarrod. "I don't want to hear your excuses! How many died in Scotland? My *partner* died there! Now Caine's brought his special brand of fucking havoc here. He needs to be stopped."

Jarrod strode over to the woman. "He needs our help, Suzi, to stop all the things conspiring against him! You don't have to be a part of it, but the threat is not Alex. Far bigger dangers are out there. Go back to Sydney HQ and help clean up."

Suzi shoved Jarrod, who obligingly stepped out of her way. "I will clean up Sydney and I will keep doing my job. But whatever other dangers exist, Alex fucking Caine is a threat to all of us. To *everyone*! I'll be front and center of the team tasked with finishing him."

Jarrod's eyes narrowed, but he bit back a retort. "You do that," he said instead. Chang wondered what he had been going to say first. She jumped when he turned to her. "You're with me."

"With you?" Jean asked.

"You have the tech to track down Hood and Darvill."

Jean pulled the tablet from her bag, shaking her head. "But they disappeared…Oh. They're back." She looked up, tried to ignore the trembling in her hands. "Not too far away."

"Good. Keep an eye on them while we travel."

"Where are we going?"

Jarrod laughed. "Wherever they are! We need to know if they've brought Alex and Silhouette back from wherever they went."

"And if they haven't?"

"We go to Melbourne. We need the services of an Armor HQ to help us figure out how to find Sil and Alex."

Jean swallowed, reluctant to ask the next question. "And if Hood and Darvill do have them?"

Jarrod's face darkened. He ignored the hiss of hatred from Suzi. "We'll cross that bridge if we come to it."

Alex and Silhouette staggered through a wooden door in a garden wall, moonlight limning everything in silver. They stepped over a dormant flowerbed onto a well-manicured lawn. An old red brick house, leadlight windows and a thatched roof, squatted at one end. The other end of the garden led to a pond and a small wood beyond.

"Gotta be England," Alex said, rubbing himself against the cold as his breath misted the air. He wished they had emerged somewhere in Australia, though he wondered how safe his home country was. In truth, he wondered if anywhere was safe. "Come on." He set off at a trot for the woods.

Silhouette tugged his sleeve. "Wait."

A small shed stood beside the pond. She slipped inside, emerged with a glass jar. She dipped the jar in the pond and held it up to the moonlight to squint at it. "Looks pretty clean. Won't kill us anyway." She took healing powder from her pouch and put a pinch in the water. It fizzed and turned dark purple-brown. She swallowed half with a wince, handed it to Alex.

He took it, gulped it down. The familiar bittersweet buzz spread through him almost instantly. His aches, pains and cuts immediately reduced, the sliced flesh of his chest sealed up. "That stuff is a winner, seriously."

Silhouette looked him up and down. "Wait there."

She went back into the shed and returned with a blue all-in-one overall like mechanics wore. "Try this on."

Alex pulled it over his training pants, zipped it up. "Bit short in the arms and legs, but not bad. How do I look?"

Silhouette couldn't suppress a laugh. "Like a fucking hillbilly. We need to find you some shoes."

They stared at each other for a moment, Silhouette's laughter fading. Alex stepped forward, dragged her into an embrace and kissed her. She was hot against his lips. He couldn't remember anything feeling so good.

"You came to Faerie for me." It was a hard concept to process.

"And I got you out. We're a fucking team, Iron Balls. Unstoppable."

Alex shook his head, despair flickering at all his edges. "I don't know about that. All the time I'm alive, this is alive." He tapped his chest. "They won't give up." In the night shadow of a garden shed, he told her everything he had learned.

"Her husband's *heart*?" Silhouette breathed. "That's insane."

"She will never give up."

"Then we kill her. When Uthentia had you, we didn't give up. Trapped in Obsidian, we didn't give up. We won't now. And we have more immediate concerns with Hood."

Alex's heart rate doubled at the mention of the name. "How is he back? Is Darvill really that fucking stupid?"

"Apparently."

"They came to Faerie, too. What the fuck...?"

"I think he's bound with Uthentia still," Silhouette said. "That means he has all those Fey connections. All that knowledge."

Alex stared at his chilled feet, pressing into the soft grass. "So Hood will be back as soon as they realize we've left and he'll be gunning for me. And he's indestructible. And as soon as she's able, the Lady will be coming for me, too. When's the next thin day?"

Silhouette grimaced. "Not long, probably."

"Aren't they six weeks apart?"

"No. The primary thin days are the solstices, equinoxes and the quarter days in between. You know, Beltane, Lammas, Imbolc, all that shit. But those are only the primary thins. There are others."

"How many?"

"It varies. Things like February twenty-ninth on leap years, blue moons, planetary alignments. All that stuff."

Despair redoubled in Alex's veins. "How many fucking days are there? Why do the Fey care about the stone when they have so many opportunities?"

"They want nothing less than free rein, I guess. They either come and go on a thin day, which is like a blink in time for them, or they have to stay until the next thin day, with massively reduced powers. With the stone, they had full power and free rein all the time. That's what they want back. I'm guessing the Darak as part of you is not enough. It's only useful if you're with them, like how they stole you away to Faerie in the first place. But if the Lady gets the Darak back, revives the Lord…who knows how much power they'll regain."

"Which brings us to something else," Alex said. "I'm still shackled. Whatever that bitch has done to me is still in place. I have no power, Sil." He heard the whine in his voice, the vocalization of his desire to give everything up, and he hated it.

Silhouette hugged him. "I know. We'll fix that. It's complicated magic, I can't unweave it. But I'm sure someone will be able to."

"You said you know a Fey, now?" He had trouble understanding how that had happened, but could only process so much information at any one time, so chose not to question the details.

"Yeah, but he's in Sydney." Silhouette took a breath, stood up straight.

"Okay, here's what we have to do. One, find an Armor base nearby. We need their protection. Hopefully they can help us hide from Hood. And undo the spell holding you. Then we can plan a course of action before the Lady comes after you."

Alex nodded, squared his shoulders. "Right. Let's go then." He paused. "It would be a lot easier if you just ripped my throat out right here and now, you know."

Silhouette slapped him, hard enough that his vision crossed and his ears rang. "Put that shit away!" Her voice contained such fury. "You will not give up, Alex. You will not leave me! We still have Hood to consider. And we'll find a way to beat that Fey cunt too."

Alex stared into Silhouette's icy blue eyes. Her fury was as beautiful as she was, as strong as her love. He couldn't bear the thought of life without her. He had to assume she felt the same about losing him. *Never give up the fight until you're out cold on the floor.* He nodded softly. His Sifu's words, Silhouette's love and fury, his own anger at how his life had become the business of so many others—all these things burned holes in his soul. He needed to use that as fuel to fight, not let it eat him up from the inside. "Let's find a phone and call the Armor emergency number. There'll be a base nearby to take us in."

Jarrod and Jean Chang watched Hood and Darvill from a distance. The two men walked along King Street as if they owned the place, the denizens of Newtown giving them a wide berth.

"They're coming this way," Chang said, her voice trembling. She watched the tablet on her lap intently.

"It's okay," Jarrod assured her. "We're safe enough here."

They sat in an open-fronted bar, windows wide to the busy street. Two schooners of beer sat before them, untouched. Jarrod patted Chang's knee under the table, doing his best to console her fears. She was incredibly brave to be staying with this, aside from the guilt she had described to him as they traveled. He would protect her. "Head down," he whispered as Hood and Darvill passed by on the other side of the road. They both stared at their beers.

Jarrod waited until they were a good few meters ahead. "I'm going to follow them. You stay here. Keep an eye on your tracker in case I lose them."

"What if you don't come back?"

"I will, don't worry. They won't spot me."

Without waiting for an answer or protest, he slipped from his stool and out into the street. Hood's shining pale bald head was easy to follow from afar. Jarrod wanted to get closer, but after all their time together in Obsidian, Darvill was sure to recognize him. Instead, he relied on his Armor training to tail a target. Easy enough in a crowded suburb like Newtown.

The men paused and consulted some notes. Darvill pointed. They crossed the road, heading for a side street. Jarrod hurried after them, paused at a shop, acted as though he was window shopping as he watched Hood and Darvill's reflections in the glass. They stopped again a few doors along the side street, exchanged a few quick words, and went inside.

Jarrod moved along behind them. Diagonally across from the shop Hood and Darvill had entered was a back door alcove with large, wheeled bins crammed into it. Jarrod slipped behind the bins, wincing at the smell of rotten refuse. He settled into the shadows and watched. It was a black-painted store, a square plate glass window with stencilled script, *Leather & Lace*. His eyes roved the mannequins on display—leather and lace indeed, corsets and masks, whips and high, shiny boots. What the hell were they doing here?

He started at a burst of noise from inside, a scream. Another crash and a splintering sound like a door being kicked in. He quickly looked out from his hiding place. No one else in the quiet side street. He couldn't risk himself by intervening, Hood was far too dangerous. Armor was well versed in the history of Alex's adversaries. What a fucking mess. Hood should not be walking the streets. He thought Darvill had learned something working with Alex against the Hierarchy. Clearly not. But there was nothing he could do now. Darvill and Hood didn't have Alex and Silhouette with them and they were obviously searching for something.

Where had they been when they vanished from Chang's tablet? Had Silhouette gone to Faerie? Would she ever make it out alive if she had? So many questions. Jarrod suppressed an impotent rage. Patience. Answers would come.

He hunkered down as movement in the shop caught his eye. Darvill and Hood emerged onto the narrow footpath.

"Useless!" Hood said.

Darvill raised his hands, palms up. "I told you, I could only track Silhouette's recent movements. They confirmed she'd been here."

"Yes, but before she went to Faerie," Hood said, exasperated. "We know that and we know they got away from there. We're still no nearer!"

Jarrod bit down on a surge of joy. Here were answers! She went to Faerie and *they* got away. Had Silhouette really done it? Saved Alex? He felt great pride for his half-sister.

"That Fey fucker in there gave her the means to get to Faerie," Darvill said. "And we know he gave her a Fey artifact to help her. All information is useful."

Hood laughed, a horrible, guttural sound. "That Fey fucker won't be helping anyone else."

"Or his little helper. How many pieces did you leave them in?"

"I didn't count. But I am developing quite a taste for killing Fey." Hood tapped his head. "My passenger here is rather enjoying it. For all his power, I think they rather abused him in the past."

Darvill's eyes narrowed. "Are you controlling him, Dad? Really?"

Hood laughed again. "I wouldn't go so far as to say controlling, but I'm getting a better handle on it by the hour. I will never bore of mayhem and murder though, so don't think I will. I have a new lease on life, son! As do you, it seems, with your swordplay."

It was Darvill's turn to laugh. "Fair enough. As long as you remember I'm on your side."

"So, what now? I want to kill Alex Caine, Claude. These delays are interminable."

Darvill nodded, lips pursed. "I have a lot of info on both Alex and Silhouette. I'm good at finding things, but this is…difficult." He gestured into the shop. "That prick said Silhouette went to Faerie from a nearby gate but could have emerged anywhere. I can't search on that scale without help."

"So what do we do?"

"Let's convene some friends back home to help me pinpoint just where in the world Alex and Silhouette have emerged. It's a big delay, but we will find them again."

The two men strode away, Hood cursing and bitching as they went. Jarrod sat in the stinking shadows and chewed his lip. It was a race against time to see who could get to Alex and Silhouette first. He had to mobilize a defense for them. He waited until Hood and Darvill were long gone before jogging back to the bar and Jean Chang.

"They're heading back towards the city," she said as he sat down.

He picked up the beer he had left behind, drained it. It was still cold and refreshing. "Yep. We have to go to Melbourne HQ and get some help."

CHAPTER SEVENTEEN

Alex and Silhouette sat in a comfortable room in London Armor HQ. One of the oldest, in a maze of catacombs beneath the city near the Thames, the aged bricks and arched ceilings were at odds with the modern equipment and industrious staff.

A man walked in, wearing a smart suit, polished shoes. He was clean-shaven, middle-aged and confident. *Looks like a corporate CEO*, Alex thought and immediately bristled. Even though his magic was bound, his vision was still preternaturally good and he probed the man's persona. He was masked well, clearly a lot more than he appeared, but that was a given for most of the Armor personnel Alex had met thus far. They all had some arcane skill, some aspect of themselves best hidden from the general populace.

The smart man extended a hand. "Gavin Crookshank. Commander here. Excuse the ridiculous get-up, I've come straight from a meeting with the PM."

Alex shook. "Alex Caine. This is Silhouette. The PM?"

Silhouette shook Gavin's hand. He gestured for them all to sit. "Usual bollocks, nothing relevant to this situation." Old leather armchairs and couches were spread around the room and they sat facing each other across a low coffee table. "Sydney is destroyed," Gavin said.

"Destroyed?" Alex tried to parse that information and came up blank.

"Armor HQ in Sydney, I mean, your local base. It's been devastated."

"By Hood?" Silhouette asked.

"Yes. Apparently he and Claude Darvill tracked it down after ransacking your house and tore the place apart. Everyone's dead."

"Everyone?" Alex felt the blood drain from his face. More deaths as a direct result of his fucking life.

Silhouette stood, stricken. "Jarrod!"

Crookshank raised both hands. "I'm sorry, no, Jarrod is safe. Sorry, there's so much in my head right now. I'm trying to get to the point quickly. There were four operatives from Sydney out in the field, and Jarrod was one of them. Everyone else there at the time has been killed. There may be others who are afield and yet to check in."

Silhouette sank back into her chair. "The Commander?"

"Dead, I'm afraid. A team from Melbourne is there now trying to get all the details. Jarrod and a friend are on their way here as we speak."

"Jarrod's coming here?" Silhouette's mood visibly improved.

Alex was pleased for her. To lose her half-brother so soon after finding him would be devastating. But so many other lives lost. A fire grew in his gut, started to push back the black shadows of despair that lived in every corner of his being. Anger had ever been his greatest motivator. It may well still be best for him to die, to remove any threat from the Fey, but he would not let that happen until Hood and Darvill were dealt with. He had no idea how it would happen, but he would finish them both, properly and finally, one way or another.

Crookshank pulled a photo from his inside jacket pocket. It showed an Asian woman, her hair a jet-black bob around a very thin face, the cheekbones knife sharp. "This is Jean Chang, used to be Darvill's right-hand man, before that a board member for Black Diamond, Hood's organization. She's defected, teamed up with Jarrod. They have some intel and tech that will help us track Hood and Darvill, apparently. We'll know more when they get here." He dropped the photo on the table between them. "Now, let's talk about you. How the fuck did you turn up in Surrey? Last we knew, Alex was abducted by Fey and you, Silhouette, had done a runner in Sydney."

Alex laughed, without much humor. "Long story."

"Right now we have time. I need to know everything."

Alex nodded. He needed allies and he needed help on many fronts. He took a deep breath and started the story. Silhouette filled in details of her activities and before long they had poured out everything they knew.

"Get that?" Crookshank asked the ceiling.

Alex turned and looked into the glassy eye of a camera above him. He scanned the room and saw others, covering every angle. No surprise really. A voice came over a hidden speaker, broad East End accent. "Got it. Orders?"

Crookshank tapped his lips with clasped fingers. "All points looking for Hood and Darvill, obviously. I need an up-to-date list of thin days. I need every Fey expert on the fucking planet in this base yesterday. And send in Parker, she's the best authority on the Fey I know. We need to unshackle Alex asap. Oh, and get some tea and biscuits sent in, for fuck's sake. What are we, savages?"

"Righto."

Crookshank turned his attention back to Alex and Silhouette. "We'll sort this. Firstly, Mr. Caine, we'll get you out of that Fey enchantment. Hopefully we'll have some time to deal with Hood before we have to face the Lady. She will come for you."

Alex remembered the Lady's power, remembered the pain she had inflicted. "Yeah, she will." He hoped they got to deal with Hood first too, because then he had a definite defense against the Fey if he needed it. Silhouette put her arm around him, as if reading his mind. Her eyes were hard. He turned, kissed her, and made a mental promise that he would do everything he could to defeat the Lady before he took advantage of his final solution. He didn't want to leave her, but under no circumstances would he let them take him again. And even as he made that promise to himself, a dark shadow in the corner of his psyche cajoled him to end it all. The escape of oblivion so close, if he just took a quiet moment to seek it.

"Ah, tea."

An Armor operative came in with a tray. She smiled, a friendly face under a bob of straight brown hair. She was short, all curves and soft warmth, exuding an air of safety and calm. "Would you prefer something else?" she asked.

Alex smiled. "Tea's fine." He held up a hand as she reached for the pot. He served them all, grateful beyond words to be somewhere safe for the time being.

"This is Emma Parker," Crookshank said. "Don't let the tea delivery fool you, she's a formidable operative."

Emma actually blushed. "Oh, Commander."

"Tell 'em about the time you killed two feral minotaurs barehanded."

Emma laughed, flapped a hand. "They don't need to know about that."

Alex looked her up and down. She was well built, leaning towards chubby, but moved with the power and grace of a fighter. Proof to never judge a person by their outward appearance. He'd be happy to have her beside him in a fight.

"Bloody fantastic shot too, sniper extraordinaire," Crookshank went on.

"Commander, hush. Go." Parker pushed at his back and ushered him out of the room. He winked back over his shoulder and shut the door behind himself. "Don't mind him," Emma said. "He's a goofball."

"Interesting crew you've got here," Silhouette said. "Almost makes me homesick."

"Welcome home," Emma said. "Sorry about the circumstances. Now, let's have a look at you." She turned her attention to Alex. "Got anything on under those overalls?"

"Er, yeah, I'm wearing some training pants."

"Right. Off with the overalls then. It'll be easier for me to see this magic that's bound you up."

Alex raised his eyebrows. "Oh, right, you're the...er..."

"Oh, sorry! Yes, resident Fey expert. Bloody Crookshank might have mentioned that, eh? The actual relevant part of my skillset. I've studied the Fey for decades, since my mother and I were taken by them when I was a child. I'm one of the few to ever escape."

"You got out?" Silhouette asked, eyes wide. "As a child?"

Emma's face darkened. "No. I got taken as a child. I was there for fifty years, escaped not much older than when I went in, physically at least. Fey magic."

"When was that?"

"I was taken age six, in nineteen twelve. Got out in fifty-three, picked up by Armor. My arcane skills were well developed by then, secretly, of course. That's how I got out. And I've been improving ever since. I know I only look about thirty-something, but you know how it is. Anyway, long story. Suffice to say I have extensive experience with the Fey and their enchantments. Now hush, strip and let me look at you."

Alex stepped from the overalls, stood awkwardly. "You need me to...?"

"Turn your head and cough?" Emma said with a giggle. "No, sit down. Relax."

Her soft face hardened as she became serious, focused. Alex watched her shades, her arcane power formidable. She probed, pushed her mind through him, her touch like a doctor palpating for lumps, but on the inside. "Fucking hell," she whispered after a while. She looked up sharply. "Sorry! Potty mouth."

Silhouette and Alex laughed together. "Seriously, don't worry about that," Alex said. "But why fucking hell?"

"This is intricate stuff."

Alex nodded ruefully. "Thanks to the Lady herself."

Emma pursed her lips, held out one hand. "May I?"

"Sure."

She stood, moved around the table and put her palms flat on Alex's chest. Her hands were hot, sent a thrill through him, but it was her arcane power that really buzzed. Emma closed her eyes and pushed and pulled against the magic that was wound through him like hundreds of meters of filament-thin wire. Eventually she stood back with a sigh. "I can undo this, but it'll take time and I need help. Enjoy your tea. I'll set up a lab and come back for you when the others get here."

"Others?"

"The Commander has ordered in all the Fey experts. No one has quite the experience I do, but there are some skilled people in Britain and we'll have to all muck in to unwrap that particular present. Chin up, we'll fix you."

Darvill watched his father with narrow eyes. Hood dug around in his penthouse suite desk. Behind him, the view from the top of Black Diamond Tower was impressive, across the Docklands of London. Claude had rarely been in the building, always kept at a remove from the business side of Hood's operations. He wondered if he would ever get to be a field agent again. Or if Black Diamond would ever be the same with this new, changed Robert Hood.

"Did you see their faces?" Hood said with a chuckle as he rummaged.

"I guess they never expected to see you again. I told them to invoke Lazarus, after all."

"Yes, well they know I'm back now."

"Well done not killing anyone, Dad. But I think you bloody terrified them."

Hood laughed. "My staff are used to being terrified of me one way or another. But yes, I did very well not killing them. There's hope for me yet, eh?" He stiffened, head tipped back. Strange words slipped between clenched teeth and he slapped himself hard across one cheek. His body relaxed and he grinned. "Well, getting there, anyway."

Darvill watched as his father continued to hunt. The man had been a painful absence in Claude's childhood, then a hero of sorts once he took the grown Darvill under his wing. As if that wasn't a conflicted enough state, now he was some kind of insane monster. Claude frowned. Just how much of the old Robert Hood was still in there? He shifted, felt the reassuring weight of the sword across his back. Then he remembered using that sword, against the Fey in Faerie, against that freaky bastard in Newtown, and smiled. He hoped there was enough of Robert Hood left, because if Claude Darvill was anything, he was his father's son.

"Ah, here it is." Hood shut the drawer and grabbed a small leather wallet from the desktop. "Right in bloody front of me. Come on then."

Hood led the way back to the lift and an electronic pass from the wallet allowed him to select the lowest button on the lift's panel, marked only with a combined Greek symbol.

"The Alpha and Omega?" Darvill asked.

"The beginning and the end. It's just private rooms, but it's where any arcane activities outside the labs take place. Very private, very secure."

The lift carried them down through the building, past all the office floors, beyond the car park levels, underground labs and warehouses, to the very deepest basement.

"Just how arcane are you really?" Darvill asked. "I remember growing up with Mum, on the few occasions you visited, you teaching me about business but encouraging my esoteric studies. You groomed me to be your man in the field all along. But are you really lacking in magic of your own?"

Hood smiled darkly. "I've dabbled, son, nothing more. It's the power of the almighty currency I've always lusted after, you know that. And now…" He drifted into silence.

"And now?" Claude prompted.

"And now I have an even greater ability to get everything I want." He looked up, laughed. "You know, it's slightly sad that I feel as though I'll have to move away from running the business. Oh, don't look so dismayed. The board can run this bloody place and it'll always supply our financial needs. You can go back to what you love, finding me all those lovely things to trade. But I think I might move into a more active role in the outside world. I have a hankering to get my hands dirty more often. And perhaps we can do more of that together now, eh?"

The lift pinged, the doors slid open. They stepped out into a large open space, completely dark. Hood flicked a switch and soft lighting swelled from lights concealed in gaps where the walls met the ceiling. Everything was black, walls, floor and ceiling alike, no furniture of any kind. Hood's phone beeped. "Yes." Pause. "Good, send them down. Yes, all the way to the bottom, it's unlocked."

"You sure you can trust this team?" Darvill asked.

Hood shrugged. "Who knows who you can trust these days? But they definitely know their business. Like I said, my best people are here. And we have no idea where in the world Caine will have emerged, so we may as well start where I'm most familiar with things."

The lift opened and five people walked out, two women, three men, dressed in long black coats. They all wore sunglasses.

Darvill laughed. "What is this, the fucking Matrix?"

One of the men turned towards Hood with an angry expression. "If you don't want our assistance…"

Hood waved a hand, laughed. "Settle down, everybody. We're here to do a job. Claude, these people have considerable power. They're here to help and they're being paid very well for it. Set up your scrying. They're your signal boost."

Darvill shrugged. He moved to the middle of the room and sat on the floor, put his satchel on his lap. He removed the items he needed: crystal wand, chalk for marking sigils, the psychotropic drug that aided his work so well, concealed in capsules marked "vitamins'. His hand brushed against something sharp. "What's this?"

He turned his satchel into the light, tipped open one edge for a closer look. His heart rate increased as he recognized the small electronic tracking device clipped under the satchel's stitching. "Fucking Jean Chang!" He held the chip up for his father to see.

Hood rumbled laughter in his chest. "Clever little bitch. What good will it do her?"

"She could be moving against us somehow."

"It would be a bonus if she came to us, no?"

Claude shook his head, stared at the chip in disbelief. Chang had been so good, such a great assistant. He felt utterly betrayed. "No, not really, because she might come with trouble." He held up a hand. "I know, I know, you're prepared to face anything. But I think we should keep every advantage we have." He put the chip onto the hard floor and ground a knuckle into it, crushing it beyond repair. "Enough spying on me, Chang!" He was going to enjoy exacting his revenge on her. What a cheek, really, to be spying on him. On *him*! What did she think she could do? Maybe she had found some allies. Armor perhaps. No doubt whoever it was had been following their movements, but it would do her no good. He marked his sigils on the black floor, set up his divining circle.

When everything was ready, he turned to the five people standing impatiently behind him. "Sit around me and do your thing then. This is going to take considerable effort. And time."

They moved into position, sat cross-legged on the floor. Darvill moved between them, drew lines from each in chalk, across and back. Eventually, he had a pentacle marked out, each of the five sitting at a point and his own circle contained in the pentagon in the center of the five-pointed star. He moved slowly around the group, drawing a final circle around the whole thing, containing them all within its boundary. He moved back to his central position and sat down.

"Keep focused." He put a capsule in his mouth, bit down on it. Bitter powder scattered across his tongue. He sucked at it, swallowed repeatedly. He focused his attention on the psychic signatures of Alex and Silhouette, cast his mind out into the world like a fisherman slinging a net. Only his net was incalculably massive. The world was more massive still, however, and he balked at the thought of just how long this exercise might take. Cold momentum flooded his consciousness, wild and uncontrolled. As waves of psychedelic color swam through his mind, rushes of ecstasy through his veins, he focused his magic. The power of the five people around him, their combined attention, amplified by his sigils and circles and his own skills, lifted him and rushed through. His mind expanded, became the world. He gasped, hung on to the sensation, forced his desire over the drug, the magic, the personalities of those helping. He leaned forward, placed his hands on the drawn symbols and searched the aether for Caine and Silhouette.

Within moments he cried out, surprise and confusion, gathered himself quickly so he didn't lose his grip. He breathed deeply, controlled the energies, and tightened his focus. He had barely started searching. Was this really possible? He started to laugh, soft at first, rising to a deep, booming sound in the basement room.

Hood moved impatiently, his face furious. "What the fuck is going on?"

Darvill stood, the magic breaking, shattering away like glass behind a bullet. "They're here. Right here in London!"

"Are you serious?"

"I think we just got very lucky, Dad. They're in a complex of some sort, probably an Armor base. I could see right through the shields, the same style as Sydney. There's an entry point beside the river, at Embankment. Not far from the London fucking Eye." He grinned broadly, rushing equally on the good news, the magic, and the drug.

Hood's concern spread into a grin of his own. "You're sure?"

"Without a doubt."

"Ha! Excellent! Well, we'll be off in just a moment then." He turned to the five mages seated around Darvill's markings, all looking up at the pair with confused expressions. They had certainly expected a much longer job. Hood walked to the nearest one and crouched, hooked one elbow below the man's chin. Before he could protest, Hood wrapped his other arm around the man's chest and wrenched his elbow up, tearing the man's head off. Fountains of blood arced across the room.

The remaining four leapt up in a panic, frantically uttering the words of spells. One drew a revolver and pumped bullets uselessly into Hood's chest, her eyes wide in shock. Darvill ducked, moved to block the lift, the only way out. As one mage bolted from the group towards the elevator, Darvill whipped the sword free over his shoulder and separated the man in two above the hips. The mage's face was a mask of utter bewilderment as he died. Darvill shook his head, half smiling. "This is why you insisted we do this here," he muttered and crouched to avoid another burst of gunfire and blasts of arcane fire while his father had his fun.

CHAPTER EIGHTEEN

Alex felt like a lab rat, stretched out on a cold metal table. He grimaced at the discomforting sensation of threads of magic being drawn from his body, like worms coaxed from the earth. But he watched intently, studied the shades and magesign to learn the complexities. He would never be a victim to this entrapment again. And he began to learn the flavor of the Lady's sorcery from watching its deconstruction. That would potentially be useful against further enchantments and spells she threw at him. But it was such an unpleasant sensation.

"Stop wriggling!" Emma's voice was sharp, but her face remained calm, eyes closed. "You make it harder. Just lie still."

Alex calmed his breathing, tried to sink into a meditative state despite Emma's intimate ministrations. "Sorry."

Three other operatives around the room concentrated, lent Emma their power and focus, amplified her ability, juggling the arcane threads between them like a complex, etheric dance. Silhouette paced impatiently near the door, refusing to leave, but told in no uncertain terms by Emma to keep out of the way.

"This is just the most amazing enchantment," Emma muttered, almost to herself. She was clearly impressed. "It's intricate and really quite beautiful."

"But you can clear it all?" Alex asked.

"Yes, yes, of course. Just takes time. It's like unpicking a series of knots in fishing line, but the line is finer than hair and the knots are buried throughout your body. I wish I had more time to study this before I removed it."

"Don't you dare! Please. Just free me." Alex winced at the desperation in his voice. Magic was something relatively new in his life, but it was a part of him and he wanted to be himself again, back in control. The weakness, the vulnerability, was more than he could bear.

"Hush, I'm working as fast as I can. I know there's more at stake here."

Alex gasped as something burst free, the shards of the Darak suddenly warming and pulsing. Emma made a noise of satisfaction.

"Feel better?" she asked.

"Definitely." He tested the boundaries of the enchantment, felt his arcane energies move more freely. But they were still trapped.

"Easy, tiger," Emma said. "Don't push against me. That's only one part of many. But I'm getting the measure of it now. Patience."

She worked on, the other operatives concentrating hard to balance and steady her efforts. They all had sweat standing out on their brows, all began to frown with the exertion as time passed. More and more ganglions of the Lady's binding sprang free. Every time, Alex felt his strength returning, his abilities re-establishing themselves. He saw how the thing worked and marveled at its intricacy. His body ached. The removal of each strand of shackling left behind a deep, bruised sensation in his very nerves as well as his flesh. He wanted to stretch and move, use his muscles to physically shift the inertia building through his limbs.

"Keep still, damn you!" Emma Parker's frown was deep, her concentration total.

"Sorry, sorry."

Movement at the door deepened Parker's frown. Alex didn't dare move, but heard a whispered conversation and Silhouette's constrained noise of joy.

"I'll be right back," Sil said. "Jarrod's here!"

The door clicked closed before Alex could reply. He was pleased for her, and, if he was honest, pleased for himself too. The big Maori had been invaluable in Obsidian. He was glad to have the man around again.

Pain lanced through his chest, made him arch involuntarily off the metal surface. He cried out, drowning Emma's shout of surprise. She barked orders at the operatives around her and Alex felt incomprehensible magic wrap around him.

"Contain that shit!" Emma screamed, her demure English demeanor shattered with her frenzy. "If you let that out, it'll tear him apart."

Alex's veins swelled and bulged, his joints popped and shifted. Fire burned through every fiber of his muscles. He bucked and squirmed on the table, ground his teeth, sounds of agony escaping his throat. "The fuck is happening?" he managed, but no one answered.

"Hold him still!"

More people burst into the room and heavy hands slammed Alex down, held him fast. Emma Parker leapt up, straddled his legs, hands on top of each other over the Darak like she was about to start CPR. Her face was a mask of furious concentration and her magic fell over him like a blanket. She probed and pushed, her mind chasing something unseen and unknown but excruciatingly painful through his body.

"Help me!" Parker said through clenched teeth.

The arcane energies of her assistants intensified. Alex felt their strain, knew they were all close to breaking point, like a wire stretched so taut it might snap with a metallic twang any second and whip and curl away.

Through the pain he tried to feel what they were chasing, tried to get a grip on whatever ran rampant in his body. Something like a spark rushing along the length of a dynamite fuse arced through his chest, burned into the shards of the Darak. He howled in pain, the incinerating heat of it almost stripping his consciousness away. He refused to pass out, pressed back against the darkness closing in from the edges of his vision and mentally clamped down on the rogue enchantment.

"That's it!" Emma cried triumphantly. "Hold that fucker still!"

Her eyes were wide now, but she looked well beyond his body, deep into some eldritch realm. Her magic was powerful, the pressure of her will soaking over his own in a tidal wave of intent. She reared up, knees astride his hips, arms raised high like she was about to slam down onto him, but she froze there, her concentration acute, diamond hard and focused. The fire in Alex's chest pulsed left and right, strained for an exit like a cat trying to bolt a closed room. Emma's mind refused to let it go. She slowly brought her hands together, like she was crushing a giant ball between her palms, and the magic screeched and thrashed against her. But her will was stronger. She compressed it away to an incandescent point and tore it from him.

She staggered back off the bed and Alex rolled onto his side, curled up in a fetal ball, gasping for breath. Slowly, the burning subsided. The other operatives around the room fell to their knees or collapsed back against the wall, sweat-streaked and fighting to breathe.

Emma moved around to look Alex in the eye. Her short brown hair was plastered to her forehead, but her eyes were alive as she smiled. "That was bloody amazing. You okay?"

Alex nodded, slowly unfurled his body. He sat up, pressed a hand to his chest. His body surged with his own power and he realized all the Lady's magic was gone. "You did it!" He grabbed Emma and pulled her into a rough hug.

"Steady on, sunshine." Emma pushed him off, but her grin was forgiving. "In truth, we did it. I couldn't have held on to that without you. That was some bloody strong juju."

"I'm so glad to be free of it."

"You're all back to normal?"

Alex shrugged. "I think so. Hang on." He gathered his power, drew against his elemental expertise and sought all the heat in the room, the air dropping to a chill. He agitated it into a single point in his palm and threw a fireball against the wall. Flames burst and curled back on themselves, heat pulsing forth like an explosion. With a laugh, he changed tack, drew air away from the fire and it popped out, deprived of fuel. The room was suddenly very warm and dry. Everyone backed away, eyes wary. Except Emma, who stayed right beside him, one eyebrow raised.

"What the bloody hell was that?"

Alex smiled, looked away from her haughty expression. "That, Emma, was really, really good. Thank you."

She shook her head. "I'd rather you kept that to..."

Her words were lost in a blaring alarm and flashing red lights. A brash voice burst from hidden speakers. "Breach! Breach! Breach!"

Alex stumbled to his feet, pulled on the black combats, T-shirt and boots he had been given. "What the hell is happening?"

Emma ran to a desk on one side of the room and talked urgently into an intercom. Sounds of screaming and gunfire erupted from the other end of the complex. "We seem to be under attack! No one is answering. This way."

She dragged Alex across the room and jumped back as the door burst open. Silhouette appeared, Jarrod a hulking presence behind her, and beside him a small Asian woman with an expression of terror. "It's Hood," Silhouette said, eyes wide.

Alex's mind tumbled over in neutral. "The fuck? How did he find us?"

"How did he find this base, let alone you?" Emma demanded. Her face changed, a decision made. "Irrelevant. They're here and getting closer. We need to get *you* out." She gestured to the other operatives in the room. "You lot, that way and intercept. Alex, you and your friends, this way." She pushed past Silhouette and moved along the corridor away from the sounds of mayhem.

Alex paused in the doorway, torn. "I have to finish him!"

Silhouette shook her head. "Not here. Not now. You haven't had a chance to recover."

"Emma undid the magic, I have my power back."

"You remember Iceland?" Silhouette said. "What it took to take him down? And what he is now? Fuck, Alex, we don't *know* what he is now. This is not the time or place for a battle."

Alex started and stopped several replies, frustration grinding his mind to a halt. He knew Silhouette was right, but he wanted Hood finished so badly. And how many more were dying right now?

Emma Parker strode back to them and slapped Alex hard across the cheek. His skin sang with pain as she winced and shook her hand. "I did not just spend three hours unbinding you so you could waltz to your bloody death! This way!"

Alex nodded. He couldn't really argue with that.

They ran, Jean Chang following Emma Parker, Alex and Silhouette behind her, with Jarrod bringing up the rear.

"Good to see you again," Jarrod said with a wide grin. "You are nothing if not exciting company."

Alex cast a rueful look back over his shoulder. "Life and soul of the fucking party, that's me."

A stutter of quick explosions rocked the complex, resounding in their ears with concussion. The corridors rang with shouts, screams, gunfire and bursts of arcane energy. Alex grimaced—more lives taken at his expense. How much more blood on his hands?

Parker led the way into a room at the end of the corridor and shut the door behind them, locked it. She shifted a desk to reveal a trapdoor in the floor. She turned a sweet smile to Jarrod. "Be a dear, would you? Bloody heavy, that is."

With a nod, Jarrod stepped up and hauled the trapdoor open with a grunt. Old stone steps led down into darkness. Emma pulled a mini Maglite torch from her pocket and started down.

"Close it behind us."

Alex let the others go ahead of him while Jarrod held the way open. He paused.

"Go on, bro," Jarrod said.

Alex looked back towards the corridor, tried to see through the walls awash with flashing red, tried to hear over the wailing klaxons. "They destroyed Sydney," he said, bereft. "Now they're here. How many are dying?"

Jarrod put one large hand on his shoulder. "As many as it takes for us to get away."

Alex winced. "Why am I worth that?"

"Can you imagine anyone else able to stop them? But you have to prepare. Now isn't the time. They're right." He nodded down the steps towards Emma and Silhouette. "Trust them. Trust me. We will avenge every death, my friend."

With a shout of impotent rage Alex turned and hurried down into the cool depths under the base. Jarrod followed him, slammed the heavy door behind him and plunged everything into a Stygian black. They ran to catch up to Emma's dancing flashlight beam ahead.

Claude Darvill leaned against a flame-scorched wall, panting for breath. His right hand gripped his left shoulder where a bullet had scored a deep furrow through the flesh. Blood oozed between his fingers. Something burned on his back, an eldritch heat, and his right ear rang with a sound that blanked out anything else on that side. His sword hung in his left hand, covered with the blood of Armor operatives. Bodies lay hacked and torn to pieces all around him. He wondered how many had died since he had released his father. The thought was both empowering and frightening. How long could he survive these incursions against trained and dangerous professionals? It was only by using his father as a shield that he had avoided more damage and now he simply waited while the indestructible Hood rampaged. His father might be unstoppable, but Darvill himself was fragile flesh.

He wondered again where all this would lead. What would happen once Caine was eliminated? That driving urge clearly usurped any other thought in his father's mind, but there had to be something after Caine. Perhaps he should go it alone once more, liaise with Black Diamond and get on with his own life while his dad got on with his. Whatever that might mean.

There was certainly a thrill and a sense of power to their current activity. Given that Hood was literally untouchable, there seemed to be nothing he couldn't do. Some had managed to slow Hood with magical attacks, but even those were watered down against the man's abilities. Thanks to his passenger, apparently. And that terrified Claude.

He tensed, flicked the sword back into his right hand and crouched as movement caught his eye through the swirling smoke and dust. A middle-aged man in a suit walked into view, but he moved strangely. Hood appeared behind, his hand locked about the back of the man's neck.

"Tell him what you told me," Hood barked.

The man tried to look around, winced as Hood crunched his neck in vice-like fingers. "I don't know where he is!"

Darvill raised an eyebrow. "You don't know where Alex Caine is?"

"No idea."

"What's your name?"

"Fuck you."

"No, seriously, I need something to call you."

The man shook his head, his eyes showing he had already accepted defeat. "For what it's worth, my name is Crookshank. But I'd rather not hear that pass your lips."

Darvill laughed, genuinely amused by the fellow. He imagined him on a country estate, shooting grouse and guffawing at jokes about the plebs. "I know for a fact Caine was here."

The man sneered. "Bully for you, you fucking psychopath!"

He howled, arms curling up, fingers clawing at the air as Hood wrenched his neck again.

"Keep him alive a moment longer, Dad." Darvill drew the preternaturally sharp edge of his sword across Crookshank's collarbone. The blade sank through skin and deep into the bone, blood welling out to soak the man's shirt. He howled again. "Mr. Crookshank, I need to know where Alex Caine is."

Crookshank's face was suddenly furious, his eyes alive with passion. "I know who you are, Darvill. You will be stopped!"

Before Claude could say or do anything in response, Crookshank grabbed his wrist and twisted the sword around. He lunged forward, planted the point into the side of his chest and threw himself into it. He gasped and gargled blood as the blade punched through and out the other side.

Hood jumped, dropped Crookshank as he looked with strange curiosity at his arm. The sword point had caught him just below the elbow and there was a tiny puncture in the skin. No blood, simply a gap. It closed over almost instantly.

Crookshank collapsed to the floor, shivering and spasming, clawing at his ribs where the sword hilt was lodged. His eyes were wide, his breath wet and short. He struggled a few moments more and fell still.

Claude leaned down, retrieved his weapon. "Well, that's bloody annoying. Gotta say, that's some impressive strength of will, doing that."

Hood nodded absently, still looking at his arm. "That bloody thing cut me."

Darvill deliberately avoided his father's eye. "Yeah. It made a small mark in your neck that first time too. You didn't notice that?"

"No, I didn't."

Darvill shrugged. "Both times it's healed up immediately. This thing rends people in half with barely any effort at all. You saw how easily it went through him. Hardly a surprise it can nick you."

Hood's face darkened. "Nick me? Nothing should be able to damage me. I burned for months in fucking magma and nothing happened."

Darvill wiped the blade on Crookshank's suit, slipped it back into the scabbard across his back. "This is no normal weapon, Dad."

"We need to destroy it. Anything that can hurt me needs to be destroyed."

Darvill laughed, desperate to head off his father's attention to the only thing that gave him any comfort. "Sure. But let's be done with Caine first, yeah? I feel like I need something up to the job of dealing with him and his Kin bitch. Let's make sure that situation is dealt with and then you can have the sword. Do what you like with it."

Hood's eyes narrowed. "You wouldn't be thinking of using it against your old dad, would you, Claude?"

"As if I'd have a chance! You saw how little damage it did to you. That would have gone right through a normal arm. It sinks through bone like butter. You'd tear me to pieces long before I'd caused you any grief. And besides, you just heal up instantly." He laughed, realizing the truth of his words as he said them. This sword was useless against his father. He laughed again. "Anyway, you're my dad! We're on the same team here. I don't want to hurt you. We're un-fucking-stoppable, right?"

Hood twitched, slapped at his face again, an action that was becoming something of a habit. He muttered, looked around wildly, muttered again. He turned back to Darvill as if nothing had happened. "We really are quite the team. But if I ever ask for that sword, you'll give it to me."

"Sure. But I'd really rather hang onto it. It's a powerful weapon and I need something like it to defend myself, given what we're up against." He gestured around at the fallen Armor operatives. "You know, it can deflect magical attacks?"

"Can it?"

"Yeah, just discovered that aspect now. You know how the Jedi in *Star Wars* deflect blaster shots with their lightsabers? It's like that. It's amazing."

Hood tipped his head to one side. "I honestly have no idea what you're talking about." He turned away, their conversation seemingly forgotten. "So, he's not here."

Darvill nodded, lips pursed. "He most definitely was here, but once we moved I couldn't keep him in mind as easily. The wards here are strong,

I have to stop and concentrate to see through them. So either they left before we got here, or somehow escaped while we fought our way in."

Hood punched a wall. It was solid brick, but his fist went right through, showers of stone and clouds of dust bursting around it. "Fucking hell! Well, we'll have to find him again. We know he's in London at least, yes?"

"He is right now. They haven't had time to get far."

"So, you can use your divination stuff to find him again, without the need for extra help."

Darvill smiled. "Yep. Just as well, considering you decimated the help."

Hood laughed, flapped a hand dismissively. "I'm sure we could find more if we wanted."

CHAPTER NINETEEN

Alex picked up the cool pint glass and took a long draft of beer. He had never been a big drinker. Staying in shape, in control, being a fighter, had always been his driving passion. But a few drinks right about now seemed like a good idea. The others around the table nervously drank their own brews. Jarrod and Jean Chang huddled over a tablet, tapping and frowning. Alex and Silhouette kept their eyes on Emma Parker. She spoke softly and quickly into her phone, nodded regularly.

Eventually she hung up, took a deep breath and downed her double gin and tonic in one gulp. "Bloody lovely," she muttered. "Just a minute." She went back to the bar.

"Not going to tell us what she learned?" Silhouette mused.

Alex smiled, despite the recent trauma. This Emma was a good person to have along, a grounding influence.

Jarrod and Jean Chang looked up from the fingerprint-smudged tablet, clearly frustrated.

"Well?" Alex asked.

"Definitely lost touch," Chang said, frowning. She seemed on the verge of tears.

Jarrod put a protective arm around her, massive across her too thin shoulders. "We knew we'd lost them in Australia, but they obviously made quick work of getting here. The tech is certainly top notch, but not good enough to track over that kind of distance. It can definitely track within a few hundred kilometers, though, and we know they're not that far away. So we've lost them."

"Tech failure?" Alex asked.

Jean shrugged. "Maybe. But I doubt it. It's robust stuff. I suspect Claude finally found the bug and destroyed it. I'm surprised I got away with it this long really. Which means he knows I betrayed him."

Silhouette reached across, patted Chang's hand. "You'd already run out on him. Betrayal enough, I'm sure. You did the right thing."

The tears breached. "I helped him release Hood!" The strain in Chang's voice was heartbreaking.

Alex moved around the table to sit beside her. "You may have helped, but he would have done it without you. Can you tell me everything that's happened, so we're all up to speed?"

Chang sniffed, nodded, told them the whole story. While she spoke, Emma Parker returned with a tray of drinks. Once the drinks were delivered, Parker began incanting something. Alex tried to ignore the magesign buzzing around the table while he listened to Jean's story. Emma built protective wards around them all.

When Jean's tale was finished, Alex nodded. "Can you imagine what it's like for Hood to have that influence inside him? It was bad enough when it affected me from that infernal book. But I've trapped it *in* him and it can't get out. It can't move from one inanimate item to another like it used to. It's stuck in him and he's indestructible." He sank his head into his hands. "What the fuck have I done?"

"You did the right thing," Jean said. "It was Darvill and me who let him out!"

Alex looked up, stared hard at Jean Chang. "Darvill let him out. You were ignorant to what was happening. It's his fault. Not yours. You're trying to make it right now. That's all that matters."

"I always knew I worked for a company that was less than altruistic. But this…"

Emma Parker downed another G&T and slapped a palm on the table. "Shut up, all of you. There's no time for this bloody melancholy. We're all up to speed on where we stand and that's where we stand. Lamenting how the bloody hell we got here and whose fault it might be is fucking silly." She blinked, clearly more affected by the alcohol than she was prepared to admit. "We've all had some serious shocks recently, not the least of which is the utter destruction of the oldest fucking Armor base in history. London is decimated, we know that. I've just spoken to Edinburgh and York, the other major bases in Britain. They're on the case, trying to track Hood, formulate plans and what have you. They're also thinking about the Fey threat, which is something we need to be aware of too."

Alex winced. "When's the next thin day?"

"Comet transition. Friday."

Alex blanched, eyes going wide. "Friday? That's less than a week!"

"What's a comet transition?" Jean asked. "And why is it a thin day?"

"Any day of cosmic significance is a thin day, as well as the recognized eight pagan dates." Parker made air quotes with her fingers as she said pagan. "A wet moon, blue moon, conjunction, eclipse, all that stuff, they're all thins. Our bad luck. There's a major comet passing between the sun and Earth. It's rare and significant, therefore a thin day. We still have no idea why events like that qualify, but they do. I rather hoped we'd have an astronomically peaceful time of it, and several weeks until the next thin, but no such luck. So we have to prepare."

"Can we hide out at Edinburgh or York?" Jarrod asked.

"No, they won't have us. Hood and Darvill have destroyed two Armor bases already, so they won't take the risk. I've built a shield around us that will hide us from prying eyes, but only for short periods of time. We have to keep on the move. Darvill has proven he can find you two very easily, even through Armor wards. All bases are rebuilding their protections, so it won't be as easy for him again, but they're still not prepared to chance it. They'll give us field support, but we have to keep moving. It's the only way we can be safe." She picked up her glass, frowned at the lack of contents, put it down again. "Well, relatively safe."

"You're staying with us then?" Alex asked.

Emma smiled. "Yep, you're stuck with me. I'm your local liaison."

"I'm glad to have you along." He meant it and hoped she recognized his sincerity. "Thank you. And I'm so sorry about…" He gestured back over his shoulder in the rough direction of the Thames.

Emma nodded, face hardening. "Thank you. We lost a lot of good people there. Not sure how many got out, but certainly not many have checked in so far. We're waiting on back-up which is on its way from York and some of the nearer sub-bases."

"I'm so sorry." Alex dragged his hands over his hair. So many deaths. So many friends and lovers, family and colleagues. All those souls lost to the Void after Obsidian, all the Sydney operatives, now London. He felt every one of them like a weight sharply hooked into his conscience.

Silhouette moved closer, put her arms around him. "It's not your fault."

Alex looked up sharply. "It is my fault!" Several people in the pub turned, surprised by the loud outburst, then quickly looked away again. "It is my fault," Alex said again, more quietly. "All of this. I got tangled up with Patrick fucking Welby and everything, all of this, has happened because of it. Everything then, Obsidian, now Sydney and London. All because I couldn't take my own advice and tell Welby to fuck off and leave me alone."

"It wasn't that simple. And lots of other stuff has happened." Silhouette kissed him. "You found me, for one. And think of all the people you *freed* from Obsidian. You had Uthentia beaten and contained too, until Darvill screwed things up by letting him out. It's not all bad. Didn't you just tell Jean to throw off guilt that wasn't hers to carry?"

Alex and Jean shared a look, a crooked smile. Her tear-stained eyes were soft and he knew they shared something these others couldn't comprehend in detail. Perhaps he and Chang could support each other somehow. He nodded softly, reached out to squeeze Jean's hand. She squeezed back, looked away, fresh tears over her cheeks.

"It's pretty bad, though," Alex said with a humorless laugh. "Pretty fucking awful, really. But I tell you this, I will defeat Hood. He's my fault and I will find a way to finish him. I have to. And I have to do it before Friday."

Silhouette frowned. "Why before Friday? Dealing with Hood and dealing with the Fey don't have to happen in that order."

Alex shook his head, looked away, unable to hold Silhouette's gaze. "Apart from the damage Hood can do in the meantime, I have a definite way of ending the Fey threat. But I refuse to die before Hood is handled."

"Alex, fuck that!"

"No, don't make this about us, Silhouette. The entire world could be overrun by Fey again if they find a way to get this." He jabbed a finger into his chest. "But if I die, it dies, and that threat dies with it. It's a final solution. But I can't let it happen until Hood is dealt with."

"And what if it's not a fucking solution?" Silhouette's eyes were dark with fury, but wet with sadness. "What if you die and that stone is still available to them somehow? Then what?"

Alex reached for her, pulled her back into a hug even though she tried to resist. "I love you, Silhouette. I love you so much. But if we can't find another answer, this is all I've got. I can at least make some kind of amends for what I've done."

Silhouette relented, gripped him tightly for a moment before pushing away. "I won't accept that. We need to find a way to deal with Hood *and* the Fey. I'm not losing you."

Alex shrugged, stared into the last inch or two of beer. "I'd love to find a way too, but I don't know if we can."

Emma Parker slapped the table again. "Once more, enough melancholy. Action plan time. My shielding is centered on you two, because you're the ones Darvill knows and is tracking."

"He also knows me very well," Jarrod said. "And Jean. If he can't find them, he might try to track us. Do they know we're here?"

"I don't know, but let's assume they do. Therefore, you four have to stay close together to stay under the umbrella of my protection. Not in each other's pockets or anything, but always within, say, ten meters or so of each other. If we need to split up, I can try to accommodate that with my shields. And I'm sure you can do a certain amount of warding on your own. The key is to keep moving, never more than a few hours in any one place. That way it'll be very difficult for Darvill to home in on us. To that end, the Armor sub-branch in Bristol is sending up a big motorhome. It'll accommodate us all and we can stay on the move and not worry about being still for too long."

"Seriously?" Alex couldn't keep a slight smile from his face. "We'll be like Scooby and the gang in the fucking Mystery Machine!"

"So be it. We can sleep and move by driving in shifts, never stay still long enough to get found. Meanwhile, I can move fairly freely, liaise with Armor and start to formulate plans."

"Any idea what those plans might be?" Alex asked. "We have some pretty big tasks here."

"What about using those two big tasks against each other?" Jean said, almost too quietly to be heard.

"Speak up, lass." Emma leaned forward, brows knitted. "What are you thinking?"

Jean looked nervously around the group, fumbling with her bag as she returned the tablet out of sight. "Well, er…" She cleared her throat, drew herself up. "I mean, if one big threat is the Lady coming for Alex on the next thin day, then we only have to wait until Friday. If Hood is desperate to see Alex dead, which he is—it's an obsession like you wouldn't believe, nothing matters more to him—then perhaps we can use that."

Emma shook her head. "Not with you, love."

Alex smiled, gripped Jean's shoulder gratefully. "I am. Good thinking. If Hood is desperate to see me dead, he won't want anyone else to get the pleasure of killing me. That means if we stay on the run until Friday, when the Lady is going to be gunning for me, and somehow put her between me and Hood, then Hood will surely do all he can to get to me. The way he is now he could probably take out the Lady. He nearly did in Faerie, after all. We could potentially use him to eliminate the Fey threat. Or perhaps, even better, she'll be able to take out Hood. Either way, we're left with one problem instead of two."

Silhouette laughed, a derisive noise. "That's the plan?"

"It's *a* plan," Alex said. "Which is something. Sort of. I have no idea how to face up to the Lady, no idea how powerful she might be, but she already completely annihilated my ability to resist her once. I'm prepared for that now, I've seen that magic in detail and can deflect it, but what else might she have? I don't fancy giving her the chance to try anything. Setting her and Hood against each other is a bloody good idea if you ask me. One or the other of them will come out worse and only leave us one threat to deal with. Or we can finish them both while they're occupied with each other."

"I suppose so. Desperate fucking measures."

Alex squeezed her. "Desperate fucking times!"

"It's good to see you thinking about fighting, Iron Balls. Do not give up on me. On any of this."

"I won't give up until there's no other choice." He turned to Emma. "Can Armor start looking into that possibility, do you think? Can they suggest a strategy? A place where it might be safe for us to engineer this fight? We need to make it happen far from people and property, because we know very well Hood has no qualms about collateral damage. I'm sure the Fey don't, either."

Emma nodded. "Yes. Okay. Bloody hell, that's a plan I wasn't expecting, but it's something to work with. And we have some time. Apart from anything else, if we can organize this and get everyone in the same place at the same time, we can hit them all at once with everything Armor's got. And when it's organized, Armor's got a *lot*. Come on then, let's keep moving. I've arranged a rendezvous with our new motorhome for an hour's time, across town. I'll contact York on the way."

Claude Darvill ground his teeth and tried to ignore his father's incessant blather. The man had been an impatient bastard at the best of times before his transformation. Hood paced and whined and chattered and, occasionally, became distracted by his passenger. Again, Claude had tried to establish just what or who that passenger was and how much control Hood had over it, and again Hood headed off the questions.

It was quite amusing, however, to see the man who had been such a stalwart for business and profit, so controlled a capitalist, such an excellent player of people, distorted into a monster of rabid passion and violent energies. Claude had to admit he rather liked this new and improved version of his father. But he remained determined to keep a distance once this Alex Caine situation was past. Leaving his father to his own devices had to be the wisest choice. Black Diamond could run itself, managed by the board. The fortune the company wielded was more than enough to keep Claude and his father while they enjoyed their various, and separate, adventures in the outside world.

But first, Caine. To think they had come so close so many times, yet repeatedly missed the bastard. And that Caine had landed almost in their laps through sheer luck and still managed to slip away. Darvill would never quite match his father's desire for Caine's demise, but he was coming close.

Concentrate. He breathed deeply, let the drug course through his system. He had been using this particular psychotropic a little too much lately. He wondered absently if it would have any permanent effect. It was certainly less effective in conjunction with his magic. Perhaps his body and mind were getting too used to it. He would have to find an alternative.

Snags and ripples distracted him. He could sense places where Caine had been, places not too far away. But nothing concrete, nothing clear. He should be able to pinpoint them with crystal clarity, but his searching was occluded, like trying to find a darkened house on a mist-thickened night.

"Still nothing?" Hood was back from his latest sojourn arguing with his passenger.

"Obviously not," Darvill snapped. "Or I wouldn't be sitting here trying to fucking concentrate."

"They're using shields similar to the stuff protecting the Armor bases?"

Claude nodded, eyes closed, tried to maintain his spell. "Yes, similar, but adjusted. Even that London base is already under a new set of wards I can't see through very easily. But we know they haven't returned there, they wouldn't be that stupid. I keep getting hints and echoes, but they must be moving around. I can't pin anything down."

"Then we have to change tack." When Claude didn't answer, Hood shook him roughly by one shoulder. "You hear me? Change tack!"

Claude hissed annoyance as his magic shattered and spiralled away like the glassy surface of a pond destroyed by a thrown rock. "Yes, we'll have to now, or I'll need to start over." He winced, gripped the bridge of his nose between forefinger and thumb. Fatigue chewed at his bones. Too much running around, too much fighting, too much magic. Not to mention his injuries and lack of proper sleep.

Hood clapped his hands together. "Not to worry, son. I've got a plan."

"Do you?"

"Yes. Well, the start of one at least. We're going to need to get some help, so let's organize some subcontractors."

"To do what?"

Hood grinned, like a kid let loose in a toy store. "We shouldn't be running around trying to catch Alex fucking Caine like a couple of dogs on a fox's trail. Let's make Caine come to us."

Alex sat half turned in the driver's seat of the parked camper van, watching Emma brew another cup of tea. Her capacity for imbibing the stuff was almost supernatural. At least once an hour she would announce it was "Time for a cuppa!" and insist they pull over somewhere. Traffic whooshed by on the main road, making the van rock slightly in the narrow rest area where he had pulled up.

"I can't help you with this situation, I'm afraid," Emma said as she doled out tea bags into plastic mugs. "None of my experience encompasses this sort of thing."

"There must be a way to make his stone worthless to the Lady," Silhouette said. "Surely!"

Alex shook his head, self-consciously removed his rubbing hand. "It's part of me. It's like suggesting there must be a way to remove my heart." The irony of the statement, the Darak being part of the Lord's removed heart, was not lost on him. But that level of magic was beyond them all.

Silhouette leaned forward on the passenger seat, reached across to put both hands on Alex's knees. "But there is a way to do that, sort of! Modern science, artificial hearts, all that shit."

"She has a point," Jarrod's voice rumbled from the back, slightly muffled as he reclined on the narrow sofa. "There are all kinds of ways to replace organs these days. Maybe there is a magical equivalent. The Lord did it, right?"

Alex frowned, remembering the pain of the Lady's ministrations, the experiments of her underlings. "They had me in a lab, cutting, poking, casting all kinds of enchantments over me. If the Fey themselves can't figure out a way…"

"But the Fey are half blind," Silhouette interrupted. "They're arrogant, trapped in their own paradigm. Perhaps we can bring a non-Fey mindset to bear, think of something they wouldn't consider."

"The Fey will find a way." Emma turned, began handing out steaming mugs. "Their mastery of magic is unlike anything we can imagine. It will take them time, that's all, to figure it out. But Silhouette makes a fair point. Perhaps we need someone else on the case. The Lady knows this stuff inside out and she couldn't find a way to get her stone back yet. So who do we know who might have a clue? Who can help us beat her to the solution?"

The vehicle sank into silence as people sipped tea and thought. Faces were glum.

"What about the Umbra Magi?" Silhouette asked eventually.

Alex looked up, surprised. "What about them?"

"They helped us enormously when we originally had to deal with Uthentia. I mean, I know they kinda fell through after a certain point, but they have amazing stores of knowledge and incredible magical ability. Could be worth asking them."

Alex pursed his lips. "I suppose it could. How would I contact them?"

"You had that link with Meera, remember? Contacting her telepathically. Is it still there?"

Alex shook his head. "No idea." He closed his eyes, concentrated. Being trapped by the book that Uthentia was using, desperately trying to find a way free from its curse, seemed like a lifetime ago. It really wasn't all that long, but so much had happened. He found himself sinking into despair, thinking again about the peace of oblivion. And every time that desolation rose in his soul, the icy touch of the Void rippled through to his core. Appealed to him. But he owed the world an end to Hood before he could allow that and if he could fathom a way to remove the Lady and the Fey from his life, he would try it. There was the slim possibility that all this could end, even if he couldn't see the route there. He focused on Meera's face—the woman's skin such a dark black, her eyes so vibrant. Her bald head, the way it would shine in the slightest light. She had been very useful to him before, supplying information via the secretive Umbra Magi group, directing him in his search for the Darak. He hoped she could help again. He cast his mind out, let his power through the Darak swell up and float free. Mentally, he called out into the aether, *Meera, can you hear me?*

He waited, feeling foolish. Nothing echoed in his mind. *Meera, it's Alex Caine. Are we still…connected? I really need you.*

He waited again. Still nothing. With a sigh he opened his eyes. "Nothing. It's like I'm just shouting into…"

Alex?

His eyes popped wide, her voice crystal clear in his mind. "Wait!" He concentrated again. *Meera, you can hear me?*

Of course. Are you okay?

Not really. I've got a bit of a situation and I was wondering if maybe you guys could help me with some information.

I can feel where you are. You planning to stay there?

Not for long, but I can if you…

Wait. I'll be there.

The connection severed and he looked up, surprised. "She's coming here."

Emma frowned, turned sharply. "From where? We can't stay here long, you realize. We're sitting bloody ducks if we're not careful."

"I don't think we'll need to wait long. These Umbra Magi are…" He was interrupted by a light tapping on the camper's side door.

Jarrod bolted upright, face stern. Jean Chang shrank back in the seat across from him. Emma Parker raised one eyebrow.

Alex grinned. "Told you." He opened the door.

The small woman smiled, her slight build completely belying her ability. Alex had seen her fight, albeit briefly, when she had delayed the Subcontractor to allow him and Silhouette to escape that time in London. He had felt her considerable power. "Hello again," she said.

Alex stepped back, gestured into the cramped confines of the van. "Hey. Thanks for coming."

"You caught me at a good time. Master Cai is about to start classes, but I was able to slip away."

"Thanks. Silhouette you know. This is Jarrod, Jean and Emma."

Meera nodded to each of them. "Hello, all. So, what's the problem?"

Emma stepped forward. "Sorry, just a minute. Where the bloody hell did you come from so quickly?" She smiled, but suspicious curiosity burned in her eyes.

"We have a talent at translocation," Meera said. "It takes a long while to develop, but we have time. And very experienced teachers."

"That's a bloody useful skill! Can you teach me?"

"I could, but it would take a long while."

Emma stepped back, looked Meera up and down. "I think Armor could use a good long chat with you and your people."

Meera nodded subtly. "You're Armor? We know about you lot. You do great work most of the time."

"Most of the time?" Emma's tone was indignant.

"Yes, most of the time."

"The Umbra Magi are a scholarly group," Alex said, hoping to head off any argument before one could begin. "They tend to simply observe and collect information. Right?"

"Right," Meera agreed. "We try to be impartial to events, just make sure knowledge is preserved. So, what's the situation here? I'll be happy to help if I can."

Emma made yet more tea while Alex relayed everything he could about their current situation. Meera sat quietly, listened intently, not interrupting once. By the end, she nodded and sat in quiet thought. Eventually, she said, "I think your situation is unique, Alex. No one has done what you've done. I don't know that anyone would have a clue about undoing it."

Alex knew he looked crestfallen, though he tried to remain calm. "Fair enough. Oh well, thanks anyway."

"That's not to say someone couldn't formulate a theory. There must be people with knowledge that skirts the boundaries of your predicament."

"You know, well, everyone, right?" Silhouette asked. "Someone out there must have an idea."

Meera shrugged. "We know many people, we're in touch with many traditions. Bonding with a power stone is something I've never heard of before. The fact that it's a part of the actual heart of a Fey Lord is astounding. So many complicating factors. But, in essence, all you need are two things: to remove the stone from Alex and destroy it. The first may be easier than the second, as it is indestructible, you say?"

"By all accounts, yes," Alex said. "The Eld were able to section off part of the anchor stone, the Lord's heart, with massive magics. That's what created the Darak from the main organ. And banishing Uthentia split the Darak into three pieces. Twice that happened. So it can be separated from itself, but the pieces can't be destroyed. At least, that's what I understand. But if the Darak could be removed from me, maybe it could be cast into the Void along with the Lord's heart. We know it's out of reach of the Fey that way, at least." Despite everything, Alex ached at the thought of losing the Darak, the thing that had given him such power. He couldn't help wondering if perhaps there was a way to keep it, but knew that was a ridiculous desire.

Meera pursed her lips, sat in thought again. The van was quiet as the others waited, politely silent. Eventually, Meera looked up. "Let me talk with our scholars. I'll see if there's anything or anyone they can suggest. I don't know if there will be."

"I understand." Alex leaned forward, put a hand on Meera's thin shoulder. The corded muscle beneath his palm was steel hard. "Thank you."

Meera smiled, patted his hand. "You do get yourself into scrapes, don't you, Alex Caine."

"I guess so."

"I'll contact you when I can."

"Okay."

Meera stood, stepped slightly aside to be further from the others. "Nice to meet you all." With another smile, she dipped her head, magesign flooded the space and she was gone.

Emma Parker hurried forward and closely inspected the floor where Meera had been. "Well, bugger me!" Her own magesign pulsed forth as she tried to sense the Umbra Mage's magic. "Seriously, bugger me."

"They're good people," Alex said. "They helped me before."

Emma stood, sniffed. "Well, let's hope they can again. Come on, we'd better move along. That burst of magic will be like a yell right into Claude Darvill's ear."

Alex nodded, started the van and pulled out onto the busy road. They continued their arbitrary journey north. He passed a sign that read *York 14 Miles* and sighed. He was a rat in a maze, running around like a fool. How long until the experiment reached its inevitable, fatal end?

That's Curly organized!" Hood sat back in his tall leather chair, clearly pleased with himself.

"Curly?" Claude asked, wincing as he replaced the dressing on his injured shoulder.

"Yep. Top bloke. In charge of a mercenary army I've used a few times.

He's got dozens of men under his command. Amoral and ruthless, they'll do anything for the right price."

Darvill raised an eyebrow, and even that hurt. "Anything?"

Hood smiled, linked his fingers behind his head. "Yes. Anything. There was a situation in Scotland not too long ago and I really tested their resolve and loyalty. They passed with flying colors."

"And why are you calling him now, Dad? I'm not sure what you're planning here."

"Power is available to the man with money, son. I've always told you that. I've let you go off getting all the arcane skills and having all the adventures, but real supremacy in this world is not magic or amulets or special drug-fueled divinations. Currency is the ultimate authority. Wealth is the god-maker."

"Right. I'm well aware of your personal philosophy. But I'm still a long way from seeing your point."

Hood laughed, rocked back in his chair, heels slamming onto the corner of his desk. "We need henchmen, Claude!"

"Henchmen?"

"Are we not the villains of the piece? I'm sick of running around trying to catch what we want. We need to act smart. I have this newfound power at my command, which I will use, don't doubt that. But it's not the ultimate authority. My philosophy, as you call it, remains unchanged. Real strength lies in the ability to buy what you need. Firstly, I have bought, once again, Curly and his crew. Now we have dozens of highly trained and perfectly ruthless military personnel at our disposal."

"Good for us. Are we getting anywhere nearer to the point?"

"I want Alex Caine's fucking guts around my neck like jewelry. I have the army now, which means I can start to implement a plan. We need a place, a well-populated place, and we need to arrange something Mr Caine can't resist. You told me how affected he was by the deaths around Obsidian, yes?"

Claude sat forward, elbows on his knees. He was more tired than he had ever been, but he was becoming interested in Hood's ramblings. Was it possible his father had started thinking more clearly than ever? "Yes, that's right. Before I was pushed out by Armor, after they'd finished debriefing me, I talked to their doctors. Caine was showing significant signs of post-traumatic stress, apparently."

Hood nodded vigorously, grinning. "Excellent! Come on then, we have a lot to organize."

CHAPTER TWENTY-ONE

A lex drove the motorhome into a marked bay and parked. There was something fundamentally depressing about a campsite in the north of England at any time of year, but especially in the winter, the air still frigid. Even with clear skies and ocean views, it felt like somewhere caravans went to die. At least it hadn't snowed yet.

Some people sat in front of their vans or mobilehomes, wrapped up defiantly in winter coats. The ubiquitous striped deck chairs housing a scattering of tourists, mostly of retirement age or older, but the place was largely deserted. Some offered waves as Alex had driven slowly through to their assigned spot. Others offered narrow eyes and unspoken warnings of a distinct lack of patience for young people and loud music.

Or perhaps he was just projecting. Why anyone would try to holiday like this at one of the coldest times of year was utterly beyond him. But there was something distinctly British about it.

Jarrod hooked up an extension cord to the power outlet so they could have electricity while Alex strolled away to stretch his legs, have a moment alone. A cold wind blew in across the North Sea. It brought with it the scent of brine and seaweed, an almost nostalgic smell, some genetic memory. Alex stared out over the iron-gray water churning across the pebble beach below. A cliff path led right by the campsite, irregular wooden staircases leading down the hundred meters or so to the water's edge. Some people braved the conditions to fish at the shoreline, grinning at their own bold stupidity. A handful of kids played with the stones. Some built castles where the pebbles gave way to a gritty, multi-hued sand. Such simple lives. No idea of the magic that permeated the world, of the monsters that stalked the night.

"Car'll be here in ten minutes. Take me to York." Emma Parker came to stand beside him.

Alex nodded, tired of talking. Tired of thinking, running, fighting. He had never given up a fight in his life, but this one seemed like it would never end.

"I'll find out what I can for you there, I promise." Emma reached up to pat his shoulder.

"Thanks."

"With us and your Umbra thingummy pals on the case we'll come up with something."

Alex laughed, a derisive noise. "Come up with a way to defeat an indestructible man and a queen of the Fey? Sure."

"Don't be so defeatist, Alex. You beat Hood before, you escaped the Lady. It's far from over."

"Why don't they just take over?" Alex asked.

"Who?"

"The Fey. They have so much fucking strength. Even taking into account the thin days and their reduced power then, they could rule this realm, no? Why are they so restrained, secretive?"

Emma chuckled softly. "Don't underestimate us human warriors, Alex. And the Kin, for that matter. The Fey know their greatest power lies in shadows. They hide and roam on the thin days when they can play havoc on a subtle scale. If they made themselves too obvious, a paradigm shift would happen in this plane. Imagine if suddenly everyone knew the Fey were real, knew the magics in the world. The arcane among the humans and Kin could rally and start to fight in the open. Magic would become everyday and those without talent would learn it or serve those who had it. We would bring war to the Fey every thin day and they would lose their edge of fear and free rein. And our realm would lose its attraction for them anyway. They revel in corrupting our supposed order, our mundane world. There's been a kind of truce in effect for centuries. Fey power is reduced and we accept any collateral damage. You'd be amazed how much of Armor's time is taken up heading off incursions on thin days and protecting people who have no idea they're even under threat."

"Does it really work like that?"

Emma swept her arm, taking in the campsite and the beach, perhaps all of England. "Look around you. Life goes on. We've got things relatively contained. Of course, this is why the Fey want free rein in our realm again. If every day were thin, if their influence never waned, they would most certainly stride across this world and live for the chaos they would cause, our order be damned. And there's very little we could do against them then, I suspect. The full might of Fey against the arcane among humanity and Kin. Who knows what other races and creatures might ally with us? Or with them. But it would be messy. It would be apocalypse."

Alex rubbed at his chest. "And that's what they want from me. I'm the instrument of their apocalypse."

"Maybe. But only if they get you. They've been infinitely patient, waiting for their time to come around again. And then you show up and in the space of a few months you've fucked them right up. Their anchor stone is gone forever, the Lord's heart. All that's left is that collection of shards in you, and you've even made that vulnerable. Do you realize what an achievement all that is?"

Alex laughed, shook his head. "I certainly didn't mean for it to happen that way. I had no idea…"

"Of course."

"I'm all that stands between the Fey and their apocalypse. If we can't do this…"

"I'll be first in line to kill you."

Alex looked sharply down at Emma Parker's kindly face. Her eyes were hard as flint. "Really?"

She nodded, no hint of a smile touching her lips. "I like you, Alex, and I will fight with you and do all I can to get the best result here. But Armor Command is unanimous and I endorse their view. If it looks like we can't win, you have to die. And that stone with you."

Alex swallowed against the rush of adrenaline at her words. "That's… actually quite reassuring."

"I know you have all kinds of conflicts and feelings, Alex. Of course you do. But I have the benefit of pragmatism. I don't love you like Silhouette does. I will kill you as soon as look at you, should the need arise."

Alex nodded slowly. "And I would let you."

Emma reached an arm around his back, gave him a squeeze. The top of her head only reached his shoulder and she pressed it against his arm. "Attaboy. You deserve to know the truth and I know you get it."

They stood for a few moments, Alex enjoying the warmth of Parker's hug. She suddenly disengaged herself. "Anyway, enough of that old bollocks. For now, we're still fighting. York is only an hour that way, straight down the A64. I'm going to the Armor HQ there to collect anything they've got for me, get a handle on proceedings. You lot stay here, don't move too far apart. I know it's restrictive, but it's the hand we've been dealt, so we play it."

"How long can we stay?" Alex asked. "Everyone is really tired."

"I know. Before I go I'll rebuild the shields and they should keep you covered for a few hours. I suggest you all rest. I'll be back before midnight, so get some sleep between now and then. We'll move on after that. Use the power here to cook up a proper feed. There's a mini-mart thing over there, so you should be able to get all you need. Stay together!"

"We will."

Tires crunched gravel. They turned to see a black Land Rover with darkened windows pull up to the camper van.

"Ah, my ride." Emma trotted over and hopped into the passenger seat. She leaned out before closing the door. "You lot, eat, sleep, stay together!"

As the Land Rover drove away, Silhouette came and wrapped her arms around Alex. "What were you two talking about?"

"Emma was just reassuring me that we're going to keep fighting. We're not going to let the Lady win. That sort of thing. You know what she's like."

Silhouette looked up at him, suspicion in her eyes. "That's all?"

"Yeah, what else?"

She shrugged. They held each other and watched the ocean for a time before Alex's stomach refused to be ignored any longer.

"Let's cook up a feed," he said and led her back to Jarrod and Jean. Together they wandered towards the campsite shop in search of sustenance.

Alex dreamed of a fight he could never win. Hood leered and laughed in his nightmares, beating on Alex with brutal efficiency. Nothing Alex did in defense worked, no strike he threw landed. His limbs felt heavy and sluggish, his breath constricted in his throat.

Hood held him down, pounding again and again. Pain cracked through Alex's skull, but consciousness stayed with him. Hood laughed and looked across Alex's broken form.

Hello there, he's all ready for you.

The Lady leaned over, upside down to his view, her face a rictus of woody fury, eyes burning amber. *You lost the Lord's heart!* she hissed, and slammed sharp fingers into Alex's face.

He cried out, tried to swat her hands away, but Hood sat on his chest, used his knees to trap Alex's arms tight to his ribs. Alex squirmed and thrashed as Hood shifted his weight back, tore off Alex's shirt.

The Lady reached in, her long, stutter-moving fingers scratching at Alex's chest. White-hot agony lanced through every millimeter of his nerves, his body alive with fire, as she plucked out each shard of the Darak.

We found a way, she said, laughter rippling through her words.

The Lady and Hood spun away from him as he staggered to his feet. She juggled the three shards of the Darak as calliope music played far too fast from somewhere, a cacophony of idiocy. Hood pranced by, tumbling and back-flipping, laughing as he caught the shards and juggled them too.

The pieces became crows that flapped furiously forward, wings battering Alex's face. He tried to shoo them away, but his arms were still stuck to his sides. He looked down to see the skin of his ribs merged seamlessly with the flesh of his forearms. He screamed. His hands melted into his hips, his legs bonded together. He fell face-first to a hard, black obsidian ground, writhing useless as a maggot, his body a lump of swollen, pasty flesh.

Cracks appeared and wan blue light flickered at the edges. Icy nothingness came through the fissures as the Void yawned for him, sucked him away from everything he knew.

He howled as pain and loss and grief and guilt flooded his senses.

"Alex!"

He gasped, sat up, cracked his head against something hard, slumped back down.

"Alex, it's okay. You're safe. You're dreaming."

Silhouette.

Alex dragged breath into his lungs, opened his eyes. He lay next to Silhouette in the cramped bed above the front seats of the motorhome. Pale light from a small lamp glowed below him. At the other end of the camper, Jarrod and Jean, propped on their elbows beside each other on the bed where the small table turned over, looked concerned.

"You okay?" Jean asked.

Alex nodded. "Sorry, guys."

Silhouette stroked his hair. "It's okay. If anyone doesn't need to apologise for nightmares, it's you."

"It's after eleven o'clock," Jean said quietly. Alex noted she was still terrified, nervousness in every syllable. The poor woman still thought herself the odd one out in the team. "Should we get up?" she asked. "We've slept for five hours."

"Did you sleep?" Alex asked.

Jean smiled, abashed. "Well, not really. On and off, maybe an hour or two."

"Jarrod?"

The big Maori laughed. "Like a log. I've been at this game a long time, learned to crash whenever I get the chance. It's a useful skill."

Alex swung his legs off the bed, dropped to the camper floor. "You're right, Jean, Emma will be back soon. We should get ready."

Silhouette dropped down behind him, silent as a cat. She put her arms around his chest, hugged him. "You okay?"

"I will be."

Alex, can you hear me?

He jumped, momentarily reliving the dream before he recognized Meera in his mind. "Just a minute, guys." He tapped his head by way of explanation. *I can hear you.*

Are you okay?

It seemed like a lot of people were asking him that lately and he was pretty fucking far from okay. *I'm fine, thanks. You got anything?*

Not anything much, I'm afraid. But since we first came into contact with you, some of our people have been closely researching the whole Fey, Uthentia, Eld and Darak history. There's a man there in England who is something of an expert historian on the subject. He claims to have fairly extensive knowledge of the Eld and their magic.

Alex felt a brief surge of hope, but it died quickly. *Will that help me?*

Anything you learn is good, Alex. Knowledge is power. If you can understand something of the Eld's history or magic, it might help you figure out a plan.

Is he one of yours, this guy?

Meera chuckled, a strange sound that rang inside his head. *No, but he's worked with us before apparently. He's…eccentric. Very old. But he's agreed to chat with you. I warn you, he'll only trade his knowledge for yours. You'll need to share your story with him in great detail, but he'll hopefully share some stuff back. That's how he works.*

Alex nodded, accepting the truth of Meera's words about knowledge being power. *Thank you, Meera. I really appreciate it. Where is he?*

By the time Alex had relayed Meera's message and they had looked up the location on a road atlas from the glove box, Emma had returned. Alex went over it again for her, pointing to the map.

"That's the Lake District," Emma said. "Lovely part of the country and not all that far from here." She tapped the map with a forefinger to point out where they were.

Alex frowned. "It's on completely the opposite side of the country!"

Emma laughed. "This is England, dear boy, the original terrier nation. We may have a big attitude and a big reputation, but we're a small bastard. That's only three hours drive or so. Easy!"

"Fair enough." Alex closed the map. "And what about you? What have you learned?"

Emma pulled a phone from her pocket. "Couple of things. Armor is working on securing a location for our big fight. If we can have a place ready, the Lady will come and find you there and we can lure Hood in as well. We'll have masses of personnel and the advantage of picking the battleground. But it needs to be a long way from people and civilization, of course. Current thinking is somewhere in Snowdonia National Park in Wales. Which fits bloody well with that." She tapped the atlas held loosely in Alex's hand. "This contact your Meera lass has found is probably a bit nearer to Snowdonia than we are now. We can keep moving and continue in roughly the right direction. Handy, what?"

Alex nodded. "Sure, I guess. But what are we going to do when we all get to the battleground? I mean, I love a good fight, but this is one where the combatants are a bit much to handle."

"The boys and girls at HQ are working on that too. Trying to find out as much as they can about ways to control the Fey and maybe contain Hood. They're working on a kind of trap for him. He's incredibly strong and very hard to harm. A lot of magic seems to bounce off him, so they're erring towards entrapment first and dealing with him later. But they're amassing mundane and arcane firepower too. With any luck they'll get him *after* he's taken out the Lady for us. Details, though. Lots of stuff still to figure out."

Alex held up a finger. "Wait a minute. Hard to harm? He's fucking indestructible. He survived trapped under rock in a pool of molten magma for months!"

Emma grinned, held up her phone. "Well spotted, that man! Look." She tapped up a video and set it to play.

Alex felt the others crowd around behind him to watch. The soundless footage was grainy and occasionally interrupted with bursts of static. It showed a double rank of operatives in Armor black, one row crouched in front of another row standing. The crouching row fired assault rifles while those standing worked together to cast some form of combined magic. The ripples of their spell caused interference in the film, affecting the security camera above them from where the footage came. What they fought against could not be seen from the camera angle, but it seemed obvious.

"This is Sydney," Emma said. "Watch closely."

Robert Hood slowly emerged into frame, leaning against the magic, straining to reach the operatives. The bullets seemed not to bother him at all, his clothes dancing and flinching in the barrage. He stretched fingers hooked into claws towards them.

Suddenly those standing bucked and pirouetted, gunfire tearing them apart.

Jean Chang gasped and stepped away, hand over her mouth.

"Oh, sorry," Emma said quietly. "Should have warned you. Gonna get worse. But keep watching."

As Jean moved back to see, the tiny black and white CCTV Hood rushed forward and tore into the Armor operatives, ripped them to pieces with his bare hands.

Jarrod whistled softly through his teeth. "Fuck me."

Jean sobbed through her fingers, but kept watching. Silhouette squeezed Alex's hand. He ground his teeth and stared. Lives lost for him, blood on his hands. And lost so violently, in such terror and distress. He had to end this.

"Watch closely!" Emma said.

A woman came running into shot with a sword held high. She sliced it down across Hood's neck and shoulder. He spun to face her as shots shredded her and she fell back, dead before she hit the ground.

Emma tapped the video to pause it. "Watch. It's not clear on this small screen, but look." A small cut could be seen across Hood's shoulder. Emma played the video again and the wound closed over, leaving no trace it was ever there.

"That sword cut him," Alex said, stating the obvious. "Not badly, but it left a mark. A fucking sword?"

"No ordinary sword, obviously," Emma said. "Sydney is a bloody mess, of course, but we're trying to search records and find out what that weapon is. We'll have the info soon. I don't suppose you know about it, Jarrod?"

The big man shook his head. "I've seen it before, in the weapons archive there. But not my department."

"Hmm. Fair enough. We're also checking all the other Armor magic item archives to see if there might be more things that could hurt him, but we're short on time and personnel right now. Anyway, watch."

Hood strode away and the camera showed nothing but the desecrated bodies of the dead. Then Claude Darvill appeared. He took the sword's scabbard from the dead woman's back, picked up the blade and slipped it in before following his father out of frame.

The weapon reminded Alex of a heavier, slightly straighter version of a Japanese *katana*. "We need that," he said quietly. "I need that."

"And Claude has it," Silhouette said. "You think maybe he saw what happened and figured it might be useful against his dad at some point?"

Alex nodded, rubbing his chin. "Claude is a smart fucker. I bet that's exactly why he picked it up. Plus, it's clearly an incredibly powerful artefact and probably priceless."

"Hood will never let him hold on to that," Jean said. "If he realizes it can damage him, he'll want to have it or destroy it."

Alex pursed his lips. "Sure. But if anyone can talk Hood around, it's Darvill. Regardless, if it's not destroyed already, it's in their possession, yes?"

"Exactly," Emma said. "Hood can be hurt, albeit not badly. That weapon should have cleaved him in two, but still...And Darvill or Hood have the weapon. We draw them into our battleground, they'll bring that thing with them. It could end up working to our advantage."

Alex sat down on the narrow bed recently vacated by Jean and Jarrod. For the first time he felt a sliver of hope, saw a tiny ray of light through the darkness of despair. Could Hood really be hurt? The blow the Armor operative had struck would indeed have sliced a normal man in two, even with a regular *katana*. A powerfully magical one had barely scratched the bastard. But it *had* scratched him. Dare he believe there was a chance? "What's the plan now then?" he asked.

Emma slipped her phone back into a pocket. "I suggest we move on, go and see this contact Meera gave us. While we collect whatever knowledge he has, hopefully Armor will finalize the battleground and learn more about the sword. Some of the files from Sydney were corrupted, so they're having trouble accessing the data."

"And then?" Silhouette asked.

"Then we have as much information as we can get and one day to prepare the arena before the thin."

Jarrod moved to the front of the camper, slipped his bulk into the driver's seat. "My turn," he said. "Let's hope whatever we gather over the next twenty-four hours is enough."

Emma slapped his shoulder. "Chin up, big fella. We'll get it done one way or another." Her eye caught Alex's as Jarrod started the engine and they shared a subtle, conspiratorial nod.

TWENTY-TWO

The man Meera had put Alex onto was called Halliday. No first
name, no more detail, just a surname and an address. The drive
there was relatively peaceful and the undulating farmland, hills
and woods of the Lake District opened up before them as they left
the A66 and headed south towards Ambleside. Narrow roads led them
past lakes and rolling green, all monochromed in the moonlit dark.
Eventually they came to the pale gray and brown dry-stone walls and
dark slate roofs of the small town. Many houses were whitewashed,
gleaming in the night.

"What a beautiful place," Silhouette said.

"Never been before?" Emma asked.

"No, not in all my years in Britain. Of course, everyone's heard of it.
People always talk about a holiday in the Lake District. I can see why."

Alex sighed, watched the quaint old town slide by. "I wouldn't
have minded a holiday here."

Silhouette turned from the window, brow furrowed. "Enough of the past tense, Iron Balls. We can still holiday here."

He smiled, but knew it didn't reach his eyes. "Sure."

Silhouette put a palm against his cheek. "When this is all over…" He opened his mouth to speak and she slapped him gently. "When this is all over, you and I will come here and have a fucking holiday, Alex. If anyone deserves one, it's us."

He looked into her icy blue eyes, intense under her blonde fringe. She was so beautiful, it made him ache sometimes. And so strong, so smart, so brave. He loved her so much. He nodded. "Yeah." He took a deep breath, forced himself to remember that he was a warrior, a fighter who never gave up. "Yeah. We will."

She smiled, kissed him.

"This is the address," Jarrod said from the front.

The road was too narrow to park their big vehicle, barely enough room between the walls of houses for two cars to pass, so Jarrod drove on and found a pub with a car park. He pulled in and killed the engine.

"We'd probably get on his wrong side if we disturbed him in the middle of the night," Emma said. "Let's rest again. It's only a couple of hours till morning."

They settled into a tense and restless wait. Alex dozed on and off, too hyped up to sleep properly, and still spooked by his nightmares. In these quietest moments, in the dark, the Void dragged at his core. He felt the weight of every life, of every person who had died because of him, hauling at his soul. Everything in which he was embroiled seemed insurmountable, massive against his tiny insignificance.

The others tried to sleep, each with varying success, except Jarrod, whose snores rolled through the vehicle almost immediately. But otherwise they were all quiet, meditating on their own little corners of darkness.

Morning came around and Alex managed to wait until a little after eight before his impatience got the better of him.

"Probably best if we don't all go in," he said. "Don't want to scare the guy with a crowd."

"Mind if I come with?" Emma asked. "I'd rather like to meet this Fey expert, given my own area of interest."

Alex looked over to Jarrod and Jean. "You two mind waiting? Me, Silhouette and Emma can go see this guy."

Jarrod shrugged, nodded. "But what about the shields?"

"I can fix up two ward domes," Emma said. "If you guys stay in the van here, I can keep you covered."

"Fair enough."

"I think Hood is quite distracted anyway." Jean's voice was quiet.

She was still so nervous. Alex wondered what he could do to help her feel a part of the team. He understood the crushing weight of guilt, but hers was unnecessary. "Why's that?"

She held up her tablet, the screen scrolling slowly with text. "I've been checking the Black Diamond servers. I wondered if I could learn anything. I mean, I've lost my tracker, but I figured Hood and Darvill might be drawing on Black Diamond funds and contacts."

Alex smiled, impressed with her initiative. "Bloody good thinking. You still have access?"

"Yeah. I don't think it's occurred to them to cut me off. I guess they're too busy with other things. Anyway, all my passwords are still active and I've been collating information while we drove and, well, I couldn't sleep. I don't know if Darvill is still trying to scry for us or not, but there's been lots of activity under Hood's personal access codes."

"Activity like what?"

"He's been communicating with a mercenary team he's used a lot. In fact, he used them when he was originally trying to hunt you down back before…"

"Yep. Go on." Alex didn't need reminding of the events that led to him creating a monster in Hood. Or more of a monster, as Hood's past was a long way from angelic.

"And he's been moving massive amounts of funds, paying contracts to engineering and shipping companies, and lots of money going into offshore accounts." She smiled awkwardly at the last comment.

"I'm guessing the offshore accounts are untraceable," Silhouette said.

"Yes. In my experience, they're usually used to pay off illegal goods or activity. He's busy getting up to no good."

Alex ran one hand back over his close-cropped hair. "I don't know if that's good or bad. Too much to hope he's given up on me and been distracted by something else."

"Definitely too much to hope," Emma said. "But he's up to something. Jean, how much detail do you really have there?"

"Not a huge amount, but I can keep trying to decipher his activity all the time I have access."

"And can you share your findings with the Armor HQ in York?"

"Sure, if you give me contact details."

Emma pulled a business card from her wallet, handed it to Jean. "Email address on there. Send a message asking to liaise and share information. Include the phrase "Taking the Hood off", capital H, in your email. That's the code we're using. They'll know you're legit then. You can encrypt messages from your device there?"

"Of course."

"Good-o. That all right with you, Alex?"

Alex laughed, nodded. He really liked this small English woman. She was a formidable force. As was Chang, if she would only shake off the guilt. "Sure thing."

They left Jarrod and Jean deciphering what she could and walked the couple of hundred meters up the road to Halliday's home. Most of the houses they passed had whitewashed walls, but the dark gray slate roofs, spattered with the moss of ages, persisted. Halliday's address seemed to be one of the oldest dwellings, small and squat, the walls bellying out under the weight of years. The windows were leadlight squares of thick, warped glass. A heavy front door of dark oak stood before them, the knocker an old brass plate and ring. Alex knocked.

Nothing happened and he began to worry. They didn't have more time to wait. He reached up, about to knock again, when a voice came through the door, deep and gravelly. "Wait a fucking minute, impatient cunt."

Alex stepped back, cast an amused glance at Silhouette and Emma. They both smiled, quickly suppressing the grins as the door opened.

"I'm an old bastard, don't expect me to move fast. Especially this bloody early in the morning." Halliday was a short, wizened man with an explosion of gray hair standing off his head in every direction. His skin was pale, stretched over bent bones, his fingers crooked, knuckles swollen with arthritis. His fingernails were freakishly long and thick, yellowed like the talons of some ancient beast. A ripe, tangy odor washed out of the house, deeply unpleasant.

Alex opened his vision, surreptitiously scanned Halliday's shades. They reeked of age, counted in centuries. His magesign was masked, but too loosely, too casually to really matter, like an elderly man who combats the annoying social demand of clothing with open flies and suspicious stains. Which was also an accurate description of Halliday's actual clothes. But the man's power was evident, albeit hard to define. Alex swallowed, braced himself. "My apologies. I didn't mean to rush you."

"You didn't. I don't fucking rush for anyone. Satan himself could demand my presence and I'd take my own sweet fucking time walking to hell. Come in, come in." He turned and shuffled away, into the shadows of the house.

The three of them stepped inside, paused to let their eyes adjust to the gloom. Silhouette wrinkled her nose, turned to whisper something to Alex. He quickly raised a finger to his lips, sure the old man would hear a rat fart though completely unsure why he thought so. Already Halliday had known he was about to knock again, so he could presumably see through a solid door. Silhouette smiled, winked.

They followed the old man into a lounge room, Alex having to bend slightly to avoid cracking his head on low, dark wooden ceiling beams. The room was buried in books, stacked and scattered everywhere. Barely any carpet showed. They picked their way through, tiptoeing from one patch of barely clear floor to the next before all standing awkwardly. Halliday slumped into a battered leather armchair, scuffed and bleached. He farted loudly.

"Just kick aside some space and sit on the fucking floor. I'm not used to having company." He flapped a hand as he spoke, then dug out a tin from the side of his chair and busied himself rolling a cigarette.

Alex, Silhouette and Emma carefully restacked various tumbles of books and managed to clear enough room to sit cross-legged, knees pressed against each other. By the time they were settled, Halliday was staring at them, puffing fragrant blue smoke into the room. Alex realized the old man was smoking a joint, the aroma of marijuana strong. It was a blessing over the far less pleasant smells of the house and Halliday himself. Alex smiled. Halliday scowled.

The silence grew slightly uncomfortable, so Alex broke it. "Meera said that perhaps…"

"I know what fucking Meera said. I was there when she bloody said it."

"Right. So, you're an expert on the history of the Eld, is that right?"

"I would be fucking surprised if anyone alive or dead knew more about them bastards than me. Question is, why should I tell you anything? What do you want to know exactly?"

Alex frowned. That was a good question. "The truth is, sir, I need to know just about anything I can about them."

"Don't call me sir, I'm not a fucking knight."

"Right, sorry. Er…Basically, I would be extremely grateful for any information you could give me about the Eld, their magic, the Darak. Anything."

The old man nodded, puffed his joint thoughtfully. His eyes were rheumy, bloodshot, and almost lost in folds of skin, but they were sharp and bright. "So again. Why should I tell you anything?"

"You appreciate a trade of information, right?"

Halliday laughed, a phlegmy sound. "I do. But what the fuck could a young cunt like you possibly have to trade with me?"

Alex's resolve hardened. This old man was a rude and arrogant prick. Enough polite entreaty. "You think you're some hot shit fucking authority?"

The old man's eyes widened. Silhouette put a hand on Alex's forearm, opened her mouth to speak.

Alex shook her off. He pulled up his T-shirt, exposing the three shards of the Darak. "You think you're the foremost expert on this stuff? This is the fucking Darak and I've met one of the Eld. Think you might like to trade your fucking secrets now, you old son of a bitch?"

Halliday's eyes widened further as he leaned forward to stare at Alex's chest. He pointed with his half-smoked joint, mouth opening and closing soundlessly a couple of times. He leaned back again and tipped his head up to the ceiling. Claggy laughter bubbled out and his entire body shook with mirth. After several moments, he pulled himself together, wheezing. He drew a huge toke and blew smoke into their faces. "Well, fuck me. I honestly thought I'd reached an age where nothing could surprise me. Well done, Alex Caine. Fucking well done. Tell me everything, however long it takes, and I'll share what I know afterwards. It'll be worth it."

Alex nodded, pulled his shirt back down. "I don't know how long we have…"

"However long it takes. That's the deal. After all, your story, your first-fucking-hand knowledge might have some bearing on what I think I know, yes?"

Alex was pleased to hear Halliday say that. For all his arrogance and rudeness, he showed the attitude of the true scholar, the eternal student. No matter how good a person thought they were, there was always more to learn. Alex's experience as a martial artist had taught him that early on and it remained true. "Fair enough," he said. "It all started when a British mage approached me and asked if I could read this particular book. My arcane vision has always been better than most, you see."

The story took several hours to tell. Alex shared everything about his battle with the book and Uthentia, how he thought he had ended Hood, his entrapment and escape from Obsidian, and all the events leading up to his current situation. Halliday interrupted often, but always with pertinent questions and requests for clarifications. The old man had a notebook and fountain pen and scribbled throughout Alex's recounting. By the end, he had smoked more weed than Alex thought anyone could safely imbibe without passing out, but the old man was as alert and focused as ever.

"And that's when Meera suggested we talk to you," Alex finished.

Halliday nodded, staring at his notes. He quietly rolled yet another joint, ruminating. Eventually he looked up, lit the joint and inhaled deeply. "Well, fucking hell. That is quite the story, innit."

Alex smiled. "I guess so."

"Leaving that Fey Lady bitch out of it for now, seems to me you've two fundamental problems that are actually kinda the same problem."

"Yeah?"

"How to destroy the indestructible."

"Well, destroy Hood, certainly."

Halliday shook his head, wagged his joint at Alex. "Don't be thinking you don't need to destroy the Darak. All the time it exists, the Fey will want it." He wheezed laughter at Alex's frown. "Of course they will! Even if you kill the bitch, others will take her place. They will always want to either reclaim their ability to pass freely between worlds or resurrect their Lord. Or both. And yes, you also need a way to destroy Hood. That sword you mentioned, the one that cut him?"

"Yeah. I'm really keen to get hold of that."

"I agree. You need that like I need an ounce of fucking weed a week. In other words, badly. It might give you a chance against Hood. But you can't discount the use of magic to trap him either. Like that Armor crew what slowed him down until his boy shot 'em all."

Alex had shown Halliday the video from Emma's phone while he spoke. "I thought about that too."

"My people are working on it," Emma said. "Hood is incredibly strong and hard to harm, but he doesn't seem immune to all arcane assault. They're working on containment spells and the like."

Halliday sucked his black and yellow teeth. "Good. That's a good approach. But his son does have some magic, and don't forget about simple mundane firepower. You said he's employing mercenaries. You have to account for all of that. But there's different degrees of indestructible, ain't there. And different ways of dealing with things. Reducibility, for example."

"What do you mean?" Alex realized his hand was resting on his chest again. The old man's words about having to destroy the Darak had seeded a deep fear in him, that he had first felt when talking to Meera the day before. He wanted to be free of the curse of everything that had happened since Welby asked him to read the Uthentia grimoire, but he was reluctant to give up the influence he had gained from binding with the power stone.

"Well, that stone in you is a part of the Lord's heart, right? Neither can be destroyed, but they were separated from each other. With big enough magic, things can be parted. The Eld used enormous magic to scallop out that Darak from the Lord's heart. That was their masterstroke, really, using it against itself. They used its power to shift the heart to the Void and subsequently banish Uthentia. Massive magics at work that fucked that stone up proper, split it, but still didn't destroy it. And even though they tried to hide the pieces, you found them, made them whole again. Used yourself to actually increase the innate power of the Darak."

Alex took his hand away from his chest. "Sure, but I don't know where you're going with this."

"I think I might have some records of the magic the Eld used to split the Darak from the Lord's heart. If I do, then perhaps understanding that might give you some insight into ways of destroying or separating that part of you. You need to be free of the Darak, son, because the Fey will always want it. You need it *out* of you. And it must be destroyed somehow, or the Fey *will* find a way to get it back. We can't allow that. But if it's indestructible, how do you manage that? I don't know. Maybe this magic will help you think of a way."

"And you can share it with me?"

"I didn't think I could help much until I heard your story." Halliday shifted his overstuffed ashtray from a pile of books by his chair and handed Alex the top tome.

Alex took it, heavy and leather-bound. He saw and felt immediately the magesign of the thing, swirling around like smoke, creeping over his hands and up his arm. "This is a grimoire," he said softly.

Halliday nodded, his eyes narrow.

Alex opened the book to see arcane script sweeping and curling across the page. He remembered his first ever encounter with such a tome, the gift from Welby that had given him his mastery of elemental magic. Then, in Peacock's bookshop, Welby had led him to the Uthentia grimoire. The book that started everything, that fucked up his life. It was also the book which set him on a path to realize his true magical potential, which caused his meeting with Silhouette. It was easy to hate Welby for bothering him after the fight in Sydney that night, but Alex had to accept his own part in events. And the natural course of things beyond any of their control. His Sifu's words drifted to him across the years. *You get hit, you accept it and move on. You can't block a strike that has already bruised you, you can't undo an injury that has already occurred. If you pause to think about how you can change the past, you get hit again. So you accept, you fight on. Never then, never later, always now. Always fighting. Until the fight is over.*

His teacher's lessons had always been about more than simply training to fight. It seemed they became more relevant to his life by the day.

He drew a deep breath and let his vision open, let his mind sink into the script, understand the words. Only arcane sight could decipher the meaning, and his was great. Slowly the significance leached up from the page. He read the first paragraphs about the meeting of the Eld and how this grimoire contained their magic. "I can read this," he said.

Halliday sat back, lips pursed. Eventually he nodded. "I can't. No one I know can. But after your story, I thought maybe you could. Your vision is truly something special."

"So I've been told."

"And you know it to be true. Is it a book of Eld magic?"

"Yeah, it is."

Halliday barked a short laugh. "Ha! I knew it. I had no way to be sure. I tried so many times to read it. But it felt like Eld work. I always knew it would explain how they did what I always knew they had done." The old man's eyes grew distant.

"You okay?" Alex asked.

Halliday shook himself. "Just remembering what I went through to get that book. It did not come cheaply or fucking easily, but some things are worth great cost, no?"

Alex closed the book, ran his fingers over the ancient smooth leather cover. Grimoires were powerful artifacts, not only containing information about magic, but vessels of transmission. Welby's greatest gift to Alex had been the elemental grimoire. By reading it, Alex had absorbed mastery over the elements, skills which became an intrinsic part of him. Already he felt the beginnings of the Eld magic nestled into his brain from just the first page of this tome. Rare and priceless, grimoires contained the very essence of magical ability. Being able to read them, decipher them, was the real challenge. So many of the greatest were opaque, even to the greatly skilled. But Alex had yet to discover one he could not decrypt.

"I need to read this book," he said. "And it's big. Might take a few hours. Once I've read it, I'll have the magic inside."

Halliday nodded, taking a last draw on his current joint. He stubbed it out. "I know how they fucking work. But take it. It's yours."

"That's a priceless thing," Emma said, awe in her voice.

Halliday laughed. "Fucking money! Do I look like I spend money on anything? Knowledge is all that matters." He looked back to Alex. "You can have that on one condition."

Alex smiled. "I promise. If I survive this, I'll come back and tell you everything."

Halliday nodded. "Now you're getting it. Go on, fuck off. I am well overdue for a nap. You can see yourselves out."

They stood. Alex leaned forward, reached out a hand to shake. "I really appreciate your help. I can't emphasize how much."

Halliday slapped his hand aside. "Go on, fuck off." But the old man was smiling as he spoke, the first time his face had cracked from a seemingly permanent frown since they had arrived.

Alex grinned, stood straight, narrowly avoiding a low ceiling beam. "I'll do my best to come back."

"We promised ourselves a holiday back here anyway, remember?" Silhouette said.

"We did." Alex felt an expansion of hope in the shadows of his despair. He had no idea if it would last, but perhaps there would be something in the grimoire that might give him an edge. His optimism was tainted as they left, however, as Halliday's words echoed in his memory. Words that filled him with dread. *Don't be thinking you don't need to destroy the Darak. All the time it exists, the Fey will want it.*

CHAPTER TWENTY-THREE

Alex, Silhouette and Emma returned to the camper van. Jean and Jarrod had folded up the end bed and returned the table to its place. They sat huddled over Chang's tablet.

Jarrod looked up as they entered the cramped space. "Any luck, Alex?"

"Maybe. I gotta concentrate." He clambered into the small bed area above the driver's cabin and opened the grimoire.

Silhouette watched him, entranced by the tome. She fervently hoped he would get something from it, something truly tangible. Deciphering arcane text was a painstaking, exhausting process, even with his overly developed vision. Reading an entire grimoire was the mental equivalent of running a marathon. But he had no time to spare. She wished she could do something to help, but this was down to him.

Emma Parker moved behind her, stepped up to look over Jean Chang's shoulder. Silhouette frowned. Parker was an incredibly capable operative, but something about the small woman put her teeth on edge.

There was a coldness under that jolly English façade that made Silhouette uncomfortable. Parker was the kind of woman who would stamp on a puppy without a moment's thought if she thought it was for the greater good. Silhouette could easily imagine the bitch stamping on Alex.

A wry smile twisted Silhouette's lips. Old Iron Balls was her puppy and she would never let this Parker stomp on him. The trouble was, Alex would probably go willingly, given his current state of mind. Silhouette needed to keep him focused on fighting. She had watched him fluctuate between despair and determination so many times during the course of recent events. She had to keep pushing him towards the positive. He turned a page, brow furrowed in concentration. *You can do it, Alex*, she thought. *Don't you dare give up on me.*

"Anything?" Emma Parker's tone was friendly but tight. The woman was clearly more and more on edge as time passed.

Jean Chang shrugged, her expression annoyed. "Yes and no. I've been tracking all the things I can. Hood has been paying money into all kinds of accounts, drawn huge sums of cash, which is almost certainly for untraceable payments and bribes. He's contracted a freelance engineering company in the London Docklands, funneled cash to his mercenaries. But I can't pin down exactly what he's doing. There are significant details missing."

"Or hidden," Silhouette said.

Parker looked up sharply. "What's that?"

Silhouette smiled crookedly. For all her officiousness, this Emma Parker could be bloody dense. "He's onto you, Jean. Feeding you enough information to keep you busy, but not enough to crack what he's up to."

Jean's eyes widened then narrowed. "Shit. There's maybe a level of encryption I haven't found." She turned back to the tablet, began studiously working.

"Well done," Parker said. "But I wonder if it will help us at all."

Silhouette smiled, as cattily as she could. "Any information is worth something, right?"

"Yes, indeed. With that in mind, I'll get on the blower to Armor in York." Emma pulled out her phone and stepped from the van as she dialed.

Silhouette moved to sit beside Jarrod. "How you doing, my big little brother?" She squeezed one huge bicep through his light jacket.

He flexed for her quickly before embarrassment flooded his face. "I'm feeling pretty useless, truth be told."

"Yeah, me too. We're treading water here, huh."

"I guess. But I've a feeling we'll be busy enough soon."

Silhouette watched Jean tap away. She nodded towards the thin woman. "Keep an eye on her, eh? She's struggling, needs someone to look after her."

Jarrod watched Chang for a moment. "Yeah, I'm on that. She'll be okay."

Silhouette scowled towards the door. "And keep a close fucking eye on Parker, too."

"She's on our side, Sil."

"Is she?"

"What do you mean?"

Silhouette shook her head, patted her brother's shoulder. "I don't know, exactly. Just watch her. Closely. I don't trust the bitch."

"Okay."

Emma Parker stepped back inside. "Snowdonia is organized. I've got GPS co-ordinates. It's well removed from civilization, but easy enough to get to. The few people nearby are being evacuated now. We've got battlemage teams moving into position and working on containment magic against Hood and the Fey. We just have to get everyone there. Then Armor will bring the war machine to all of those bastards."

"And how do we get everyone there?" Silhouette asked.

"Well, the Lady will home in on Alex like a moth to a flame. She'll come barreling to wherever he is, no doubt. We need to lure in Hood at the right time and lead them together. Hopefully, our pal Jean here will get some more information on that for us."

Jarrod made a low growling sound in his throat. "In a way, I preferred it when Hood was gunning for us. This is too quiet."

Silhouette agreed with him. But there was nothing they could do about it. "We'll just have to wait for now. How long till the battleground is ready?"

"Just a few more hours. Well before the Lady is due."

"Let's hope Jean can track Hood before the thin then," Silhouette said.

Alex's reading began to turn his brain to porridge. New magic built its way into his consciousness, arcane knowledge nestling into him like maggots into rotting flesh. The acquisition of powers was a particularly discomforting process, like swallowing nails. At the end of every line, the turn of every page, he wanted to throw the book aside. But this was how it worked. Nothing this valuable, this strong, came easily. And he had no time to spread it out and ease the process.

He marveled at the ingenuity of the Eld. The method they had devised of corrupting the incorruptible was a masterstroke. Using eldritch energies to create slight shifts in realms, brief moments of *other* through the space the indestructible occupied. Things that could not be destroyed could be divided that way, though only briefly. It was utilizing that brief division that posed the biggest challenge. The magics were mind-bendingly complex, but he began to understand them, even though separation of the supposedly indestructible was a hair's breadth from impossible. Alex began to internalize it. Controlling it, that was something else. And it needed a fine wielding hand. He looked at the remaining pages, nearly half of the book still unread. Such dense, complicated sorcery.

He rubbed his eyes, blinked heavily. Hood would be coming any time, the Lady not far behind. He would find himself in the middle of a maelstrom of violence and had to be ready. His brain needed rest, but he didn't have the luxury. If Armor were preparing the war, he would be prepared to stand at its head.

He paused in his reading to consider how they might tempt Hood to them. He had half listened in on Emma's report, Jean's consternation.

The fight would be in Wales, the Lady would come there, but would it be enough to simply reveal themselves to Hood? Previously, Alex thought that would have sufficed. Now he had a bad feeling about it. He shook his head to clear his thoughts. First and foremost, he needed to get this magic inside. He could think of ways to draw Hood in later.

"Oh."

Alex's gut ran cold at Jean Chang's tiny sound. All eyes turned to her. Chang's face was ashen, her lip trembled.

Emma Parker moved to put a hand on her shoulder. "What is it? What's happened?"

"This." Jean held up her tablet. The screen was blackened, with a large block of white text stark against it, clear enough for Alex to read from the other end of the van.

Figured it out yet, Chang, you back-stabbing bitch?

I'm sure you haven't, you useless slag.

I suggest you tell your friend Alex to watch the news.

"Watch the news?" Alex said. "What the fuck has he done?"

Emma raised both hands as the mood in the van electrified. "Let's be calm. Don't rush into anything."

Alex jumped down from the bed. "Fuck that. There'll be a television in the pub."

Without waiting for an answer, he marched out. Fingers slipped into his and he smiled tightly at Silhouette right beside him. "Promise me you'll think this through and we'll deal with it together," she said.

Alex kissed her, unsure he could promise her anything of the sort. Jarrod, Jean and Emma were hot on their heels as Alex pushed open the pub door and strode in…It was busy with an early lunchtime crowd. He walked up to the bar.

"What can I get you fine people today?" The barman was a big man gone soft, his nose swollen and veined in accordance with the volume of his own supply he had enjoyed. His hands rested on top of two of the many pumps ranged along the highly polished, dark wood bar.

"You have a TV here?" Alex asked.

"Sure." The barman pointed.

Around the corner, in a lounge area to the side of the low-beamed main bar, several tables and chairs were scattered. Groups of people sat, some eating pie and chips or fried fish, some drinking, all watching a soccer match on a big-screen television.

Alex walked directly up to the set. He looked all around it as people complained he was blocking their view. "Where's the remote?" he demanded of the nearest person.

"Get fucked, pal, we're watching the match."

Alex felt fury rise, his face twisted. "This is more important than a fucking game!"

The barman barreled out from behind the bar as Jarrod put one huge hand on the drinker's shoulder to prevent him standing up to Alex.

"I think you lot better go," the barman said, eyes betraying his fear. He had obviously been in the business long enough to know when something was about to kick off.

Others in the lounge area stood, started shouting over each other. Faces appeared from the bar, peering around the corner.

"How do I change the channel on this fucking thing?" Alex roared.

Silhouette reached for his hand. "Alex, calm down."

He shook her off, about to reach for the barman's throat when Emma Parker stepped forward. Her voice was bellowing, momentarily stunning from such a small and unassuming woman. "Ladies and gentlemen, please bear with us. Something extraordinary is happening. We need to see a news channel."

Unnoticed in the commotion, Jean Chang had figured out the set and the channel changed. Amid hollers of annoyance and threats of violence, several programs flicked past before settling on the BBC. A harried-looking woman in a suit held a microphone. Behind her was a huge building site of some description. Clearly visible, towering up in the background, a massive crane held a bus suspended some thirty meters or more off the ground. Hands waved desperately from the bus windows. The angry vocals in the room drained away as people watched the bizarre spectacle, the reporter's voice too low to hear.

"Turn it up," someone called out.

Jean raised the volume, the reporter's voice suddenly strident as the pub dropped into silence.

"…police are saying this may not be a terrorist attack. They suggest, however, that there is a distinct motive at work. The site of a massive building development on the edge of Canary Wharf was raided around two hours ago by a team of soldiers in black balaclavas, carrying automatic weapons in plain sight. These people were not, repeat, *not* the British Armed Forces. This footage was sent to all news networks less than half an hour ago." The picture changed to show several shots of the soldiers described rushing every entrance of the large site, herding all the people working inside into one area near a cluster of prefab buildings. The reporter continued to talk over the images. "As you can see, the assault was swift and brutal. We've edited out two portions of film where workers tried to question the instructions they were given and were gunned down instantly. We know at least three people have been shot, presumed dead, quite possibly more."

Alex blanched. "Oh, fuck me…" Silhouette squeezed his hand, her grip enough to hurt.

"The school bus was driven in by a man with his face concealed in a similar fashion to the attacking force," the reporter went on. "It was fixed to the crane and winched high. There are at least thirty children on board aged between eight and eighteen, possibly more. From my position, I can hear their screams and shouts for help.

"The soldiers who secured the area are guarding every entrance behind metal barricades. You can see one such barricade behind me, and at least three heavily armed personnel behind it. When a Channel Four chopper tried to get a look into the site moments ago, it came under heavy fire and had to make an emergency landing in the street outside. We're unsure if anyone was hurt in that incident. We have been unable to get any vision inside the site. Snipers inside are taking aim at anyone they see in the windows or on the roofs of the surrounding towers."

The shot returned to the reporter's harried face outside the site. "The police are working on clearing the area and all nearby buildings. Where I'm standing now is as close as I'm allowed to go. No demands have been made. I heard from one police officer a few minutes ago that SO19 and the Army have been called in and are even now establishing a perimeter. It's likely we'll be moved along at any moment, but I will keep reporting until I'm no longer permitted to do so."

"What the fuck is he doing?" Jean asked.

"I think it's pretty obvious," Alex said. "He wants me to go to him."

"Really?" Emma asked.

"Dude, who the hell are you?" one of the diners asked. "You have something to do with this?"

"I'm getting new information," the reporter said, one hand pressing her earpiece to hear more easily. Army personnel appeared behind her, moving along other reporters and bystanders. Two men in full infantry gear jogged up to the reporter as she spoke. "There's been a ransom demand. No, my apologies, not a ransom. But a demand." The Army personnel yelled at the reporter to move along. The picture shook and tilted as someone out of shot dragged at the camera operator.

"We're cutting back to the studio for breaking news," the reporter said, desperately trying to look into the moving camera as she spoke, then static.

After a second, the picture resolved to a studio. A dark-skinned man in a gray suit sat behind a desk. "We've just received this video from the people who have taken control of a London building site and suspended a school bus full of students more than a hundred feet above the ground. Apparently, every news agency has received the same footage and it's spreading at a furious rate across all social media."

Another moment of static, then the screen filled with Robert Hood's insanely grinning face. "Hello, world!"

Alex felt his knees weaken for a split second before rage washed through him. "Fuck!"

"I suspect you're wondering what on Earth is going on," Hood said. "I do apologize for making this so public, but who doesn't love a bit of drama, eh? I bet you're all wetting your pants in excitement. So sorry to disappoint, but this is actually a rather personal campaign. Are you watching, Alex Caine?" Hood leaned close to the camera, his face distorting. "I want you! Come to me, or this bus drops and all those kiddies die. Can you handle that, Caine? Another bus load of lives to add to your tally? All so young. I think not! Anyone who approaches this site will be shot, except Caine. Only you are allowed in, Alex. You coming?" Hood's face twisted into a moment of deranged laughter before he pulled swiftly back from the camera. His features contorted, he slapped himself violently twice across the cheek and the film cut.

The picture returned to the newsreader at his desk, his eyes betraying shock at the demand from Hood. "So...so there you have it. Apparently, someone called Alex Caine is at the heart of all this. We are looking into that now and will report more on this bizarre situation as and when we can."

"Are you him?" someone yelled.

"The fuck is this?" another said.

Alex turned and forced his way past grabbing hands. Silhouette ran with him. "Alex, you can't go."

"Thirty children, Sil? Or more? I have to go."

Emma Parker hurried up to his other side. "We have to plan this. We can't go blundering in. We have a plan we need to stick to."

Alex turned to her, his eyes dark with anger. "No, *you* can't go blundering in. No one can. Except me. You heard him." He strode into the pub car park, his friends quickly gathering around him. People crowded in the doorway behind them.

Alex looked to Jean Chang. "You can send him a message, right?" She nodded. "Tell him I'm coming, but it's going to take me a while to get there."

"Alex, no!"

"What else can I do, Sil? I will not have more lives lost on my account. Children! He's calling me out. When that happens, I fight. Haven't you been telling me all along to fight?"

"Not like this. Not on his terms!"

"There are no other terms. Fuck it, Sil, let Hood kill me! Then the Fey threat is gone, right? I'll take him down with me if I can. If not, he's Armor's fucking problem. But no more deaths on me!"

"Alex, please…"

A motorcycle pulled into the car park. The rider put the stand down, pulled his helmet off and hooked it on one handlebar. He watched the fracas with an interested expression.

Alex pushed past Jarrod and Silhouette. "I need your bike, mate." The biker laughed. "Get fucked!"

Alex saw the keys still in the ignition. The biker saw Alex's face and made to step back onto his vehicle. As he raised his leg, Alex gathered his magic and pulled all the air around them in one stiff column of wind, forced it into the biker's chest. The man flew back, hit the ground with a grunt.

Silhouette and Emma ran over, pulled at Alex. Jarrod started towards him. He drew the air back and forced it into a shield between them. As his friends staggered away and fell, he paused, shamed by Silhouette's stricken expression.

"I love you so much, Sil." He grabbed the helmet, jammed it onto his head as he hopped onto the bike. As Jarrod ran for him, and Silhouette and Emma picked themselves up, he turned the key and hit the starter.

The biker was on his feet, running for him in a spitting rage. Without another glance, Alex kicked the bike into gear and roared away. He hit the brake, slewed around a car passing on the narrow street, and shot towards the main road.

He knew which way was south. That would get him towards a motorway in the general direction of London. He would have to find his way from there. The roads in this country were well signposted. He had gained a lot of knowledge from Halliday's grimoire. Not nearly enough, probably, but a lot. He twinged inside at the realization he had left the valuable book in the camper. But there was no more time for reading. His friends would protect it for him. His friends. He hoped they would forgive him, but no more deaths on his hands. No more!

Maybe he could figure out a way to make the magic he had absorbed work. He hammered onto the main A591 at dangerous speed, wondering what he could come up with in the way of a plan before he reached Hood. He figured that even with a fast bike it would take him a few hours to get there, so he had time to think. And hopefully Jean would convince Hood to wait.

Silhouette screamed inside and ran for the van. "We'll never keep up, but we have to follow!"

No one argued with her. Parker was babbling into her phone already, barking orders about tracking but not intercepting. She quoted the motorcycle's registration number. Silhouette reluctantly, and silently, admitted that was good thinking. She hadn't seen it. Hell, she didn't even know what type of bike it was.

"Yamaha F1," Emma barked. "Red and charcoal."

Oh, fuck you, bitch, Silhouette thought.

Jarrod moved past her. "Let me drive, yeah? You're too emotional."

She was about to chew him out for even suggesting such a thing when she realized that only proved him right. "Yeah, okay." She dropped into the passenger seat as Jarrod backed the van out and followed Alex.

The bike was long out of sight. The biker stood halfway along the road, yelling into his phone. He hammered on the side of the van as they passed, his eyes wild. Probably shocked by Alex's magic gust as much, if not more, than by the blatant bike theft.

Parker talked rapidly to whoever was on the other end of the line, something about how slow they were. *Come on*, Silhouette thought. *Do something to help us.*

"We'll catch up somehow," Jarrod said, one hand briefly patting her knee. "He's got back-up in you and me. Just like Obsidian."

"I hope there's something we can do."

Jarrod grinned. "That Hood fucker said they'd shoot anyone who approached the site. They'd have to see us though. We've got skills, right?"

Silhouette couldn't help a slight smile, despite her worry. "Yeah, we're badass."

"We'll get there and we'll help him."

Emma appeared between the seats. "Righto, lovelies, bit of a fucking spanner in the works, obviously. Still, we play the cards we're dealt. There's no way to get the teams from the battleground we'd organized all the way to London to face Hood now. And we can't have massed magical battles in the heart of the capital anyway. We need to try to draw Hood back up here and stick with the original plan."

Silhouette opened her mouth to protest, but Emma held up a hand to cut her off. "We're not going to let him face Hood alone. You might not like this, but it'll be best to let that bus drop."

"What?" Jean Chang's voice from the back was high with shock.

"Far bigger things at stake here. It's all about acceptable collateral. I know that's a terribly harsh thing to say, but bear with me. Jarrod, get us as far as Stafford. One unit of Armor battlemages will meet us there with a chopper and we'll get to London ahead of Alex. Another chopper is heading off to track and follow him. It's more than four hours drive from here. Three even if he continues to ride like a maniac and doesn't crash or get pulled over."

"He's a good rider," Silhouette said. "Had bikes since he was a teen-ager."

"Well, at least he shouldn't stack it then."

Silhouette's eyebrows rose. "Can't you lot tip off the police and have him caught?"

"Well, we could, but it might complicate things too much. Alex wouldn't let them take him, would he? Might get messy. If they do catch him, we shouldn't have any trouble taking over, but best to keep this in-house. We'll try to track and intercept him before London but that could be dangerous. Anyway, assume he makes it to London. We'll be there first. We can get him then, rather than try to catch him while he's riding and risk an accident. Then, we get him away again. If London Armor hadn't been destroyed, we'd have plenty of operatives there, but we've a bit of a hole in our defenses in old Londinium right now. So we'll cope as best we can. If we can find a way to stop him along the way, we will. If not, we wait for him to arrive and spirit him away before he engages Hood."

"And let all those children die?" Jean asked.

"I'm afraid so, dear. We can't risk the operation."

"You're a cold woman," Silhouette said, though she begrudgingly had to admit that Parker probably had the size of their situation about right. She didn't like her, and didn't think for a minute she would treat any of them any differently to those poor kids if the situation demanded it, but Parker was bloody efficient under pressure and a solid leader.

Parker squeezed Silhouette's shoulder. "I am cold, I know. Have been for many long decades. Believe me, I don't sleep well at night sometimes."

TWENTY-FOUR

Alex roared along the M6 past Coventry, heading for the M1 junction that would take him directly to the heart of London. It would be late and quite dark by the time he arrived, but maybe that would be for the best. Less chance of cameras getting much coverage. He glanced at the speedometer shuddering around the 130 mph mark. He made a quick mental calculation. He was travelling at over 200 kph. He fervently hoped no police took notice of him. The last thing he needed was a highway patrol chase.

Grimacing with indecision, he eased off the throttle a bit and dropped to a steady one hundred. But that was still thirty miles per hour over the legal limit. Fuck it. He cranked the speed back up. Take his chances with the cops and get to London as quickly as possible.

Hammering through the winter night, he was so cold. He gathered his magic, used elemental control to warm his hands, to build an eldritch shell of protection around himself from the biting winds. And he marveled at how casually he did so, how easily magic had become an intrinsic part of his life. He didn't want to lose it. But he was prepared to lose everything.

A helicopter swept overhead and he frowned. A moment's adrenaline burst at the thought of police air patrols passed, yet he still felt concerned. The chopper was plain black, too high to be paying much attention, but he was sure he had seen it before. Probably Emma Parker had got Armor onto him.

Why couldn't they just let him go? He had enough of trying to operate within the group, follow some plan, organize some elaborate fucking strategy. Sometimes you just had to stand up and fight. He would do all he could to destroy Hood, he owed that to the world. But there were surely plenty of others within Armor with skills enough to handle the bastard. It felt nihilistic to think so, but it had to be the truth. He had spent so little time exposed to this wide and confusing arcane underworld, but one thing he had realized was there were an awful lot of powerful people out there. Organizations like Armor and Meera's Umbra Magi group. They could manage.

He had a clarity of thought born of that simple realization. Go to Hood, save the children, kill Hood or be killed. The best result would be dying at Hood's hand *and* taking the evil fucker with him. That would end Hood's threat to the world and remove Alex's presence, finally ending the risk of a Fey takeover Alex had started when he went off in search of the Darak shards in the first place. A fitting closure.

He shook his head as he rode. What were the chances of that? Nothing ever seemed to finish cleanly and completely in his life anymore. But he had to try. And apart from anything else, he would not let those children die. He could be heading into his final fight, a battle he could never win, but he was strangely calm about it.

The chopper passed over again, slightly lower. Fucking Armor. Or was it the police, in an unmarked aircraft?

A sign indicated the junction with the M1. Alex swept around the long right-hand bend, weaving between startled drivers. He merged onto the main road and saw a sign for services, Watford Gap, not too far away. His eyes narrowed and he wound on the speed, pushing the bike to give all it could. Wind howled past the closed visor of the helmet.

As he approached the services turnoff, the chopper swept past again. Police or Armor? Did it matter? He needed everyone to back off and leave him to it. He cut his speed and indicated for the exit, slowing enough for the chopper to notice. From the corner of his eye he saw it bank. *That's it, come on, you pricks.*

He pulled into the services and rode slowly across the car park. He smiled at the sight of several other bikes parked up near a fast food joint, pulled up next to them and ran in. He didn't dare glance back, but the noise of the helicopter was suddenly intense as it came low over the car park for a moment before lifting away again. He hoped he hadn't made a mistake.

The fast food joint was busy, queues lining up for burgers and chips. He saw a group of bikers in one corner, lounging around a table, talking and laughing. Another leather-clad rider sat alone across the room. They had all been big sports bikes outside, any one of them would do.

Alex sat at a table behind the lone biker, breathing deeply to calm his nerves. He went through the mental exercises he had learned from Silhouette, the methods of gently coercing a person's thoughts. He sent his will into the mind of the man, who was thankfully about his size, dressed in all-in-one red racing leathers. *You need to piss. Go to the toilet.*

The biker sniffed and stood. He walked off, rubbing at his temple.

Alex's skills with this stuff were heavy-handed and far from practiced, but he seemed to have got away with it for now. Without waiting too long, he followed. The biker stood in the bathrooms, the zip on the front of his leathers pulled all the way down, a confused expression on his face. He turned to leave again, pulling the zip back up, and started as he saw Alex right behind him.

"Hey." Alex lifted his own stolen helmet. "Just pulled up beside the bikes out there. Which is yours?"

"Ducati 1098." The man was clearly very pleased about his ownership, smiling and lifting his chin like a proud dad.

Alex whipped out his other hand, cracked a punch across that chin with casual expertise. The man crumpled without a sound. Alex caught him and lowered him to the ground. "Sorry, mate." He quickly pulled off the man's boots and started stripping the leathers.

The biker mumbled and began to come around, his eyelids flickering as he fought to regain consciousness. Alex, genuinely sorry for the violence, tried the mind tricks again. *Stay asleep. You're so tired, you just want to sleep.* The man's eyes settled and he slumped again.

Fighting him out of his leathers was harder than Alex had anticipated and he desperately hoped no one came into the bathroom. Eventually the poor fellow lay on the tiles in his underwear and a T-shirt and Alex stripped off his own clothes, clambered into the leathers and boots. They were slightly too large, but that was good. He'd have never got in them if they were even marginally too small. Heavy, armored leathers were unforgiving in size.

He patted the pockets, momentarily alarmed, before finding a single key on a rubber Ducati keyring. He offered the man on the floor one more silent apology and dragged him into a stall. He sat him up on the toilet seat and pulled the door to. It was a poor job, but would do for the short term. Alex pushed his helmet back on and strode from the diner.

He slipped the key into the Ducati as he stepped over it, hit the starter button, pushed it backwards as it roared to life. He sped across the car park and away, heading for the southbound entrance to the motorway again. He looked around as much as he safely could as he shot down the on-ramp. The chopper was nowhere to be seen. Hopefully he had bought himself some respite from the chase.

Emma Parker was red-faced with rage. Silhouette had never seen her bold and brash façade quite so rattled. "What the sweet fuck do you mean, you've lost him?"

They sat in their own helicopter, a team of four Armor battlemages silent beside them, waiting for directions from the quick-response team. Emma ranted and raved over the phone a moment longer before finishing with, "Well, we'll go directly to bloody London as planned. Try to find him again, you imbeciles."

She stabbed the button to end the call, blowing air out in an overly dramatic sigh of exasperation. "Right. Fucking idiots." She leaned forward to address the pilot. "Docklands, site of the incident. Go." The man nodded and the rotors roared. As they lurched into the air, Emma sat forward to shout over the noise. "Clever bastard, Alex. Led the chopper following him into a service station. They had to put down somewhere else to get to him, but he'd gone. Stole someone else's bike and clothes. Took them a while to realize because they saw his original bike still out the front and assumed he was eating. Dickheads. As if he'd stop for a fucking snack! We have no idea now where he is. The chopper may eventually spot him again. Idiots! Anyway, what's done is done. Maybe Alex thought that chopper was going to try to intercept and that's why he shook them off. They obviously got too close. What the fuck was he thinking, really?"

"Who knows what he's thinking?" Silhouette pushed down pangs of worry. Poor Alex. "He's kind of out of his mind at the moment, everything is stacking up on him. That chopper had him spooked and he did something about it."

Parker nodded, lips pursed. "Oh well, on to London. Hopefully we'll get there first and stop him going to Hood."

CHAPTER TWENTY-FIVE

A lex decided to stop pushing his luck and rode through London as close to the speed limit as he could. He seemed to have shaken off the black chopper and avoided the police for the rest of the journey. London streets and traffic were too dense for high speed and he was far more likely to be caught by police in the confusing tangle of narrow roads and complicated signage.

Twice he had stopped and asked for directions to Canary Wharf. He finally had a good idea of how to get to that part of town and hoped the rest would be obvious when he got there. He had also been turning over and over in his mind the magic he had learned from Halliday's grimoire. It was incomplete, large chunks of it semi-formed and all the more dangerous for that. But he felt like he could at least apply some of the principles. He hoped it would be enough to hurt Hood. Enough to kill the bastard properly at last. Well, maybe kill was the wrong word. But end him, certainly. End his influence in the world.

He pulled the bike to a halt at the sight of yellow cordons and

Army personnel a block ahead. The road was closed, heavily guarded. He was obviously close. An armored vehicle and heavy assault rifles were on clear display. He stood the bike on its stand, hung the helmet on a handlebar and looked around. No point trying to get past them, everyone so on edge. And he certainly wasn't about to tell them he was the Alex Caine their resident lunatic was after. He would only be dragged into their plans and their strategies and fuck that. He could use his invisibility skills, but didn't relish wandering the streets beyond the cordons looking for the site. They had probably closed a large portion of the city. He needed a high vantage point.

Massive shining tower blocks stood all around the grid of roadways, watercourses here and there between them. The buildings were pixelated in the night, random windows still lit by late workers, or left on by people unconcerned by the power they burned. One building had a kind of wirework trellis all up one corner, some architecturally pleasing modern-industrial affectation. Alex smiled slightly at a memory of Canada, when he had been on the hunt for the Darak with Silhouette. It seemed a lifetime ago. The way she taught him to harness his magic and race across rooftops, jumping street-wide gaps with ease. *I feel like Batman!* he had told her.

He looked up at the heavy metal trelliswork. *Time to get my Batman on.*

Moving around the corner, masked from the army cordon by the building, he centered himself and gathered energy. His shields of invisibility enveloped him and he disappeared from view. Once concealed, he let the magic of the Darak, the power intrinsic in his being, flood through him, empower his muscles. It felt so good to be unfettered from the Lady's hideously restrictive harness. "Death or glory," he whispered to himself. "Or both."

He leapt up, preternaturally enhanced muscles lifting him several meters in the air to catch the metalwork. Breathing deep, using a level of focus gained over years in training for the ring, he jumped and sprang, hand over hand, climbing the building like a super-powered ape. The chill air cooled further as he rose, a soft breeze became a stiffer wind. In only a minute or so he had gained the roof, the cityscape of London spread out below him like a three-dimensional model map. The twisting snake of the River Thames was a thick, dark line in the night. He jogged across the roof, scanning from each side, looked for anything like the site he had seen on the news report. The yellow cordons were everywhere, the streets inside strangely still and quiet. He used them to triangulate his position, guess the direction of the site somewhere at their center.

Steadying his suddenly hammering nerves, he ran for the building's edge, gathered all his strength and power into his legs, and leapt. He sailed out into thin, cold air that whistled past him as he dropped, heading for the next roof over. The dive was massive and he felt a moment's panic at the thought he would never make it, before the next building came up to meet him with a shocking, jarring impact. He forced his magic to harden his bones like steel and tucked and rolled, skidded across the rooftop and gained his feet again running. Without pausing to think about it, he ran again, leapt across the next street and grabbed a window cleaning cradle hanging halfway down the side of the next tower block. Letting the adrenaline rush through him, empowering him along with his magic, he clambered hand over hand up the cradle's cables to the next roof and ran across. And there it was.

A massive hole in the ground, the foundations of some enormous building project, fenced off with ten-meter-high, corrugated-steel walls. Rough roads criss-crossed the site, demountable huts and earth-moving vehicles scattered around it like toys. And in the middle, the giant crane, school bus suspended below it. From his vantage point, even the crane and bus looked like children's playthings far below. The bus swung gently in the breeze.

In all the streets directly surrounding the site, army and police swarmed in tight gatherings, checkpoints at every junction. There was no way Alex had the skills to survive a drop into the site from the top of a tower block. He needed to get to ground level and avoid the patrols.

The last time he had used his invisibility skills, the Fey had found him with other preternatural senses. But against humans in the streets of London, he had no need to fear. The roof had a stairway access marked with a large green EXIT sign. With a mighty kick, he smashed the door inwards and ran, circling down and down, flight after flight of stairs. Panting, he finally passed a door marked G. He tried it and found it unlocked, leading into the lobby. The site was opposite, the huge glass front of the building he was in facing directly into one of the barricaded site entrances. Hood's mercenaries huddled behind it.

Alex walked across the office foyer, invisible in his shields, and tapped the large green plastic button to open the doors from the inside. They slid soundlessly apart. One of the guards opposite noticed the movement, his attention sharpening for a moment. Completely oblivious to Alex striding across the road straight for him, he settled back down again.

Alex heard a chopper coming in low and fast as he stepped around the barrier. More Armor? he wondered. Or perhaps TV crews trying to get a look again. Shots rang out and the chopper veered away, the sound of rotors becoming muffled by architecture.

Alex would not allow any more innocent deaths to be caused by his situation, but a few less than innocent deaths might be in order. One of these bastards had driven that bus in here. None of them deserved a second's mercy. He slipped silently behind one of the two guards, used his power to harden his hand into a steel-like weapon, and slammed it down onto the man's balaclava-covered head. As he crumpled, Alex snatched his weapon and squeezed a volley of bullets into the fellow's startled partner, made him dance and twitch backwards to drop dead on the muddy ground.

Reaction to the gunfire was immediate. The site erupted into shouts and a flurry of movement. More shouts and the pounding of running feet outside in the streets. Mercenaries poured from one of the huts near the crane and rushed for their fallen comrades. Alex walked out into the middle of the site, stood directly beneath the bus, tiny and artificial-seeming high above him, and dropped his shields.

He raised his arms and his voice. "I'm here, Hood, you fucker! Come and get me!"

From the Army station where they had been waiting, watching CCTV monitors, Emma Parker cursed. "Fuck! He's already in. How did we miss him? Bloody understaffed, we are!"

They scrambled out and ran towards the site. Silhouette caught Jarrod's eye and he gave her a subtle nod. She smiled slightly. Time to be rid of Armor and work only in Alex's interests. First opportunity, they would slip away.

"Sit rep?" Emma demanded.

One man stepped forward. "We just found the bike, but Caine slipped away again. He somehow gained entry to the site unseen and called out Hood. Looks like he killed at least two of Hood's men getting in there and totally immolated a bunch more when they ran at him. He literally threw a massive fireball at them from what we could see. The fight is on in there and Alex is yelling for Hood to step up."

Parker nodded. "Right, this is beyond us for now. Assume Hood will kill Caine and make sure we have all surveillance in place to track Hood and Darvill when they leave."

Silhouette couldn't believe her ears. "The fuck did you just say?"

Parker ignored her completely, pointed to another operative. "Get on to the Snowdonia team. Tell them we probably won't need the battleground after all. Caine dies here, the Darak dies with him and the Fey threat is averted. Saves us having to consider our own final solution, at least. Tell the team to maintain position until they hear from me, but be ready to redeploy wherever Hood goes. If Caine dies, Hood's the only real threat left. Of course, stay prepared on the slim chance Caine prevails."

"You fucking bitch!" Silhouette raised a hand to slap the smug look clean off Parker's face and someone grabbed her arm from behind.

"Calm down, please, Silhouette. I'm dealing with the situation presented to me."

"Fuck you! What was your final solution? Kill Alex yourselves and deal with Hood on your own? You think you can do that?"

Parker held up placatory palms. "We did all we could to give Alex a place and do this with him. But we were never going to let a situation this dangerous get out of control."

"You actually prefer this outcome, don't you?"

"Preference is irrelevant. I'm reacting to circumstances." Parker strode away, pulling her phone from her pocket as she went.

Silhouette shook with rage. She whipped her arm from the Armor operative's grip.

"Leave her," Jarrod said quietly. "Alex needs us."

Not taking her eyes from Parker's retreating back, wishing all kinds of agonizing deaths on the heartless bitch, Silhouette nodded. "You keep that fucking battleground in place!" she screamed. "Alex will survive this and the original plan is still gonna happen!"

Parker glanced back at her and shrugged.

Silhouette turned with Jarrod and strolled from the group. Several operatives tried to block their way. As one, Silhouette and Jarrod struck out left and right, knocked Armor personnel aside like bowling pins and pounded down the street. They shifted as they ran, Silhouette easing into the warm, powerful comfort of her panther form, Jarrod into his large black wolf. They hammered along the road, keeping to the shadows, and headed for the building site.

CHAPTER TWENTY-SIX

Alex stood under the hanging school bus, panting from exertion, his breath condensing in swirling bursts in the frosty air. But he rushed on adrenaline to a degree he had never known before. His magic coursed through him in tidal waves of exhilaration. Two clusters of burning bodies lay churning black smoke up into the night from two groups of Hood's mercenaries who had dared to move towards him. No more innocent life at his hands, but he was sick of fucking around. These lives were far from innocent.

Many more mercenaries gathered around the edges of the site, more than a dozen guns trained on him. If they decided to shoot, he was done for. No magic he had could withstand a barrage of automatic weapons fire. Besides, if they did gun him down now they would be doing him a favour. Ending the Fey threat, ending his fucked-up life and he would die standing up to a fight, the way he had always lived. He had nothing left to lose. But he had counted on Hood's determination to face him personally and he had been right.

Hood's voice rang out. "Leave him! He's mine alone! Anyone shoots him and that gunman will suffer horribly at my hands for *years*."

Hood emerged from a foreman's hut and strolled to the center of the open muddy space. He wore a dark suit and shiny shoes, his pale bald head almost glowing in the overhead lights. He spread his palms to either side, parody of the iconic Christ. "You came!"

Alex let his magic build up inside like flood waters against a dam, but held it in check. "Let's do this, you fucker."

Hood laughed. "Oh, no time for a chat? You're not glad to see me?" His voice rose into a furious shout. "After what you fucking did to me? Do you have any idea of the extent of my agony? I cannot be harmed, but I still feel. Can you imagine what it's like to burn constantly?"

"It's a better fate than you deserve."

"Do you *really* think so?"

Alex felt his body swelling with arcane energy. "You wanted what I had for no other reason than personal greed and you sacrificed *children* to get it. You think you deserve anything less than some kind of hell?"

Hood flapped one hand. "Heaven, hell, fuck all that. Children's stories. We may write great works of literature and paint chapel ceilings as we try to convince ourselves we're some higher form of life, Alex Caine, but we are animals, pure and simple." He gestured expansively around himself. "This? This is still the jungle, you know. We've manipulated it and we convince ourselves we're *civilized*, but we've just changed the savannah for fields of brick and glass. Look past the surface and all the old rules still apply. We feed on each other, *prey* on each other, and the strongest predator rules the land. And that's me, Caine. The strongest predator."

Alex could contain his power no longer. "No, you're not!" he yelled, and sprinted forward. He shot his hands out in front of him, let his magic out in a searing blast of wind and fire, a column of incandescent heat like the exhaust of a jet engine. It engulfed Hood and blackened him instantly, burned his clothes away and lifted him, pounded him back into a cement footing of the new building's foundation. A mercenary crouched in the way was collected by Hood and smashed, blood bursting out to sizzle and vaporize around Hood's burning form. Alex powered on, met Hood a fraction of a second after Hood met the footing and the mercenary. Alex hammered blows into Hood's stunned face, used his power to harden his fists into steel.

The flames around Hood seared Alex as they died away and Hood's skull shifted and cracked with Alex's blows. But his head popped back into shape after every strike and Hood spread his mouth wide in a laugh of insane joy. He grabbed Alex below the arms, lifted and threw him like a doll across the site.

Alex tumbled through the air, hit the muddy ground and rolled, grunting as breath escaped. He moved with the momentum, came up onto his feet and dug his heels in, sprinting back to meet the pale and naked Hood head on. He ducked under Hood's sweeping punch and whipped a leg around, hard and low. Hood's feet flew out from beneath him and he hit the deck with a cry of surprise. Alex fell upon him, raining blows, letting the focused energy of his magic gather in the Darak shards. He recalled what he had learned from the Eld grimoire, the incomplete lessons in their huge magic of separating, and barked out the eldritch words.

His will slammed into Hood and Alex used the spell like a thousand tiny sharpened crowbars to pry into the very essence of his enemy, open miniature realmshifts in every part of the bastard. Hood screamed as his body bucked and flaked. Scales of flesh lifted from his face, neck, chest, his torso twisting and undulating under Alex's ministrations.

But the magic was too strong, too uncontained, like trying to hold together a flock of tiny birds that only wanted to fly in a thousand different directions. As Alex struggled to manage the focus, Hood hooked one arm up from the ground and cracked Alex in the side of the head.

Pain whined through Alex's skull, his vision darkened and crossed and he staggered up and away, thinking only to remove himself from that hurt, that sensation like a car had driven into his temple. Hood's strength was unbelievable, even against Alex's enhanced state.

The two men stumbled apart, both gasped for breath. Alex shook his head, sucked air deep into his lungs to push aside the ringing in his ears, bring his blurred focus back to clarity.

Hood looked at his hands as his flesh resealed, closed over, leaving no trace of the splits Alex had forced into it. There had been no blood.

"What the fuck was that?" Hood asked, eyes wide, manic grin still splitting his face. "Fuck me, Caine, did you manage to actually injure me?"

Alex sneered. "I have weapons you couldn't possibly imagine." He sucked another breath, his vision clearing. He drew on his power again, re-found the enchantments he had absorbed and launched another blast of separating magic at Hood. The thin, pale man threw his hands up, howling again as his flesh ruptured and writhed. He thrashed around, as though trying to beat away a swarm of invisible locusts.

Alex strained, mind threatening to crack as he tried to hold onto the spell, pulsing and random, bursting out in all directions. He felt his own skin begin to blister and tear. Unable to properly direct the magic, it exploded out all around him in a supernova of destruction. Hood staggered back and Alex drove on, tried to keep the pressure of the attack forced forward. As Hood moved near two wide-eyed mercenaries crouched by a foundation wall, the sorcery engulfed them and they ruptured in a spraying cloud of blood and fragments of flesh, bone and clothing.

Hood straightened, tipped his face to the night sky and howled. He flexed his whole being, like a naked, scrawny, pale parody of a bodybuilder posing for the win. His flesh fought back against Alex's ministrations, splits narrowing, flaps of skin lying back down.

Alex yelled incoherent denials, tried to increase the strength of his attack and felt it tearing him apart even as Hood hollered again, desperately resisting. Alex staggered forward, swung one arm back low and swept a mighty uppercut under Hood's chin.

With a sickening snap and crack, Hood's head whipped back and he shot up and away. Alex's Darak-enhanced strength lifted Hood and threw him high and far. He flew back out of sight, tumbling over the concrete blocks of the new building's base. Alex gathered his strength into his legs to spring up after and a voice cut through his concentration.

"Fuck you, Caine!"

Alex turned and narrowly ducked a sweeping slice from Darvill's arcane sword. Sudden, aching desire swept through Alex. He didn't think for a second he had finished Hood and this blade was the weapon he needed. His new magic was too strong, too wild to control. He needed to wield it like a scalpel but was only able to swing it like a club. But this sword, in conjunction with the blunt instrument of his new power, could maybe do it.

Darvill snarled, a spitting rage, and swung again. Alex ducked, rolled and came up beside Claude, shot a punch out for the man's jaw. Darvill tried to move, partially successful, the blow glancing obliquely. Darvill staggered, his legs jelly, but he didn't go down. Alex grinned, the rush of victory washing through him, and he dived forward to snatch the sword from Darvill's grasp.

As his fingers reached for the hilt, a freight train hammered into his ribs, slammed the breath from his lungs and drove him barreling away from Darvill and that valuable prize. Wheezing a breathless cry of frustration, he twisted and rained blows into Hood's grinning face.

"I'm not that easily beaten, Caine!" Hood returned the strikes and the two of them fell to the floor, tumbling and sliding in the mud, swinging wild blows that failed to connect.

Alex rolled to his feet, ground one into the earth and swung the other to kick Hood hard as the man tried to stand. Alex's attack slammed into the side of Hood's neck and sent him spinning over and away to sprawl again in the mud.

Hood jumped up and faced Alex. The two of them crouched, facing off some five meters apart.

"Claude, fuck off!" Hood snarled. "This is my fight, none of you get involved."

Alex drew his power again, desperate to refine his ability enough to truly rupture Hood's presence.

Without taking his eyes from Alex, Hood gestured towards the crane. "Go, drop the fucking bus! I want Caine to see those children die before I kill him."

Darvill's eyes widened and he grinned. "Will do!"

Alex let a burst of gathered magic out. He pulled together fire and air with it, engulfed Hood again in jetting flames and disrupting Eld incantations. Hood lifted and flew once more, screaming and writhing, to land blistered several meters away. Alex ran him down. He caught sight of Darvill racing for the crane. He could not let those children die. He was no fool, he saw what Hood was doing. Hood knew Alex would try to save the children, be distracted in his efforts and that would give Hood the chance to finish him off.

So be it.

Alex felt his strength begin to waver from wielding such massive volumes of magic. He dropped the devastating Eld spell, grabbed Hood by one naked ankle and let one more wave of power strengthen his muscles to wrench Hood from the ground and swing him like an Olympic hammer. He let go and Hood sailed, howling in rage, far across the site, to crash into a stack of steel reinforcing frames. With a deafening clanging, they collapsed and Hood tumbled to become entangled in a clattering trap beneath tonnes of metal.

Alex turned and ran to chase down Darvill. Darvill leapt up to the crane base and began clambering up the ladder, heading for the high control booth. Alex skidded to a halt. The element of air had been his friend all this long day. He could use it again. He concentrated to gather a wind to sweep Claude clear off the ladder when Hood's voice rang out from far across the site as he struggled to extricate himself from the twisted steel.

"Oh, fuck this! Men, *finish him!*"

Panic pulsed in Alex and he ducked and rolled as gunfire barked out from every direction. Rerouting his gathering of elemental air, he switched it to elemental earth and forced apart the ground beneath him, dropped with a grunt into a sudden hole as bullets tore the air above him. Trapped in a bunker of his own making, he realized it was over. Pinned down by gunfire, unable to stop Darvill, unable to save the kids, unable to use the new magic to truly finish Hood. He had failed on every count.

A man screamed in agony, gargling to a sudden, wet silence. Alex imagined squads of Hood's mercenaries would pound across the site and fill his hole with searing lead, but that sound gave him hope. He peered over the edge and saw a large smoky gray cat leap from one savaged mercenary to rend the throat of another even as that man tried to draw a bead on her. Silhouette! Exultation and fear washed together in his gut. She had come to save him, again. But now she would probably get herself killed.

Gunfire exploded chunks from the cement right above where Silhouette fought and Alex spun to see the mercenary trying to shoot her torn asunder by a huge black wolf. Jarrod.

Alex scrambled from his hole, ducked and weaved as he bolted across the site. Mercenaries appeared from shadowed corners, tried to draw beads on the ferocious beasts suddenly tearing their numbers to pieces. Alex dog-legged close to one wall and slammed the heads of two soldiers together with a sickening crunch. He crouched, concentrated, gathered heat and immolated another pair as they tried to flank Silhouette's position. She leapt from one corpse and raced, low and lithe, from one shadowed enclave to the next, aiming to take out another small group of attackers. Jarrod was nowhere to be seen, but screams due to his efforts rang out.

Alex grinned. They were buying him a chance. He turned to the crane and was dismayed to see Claude clambering into the control booth, his face a mask of fury. Alex ran his hands back over his head, despairing. But maybe...

He ducked back into shadow, closed his eyes and drew every bit of energy he had left, focused on nothing but the movement of air around him. He drew it all together, gathered every breeze and zephyr. Over gunfire and screams of pain, he became aware of the high-pitched wails of terror from high above. Then a metallic *clank* and those cries magnified in pitch and volume.

Alex stood and opened his eyes to see the bus plummeting. The Darak burning like molten iron right through his chest, he raised his arms, palms open as if he aimed to catch the bus in his bare hands, and pushed all his gathered air upwards. Like a spiraling tower of cyclonic wind, he forced the air towards the falling vehicle. Several tonnes of metal and people hit his magic as though it had hit his body and he buckled, fell to his knees. His muscles and tendons creaked and split, burning lines of pain through every limb. His body shook. But he kept his hands steady, kept the magic up, and the bus bounced and rocked in mid-air, its descent not arrested, but considerably slowed. Teeth grinding together, a roar of pain and effort streaming between them, Alex squeezed his eyes shut and concentrated only on keeping as much upwardly moving air between the ground and the bus as he could, ignoring the agony of tearing muscles.

Swiftly, but not dangerously so, the bus dropped to the ground. The howls and screams from inside intensified as the vehicle hit the mud and bottomed out, bounced and sprang on its suspension, steel and hydraulic twanging and snapping as it broke under the weight.

Alex dared to look and saw a sea of wide young eyes staring back at him from the bus windows. The vehicle sat crooked and low on its broken wheels. There was no more gunfire. Silhouette and Jarrod must have finished Hood's mercenaries in their savagery. He started to smile, stunned, when Hood hit him again.

The football tackle lifted Alex from his knees and they tumbled over each other through the mud.

"You are so fucking annoying!" Hood roared and slammed his fist down into Alex's face as they came to rest, Hood astride Alex's chest.

Alex twisted, dragged what last vestiges of magic he had left to try to harden himself against the blow, but he was spent. Hood's punch glanced off his cheek, crossed his vision as pain arced through his skull. Darkness swam at the edges of his mind.

Hood raised his fist to strike again and Alex began to laugh. Weak, breathless laughter in the face of such absurdity. Hood paused. "You laugh now?"

Through his continuing laughter, Alex said, "You have no idea, do you?"

"Of what?"

Alex knew he had nothing left. "Of anything, you fuckwit. Kill me. I'm done."

Hood tipped his head to one side, a shift through his hairless brow as a half-smile twitched his lips. "It's almost less fun to know you want to die, Caine. But I'm more than happy to oblige." He drew his fist back again and a gray blur slammed into him and tore him away.

Alex's laughter stopped and he wailed, "No!" Silhouette. He couldn't let her die, not now.

He scrambled to his feet, staggered left and right under the weight of his exhaustion, damaged muscles protesting, to see Hood and Silhouette roll to a stop. She was smart enough not to stay and fight. The moment they came to rest, she sprang up and away, running back for Alex as he collapsed again. She morphed as she ran, cat form standing into human shape as she reached him. She grabbed him as he fell and pulled him away even as Hood regained his footing. Jarrod ran to them, he and Silhouette both coated in blood and gore.

"Let him finish me!" Alex yelled and Silhouette ignored him, tried to drag him away.

Hood rose, grimacing in rage. He ducked his head and made to run Alex and his friends down. Shouts and shots rang out along with the boom of a concussive explosion. Soldiers poured into the site, British Army. The good guys finally deciding it was time to move in, presumably now the bus was safe. Hood spun up and away from a grenade explosion. Dozens of heavily armed men and women poured in, some headed for the bus, others for Hood, fanning out through the curling smoke of several more grenade blasts that quickly filled the air all around. One group turned towards Alex.

Silhouette dragged him along. "Come on, we have to go!"

"But Hood." Alex shook his head, vision blurred with fatigue. His clothes were ragged, his over-exerted body mud-covered and steaming in the cold air as he poured with sweat.

"Fuck him, not our problem right now. Alex, the original plan still stands. You saved the children! You did it! Now let's get away and get Hood to face the Lady if he survives this."

"He'll survive," Jarrod said, pointing.

From their angle they could see past the smoke of grenades. Darvill and Hood, supporting each other as they ran, disappeared under a concrete overhang beside a demountable hut even as the army spread across the site in search of them. Hood glared back over one shoulder as he went.

"Like fucking rats, they'll have a bolt hole somewhere," Jarrod said.

Other soldiers swiftly herded a stream of terrified children from the bus, weapons out to meet any incoming threat.

"That fucking bitch!"

Alex looked up to see who Silhouette was talking about and spotted Emma Parker in the gateway nearest to them, gesturing frantically.

"She'll get us away from here," Alex said, shocked at how much his words slurred together.

Silhouette spat something in frustration, but Alex chose not to work out what it was. He slumped in their arms as Silhouette and Jarrod dragged him along.

CHAPTER TWENTY-SEVEN

Alex spluttered as water dribbled over his lips. A voice drifted to his ears, as if from another planet.

"Gently. Sip it."

He took the advice and the cold water was nectar on his tongue, iced pleasure down his throat. He rocked gently, a soft hum rising up through whatever he lay on, and realized they were traveling in a vehicle. A vague engine noise registered from as far away as the words.

"Gonna be bittersweet this time."

He smiled inwardly. That was Silhouette's distant voice and her special healing potion was coming. The glass touched his lips and he gulped greedily, the supersweet, acridly bitter potion washed down. He coughed, gasped a breath, drank again.

"Easy, easy."

Tendrils of warmth tickled and buzzed through his body, pushed aside the aches and jets of pain that danced through every limb. He felt muscles reknit, tendons reduce from swollen insertions. The burns on his skin, grazes, cuts and breaks from fighting, cooled and closed.

"Thanks," he said. Or did he? Perhaps he only thought it, his mind a turgid mass, sunk in a deep and black abyss. He wanted to open his eyes, but inconceivable weights hung from his eyelids. As the potion worked its magic, he smiled and let himself sink back into warm oblivion.

"Fucking lightweight," Silhouette whispered as he went, but he heard the smile in it, and the last thing he felt was her soft lips on his.

"You were quite happy to fucking sacrifice him, you bitch!"

"Not sacrifice. There's a greater…"

"Don't you dare fucking lecture me about the greater good!" That was Silhouette. "Do you have any idea what Alex has done for this world?"

"I would suggest that without Alex this world would not be in the danger it is currently in." That was Emma Parker's clipped English tones.

There was a scuff and surge of movement, scrabbling and grunts of surprise.

"I'll fucking kill you!" Silhouette snarled. "Let me go!"

"Please don't let her go, Jarrod," Emma said, fear quite evident though she tried to keep her voice level.

Alex sucked in a deep breath, forced his eyes to open. "Easy, Sil. She's right."

"What?"

He pushed himself up onto one elbow, pleased the waves of pain through his tortured body were a fraction of what he had expected. He felt pretty good, all things considered. "It was Welby who led me to the book, which led me to the Darak. Only because I could read the book was I then put on a path to find that stone. You know how it went down. And only because I did that did the Fey try to leverage me into Obsidian. And only because I cast out the Lord's heart from there are the Fey coming after me now. And Hood is a by-product of all that, created by me."

Silhouette sagged in Jarrod's grip and her brother warily took his hands from her arms. "It's not your fault," she said in a small voice.

"It is, Sil. It wasn't deliberate, any of it. But it is my fault. I need to own that."

She winced, moved to sit beside him and pull him into a hug. She cast a hateful glance at Emma. "But you would happily have given him up, not given us a chance to fight. And look what happened. We fought anyway and succeeded. And Alex saved the children!"

Emma nodded, eyebrows high. "You did. The three of you really are quite amazing. I'm stunned you managed to do that. Of course, without the intervention of the army, Hood would have finished you all off." At Silhouette's look of outrage, she quickly added, "It's only a shame he got away."

Silhouette hissed with annoyance, turned away from Parker. She stroked Alex's brow. "You okay?"

"Yeah, pretty good, thanks. That healing potion of yours…"

"I swear, I've got through more of that in the short time I've known you than in the previous one hundred years."

"Got any more?"

"Yeah, still plenty from the last purchase. But you're making a good dent in it."

Alex smiled, squeezed her hand. "Reckon we might need a bit more before we're done."

She scowled at him. "You plan to fight then? I heard what you said to Hood. You told him you were done."

"I thought I was. I had nothing left, felt like my body was about to fall to pieces. And it's true that if I die, the Fey threat is gone and others can deal with Hood."

Silhouette shook her head, hair hanging over her eyes as she looked at him. "It might be true, but it's unacceptable. *I* can't deal with it. Don't you get that?"

"Yeah. And to answer your question, yes, I plan to fight them both now. I want to live, I want to live with you. When I saw you rush in and save me again…but I will not let the Lady take me."

Emma Parker cleared her throat in an entirely British way. "If I may? The battleground is prepared. We have teams of battlemages on site, preparations to attempt to contain Hood, and everyone with a gun is on orders to shoot to kill Claude Darvill the moment he's spotted. Honestly, that bastard isn't even indestructible and needs to be rubbed out on sight. We can't underestimate him and that blade, or his ruthlessness. We also have some ideas about controlling the Lady. But there's kind of a missing piece now."

"Which is?" Alex asked, but thought he knew. Hood had gone underground again.

"How do we get Hood there?"

Alex nodded. "He's battered and run to lick his wounds. But his wounds heal quicker than I do with Silhouette's potion. He'll be in tip-top shape again already and only more infuriated. We need to get a message to him before he sets up another elaborate supervillain debacle like that bus thing."

"Indeed. So how do we get him to come to us?"

"I have an idea." All eyes turned to Jean Chang in the back, sitting tall and looking more together than she had since he'd met her.

Alex realized they weren't in the motorhome they had been using previously, but a plush, short tour bus. He lay on a comfortable bed, another opposite him, and a fully fitted kitchen to one side. Three people sat up front, in Armor fatigues, paying their conversation no mind at all. "You look like you're ready for a brawl," he told Jean.

Chang smiled, licked her lips. "What you said before about owning our guilt, that's true. Sure, I've tried to do what's right recently, but if I'd done that all along, maybe Hood wouldn't be out." Before Alex could answer, she held up a hand. "But I've had a lot of time to think. I was a powerful board member of a multi-billion dollar, multi-national corporation. I owned that male-dominated circus and I've realized I need to get that confidence back. I've watched you guys work, watched you deal with things so massive, so dangerous…I can be a part of that."

Alex nodded. "I know you've felt out of place here, and I know you feel like you're somehow responsible for things. But I made Hood, not you. Darvill released Hood, not you. It'll be good to have you firing on all cylinders. You've been invaluable to us."

"And I plan to atone for my part in all of this."

"Good. Hood would still be here if you had never become involved, you know. Darvill would have done it with or without you. Own your guilt, sure. But you're bigger than that, right?"

"Yes, I am. And so are you."

That gave him pause, and he let her words sink in for a moment. "Good. Well, step up, Chang. What's your idea?"

Jean looked around the group, her smile broadening at their nods and encouraging expressions. "Right. Well, Hood is motivated by money. He worships it. Not in some esoteric, idealistic way. He actually worships money as the highest ideal of existence. He equates cash directly with power and the more money he has, the more powerful he believes he is. He's built all of Black Diamond on that philosophy. He might be some indestructible creature carrying this despicable curse now, but he's still Hood. He still has that primary drive. He collects wealth by collecting artifacts for which people will pay massive sums of money. All along, more than anything else, he's wanted the thing that makes you powerful."

Alex put a hand to his chest. The Darak. The thing everyone wanted and the thing he was vey reluctant to lose. "But he can't have it, anymore than the Lady can, unless she can separate it from me, and remove the entropy from it."

"But Hood doesn't know that."

Alex frowned, not seeing where this was leading. "But we can hardly call Hood up and offer him a deal."

"No, not exactly. But if he was led to believe you were setting up a trade with the Fey, especially if there were many items of arcane significance involved, he would not be able to resist. He might be thinking up some new and elaborate way of drawing you in again, which we can't allow. If he got wind of the idea that you had a way to remove the Darak from yourself and you were arranging a meeting with the Lady to let her have it in exchange for some other items of great value in a kind of trade to bring about peace between you…"

"He would definitely crash that party," Alex said. "You see, Jean! You're good at this shit."

"I just know Robert Hood very well."

"Wait, though," Silhouette said. "You can't just call Hood and tell him. He'd know it was a trap."

"Yes, he would." Jean held up her tablet. "But I still have access to Black Diamond files and accounts. That means I still have access to their subcontractors too."

Alex winced at the word, the memory of his defeat in Canada at the hands of the hideous monster known as the Subcontractor. Would he ever get over that? The boom of the hotel clerk's shotgun that had been the only thing to save him. He shook the thoughts away when he began to realize how much safer everyone would be if he had died then. Except Hood would have got the Darak and the book. It was all so fucking complicated, he just wanted it over and done with. "How does that help?"

Jean tapped up a screen that showed a list. "While we drove, I've been putting together a fake deal, using contacts we've used in the past. Hood never trusts anyone and always has seers along to any deal, scrying to make sure no one is lying or planning a double cross. He knows some people he calls the home guard, with moderate battle magic skills, basically, as well as great physical training. I was never sure whether I believed all this stuff before, but now…anyway, he always arranges his deals using various members of these groups, but he never uses the same combination of employees more than once. Too paranoid about people knowing his business.

"So, I've put in fake contacts and calls, made it look like I've been sneakily using his methods and his personnel to arrange a deal of our own. I've encrypted it all, but not well enough. I know Darvill will be watching and he'll crack my encryptions and think he's stumbled onto something. The fact I'm using Hood's own people will infuriate him further. All I need to do is add a final location to the contracts and it's done."

Emma Parker made a strange noise, part chuckle, part squeak. "You really are one clever cookie, Ms Chang."

Alex grinned. "You really are. You think that'll bring him in?"

Jean shrugged. "I can't think of anything more likely. He'll want to call the shots and make you come to him. Unless we convince him he's missing out on something big and valuable."

"How long till the thin day kicks in?" Alex asked.

Parker looked at her watch. "Nine hours. I don't expect the Lady will wait a minute longer than she needs to. As soon as the realms are thin, she'll come."

"And she'll be able to home in on me?"

Emma pointed at his chest. "With part of her husband's heart embedded in you, yes she will. She'll find a gate as close to you as possible. That's partly why we set up where we did. Old country, lots of gates. Plenty not far from the chosen battleground."

"That's not long at all. How far are we from the place?"

Emma turned, shouted up to the driver. "How far from Ground Zero, Gareth?"

"About an hour."

She turned back.

Alex nodded, lips pursed. "Hood can chopper in from anywhere pretty easily, right?"

"Sure," Jean said. "When he gets this info he could be on site in less than two hours, I would guess."

"Then we'd better time this well. How ready are you to release the information for them to find?"

"It's all good to go. Take me a couple of minutes to set it in motion."

Alex nodded, stretched kinks from his neck and shoulders. "Then we'd better get to the site, see how it all looks and make sure we don't give Hood more than two hours to drop on us."

Jarrod moved to sit beside Jean. Alex noticed a soft look in the big man's eyes and had the sudden thought that perhaps Jarrod had a thing for Chang. He looked at Silhouette, a half-smile tugging at his lip, to see if she saw it too. Sil rolled her eyes at him, gave a slight shake of her head. What did that mean? He realized he was last to arrive at this particular nugget of gossip.

"What if Hood takes too long getting there?" Jarrod asked. "Or the Lady is late or whatever."

"Not a problem," Emma said. "Ideally, we'll let those two fight it out amongst themselves, at least to start with. But regardless, we get them into our terrain and if we have to fight or contain one or the other for any length of time, we will. It's a good plan. Well done, Jean."

They sank into silence as they wound into the countryside of northern Wales. Alex wondered what the near future would bring. Only nine hours until the Lady would be coming for him. He remembered how easily he had been shackled by her, how effortlessly she had trapped and tortured him. But he had seen the workings of that enchantment now and knew he could fight it off. And Emma had promised to teach him some Fey defense tricks. They had a little while to prepare.

Hood was another matter. Having faced the indestructible bastard once, he worried that he would turn out to be an unbeatable adversary. But if he could refine the Eld magic from Halliday, he might have a chance. His heart double-thumped. "My grimoire! From Halliday."

Silhouette picked up a small backpack from the floor. "Here. We kept it for you."

Alex relaxed, his knotted gut unraveling slightly. Another hour to the battleground would give him at least a start on the remainder of the complicated magic "Thank fuck. I need to read the rest of this."

He kissed Silhouette, scrunched up on the bed, and buried himself in the swirling script.

TWENTY-EIGHT

T ime passed in a dichotomy of fast and slow. While the hours seemed to drag by interminably, Alex struggled to internalize the contents of the grimoire, his sense of urgency increasing with every page. The text was dense, the concepts convoluted. But it slowly came to him. The way the Eld had scalloped away a part of something indestructible, the hard magic of the Fey Lord's heart almost impossible to compromise, was inspired. Dividing the physical without entirely dissecting the essence. Playing trickery with form and realms. Alex had first felt it when he sought the shards of the Darak, the way they had been drawn to each other, impossible to resist. As soon as he got close, the shards were attracted to each other like irrepressible magnets. He felt it again in Obsidian, when he had finally found the anchor stone, the Lord's heart, and it had drawn him forward so powerfully. He had barely been able to resist the pull, using the power of the Darak against itself, against the ground to cast the heart into the Void and use himself to replace its anchoring magic. It had nearly torn him apart.

But he understood now, better than he had when he faced Hood, how these things were separated only on a physical plane, in this realm, and ever ached to be rejoined. The Lord's heart was truly lost in the Void, the only place absolutely separate from all realms, its influence utterly removed. But the Lady could perhaps gain enough from the shards in him to resurrect her Lord and that would be disastrous. He had to prevent it, had to remove the threat from any impact it could have.

He had a final solution, the strange and unexpected side effect of his bonding. He would gladly die to remove the threat to the world if that was his last and only option. But his fight with Hood had reinvigorated his anger. He had hurt the indestructible lunatic and now he had learned more, maybe enough to truly control and refine the ancient magic and finish Hood. That was his first priority. And perhaps he could similarly find a way around another impossibility and figure out how to kill the Darak without dying himself. The more he read, the more unlikely that seemed, but he would try.

He sat back, raising his eyes from Halliday's grimoire for the first time in hours and reveled in his refreshed strong urge to live. He remembered Silhouette and Jarrod fighting for him against Hood's men. He surged with love for Silhouette. She had been the real hero since the beginning, when he became tied up with Welby and Uthentia's book. She saved him and fought for him every step of the way, had rescued him from Faerie, and still fought. She never gave up. He should learn from her example. He was no fool; he had to always remember his death was preferable to the Lady recovering the Darak. But perhaps they had a chance here. And Jarrod was a genuine ally.

Though one truth nagged at him. This new magic that churned inside him had been designed by the Eld to be wielded by the Eld. By a *team* of powerful mages. He harbored doubts he would ever be able to truly control the sorcery on his own.

He stretched stiff and aching muscles, marveled again at the healing potion. His body, broken almost beyond use from his fight with Hood and the magic of catching the falling bus, felt whole and strong again. They had arrived in Snowdonia hours before and he told the others to go, see the battleground. He had to finish reading first. He had reached the end of the book and finally felt as ready as he ever would, so perhaps it was time to see outside.

He stepped from the bus into a dark night to find Silhouette and Jarrod sitting on a bench under a canvas tent without sides. A gas lamp burned and flickered on a table beside them. Sandwiches and fruit and a gleaming silver coffee urn steaming gently covered the tabletop. They smiled to see him.

"Read the thing?" Sil asked.

"Yeah. My head feels like it's about to burst, but I got through it." He winced as the magic squirmed and burrowed in his mind, taking its time to assimilate into his consciousness. The few grimoires he'd read were old and powerful things. The process left him nauseated and discomforted every time. Probably something he would never get used to. He figured most people spent years developing enough magical ability to be able to read grimoires, built their strength slowly in order to gain the enormous advantage of those abnormal books. And even then, start with far simpler, less powerful tomes. His vision had very much thrown him in the deep end, to his detriment and his benefit.

Jarrod held out a sandwich. "Here, you need to eat. Think you've got a way to fight?"

"Thanks. Yeah, maybe I do. It's hard to really understand, let alone use, but I think I have it. We'll find out soon enough, I guess." He began to eat, realized he was ravenous and moved in for more sandwiches.

Silhouette stood, put her arms around him. "You okay?"

"Not really, but yeah, kinda." He laughed at her frown. "I want to fight, Sil. I will fight and I want to win."

"That fucking Parker was ready to throw you to the wolves."

"She has a job to do."

Silhouette made a noise of anger. "Fuck that. Where's the loyalty to the team?"

Alex crammed food into his mouth, hugged Silhouette in return.

"The only team that matters is you and me and Jarrod. You come through for me again and again, and I can never thank you enough. I'd be done in without you, a long time ago."

She kissed him. "Yeah, well I'm a bitch to get along with and you're the first to put up with me in an age. And not piss me off doing so. You, me, Jarrod. We're deadly."

"Yeah, and I think Jean is too. Where is she?"

"At the command center. She's a tech whizz and one hell of an organizer. Has them very impressed apparently. I think she's found a new job."

"She deserves it," Jarrod said. "She's amazing."

They all shared a smile and Jarrod actually blushed.

Alex clapped the big man on the shoulder, turned back to Silhouette. "We'll be okay, Sil. Just remember, Emma is here to help us, but not at the cost of anything else. She'll help the bigger picture at our expense every time if she sees it that way. Don't hate her for it, just accept that that's her role."

Silhouette shook her head, a frown creasing her brow again. "I suppose. But I don't like it. Having said that, they've set up something damned impressive here and they're definitely planning to work with you to get this thing won."

"Yeah?"

"Come on, I'll show you around. We got the guided tour while you were reading."

Alex grabbed another couple of sandwiches and Silhouette led him away. "How long do we have?"

Silhouette pulled her phone out, checked the time. "Less than two hours till the realms thin. Parker seems to think the Lady will be frothing at the mouth and hammer through immediately."

"You don't agree?"

"Who knows? Who can fathom the mind of the Fey?"

Alex had to concede the point. "Emma has a pretty good handle on Fey thinking."

"Maybe. Certainly better than any other human, but I think we should prepare for anything. For all Armor's 'expertise' they were fucking useless back at your place."

They walked away from the bus and the small tent city that made up the Armor mobile command center. Alex spotted several operatives at various stations, many other vehicles, people huddled in groups around equipment. An air of tense expectation seemed to sit over everything. People flicked him curious or suspicious glances as he passed, some openly hostile. He had to remember that many of these people had lost friends and loved ones recently and he was fundamentally responsible for that.

They climbed a shallow, grassy rise. Silhouette gestured back to the tents. "Everything is centralized there and there's a team down from Edinburgh whose job it is to wrap that up tighter than a drum. They're building all kinds of wards and shields to prevent the Fey from compromising that base. Personally, I think they'll just attack it directly first. It seems the obvious target. But Parker says, 'I've done this one or twice before, lovey' so I'll leave her to it."

Alex smiled at Silhouette's excellent impression of Emma. She managed to both imitate her perfectly and leave the words dripping with disdain. He looked out over the terrain before them. "And we'll be out here, I guess?"

Large arc lights had been set up around a wide, open space, bigger than many playing fields locked together. The grass was lush green thanks to the famous wet Welsh climate. An icy wind cut through them, threatening snow. A high ridge of peaks, curved like a dragon's spine, stood darkly against the night in the distance.

"This area is sort of ringed on all sides by high ground," Silhouette said. "The idea is that it's a natural amphitheater and will help to contain the battle." She pointed to a few distant spots where Alex could see faint lights glimmering. "There are battlemages stationed at all those points, supposedly far enough away to be safe from direct attack, but near enough to assist us."

"You don't sound convinced."

Silhouette shook her head, lifted her palms, let them drop. "We're talking Fey here, Alex. On a thin day, coming en masse, determined to fuck everybody up. It's not like picking a site for a pitched mêlée among pikemen and fucking cavalry. Seems Parker and Armor are treating this like some live-action tabletop battle game, but I really think they're underestimating the enemy."

Alex scanned the area slowly. Some of the battlemage stations were miles away in the hills, others closer in. He could see encampments all around the open space, small groups milling around with an air of feverish preparation. "It's not going to work." His words surprised him, but he heard the truth in them.

"I don't know. We have to make it work." Silhouette turned a slow circle, looked over the command center and back across the battleground. "But all this, it might be kinda irrelevant. We have to trust in ourselves, Alex."

"Yeah. And I trust in you, Silhouette. More than I can say."

She nodded. "Armor will sacrifice us in an instant. In a fucking second. We have to be prepared to do the same to them. We have to look out for ourselves and succeed, no matter how many of this lot manage to help or not."

Alex grimaced at the thought. "There are already so many deaths on my hands, Sil."

"And so many live because of you. All the lowen you saved from Obsidian, they would have died without you. The kids on that bus. It's not all death."

"But all the death is my fault."

She turned to him, took his face between her palms. "No, it's not. It's the fucking Fey. Always has been. Uthentia, the grimoire, the Darak, it's *all* Fey, Alex. All their fault. You're just another in a long line fighting it, taking up the mantle of the Eld. You have to see it like that, because it's the truth. If it wasn't you, eventually it would have been someone else.

All this would still happen, and maybe far worse, because I bet others wouldn't come close to the badass team that we make."

Alex nodded softly. Silhouette's words made a lot of sense.

"I've been thinking about this," she said. "I understand your guilt, I really do. You've been through hell and had to make terrible decisions. But it's become clear to me that this is *not* your fault. It's *always* the Fey, Alex. And here, tonight, we stand up and we fight them again." She swept an arm out to encompass everything around them. "Fuck all this. You and me, with help from Jarrod, maybe Jean. No one else matters. We'll take all the help Armor can give us, but focus on ourselves. Focus on *our* fight, on taking it to the Fey. Because this is all their fault and fuck them for that!"

Alex smiled, genuinely warmed by her words. He leaned forward and kissed her. "You should be a motivational speaker."

She laughed, her hard, serious eyes softening for a moment. "Fuck you, too, Iron Balls." But she kissed him back.

"Still gonna take me a while to feel okay about any of this. Even if we win tonight. I'll always have those deaths on my hands, even if it was the Fey forcing me along."

Silhouette kissed him again. "And I'm here to help you. Always."

"You two got a mo?"

Silhouette snarled quietly at Emma Parker's voice. Alex smiled. "Hush." He turned to Parker. "Sure, what's up?"

"Not long to go. Thought we might brief you, talk strategy, all that."

"Fair enough."

As they moved to follow Parker back to the tented command center, Silhouette said, "Remember, you and me. Nothing else matters."

Alex nodded, something roiling through his gut. It was nerves in part, he could never deny that. But it was something else too. He had a bad feeling about all this.

For nearly an hour, Alex sat and listened to Armor operatives talk about binding magic and protective wards, arcane energy offense and old-fashioned ordnance and crossfire. There was no doubt these people were committed and organized. Every step of the way they asked him for his opinion and he could do little more than agree and accept their greater expertise.

Eventually they asked him about his own plans and his ability to fight Hood. They had offered to contain Hood entirely on their own and face the Lady and her Fey army, the presence of which there seemed little doubt about, using Alex as nothing more than the bait to lure them all in.

"No," Alex said. "This is first and foremost my fight. I'm sure you can hold Hood, but then what? Keep him in some cell somewhere? It's too risky. I had that fucker trapped underground in molten rock and he got out."

"Only because of his son," Parker said. "We plan to deal with Darvill too."

"Sure, and then who else? Hood has been in contact with Black Diamond. That company is powerful and well connected, you all know that. Who knows what he's put in motion."

"Alex is right," Jean said from the back. "Hood will be taking all kinds of precautions and setting up all sorts of contingencies. He is very smart and very cunning. Don't underestimate him."

Alex raised his palms. "You see? She knows what she's talking about. Hood needs to be dealt with. Permanently. And I think I have the tools to do it now. Maybe."

Emma Parker called for quiet as several voices fought for prominence. Silence slowly settled. "We have the means, hopefully, to contain Hood. But Alex is right. He can possibly finish the bastard. Besides, this is Alex's fight and we're here to assist him." Parker smiled as Silhouette burst out a sound of derision. "We will serve the greater good, Silhouette. But we will try to serve Alex first."

Silhouette's face was sour. "The greater good. Whatever."

"What remains," Alex said, before an argument could start, "is figuring out how to draw Hood to the Lady. We need to use Hood's anger and power to decimate the Fey ranks and hopefully mess up the Lady for us. How do we do that?"

Emma Parker shrugged. "That's up to you. You need to engage the Lady when she arrives, use our forces to fight the Fey, wait for Hood to wade in. If you or he can't subdue the Lady, we'll try to do it ourselves. You need to concentrate first on getting them all together and secondly on finishing Hood—without being caught or compromised by the Fey. We'll all be assisting you in that. Once Hood is gone, the Fey are neutralized or whatever and the thin day passes, we have all the time between now and the next one to figure out what to do about the Darak. The Fey will keep coming for it, after all."

"What about getting Hood here?" Alex asked.

Emma gestured towards Chang. "Good old Jean there has everything ready to go. We've already dropped the initial hints, right?"

Jean nodded, held up the tablet that seemed a permanent part of her. "Hood, or someone at Black Diamond, has accessed the information already. They know we're planning a deal and I've left clues to get them close. I'm sure Darvill is already scrying for us."

"And if the Fey show up, we release the last and most obvious hint," Parker said. "Hood sees it and comes barreling for you."

"If he hasn't worked it out already and arrived first!" Alex said, aghast. "Or it might take him hours to get here and we'd have to hold off the Fey all that time."

"Yes. Or fight them and win, or lose, or whatever. Ideally, we'll be able to have Hood come in quickly and let him and the Fey fight it out first."

"That's…" Alex groped for the right words. "That's fucking ridiculous!"

Emma laughed, shrugged. "This isn't a situation that's easy to plan for, Alex. There are so many possible permutations, so many variables. We know the Lady is coming for you and we've picked this place. We know Hood will come when he deciphers Jean's little Easter egg. Whether they arrive together or apart, who comes first, whether they'll even fight each other, it's all out of our control. This is the best we can manage.

And regardless, Armor is ready to face whatever threat arises. We fight each fight as it happens."

"Nebulous fucking plan," Alex said. "For all your talk and strategizing, we're really just preparing for an ongoing, all-out brawl."

Parker grinned at him. "Isn't that what you do best?"

CHAPTER TWENTY-NINE

n a flat in Soho, one of many properties with no legal link to Black Diamond but which were nonetheless company assets, Claude Darvill watched his father with mounting concern. Hood sat in one corner of the lounge room, crouched by the babbling television. His body was locked in a contraction of muscles so extreme, Claude wondered if the bones of any normal man would have shattered under such duress. Hood's eyes were squeezed tight, then would pop wide, close again. He muttered and ranted in a language Darvill had no hope of understanding, the words like oiled razors slipping through his ears.

Hood sprang up, stood tall and yelled, collapsed back into a squat. "So close. Close and open, stepping through. Freedom is within reach." Recognizable words devolved into that ancient, crabbed tongue again and Darvill turned away.

Hood had been in almost total control it seemed, at least for a little while. The presence of his passenger had taken a back seat to Hood's own psyche and the absurd trap they had set for Caine. Admittedly, that had been a lot of fun at first, but Caine had once again proven himself a most infuriating adversary. It if wasn't for the bloody Army, they would have had him. But Hood's frustration at their near miss was catastrophic. He had ranted and raved, smashed a swath of destruction through a part of London Claude didn't recognize and hoped to never see again. Finally, he had managed to convince his father to find somewhere to lay low and Hood had sunk into this state of compressed rage. It seemed his passenger was getting the better of him at last. He might regain control, but there was no guarantee of that.

Darvill had recently discovered Chang was using company resources to set something up between Caine and the Fey. Something massive and valuable. And that piece of news had been the final nail in the coffin of Hood's sanity, it seemed. Claude wondered if he could survive much longer in his father's presence. And Darvill was, if nothing else, a survivor. He had a habit of getting off the ride just before it jumped the rails. This one was nearly over.

Perhaps his father would regain some kind of control, perhaps he would even find and finally finish Caine. But Darvill would no longer be his partner. There were many opportunities in the world for a man of Claude's skills. Time to go.

He moved into the kitchen, grabbed his jacket and satchel from the table. The sword he had held onto so tightly was there too, and he strapped it back on. Its weight was comforting across his back. It might have been a weapon to use against his father, but he was glad he wouldn't have to. For all his distasteful habits and the atrocities he had committed, he was reluctant to add patricide to his litany of crimes. That man curled in broken agony in the front room had been a terrible father most of the time, but he had forged Claude into the man he was today. There had to be some vestigial respect for that, at least. Much better to quietly slip away and simply remove himself from this whole situation than end up facing a devastating confrontation. Especially as Claude himself was quite likely to finish up worse off in that eventuality. Permanently worse off.

Maybe in a little while, even some years hence, he could figure out a way to make Caine pay for all of this. Now was not the time. With a deep breath, let out as a sigh of resignation, he nodded softly to himself. Harsh, but fair. In Claude Darvill's life, the safety of Claude Darvill came first.

Arms like iron clamped around his chest, pinned his arms to his sides. He yelped in pain and surprise.

"Thinking of going somewhere?" Hood growled in his ear.

"Dad, no. What do you mean? I'm just…"

Hood squeezed tighter, Darvill's ribs cracking in protest. "Don't fucking bullshit me, son!"

"You're hurting me!" Panic washed through Darvill. He had left it too late after all. He cursed himself, cursed his ridiculous need to try to build something with his father. He should have walked out on this ludicrous situation long ago, and that knowledge burned.

"Can't let you go, son, no. We need you."

"We?"

"Everyone. Us. Them. Hahaha! It's all so confusing, but clarity comes from purpose, no? And my purpose is clear. Caine must be finished. We might have failed before, but oh, so very, very close! But Caine, yes? Caine!" Hood lifted Darvill and turned him back towards the front room. "Father and son together."

Darvill cried out as Hood squeezed tighter. A blanket of darkness descended over his vision and mind, some thick presence beyond the pain. He sensed something else with them in the apartment, something terrible. As consciousness slipped away, he wondered if he felt what his father did—the presence of that unfathomable passenger inside him.

Alex walked with Silhouette and Jarrod into the middle of the open battleground. A slight hiss sounded constantly in his left ear from an earpiece Parker had given him. He had a small mic clipped inside his collar, off until he was ready to activate it, and a couple of tracking devices on his belt and boot, in case things got too hectic in the wide open space and Armor needed to pinpoint him quickly.

He flexed his hands, tingling with the early rush of adrenaline. He had stepped onto the mat, into the ring, into the cage so many times before. Walking out to fight was nothing new to him. He remembered Joseph's den in London, Silhouette's old home. The challenge he had risen to then, stepping up to fight Ataro, and the sickening bloodlust of his win. That all seemed so long ago.

He breathed deeply, kept his focus, relaxed in the knowledge the Fey might come through any minute or hours hence. No point holding any tension, it would only fatigue him as time passed. Hood and Darvill might show up any moment or not at all. It was all so bloody nebulous. So he relaxed, but remained ready.

He gripped Silhouette's hand. She squeezed back. Jarrod stood huge and implacable beside them. Alex was under no illusion of their role here. Regardless of the platitudes of Parker and others, they were nothing more than bait. This was war. A war Armor had been looking forward to for a long time if the subtext of all Parker's speeches was to be believed, an excuse to actively engage the Fey. Alex was savvy enough to recognize that. And he was also sure Armor would happily trap Hood and keep him locked away somehow if they had to. Alex, Silhouette and Jarrod could all die within seconds of the Fey's arrival, whether Hood showed up or not, and Armor wouldn't give a fuck. Alex and his friends were just more expendable soldiers in the big fight, useful but ultimately irrelevant. In fact, Armor would probably prefer it if he did die, perhaps even before the battle, thereby removing finally the Fey threat. But a couple of things kept him alive. One was the hope he could actually finish Hood forever. The other was the possibility that even if he died, the Lady would have figured out a way to save the Darak. He was sure if those things weren't so unclear, Armor would have killed him already. And he could hardly blame them for that. Yet he also knew they would gladly have him on board as an operative, if he was no longer a threat to the world. He begrudgingly admired their pragmatism. They thought like a fighter, considering only the things necessary to win, keeping all their contingencies open.

"You guys don't have to be here," he said quietly, knowing it was pointless, but needing to say the words anyway. "I'm the bait, I'm the only one who needs to stand in the wide open cold fucking night and face death."

"We're going nowhere," Silhouette said quietly. "I told you, we're a team. Stand or go down together."

Alex squeezed her hand again. He glanced up at Jarrod's profile, shadowed in the dark. "She loves me, so she's fucking mental. But you don't have to be here, mate."

Jarrod turned to look down, teeth bright in the gloom as he smiled. "I love you too, Alex." He smacked his lips in a ridiculous blown kiss.

Alex laughed, clapped the big man on one meaty shoulder. "I really appreciate your help."

Jarrod looked out over the grass again, his eyes serious. "I have an investment in this too. Almost everyone I know and care about died in Sydney at Hood's hands. And Silhouette is one of the few people left in the world who means anything to me. And we hardly know each other." He smiled again, but it was a sadder smile. "We're all pretty much family, us three. The only family we've each got, right?"

Alex nodded gently, keenly feeling their isolation even as hundreds of people watched them. "I guess so."

Jarrod returned Alex's pat on the shoulder. "Stand or go down together."

They lapsed into silence as they waited. Distant sounds drifted to them, occasional muffled shouts of orders, a muted generator, a vehicle firing up and driving away.

Alex started at Emma's sudden voice in his ear, though she spoke softly, calmly. "The day is thin, gate sensors alive. All scans on wide. The realms are close, Alex."

Alex reached up, clicked the small switch to activate his mic. "Game on," he said to Silhouette and Jarrod. "I'm leaving the mic on now."

"Trackers are sending a clear signal," Emma reported. "As there's been no sign of Hood, Chang has sent the final encryptions. As soon as they unlock that, they'll know exactly where to find us."

Alex drew a deep breath, rolled his shoulders. "Fey could come through any time. Hood's been given the information. Stay alert."

Silhouette turned suddenly, grabbed him and kissed him passionately, urgently, almost violently. "After this, we go to the Lake District," she said. "And we drink and fuck, and nothing else, for months!"

Alex laughed despite the tension in the air. "Deal. Although, we might have to eat occasionally too."

"Promise me!"

"I promise."

She smiled, kissed him again.

"Maybe I'll join you for the eating and drinking for a few days," Jarrod said in his deep, rumbling voice. "But I'll stay in my own room."

Alex grinned. Silhouette chuckled and Alex's grin became a laugh. Within moments all three were cracking up, shaking their heads, lost in the absurdity of everything.

"Oh, man," Alex said, wiping an eye.

"Try to concentrate please." Emma's voice was clipped, officious.

Alex laughed again. "Oh, fuck you, Emma Parker. Just watch your screens and what-the-hell-ever else you've got there."

They pulled themselves together, slowly calming. The minutes ticked by, the tension built again.

As the wait dragged on, the strain increased. Minutes stretched and became an hour. Alex and Silhouette shared occasional small bites of irrelevant conversation, aware that Parker and most of Armor were listening in. Jarrod remained silent and solid as a statue. Emma Parker whispered time updates every now and then, probably for something to do more than for any real point of reference. Who cared what time it was? Alex just wanted to fight. He was charged up, ready, swollen with new magic, and completely fucking sick of waiting. And he knew something was wrong. Hood, at least, should be here by now.

"Why the fuck is this taking so long?" Alex burst out. "Seriously, neither Hood nor the Lady here yet? Seems…" He stopped dead. A light glittered in the distance, blue-white and surreal. "You seeing this?" he whispered.

Emma Parker and Silhouette spoke simultaneously. "Yes."

"What is it?" Jarrod asked.

Emma's voice again. "We have a seer reporting a gate opened one kilometer west, directly behind that light. Delta group has visual, they report one person on foot."

"Fey?" Alex asked.

"Wait…can you confirm? Double-check. Okay. Alex, yes, definitely Fey. Delta can clearly see. It's making no effort to conceal itself, but is in human form. Female."

Silhouette and Jarrod each moved a little to either side of Alex as he flexed and stretched again, warming up his joints. He drew on his arcane power, felt the Darak warm through his chest, down into his gut. "Let's do this."

The figure approached slowly, bluish light swirled around her like smoke. She wore a long dress, emerald green and shining, her hair thick, equally green tresses that tumbled over her shoulders. As she walked, the full moon began to emerge over the distant hills, the night lightening subtly as it rose. The combination of the woman's shades was convoluted as she worked some magic Alex couldn't decode.

He breathed down his adrenaline. Something wasn't right here. "Any other activity, Emma?"

"No, nothing. All units stand ready. I want to know what that Fey bitch is doing! Alex, is it the Lady?"

"No. At least, not the human form she wore when she had me."

The woman got to within five meters of Alex and stopped. She smiled, her face quite beautiful in the soft moonlight that shimmered off her hair and dress, but her expression exuded disdain. "You people," she said, almost too quietly to be heard. "You are just so hilarious." She lifted her arms out to either side and the blue light swirling around her increased.

"What is that stuff?" Emma said, annoyance and incomprehension clear.

And Alex realized, too late. "It's a decoy!" he shouted at the same moment as wind pressed down from above and something snatched at his shoulders with painful sharpness. He cried out as he was whipped up and away with enough force to strain his neck and back. The ground dropped away like a stone, the glowing blue figure shrank to a dot in the night. Emma's voice was frantic, her words lost in the rushing wind, then silence but for the howl of passing air.

Alex strained to see what had him. Chitinous hooked feet drew blood from his shoulders that soaked into his shirt and he had a moment of panic as he remembered the Subcontractor before his eyes took in shimmering, iridescent scales. Wind whipped around him and thrust down at him and he realized it wasn't all due to his own forward motion. Huge diaphanous wings blurred above. The thing was a machine, the chitin actually highly polished metal, so beautifully crafted it looked alive. Opening his vision, he saw subtle magesign swirling around it, silencing its physical noise, the shades so fine, the magic so carefully crafted as to be almost invisible even when he looked for it. It had no other aura for the hundreds of arcane operatives around the battlefield to see coming. All along they had stood prepared for an invasion of Fey, then been distracted by a single one as a fucking machine swept him away.

The grip on his shoulders prevented too much movement and the air was even colder with altitude. He dare not risk damaging this thing and dropping what appeared to be thousands of meters to the ground. He recalled catching the bus with air and wondered if he could do that for himself, but didn't trust the accuracy of his ability.

Besides, the woman had been Fey. This was a Fey device. Whatever else was happening, it would take him to her, the Lady. Hood would have to wait. Maybe Armor would get their shot at him after all. He glanced left and right and realized Silhouette and Jarrod were with him, struggling against their own mechanical dragonfly captors.

"Relax!" he called out. "Let them take us wherever they're going. Save your energy to fight when we get there, but keep your shields strong. Don't let the Lady shackle your magic. We're on our own now."

CHAPTER THIRTY

Their bizarre flight was short and swift. As Alex's stomach turned with a sudden descent, he heard Silhouette cry out his name. He craned his neck to see her sweeping away out of sight. He stretched out one hand, winced at the pain in his shoulder. "Silhouette!"

Her eyes were wide in the night as she disappeared from view. The creature carrying Jarrod shot past, following her into darkness. Alex watched the ground fast approaching, fury burning up from his gut.

He was carried low over a small town and a patchwork of fields like a soft, dark green mosaic in the moonlight. Long ridges approached, ending in high, curving half-bowls, the whole landscape like four giant fingers had pressed into the earth and left their imprint for eternity. Behind the ridges, the mechanical insect carried Alex down into a long, deep valley. It rose high and steep on one side, shallower and wider on the other. A small river carved its way through. The valley floor looked like a concave closed eye from above. He saw a crowd down there, a host most definitely not human.

He shored up his shields, remembered the Lady's hideous shackling magic and built iron-clad walls against it. He hoped. He had had time to consider these defenses and silently prayed they would hold. He let his energy build behind his wards, physically vibrating with adrenaline, anger, anticipation.

The giant bug lowered him towards the valley. Hundreds of Fey in their gangly, stutter-moving form shifted in a crowd, all casting glowing amber eyes skyward to watch his approach. At the head of the valley the Lady sat astride a giant stag, massive antlers curving up before her like trees. She shimmered in her human form, her dress an arterial scarlet of swirling silk and smoke. Alex was brought to within a hundred meters of the Lady, the stuttering host milling beneath him, and the bug hovered some thirty meters off the ground. Even from such a distance, he could see the burning fury in the Lady's eyes. Behind her, three of the huge dragonfly machines stood vertical, balanced on unmoving tail and wings. Their shining, hinged legs formed a cage around each of the captives. Silhouette and Jarrod were two of them, Sil struggling angrily against the bars of her jail. Jarrod hung still, implacable. Alex's heart skipped as he recognized, between them, Claude Darvill, similarly trapped, his face a mixture of anger and fear.

Alex looked more closely at the ground, searched the throng milling in front of the Lady's stag, and there he was. Robert Hood, pale head like a tiny moon in the crowd, leering up. His eyes were dark, yet there seemed to be little emotion showing through. He stared as if dreaming.

The Lady's laughter drifted to him, before her voice rang out, preternaturally loud. "You think me so stupid as to walk into your trap, you dancing monkey? You think to *challenge me*?" Her voice cracked through the night with its rage, boomed off the valley walls. "We may be restricted in realms, but we are not fools, Alex Caine. We have wisdom of ages you could not imagine."

As she spoke, Alex searched for any advantage, any way to turn this situation to something close to an even match. He squinted for a better look at Claude and saw something long and dark protruding past the trapped man's shoulder. He could use that, maybe. His gaze drifted back to Hood as the Fey moved slowly away from him, leaving the pale man alone in a clearing in their midst. Hood wore a dark suit and black shoes that glinted in the moonlight.

"You thought to use this *man* against us?" the Lady spat. "You have gall, Caine, I'll give you that. But you think us so useless? Uthentia was ever *our* dumb beast! He may be a creature of unimaginable power and strength, but only unimaginable to *you*. He is our trained ape and always will be!"

Hood thrashed, spittle flew from his lips, his eyes squinting with effort. He growled and shouted incoherently, his face a mask of frustration and anger.

"You see how even now the human tries to master the godling inside? And tries to deny *my* sway?" the Lady said, amusement in her tone. "You will move when *I* say you may move, Hood! He thought himself in control of it. In control of the influence of Uthentia! The arrogance of it. You know yourself the futility of that, don't you, Caine? Yet remarkably, you found a way to cast off that power, and put it in this Robert Hood. No matter. He's our tool now."

Hood danced in impotent rage, as if he fought invisible assailants. The Lady barked some staccato words and he staggered, stilled, and became immobile, staring blank-faced at Alex. But his eyes were alive, burning with a furious passion.

The Lady's laughter rolled through the valley like thunder. "Funny though, his over-riding desire is to see you dead. I cannot say I disagree with that sentiment. And I've devised a way to preserve what I want from you *after* your death. Did you really think us incapable of this task? We just needed time. Magic is the air we breathe, you brief flesh. Oh, I couldn't be happier. So I plan to let Mr Hood have his desire, but under my terms. And you did so often beg me for death. You shall have it."

Alex realized the time for listening to this creature's self-indulgence was over. He didn't know if it was a bluff or not, but if she had a way to take the Darak after his death, he was a whole new kind of fucked. And why would she set Hood on him if she was lying? Now simply killing himself was no longer an option. He had to fight. And he had to win. A strange calm rose in him. Single-minded purpose, and a fight to be won.

He looked at the ground and decided he had to chance it. The drop was probably deadly, but he had learned a lot with his recent experiences. He drew on all the power he had hoarded inside and gathered every bit of air and wind around himself. He let the immense might of the Darak flood into his muscles, gripped the metallic legs that held him and heaved them apart. He dropped like a stone. The green floor of the valley rushed up to meet him in a crushing embrace.

The Lady screamed, "Get him!" and the Fey surged apart to let Robert Hood stride forward.

Alex waited until the last millisecond, heart hammering with adrenaline, and concentrated all the air he had called into a blast of wind at his back. As the ground was about to smash him to pieces, he shot forward, carried at eye-watering pace by the jet of air slamming into him, directly over the heads of the rushing Hood and the gathered Fey. The Lady cried out, her eyes going wide as he barreled towards her. He felt her magic slam into him, her enchantment designed to cancel his ability, to trap it within him. For a moment he gasped in pain, his arcane strength flexing under her barrage, but his shields held. He had the measure of her magic now. He hit her like a cannonball, sent her tumbling from her mount.

The impact completely disrupted his trajectory. He had no control over his flight and hit the hard earth with a burst of forcibly expelled breath. He tumbled, rolled, came up running. He focused only on Claude Darvill, trapped between Silhouette and Jarrod.

"Don't fight them!" Silhouette screamed. "Get away!"

"No, Sil. This is where I stand!"

He rushed for Darvill and slammed a punch between the huge dragonfly's embracing legs, cracking Darvill into surprised unconsciousness.

Alex reached in and hauled out the sword from its scabbard across Darvill's back and dropped, rolled sideways and stood behind the dragonfly to use it as a shield.

He was not a moment too soon, as the Lady's magic blistered into the ground where he had stood, a crackling bolt of electric green. Alex ducked around and sliced through the legs on one side of the dragonfly holding Silhouette. The metal sheared away like butter and Sil dropped from her cage, morphed into panther form as she fell, and hit the ground running. She bolted from sight as Alex twisted and hacked to the other side. But the mechanical beast holding Jarrod had already whirred into life, began to rise from the ground. Alex's blow clipped only the lowest leg, severing it. Jarrod began to struggle against the remaining bonds, but Alex had no time to see if he escaped as more of the Lady's crackling magic burst against him, searing into his shields and wards.

He staggered backwards, pain flaring even against his protections. He smelled his hair burning, saw his clothes crisp, and turned. He ran, ducked behind the creature that had held Silhouette, still motionless and inert.

Claude's voice called out, slurred and thick as he regained semi-consciousness. "Let me out! I can help you!"

Alex laughed. "Fuck you, Darvill. I gave you every chance you'll ever get."

Alex ran, let his magic flood his system and powered preternaturally enhanced legs up the shallower slope of the valley. Fey swarmed across the valley floor, Robert Hood at their head. The Lady stood, glorious, furious, surrounded by a nimbus of raw power. Alex breathed deep, desperate to control the adrenaline that surged through him. He was against ridiculous odds, facing the Lady and Hood simultaneously, the pair of them backed by hundreds of Fey. And Armor miles away. It was insane. Suicide.

He ducked into a crease of rock and grass as more of the Lady's sizzling magefire burned past him. "Just kill him!" she shouted. "And bring his corpse to me before he cools, or you will all pay!"

A thought flitted past Alex's mind. *Before I cool?* Perhaps her magic to save the Darak was only good in the instants after his death. If he died and stayed out of her grasp for long enough, perhaps the Darak would be unrecoverable after all. Perhaps was not good enough.

He leapt from cover as the pounding, stammering Fey forms flicker-ran and drew close. Their hands raised and crackling magefire burst forth. Their long legs outpaced Hood and he heard the man howling frustration from their midst. Alex had never felt more alive, his magic never stronger. The Darak pulsed rapidly, hammering in time with his heart, and he let his magesign surround him, let his shades bulge out into a shield of pure will. The Fey attacks burst and splashed against his defenses, dissipating in all directions. The sword he wielded felt alive in his hands, even deflected some of the assaults, Fey howling as the magic ricocheted into them. The tricks Emma had taught him, in conjunction with his own experience and the amazing weapon, were proving most effective. But for how long? He couldn't maintain this level of effort indefinitely.

Alex laughed, rushing hard on adrenaline, fear, exultation. He ducked forward, drove his mind and his magic into the earth in front of him and agitated it up into a wave of soil and rock and shale, pulling the very ground from underneath the advancing Fey like a giant rug. Some of them, sharper-eyed, more fleet of foot, leapt and dodged, avoided the tsunami of substrate. As they landed and rushed Alex, he swept Darvill's arcane blade in a wide arc, laughed maniacally as it passed through three Fey bodies with ease. They fell, gouting gore, and he had barely felt the drag of the blow. All kinds of magic hammered his shields, but for now at least, his protections held. The Fey tried to surround him, shifted into monstrous forms of tooth and claw, blasted him with arcane flames.

He moved with graceful ease, his years of training working without conscious thought. He danced left and right, shot forward and back, marveled at the deadly power of the weapon he wielded as Fey fell before him in droves. His swordsmanship was skilled. He was never more thankful for the traditional weapons training of his ancient system of *kung fu*, and coupled with this sword he felt invincible. The hilt pulsed in his hands as if alive. He switched from single to double-handed strokes and sweeps with ease, the sword a flawless partner in a sublime ballet of martial perfection.

With the more agile attackers dealt with, Alex dodged bolts of the Lady's glittering fire and ran for the ridge top before the others could regain their footing. He heard Hood's roar as the man pushed through to get to him. The words of Sun Tzu, eternal wisdom from *The Art of War*, flashed in his mind. *You can and must choose the ground over which you battle.* There was no question he was at war now and he needed to take active control of anything he could. This valley was the Lady's chosen arena. He needed to establish his own.

"Fall back," the Lady yelled. "Let the Hood creature have him!"

Even as she spoke, she threw more blistering fire at him, but Alex's senses were alive like never before. He saw with a clarity born of absolute need and easily leapt aside, sweeping the sword in a defensive arc as he moved. The sea of Fey rolled back and he stared down the steep slope into the dark, angry eyes of Robert Hood.

Hood ground his teeth, winced and peeled back his lips with the effort of trying to retain some autonomous control. Alex could see the struggle raging behind the lunatic's eyes.

"I may be somewhat compromised," Hood spat between clenched teeth. "But if nothing else, I will see you dead this night, Alex fucking Caine!" Hood staggered as some invisible bond was released and he ran forward, head low, arms pumping.

"Bring it, you pain in my arse!" Alex yelled, and ran for the top of the ridge. The ground leveled off a little before the top, became grassier, and Alex sprinted across it. He dived over the crest to find himself on a similar gradient slope leading down the other side, another thin river glittering at the bottom among rocky outcrops. He glanced left and smiled to see the river feeding into a huge lake in the valley floor. Narrow, constrained by the geography, it stretched maybe two kilometers in length. There was his battleground.

He gained his feet and ran down, traversing the steep side to make the descent easier and give him a chance to see the lay of the land, all the time heading for the center of the lake's length. The full moon rode high, illuminating the few wisps of cloud in the otherwise clear, cold sky. It limned the ground in silvery light, almost as bright as day, glittered reflections on the water below.

As he ran, movement caught his eye. He braced, raised the sword high over his right shoulder, ready to sweep it down. A smokey gray cat loped over to him, morphed into Silhouette as she reached him and gathered him into a tight hug.

"Alex, come on. We have to run."

"No. I'm standing here. This is where I fight."

Silhouette's eyes widened. "Against those odds? Are you insane?"

"I might be. No time to talk, they're coming. I don't believe for a second she really wants the Fey to fall back. She'll send Hood to occupy me while they flank me."

Hood appeared at the crest of the ridge and hollered Alex's name. He tipped forward and barreled straight towards them.

Silhouette dragged at Alex's arm. "You can't face an army on your own, Alex! Please!"

He finally paused, took her chin gently in one hand, kissed her. "I have to fight. The Lady is here and she controls Hood. Think about the implications of that!"

Silhouette nodded, shrugged. "Right. Then I fight with you." She held up a hand. "Fuck you, Iron Balls, together or not at all."

He kissed her again. "And Jarrod?"

Her face saddened briefly. "I don't know."

"Alex Caine!" Hood roared again as he closed the distance.

Alex caught Silhouette's attention, his eyes intense. "Use your cat form, keep moving, take out fuckers from the edges. Make space for me to face him."

Silhouette held his gaze one second more, nodded. She slipped into her graceful feline shape and melted away. In the night, even bathed in moonlight, she was better camouflaged than a shadow.

Alex turned and pounded down the slope, heading straight for the lake.

"Face me, Caine!" Hood yelled behind him.

Alex let momentum carry him, legs flying, hoping desperately he didn't trip and fall. As the lake neared, he cast his will towards it, used his elemental skills to gather the water together, draw its molecules tight, thicken it as his foot hit the edge. Like wet rubber, it held his weight. He put his mind at every point his foot headed and ran from land straight across without breaking stride. "Like Jesus fucking Christ!" he shouted with a laugh and sprinted across the five hundred or so meters to the other side.

Hood growled in anger and frustration, but didn't slow. He splashed furiously into the water and kept running, got deeper and deeper, grimacing against the effort of keeping up his pace against the wet drag. His head went under and Alex knew the man still ran, driving his feet into the lake bed.

For a moment, there was calm. Alex backed away from the lake's far edge, the huge body of water between him and the Fey army. They would hopefully have to come around, but even if they came through it would buy him time.

With a roar and a furious splashing, Hood burst into the air on the edge right before him, still running.

Alex raised the sword and moved backwards as he called out to Hood, "Come on then, you useless fucking tool."

Hood snarled, gathering speed. Alex continued back. He slipped his mind between the rocks at his feet. As Hood closed the distance, almost close enough to touch, Alex leapt up, splitting the rock he left behind. The stone crumbled, a fissure opened in the earth, and Hood found himself running on air. His momentum kept him moving and he fell and tumbled, flipping and bouncing with bone-jarring impact.

Alex knew the fall would do Hood no damage, but it would disorient the bastard. Alex landed, drew breath to focus and let his consciousness form the shape of the Eld magic he had learned from Halliday's grimoire. It felt stronger this time around, more natural, more contained. But it was still massively powerful, designed to be wielded by a team. It stretched and tore at the edges of Alex's mind, pushed and ground at his muscles and bones. With a howl of pain, he let it go, tried to focus it in a tight, narrow blast, intending to blow Hood into a million tiny shards.

But the release was more shotgun blast than rifle shot. The earth exploded around the tumbling Hood, bursting up like a mine had gone off. Hood flew up with it, a rag doll and screaming. He landed heavily, rolled bonelessly across the grass and rock, yelling in pain. His flesh was split and torn, his head and face striated with damage like a cracked hardboiled egg. He staggered groggily to his feet, keening in some combination of hurt and fury, even as his body reknitted.

Alex ran at him, gathering the magic again as he moved. As Hood shook his head to clear his sight, crouched for impact, Alex let the Eld sorcery out again. Hood braced as if against a terrible wind, his expression twisting in pain as his skin split and flayed. Sheets of flesh tore from his face, fluttering back behind him like leaves in a stiff autumn breeze. He opened his mouth wide, teeth exposed, lips gone, and yelled some broken, crabbed phrase in a language Alex hoped never to hear again.

Alex closed the gap and brought his sword arcing around. Hood raised both arms to protect himself and the blade bit deep into the flesh and bone, and wedged there. The weapon that had easily carved through three Fey torsos stopped dead halfway through Hood's skinny forearms.

Hood laughed, his visage hideous as skin and muscle grew back across his skull like fast forward film of mold spreading. He laughed and twisted, his immense strength lifting Alex by the sword, and he threw his body sideways. Alex refused to relinquish his grip on the hilt and it dragged for a fraction of a second before ripping free of Hood like an axe from stubborn hardwood.

Alex hit the ground and rolled. Hood glanced briefly at his cleaved forearms as they healed, eyes wide in shock and more than a little anger, then rushed forward. Alex had no time to get the sword up to defend himself, could only thrust out one leg. His heel caught Hood low in the gut and the thin man bent double over it, breath bursting out. Alex twisted, drove his upper back into the ground, used his power to turn his other leg steel hard and whipped a kick across Hood's head.

Hood slammed sideways and Alex rolled with the motion of his attack, regained his feet. He drew the sword high, but Hood was fast. He sprang back and drove both fists into Alex's chest.

Alex's vision crossed, white sparks of pain danced through his eyes as he was lifted up and back, all breath gone. He thought his heart would burst. He hit the ground, rolled, forced himself onto hands and knees, the sword blade reflecting moonlight across the grass as he pushed his knuckles down, refused to collapse. His eyes watered, his throat wheezed as he desperately dragged air in. His muscles, jelly weak, threatened to drop him face-first onto the dirt. His ribs felt cracked from the impact of Hood's fists and Alex focused on that pain, used it to drive himself on. He caught movement from the corner of his eye and came up onto his knees, whipped the sword wildly across in front of him. It thudded into something and jammed there and Hood yelled.

Alex blinked his vision clear, saw his blade stuck in Hood's upper left arm even as Hood's right arm hammered down. Alex raised his free hand and met the jarring impact as he drove his will into the limb to strengthen it. He felt his bones bend and threaten to snap, his knees dug into the earth, but he held. He wrenched the sword free, drove himself to his feet and kicked out, his heel thrusting up under Hood's chin. The indestructible bastard lifted clean off his feet, flew backwards.

"You might be strong and hard to kill, but you're no fucking fighter!" Alex shouted and ran forward. He swung the sword again, double-handed, swiping fast and continuous figure eights with the blade across Hood's fallen form.

Hood flailed both arms in front of his face, yelled incoherently as gaps were sliced open in his flesh. He kicked out, forcing Alex to jump backwards to avoid being swept to the ground. In the moment's reprieve, Hood leapt to his feet and backed up. They faced each other across several meters of rock-strewn, moonlit grass.

Alex kept his eyes focused on Hood, but in his peripheral vision he saw movement, above to the right, and further along the ridge. He circled, tried to see back the other way and saw movement there too. The Fey horde was advancing from all along the crest, splitting in two groups as they headed for either end of the lake to come around and pincer him. Any moment they would surely start to unleash magical attacks across the water. His battleground was quickly becoming compromised, but he had some time. He redoubled the concentration of his shields.

A flash of gray shot along the ridge high to one side and a flurry of movement burst out. He smiled inwardly—Silhouette running interference for him. But it was small consolation. There was little she could really do against the hundreds of Fey out there. He dodged as Hood bullrushed him, spun on his heel and dropped to one knee, brought the sword blade whistling around at the back of Hood's knee.

Hood howled and collapsed, the blade wedged more than halfway through the limb. Alex wrenched it free. Hood stumbled to his feet, staggered and tripped on his useless leg before it closed over and was whole once more. He grinned. "You may be able to nip at me like a little dog, Caine, but you are no real threat."

Alex knew his strength was waning. Fatigue started to bite deep at his bones. He drew on the Darak, focused the Eld magic, hefted the reassuring weight of the powerful sword. "I'm more of a threat… than you realize," he said, his voice a breathless hiss. But his focus was still sharp.

All things are duality, Alex, all things yin and yang. From the purely physical, hand and foot working in unison, to the spiritual, body and mind united, acting as one. All things are more powerful when combined, all things weak in isolation. His Sifu's words echoed across the years. Alex had things he needed to combine.

He ran forward, let the blast of Eld magic go. It slammed into Hood, drove him backwards, and Alex ran with it. He tried to focus the mental attack on Hood's limbs and grinned as the suit shredded away, the flesh splitting and fracturing beneath like snapped wood. Hood roared, drove his heels into the ground to return the attack and Alex swung the sword, aimed for a point on Hood's arm where it seemed the magic had done the most damage. Where Hood's flesh was broken, Alex sliced, and he yelled in triumph as Hood's left arm severed just below the elbow.

The limb spun away, hit the dirt still twitching, the fingers grabbing at air. Hood stopped, stared dumbfounded at the stump. "No!"

Alex gathered and released the magic again, ducked low with it as Hood struck out wildly with his right arm. The Eld incantation blistered into Hood's legs and Alex concentrated on a point just above the knee where the magic damaged most deeply, and swept the sword into the gap. The blade passed through and Hood fell screaming. Alex rolled up onto his feet, kicked the heavy limb away.

Hood pushed his remaining hand into the ground, rose up on knee and leg stump, his face a mask of disbelief and horror. Alex heard some deep, throbbing sound, imagined the hordes of Fey hammering around either end of the lake at him and knew he had to finish this. He drew everything he had and blasted out the Eld magic once more, hit Hood full in the face and chest with the wide, devastating blast of it. He focused on the man's neck, watched the flesh strip away at the throat and brought his blade whistling around. Hood's head spun up and away, howling his defiance and pain as he went. Alex kept the blade moving, kept his magic flowing out and hacked again, and again, divided Hood's body into pieces. The right arm went one way, the torso cleaved in two, then three parts and Alex kicked them all away from each other.

As he gasped for breath, prepared to turn and face whatever came next, the throbbing became a deafening staccato barrage and he realized choppers were sweeping low over the valley. Mounted weapons flashed as ordnance exploded into the ground. Fifty caliber rounds tore up earth, water and Fey alike, air to ground missiles burst in concussive explosions of sound and light. Blasts of magic jetted from the Fey on the ground, wrapped the helicopters in wreaths of flickering blue and green flame. One aircraft went down, its rotors decimating a dozen Fey even as it hit the earth and crumpled in a burst of metal and glass. The others passed over, banked, came around for another pass. More blasts of magic arced from their open doors as Armor battlemages cast their attacks from the air.

Alex staggered away from the turmoil, dragged breath into his lungs.

"Cavalry's here," said a voice behind him. "Your tracking devices are obviously working."

Alex spun around, sword rising, and grinned to see Jarrod. The big man was soaked through. "You made it."

"Yeah. You gave me enough room to wiggle free. Fortunately, the dumb robot bug flew over a lake and I took the chance it was deep enough to catch me."

"Good to see you."

Jarrod looked Alex up and down. "You okay?"

"Kinda. Need a minute."

They looked back across the lake to the battle in full swing between Armor and the Fey. Shadows shifted to their right and Silhouette stood up into the moonlight. She grabbed Alex in an embrace. He hugged her back. "Thanks, Sil."

She laughed. "I did pretty much fuck-all, really. Way too many. I just tried to hamper them a bit." She held up her pouch of healing powder, one eyebrow raised.

Alex poked a finger into the glittering dust, took a generous dose and rubbed it onto his gums. Not the same as drinking the potion, but still he felt its healing rush through his body. "Come on, we need to move."

"Where?"

"There's no way this is over. Armor may be engaging the Fey, but the Lady is not dumb. She'll be…"

Silhouette's eyes widened and she screamed as Jarrod grabbed her and spun around, hugged her to his huge chest. Alex turned to see as green fire exploded over them, threw them apart with blistering heat and sent agonizing electric tendrils through every part of them. "You despicable worm!" The Lady strode forward, still in human form, her dress more smoke than silk. She appeared like an avenging angel of blood, wreathed in swirling colors reflecting moonlight.

Alex rolled to his feet as her magic burned out again. He threw up his shields and stumbled back under the force of her attack, but the fire didn't get through. He saw Jarrod sprawled across the grass some ten meters away, Silhouette lying half obscured beneath the big man. He refused to acknowledge their scorched flesh and limp, unmoving forms. He turned back to face the Fey woman.

He cursed himself for pausing for breath. He knew the Lady would focus on him at the expense of all else. He felt Silhouette's powder still coursing through his veins and realized it was all that had prevented the magefire from doing to him what it had done to Jarrod and Silhouette. If Sil was dead now, after all this…Rage bubbled up in him like a volcano.

The Lady raised both hands, fingers crooked like claws, and shifted back to her Fey shape. Her bark-like skin seemed to glow green, her burning amber eyes like tiny suns, incandescent in her fury. She rose up, growing to some nine feet tall, towering over Alex as she stutter-stepped like a dancer in a strobe light towards him. "You will not deny me what's left of my Lord's heart, you pathetic mortal!"

Alex raised the sword, forced his body to respond to his will. He gathered energy and focused it through the Darak. Fatigue dragged at him like anchors tied to every limb, but he refused to give in now. This was the last chance, the final confrontation. "Your Lord's heart was a fucking abomination in the first place, you bitch! He got everything he deserved and you will never get it back!"

The Lady tipped her head back and laughed. "You think us so easily defeated, human? I don't need you alive any more. I can extract what you stole from me and my people can restore its original strength."

Alex hefted the sword, tightened his grip. "You never fail to underestimate me!"

"You dare to face *me*?" She circled him as she spoke and Alex realized she was cautious, for all her bluster. Her hands were raised, magesign crackled around her, ready to unleash, but she stayed her attack. Perhaps, finally, she had realized he really was a threat. It bought him some time, at least. But the true threat was the Darak, and always had been.

She whipped her hands forward. Green fire crackled out and Alex braced his shields even as half a dozen Fey burst from hiding and rushed him. Bitch. He should have known better. And he did know her tactics. He ignored the newcomers and ran straight at the Lady, whipping his sword across as he came. The Lady screeched, magefire crackled past him, and she leapt backwards. He kept moving, tried to run her down.

"Fey rules don't apply here! You can't run from me." Alex swept the sword back, aiming for the Lady's outstretched arms.

She whipped her hands away, ducked to the ground and morphed into some animal form. She slipped to the side and Alex had to let her go as the other Fey closed on him. He let his mind empty, let his vision work independent of thought and stepped sideways and back, forward and sideways, the sword sweeping and glittering with expert skill. Everything it touched separated without a moment's drag. Fey limbs and heads littered the ground. They gathered their magic and magefire arced from fingertips, scorched against his shields. Alex felt his wards weakening with his fatigue and their sustained attacks, felt the burn and electric sear of their assault getting through. But still he danced in combat.

It took only moments and the six Fey were down, dismembered, decapitated. And new fire smashed Alex to the ground, drove the air from his body. He rolled, tried to gain his hands and feet, and was flattened by another blast. It burned away his shields, his skin blistered, his clothes incinerated. The shackling magic came again, but Alex's defense against that held. "I've seen the shape of your magic and I can resist it!" he yelled.

Her fire came again. "Can you resist *this*?" The pain was tremendous and Alex screamed. He gathered all the elements together, blasted the Lady with heat and raging wind, exploded the earth at her feet. She threw out shields, a bubble of magic deflecting his attack as she rose above the churning earth, untouched by all his efforts.

"I have had enough of you!" the Lady shrieked, and raised her hands again.

Gasping in the last of his breath, Alex whipped his arm up, threw the sword with all his remaining strength. It spun flat through the air like a boomerang, its edge glittering in the moonlight. Alex pushed air beneath it, kept it spinning flat and true despite the work of physics against it, and it sliced into the Lady's raised left arm. She screeched as her hand was severed at the wrist and fell to the earth. The stump of her arm sprayed thick, green ichor.

Alex didn't pause, he knew he had only interrupted her briefly and she would be more furious than ever. He drove himself to his feet and ran past as she blasted at him again from her remaining hand. Magefire seared his back and he grabbed the sword from the ground, dropped and spun on one knee, sliced a deep cut through the Lady's side, just above the hip. As she screamed, he reversed the cut, came back through under her knee, and again, back through her thigh. Her leg fell in two pieces and she collapsed, wailing, dark emerald spraying into the night.

Her strength was remarkable, even so grievously wounded. She drew magic again, energy danced at her remaining hand. "I am eternal!" she yelled, and threw the blaze at him.

Alex ducked, vision crossing with the pain of previous strikes and her spell burned him, a debilitating heat across his arm and shoulder. He staggered back, fell to his knees, all strength waning.

He was spent, but he had one chance left. The Lady was broken and maimed, but far from dead and Alex could not risk his last effort on her.

"You need to live long enough to see this, bitch. Here it ends."

Alex gathered all he could of his remaining strength, focused the Eld magic he had learned and directed it inwards. Drawing it together inside himself was far easier than trying to project it out under any kind of control and he let it build, a focused, destructive force of unimaginable intensity. The sword hung limp in one hand, the other he pressed over the shards of the Darak. He focused his mind on nothing but those hard, glassy black pieces. This really was the end. Of him. Of everything. But as long as he could survive for long enough…He tightened his focus as much as he possibly could and let the magic go.

He arched back, screamed as his chest burst open. Every bit of resilience and power he had ever had, he put tightly through the Darak and the Eld separating magic atomized the three shards. The pain was blinding as his flesh vaporized, his ribs disintegrated, and the Darak became a thousand spinning grains of Fey heart.

The Lady shrieked her rage and grief and Alex drew all the winds from all directions and gathered every drop of blood, every scrap of bone and flesh and every microscopic piece of the Darak and let those winds open to the world. Air rushed by him as his consciousness receded, blew the Lady onto her back, and the cloud of gore and Darak whipped away, swirled up into the night sky.

Alex's vision faded, his thoughts began to shut down. He ignored everything except the eldritch hurricane he had conjured, kept it gusting, opening in every direction, carrying particles of his body and the Darak far and wide across the land. He followed the winds with his mind, kept them going higher and wider, into the stratosphere, across the seas, carrying every tiny part of the Darak hundreds, thousands of miles apart. Every minuscule piece of it wanted to join with every other, but the further apart he pushed them, the more their power waned, the more the attraction weakened. The Darak might still exist, but it existed across most of Europe and the Atlantic Ocean, blowing out through the clouds to rain down in a million particulate pieces, all far from each other, impossible to find, impossible to recombine.

Agony gave way to icy cold in Alex's chest and he realized he was facedown on the grass. Wind still whistled in his ears, but his mind was numb, everything muffled. Somewhere, miles away, he heard the Lady screaming and then drums. No, fireworks perhaps. Or gunfire, maybe. And he let himself go.

CHAPTER THIRTY-ONE

Cold.

Floating in a haze of ice and pain.

An angel's voice. *Fucking do something!*

Movement, buffeting winds and searing pain.

Blackness.

Something beeping like an arcade game in another room.

Visuals like staring too close at a television tuned to static.

A deep voice, panicked, desperate. *Too much damage!*

Blackness.

Another voice, female, clipped. *Contain that ward! We need more medicmages in here right now.*

The angel's voice again, racked with sobs of grief and a burning anger underneath. *Don't you fucking dare! Not you, too. Not you…*

Blackness.

Thick, cloying, choking. Coughs and stabs of blinding pain.

Blackness.

Floating in a haze of pure light. Pure dark. Total void.

Panic!

Blackness.

A t a building site in Birmingham, England, an Armor operative disguised in hi-vis vest and worker's steel-capped boots walked casually towards the footings of the hotel under construction. Deep holes, steel-reinforced, sank into darkness. The operative held a messenger bag close to his hip as he walked into the shadow of a huge pipe lowering over the hole. Concrete began to pour, thick and glugging, down into the shadowed depths. The operative watched the level of concrete begin to rise. He checked around, made sure no eyes were on him, and pulled a thin, pale arm from the messenger bag. It writhed and flexed, the fingers clutching uselessly. He threw the arm into the rising concrete. It squirmed momentarily on the surface and sank.

The man watched a moment longer, nodded, and walked away.

A black boat powered through open ocean, hundreds of kilometers from land in any direction. The boat driver checked his instruments, slowed the vessel, checked again. He killed the engines. "We're here."

A woman stepped onto the deck, wearing the black combats of an Armor Jane Doe. "You're sure?"

"Mariana Trench," the man said, "as deep as the ocean gets."

The woman nodded, used a key to unlock a steel chest at the back of the boat. She pulled out a thrashing canvas sack.

"Need a hand with that?" the man asked.

She laughed. "A hand with a leg? Sure. Save it from kicking my head in."

The man grimaced, knelt to hold the flailing sack down. "Creepy as fuck, this is."

"I've seen stranger things," the woman said, concentrating as she used chains and padlocks to secure steel weights tightly around the thing. "It's the big chunk of still-breathing torso attached to it that gets me. Okay, help me up."

Between them they strained to lift the thing and toss it over the side. They watched it sink away from view, still kicking all the way into the darkness.

"Nearly seven miles deep," the man said quietly.

The woman nodded. "I hope it's enough. Come on, let's get back to Guam. I want to go home."

A man leaned from the door of a helicopter as it passed over the open, glowing crater of a volcano. The heat buffeted the aircraft as he dragged a sack to the edge. The sack contained a single leg that kicked and bucked in his grip. The man watched it tumble down into the gently churning magma and sink away. He turned to the pilot and gave the thumbs up. The chopper banked and flew back the way it had come.

"Here we are," the guide said.

The operative nodded and pulled a canvas-wrapped lump from his backpack. It swelled and relaxed softly, as if it breathed. *Just a chunk of meat*, the operative said to himself and moved carefully across the ice to the edge of the crevasse. He looked down, past the white ice, past the blue ice deeper down, into darkness. "How deep is it?" he asked.

The guide shrugged. "No one knows. Too narrow for a person to rappel. Who cares? It's just a split in the skin of the world. What do you have there, anyway?"

The operative smiled ruefully. "Nothing. Just something that needs to never be found again."

"It's a long way to come to throw away some garbage."

"It needs to be far from anything." The man dropped the parcel into the abyss. It made no sound as it fell out of sight. He turned, scanned the horizon of mountain ridges as far as the eye could see. The sky was cobalt blue above, the air thin and crisp. "Come on, then," he said.

The guide shrugged again and turned, led the way for another four-hour hike back to the base camp and the operative's waiting transport.

CHAPTER THIRTY-THREE

Machines hissed and whirred. Magesign swam in lazy spirals, obscuring his vision. And Alex realized he was awake. He blinked, swallowed, winced at the pain in his throat and chest. He peeled apart dry lips and sucked in a wheezing breath. An involuntary sound of pain escaped him as his chest rose.

"Alex!" Silhouette appeared through the haze, her face beautiful. Tears streamed from her eyes.

Something was wrong with her. The flesh of her left cheek and ear was slightly puckered, her hair burned away from the side of her head. A fuzzy regrowth pushed through. She saw his eyes go to her injury. "It's okay, it'll heal. No scars, they assure me. Just takes a while because the magic was so strong." Her eyes were sad, some deep melancholy that persisted beyond the smile she gave him.

Alex smiled back, weakly, the effort costing him a moment's breath. "Alive?" he managed to croak out. The thought mystified him. How was it possible?

Silhouette laughed through her tears. "Yeah, you're alive, Iron Balls. Fuck me, but you're strong. You've got a cybernetic heart, an Armor magetech special apparently, someone else's left lung and a new titanium ribcage among many other things. You, I'm afraid, are definitely going to have some scars. The combination of medicmages and Armor tech is quite impressive. They really came through for you."

Alex chuckled softly, the movement an agony. "No. You. Alive." He closed his eyes to concentrate a moment on not passing out.

"Yeah, I'm still going. It's taken a couple of weeks to fix me up, but I'll be tip-top. So will you, eventually."

Alex opened his eyes, drank in her gorgeous face. "Jarrod?"

Silhouette's expression fell, new tears. She shook her head. "He." She took a quavering breath. "He shielded me. Took the brunt of her blast. He didn't survive it. My little brother saved my life."

Alex felt a new pain rise with the physical hurt. "So sorry."

She nodded.

"Didn't want to leave you, Sil. Love you. So much. But had to…"

"I know." She gently brushed a palm across his forehead. "I understand. I don't like it, but I get it. I love you too."

"So tired, Sil. Need. Sleep."

She leaned forward, brushed the gentlest kiss across his lips. He sank back down into oblivion, struggling to believe he was still in the world.

CHAPTER THIRTY-FOUR

Silhouette pushed Alex in his wheelchair through the corridors of Armor HQ in London. Workers rebuilding, painting, moved aside for them, nodded greetings.

"This place is looking good," Alex said.

"Yeah, it's nearly finished. They've had six weeks, after all." She walked around the chair to knock on a door, pushed it open and wheeled Alex inside.

A man rose from behind a desk, the office all new, smelling of fresh carpet and barely dry paint. "Alex Caine!" he said, extending a hand. "I'm John Barclay, head of York. Temporary reassignment here."

Alex leaned forward in his chair to shake. "Good to meet you."

"You're recovering well?"

"Not too bad. Walking short distances. Should be up and about like normal in another couple of weeks. Thanks to you guys and Silhouette's special potions."

Barclay nodded, returned to his seat. "And in no small part thanks to your own strength and spirit."

"I've always been a fighter."

"Indeed. First off, let me officially thank you on behalf of everyone for what you managed to achieve."

Alex smiled crookedly. "As far as I could tell, I was just clearing up my own mess."

"Not true. You got tangled up in something well beyond your control and you took a hold of it and ended it."

"I've always hated having no control over my life. Can I ask a few questions?"

"Of course."

"The Lady?"

"She was very badly hurt by you and took a lot more damage from our people, but a contingent of Fey managed to gather around her and they got to a nearby gate. Whether they'll survive on the other side is hard to say. She was truly messed up."

"She'll be madder than ever," Alex said quietly.

"Maybe, but she's got nothing left to fight for. She'll be a fallen monarch. Broken and defeated as she was, she'll command no respect over there any more, except maybe among a very few close allegiances."

"She'll probably still want her revenge against me."

"Maybe. But honestly, she was so damaged, I think she'll be very little threat to anyone. Let her stew over there in grief and the sure knowledge you beat her and the Lord. I don't think she'll be back, but we'll do all we can to stay abreast of any developments in Faerie. We learned a lot from all this and a large proportion of her Fey faithful were destroyed. Not without our own losses, naturally. Lots of people died that night." Barclay held up a hand at Alex's dismay. "It's part of the job and that was by far the biggest and most successful confrontation against the Fey we've ever had. Sure, they'll regroup and the Fey threat will never really go away. Some bastard will rise to take the Lady's place, I expect, in some twisted internal politics. But their menace will only ever be on the thins now. That's a massive achievement and worth the cost, hard though it may be to accept. *All* of the Lord's heart is truly gone. And I think you're fairly safe from recrimination. You have nothing they want any more."

"What about Hood?" Silhouette asked. "Alex killed him, right?"

Barclay raised his hands. "Well, yes and no. The pieces of Hood are still alive, and each piece seems to have something of Uthentia in it. But those pieces have all been sent to places where they will never be found again. Trust me, that's dealt with."

"Still alive?" Alex asked. "I took his head off!"

Barclay grinned. "Come with me."

He stood, strode out of the office and off along a corridor. Silhouette grabbed the handles of Alex's wheelchair and they followed. Barclay led them to a lift, down into the basement and along another corridor. A huge, circular steel door stood before them. Alex looked over the shades, the dense magesign swimming all around. Two armed guards stood either side.

Barclay nodded and a series of wards and physical barriers were lowered. The door swung silently open. Beyond the door a large room was carved into the bedrock of London. Shelves and lockers lined the walls, glass cabinets stood throughout. Barclay led them to the back and pointed to a steel box with a thick glass window in the front.

Alex raised himself carefully from his chair to look in. Hood's head sat inside. "The fuck?" Alex stared.

Hood's eyes popped open. His expression twisted into a visage of hate, his mouth working frantically. Barclay tapped a button on the side of the case and sound burst from a speaker embedded somewhere. Hood's voice was weak and burbling, cracked and croaking, unintelligible.

"He has no lungs to make air and only severed, almost useless vocal cords, but he still manages to create that sound, sometimes even intelligible words, and he threatens all kinds of horror. The influence of Uthentia is weak, but it's there. We've done some study on it, but it's not yielding us much, to be honest. The lab staff call it the Head of Raging Hate."

"Why keep it?" Alex asked, horrified.

"Why not? It's a truly unique curiosity. It's in lockdown here and won't go anywhere. And as you know, we can't destroy it."

"But surely it's too dangerous to keep around."

"Yes, in the long term. We're in touch with Armor in the US and they're talking to NASA. When the next space vehicle goes up, our friend there is going with it. At massive expense, as I'm sure you can imagine. Once it's out of Earth's atmosphere, it'll be jettisoned in the direction of the sun."

Alex laughed. "Oh, that sounds about perfect." He stared at Hood's ranting head, looked deep into the man's dark, hate-filled eyes. He saw recognition there. Hood knew who he looked at. Alex grinned, lifted one middle finger to the glass and held it there a moment. He slumped back into the chair. "Let's get out of here."

As they made their way back to the lift, Alex asked, "What about Darvill?"

"No idea. Most reliable reports have him still caught in that giant mechanical thing. It took off with him and vanished. We recorded several gates opening and closing around the area, so we can only assume he was taken back to Faerie with various other fleeing Fey."

"Perhaps the Lady will assuage her rage torturing him," Alex said, warmed by the thought.

Barclay looked down at Alex, eyebrows raised. "We can hope so, no?"

"Yeah. We're well rid of that fuck up."

Silhouette laid a hand on Alex's shoulder, squeezed gently.

"I agree," Barclay said. "The man is far too dangerous. With any luck, he'll stay trapped over there for good."

"And Jean Chang?" Alex asked.

Barclay's smile was wide and genuine. "Now there's a formidable woman. She's incredible, the things she knows and the tricks she has for intelligence and organization."

"Yeah, she's pretty cool. You're looking after her?"

"Yes. She's been working here for some weeks and is already invaluable. We'll go to see her later. She asks after you often. I promised I'd bring you by."

"She and I have had some good chats," Silhouette said, sadness quietening her voice. "She misses Jarrod terribly. They really had something, you know, however briefly."

Alex looked into Sil's eyes, saw tears hovering on the lashes. "I'm so sorry."

"Me too. But Jean will be a good friend to both of us, and we need to be there for her."

"We will be." Alex turned back to Barclay. "And what about Emma Parker?" he asked. "She okay?"

Barclay chuckled, shook his head. "She is one dangerous woman. She was front and center of the battle and led the crew who tried to run down the Lady when she was taken away. They didn't stop her, as I said, but had a decent go at it. Emma was pretty heavily injured, but she's made a full recovery. Looks like she might take over York if my re-posting here becomes permanent."

Alex nodded. Parker was hard but fair, and deserved a leadership role. "Good for her."

They made their way back to the office and Barclay ordered them all tea. "So, how are you, Alex? Really?"

Alex absently brushed a hand across his chest, felt the ridges and puckers of scar tissue through his T-shirt. His flesh looked like a relief map of the moon. "I'm physically okay. Getting there anyway. The Darak is gone, but I seem to have retained some of the power it gave me. Nothing like as much as when it was part of me, but I still have a surprising ability according to the docs here."

Barclay nodded, took a tray as it was delivered to the door. "You lived with that thing for a fair time. It's only natural you would absorb a lot of its influence. Plus you have a remarkable natural ability. I mean, you may not be catching falling buses again anytime soon, but you might one day with practice and training. But what about…mentally? You coping okay?"

Alex shook his head. "Not really. Your counselors here are great, though. We're working through a lot of stuff. And Silhouette's here. All the time I have her, I know I'll be okay. It's just, sometimes in the night…" His voice petered out as half-remembered nightmare images danced across his mind. A thousand faceless dead screamed silently at him and he winced.

Silhouette put her arm around his shoulders. "We'll be okay," she told Barclay. "It's a long road, but he's tough and I'm not going anywhere. Physically and emotionally, we'll build him back up."

Barclay nodded, gripped Alex's knee briefly in a gesture of solidarity. "You can busy yourself getting on with your life now. And we'd still love to have you on board. Plus, your vision means you'll be able to study pretty much any grimoire you can find. You have unbound potential. A lot to live for, yes?"

Alex smiled. "I'm looking forward to learning more, without the constant threat of having to survive. Be nice to take some time for myself."

"And given your level of power, you'll be around a long time to get your practice in."

"Which is just as well," Silhouette said.

Alex leaned over, kissed her. "I'm not going anywhere anytime soon. What happened to the sword?" he asked Barclay.

"The sword? You mean *your* sword?"

Alex grinned. "Well, I was hoping…"

"I think you've earned it, if you want it."

"I really do."

Barclay rummaged on his desk, handed Alex a sheet of paper. "Here's what little we know, recovered from Sydney. The lab folks here are having another look, but it's yours to collect when you're ready. It's one of three connected items, apparently. We're tracing the mythology, to see if we can figure out where the other two are."

"Three items?" Alex asked.

"Apparently so. Could be quite interesting to find out what the other two are and how they work together, yes?" Barclay winked. "Perhaps something you could look into, help us with?"

Alex smiled, nodded gently. "I'd certainly be interested."

"The team made a new scabbard for the sword," Barclay said, "as the original was lost with Darvill. It helps to mask the powerful presence of the thing."

Alex folded the paper and pocketed it to read later. "Great, thanks. I reckon it might be useful in any future jobs I might do for Armor, yeah?"

Barclay poured tea, handed them each a cup. "Quite. So, let's discuss the future."

CHAPTER THIRTY-FIVE

Alex checked the map as they drove through winding streets between slate-roofed buildings. "That fork in the road coming up, take the right and go up the hill."

Silhouette nodded, guided the car. "There it is. I recognize it from the website."

"Yep."

She pulled in through a wooden gateway onto a gravel drive and parked next to the house. A hand-painted sign by the door read *B&B RECEPTION* with an arrow beneath. They got out and walked across the driveway to take in the view. Green hills rolled down to a glittering lake, rose again on the other side. Sheep like tiny earthbound clouds moved lazily across the grass. The sky above was brilliant blue, the spring sun beating down warm and all-embracing. Birds sang, insects buzzed, multi-hued flowers bloomed in the B&B's gardens.

Alex put his arm around Silhouette. "Beautiful, isn't it?"

Silhouette slipped an arm around his waist. "It really is. We've earned this."

"I say we go and visit Halliday this afternoon," Alex said. "Partly because I'm kinda looking forward to seeing the funny old bastard, but mostly to get it out of the way. Then it's just us and a holiday."

Silhouette laid her head against his shoulder. "Sounds good. We going to take the jobs?"

"Yeah, I think so. I owe it to the organization, right? And like you said before, I need direction. Something to do. It'll be cool for us to work together. You want to join them, yeah?"

"Sure, why not. We can always quit if it doesn't work out. London or Sydney?"

"Don't know. It was nice of them to offer me the choice. And a pretty senior role for both of us in either one. In all honesty, I really don't think I'm qualified…"

"Oh, hush, you'll be brilliant at it. We both will. Like Barclay said, you'll probably be in charge of an HQ in no time."

Alex laughed. "Well, I'm definitely not qualified for that yet!"

"Their numbers are low, they're scraping the barrel." She laughed and danced back as Alex swung a playful shot at her. "You're a figurehead," she said. "You represent strength against adversity. That's why they're offering you a good job. But you'll learn and you'll be great."

"Still going to have a lot of resistance. So many people in Armor don't like me."

"You'll win them over, you charming bastard."

Alex nodded, gathered her back into his arms. "I'll try. Which would you prefer? London or Sydney?"

"I don't know. Let's worry about that in a couple of weeks, eh?" She moved away, opened the boot of the hire car. "Let's get our stuff inside."

"Sure. And then we'll walk down the road to the pub and have a drink in honor of Jarrod before we go see Halliday."

Silhouette smiled, her eyes sad. "Yeah, let's do that. And promise me one thing."

"What?"

"No fucking adventures for a little while!"

Alex shouldered his bag, took her chin gently in one hand and kissed her. He pulled away with a grin. "I'll do my best. But no promises."